Contents

The Pyramid Builders, Book 2: Sekhemkhet

By Max Overton

Writers Exchange E-Publishing

http://www.writers-exchange.com

Publisher note:
Due to formatting issues symbols such as ü, ä, é and ö have been replaced with the simple letter u, a, e and o. We apologise for this necessity.

The Pyramid Builders, Book 2: Sekhemkhet

Copyright 2025 Max Overton

Writers Exchange E-Publishing

PO Box 372

ATHERTON QLD 4883

Cover Art by: Julie Napier

Published by Writers Exchange E-Publishing

http://www.writers-exchange.com

ISBN **ebook**: 978-1-922548-38-2

Print: 978-1-922548-37-5

Setting the Scene

R eaders of my other books on Ancient Egypt will know much of what I am going to say in this foreword. You can skip it if you want, but I will try to include some words specific to this series on the Pyramid Builders as well as general information pertinent to those ancient times.

This is a work of fiction, but fiction based on fact. The closest parallel I can draw is of a dramatised re-enactment of actual events in history. I have tried to be historically accurate within this series of books, though I have had to make some assumptions that may not agree with every expert opinion. I did not want it to read like a history lesson, so I have invented dialogue, and many incidents that fill in the stories of men and women, both fictional and real, that lived and died in these years so long ago. I have also tried to make sense of tangled and sometimes contradictory lists of kings and relationships between real characters.

I have read extensively in preparation for this series, consulting the works of both Egyptologists and other authors for whom the mystery of the pyramids is the centre-point of their lives. These researches provided me with the bones upon which to hang the flesh of my novels.

I would also like to thank Sara Jane Sesay who is my first reader. She takes the time to go through my manuscript and is quick to point out any mistakes and places where my ideas need clarification.

My cover art is by Julie Napier. I have long admired her work and over the years, she has designed all my book covers.

I am grateful too to my many readers. Without readers, a writer's efforts are just a personal exercise in telling a story. I would probably write them anyway, even if nobody read them, but I like to think I am bringing enjoyment to someone.

The era of the first pyramid builders covers the third and fourth dynasties of the Old Kingdom, and even though huge stone monuments dominate the landscape at such sites as Giza, Saqqara, and Dahshur, there is still a lot that remains unknown.

The kings of this time are known, for the most part, though nobody can really agree where Sanakht fits into the king list, or whether Khaba and Huni are the same person or different kings. Even the relationships between the kings, their wives and courtiers are a matter of conjecture.

This brings us to the almost mythical person of Imhotep, First Minister of King Djoser, architect, mathematician, priest and physician, whose reputation swelled with the passage of time until he was worshipped as a god hundreds of years after his death. Nobody knows who he was or where he came from, but as influential people were usually recruited from the highest families, it is at least possible that he was related to the king.

Two words you will come across in relation to those times are 'mastaba' and 'pyramid', neither of which were words used by the ancient Egyptians. Mastaba is an Arabic word meaning a 'bench of mud' and describes the ancient mud brick tombs of the early kings. I have used the term 'Per-djet' to describe these low, bench-like tombs. The word 'pyramid' comes from the Greek, but the ancient Egyptians used the word 'Mer', so I have done the same.

Many of the names I have used in my books may be unfamiliar, as I like to use the names that would be recognised by the people of the times. Thus, modern Luxor is ancient Waset, modern Memphis is ancient Inebu-hedj. Heliopolis was once Iunu, Abydos used to be Abdju, and Saqqara was Sekera. In the same way, Egypt is derived from the Greek Aegyptos, but the people of those times referred to their country as Kemet and of themselves as Kemetu. The names of the gods differed too. Horus was Horu, Thoth was Djehuti, Osiris was Asar. Some people may disagree with my choice, but it just felt wrong to put Greek words in ancient Egyptian mouths.

I have simplified the names of the kings. Egyptian pharaohs had five names, two of which are important as far as most stories of Ancient Egypt are concerned--the prenomen and the nomen. Only the nomen was given at birth, the prenomen being a coronation name. Thus King Djoser of the third dynasty had the birth name of Nub-Hor, was known as Nisut-Bity-Nebty-Netjerikhetnebu (or just plain Netjerikhet) when he became king. Djoser was a descriptive, meaning 'sublime', and perhaps he thought of himself that way. Further back in time, in the Old Kingdom, not even these names are known with any certainty, and the kings bear only their Horus names or Nebty name. Thus nobody really knows the birth name of Djoser's successor Sekhemkhet. His Horus name was Hor-Sekhemkhet and his Nebty name was Nebty-Hetepren, so I have had to simplify matters somewhat. Generally, I have tried to keep the names by which these kings are popularly known.

How were the pyramids built? I dare say more has been written on this topic than on the whole of the rest of Egyptian history. I know I have read many books on the subject. Theories range from hauling rocks up inclined

3

ramps to floating them up in cylinders of water, from using primitive block and tackle to casting the blocks *in situ* using a limestone slurry as a cement. Some people even invoke music as a lifting mechanism or suggest aliens built them. I do not pretend to have the definitive answer, but I believe the simplest, most straightforward technique is the most likely. I am sure some of you will disagree with me, but viewed as a whole, I believe the progression of building from mud brick mastaba through stepped pyramid to immense smooth-sided stone pyramid is a step-by-step process started by master architects like Imhotep and Den and passed on to their descendants.

One last note on fictional characters. Many of the characters you meet in these books are real, lifted from the history books. They lived real lives, performed real deeds, and eventually died. Others are fictional, either created whole from my imagination, or based on other real characters from the times about which I am writing. Sometimes the two merge. For instance, very little is known about Imhotep beyond the fact of his existence and later legends told about him. He was the main architect of Djoser's step pyramid and may have been involved in the construction of stone temples and even Sekhemkhet's pyramid, but apart from this, nothing is known about the man, his ancestry, descendants or associates. Those I have had to invent. Again, I hope that my interpretation of real characters does not detract from your own ideas.

Now, enough of notes. On with the story....

Chapter 1

"I have made a decision, Tjaty Imhotep, the first of my reign," Sekhemkhet said. "I want you to build me a *mer* and associated city of the dead, like that of my father, but bigger and better."

There was nothing Imhotep could say to that but bow and withdraw with his assistant Den to discuss the matter. As soon as they were outside, Den started to talk, but Imhotep shushed him and strode along the corridors of the palace to his offices. Here, he dismissed his servants and sank into a padded chair with a sigh.

"How could you agree to that?" Den demanded, pacing the room. "You just bowed and left without a word of protest."

"He is the king," Imhotep pointed out. "What would you have me say?"

"But it is an act of madness. Every *deben* of gold that comes into the king's treasury goes out again to create a monument of stone that aggrandises the king at the expense of..."

"Let me stop you there, Den. This is why I did not want you speaking where anyone might overhear you. No matter what you might privately think, you cannot go about denigrating the king or his actions."

"So you agree with him? You think we should just turn around and build another great city of the dead?"

"That seems to be what he wants...and he is the king, after all."

"We have spent the better part of our lives creating a huge stone structure that has no purpose but to house a dead body. Now you want to spend the rest of our lives building another one."

Imhotep sighed again. "Sit down, Den, your pacing is very distracting. Attend upon my words; there is no higher purpose for us as loyal Kemetu than to do the will of our king, and no greater service we could perform than to ensure his everlasting life. Now his son, who is also our king, wants us to do the same for him. That seems like a reasonable request, don't you think?"

Den shrugged and sat down. "I suppose so."

"Do you want to resign your position as my personal assistant?" Imhotep asked. "If you do, just say so. I will not hold it against you if you want to go back to scribing. I can find someone else to help me."

Den stared. "No! No, that is not what I want."

"Then let me hear no more on the matter. We will carry out the words of our king as we are commanded."

"Of course, sir. I... I don't know why I..."

"I do," Imhotep said quietly. "I share your sentiments but I am not such a fool as to voice them publicly." He got up and opened the door, calling for a servant to bring beer. "We have just finished a massive project that has taken years to complete. Naturally, we are feeling relieved that it is over, and the last thing either of us expected was to face the same task again."

The servant appeared with a pot of beer and two cups. Setting them on the table, he bowed and left the room. Imhotep poured beer into the cups and handed one to Den.

"Time for us to start planning. What are your first thoughts?"

Den took the cup and drank thirstily. "What does he mean by bigger and better?"

Imhotep shrugged. "I think if he had something specific in mind he would have said. Bigger and better could be whatever we say it is. If we take the plans to him, he may just agree with what we set out."

"So if Netjerikhet's *mer* was six levels, Sekhemkhet's could be seven or eight."

"That's the sort of thing," Imhotep agreed. "Can it be done? Can we go higher than six levels?"

"I do not see why not," Den said. "We could have put another small level on top of Netjerikhet's; but would that have been enough for 'bigger and better'?"

"Perhaps not, but say we drew up plans for seven good-sized layers, build an enclosure wall, a mortuary temple and other structures; we would at least have something to take to the king."

Den stifled a belch, and then got up and poured himself another beer. "My spirit quails at the thought of another fifteen or twenty years building another city."

"You are forgetting something," Imhotep said with a smile. He held out his cup and Den poured more beer into it. "We built the last one not knowing what we were doing. We have learnt a lot since then. None of the mistakes we made need be repeated. In addition, we have a sizeable workforce trained in construction. It will be good to use them for some useful purpose."

Imhotep's office had baskets of scrolls and writing materials, so Den took what he needed and started scribbling notes and making calculations. For many minutes, the only sound in the room was the scratching of reed pen on papyrus or the scrape of stylus on waxen tablet. Imhotep was content to sit back and let Den work. The young man was skilled in computation and generally accurate. He would come up with figures that would need to be checked, but he was sure they would give a good indication of what was required. At last, Den threw down his pen and leaned back, stretching.

"Well, it can be done," he said.

"Bigger and better?"

"Seven levels, pleasing to the eye, cased in fine Troyu limestone."

"And an enclosure, with temples and courts?"

"That still needs some work, but yes."

"How big?"

"The *mer* will measure two hundred and twenty *mehi* on a side, square, and rising one hundred and forty *mehi*. It will be surrounded by an enclosure wall one thousand *mehi* on a side, rising twenty *mehi*."

Imhotep choked on his beer, putting the cup down and coughing hard. "That big? Perhaps you took the king's instructions too literally. The *mer* dimensions are reasonable, given the need to rise seven levels, but that is a huge enclosure. Can we scale it back so it still looks big?"

"Anything is possible, sir," Den said. "You are the Tjaty and King's Architect."

"And you are the man who will turn an idea into reality, Den."

The two men sat down to plan the city of the dead in greater detail, roughing out plans on tablets and papyrus before getting teams of scribes to carefully copy out the drawings and annotate them with measurements. After the neat plans came back to them, Den examined them carefully for mistakes, but because they had rigorously trained the scribes, there were few found. From the detailed plans, scale models were constructed out of wax and wood. It rapidly became apparent that an enclosure wall of a thousand *mehi* on a side was too large, as too many structures would be needed to fill it.

"We can do it," Den said, "but it will keep us busy for twenty years, even knowing what we do now about building these things."

"Too long," Imhotep opined. "The king is a young man, but I doubt he will want to commit to such a long project; not when there are so many other things that need attention. What can we cut back on?"

"If we keep to the same overall design as Netjerikhet's, we have the *mer*, which if it is to be seven levels, needs a base of that size. Then we need a mortuary temple to the north, a courtyard and tomb to the south. With all those in place, we need the thousand *mehi* on the north-south axis." Den examined the drawings, and the model. "We have included elaborate temples, courts and halls to east and west, but they are not really needed. If we draw in the sides, it will save a lot of stone and effort on the enclosure. There is the added benefit of accentuating the towering height of the *mer*."

"Try it. See how it looks."

Den drew a line through the old drawings and sent them back to the team of scribes with new instructions, and by the time the new model arose, both Imhotep and Den were nodding in satisfaction.

Imhotep had the model carried to the king for his appraisal. The young man walked around it slowly, bending to examine it from the point of view of a man, standing tall and looking down as if he was one of the gods.

"This is bigger than that of my father?" Sekhemkhet asked.

"It is, my lord," Imhotep replied. "As you can see, the *mer* is seven layers, whereas you father's was only six."

Sekhemkhet grunted, counting the levels again. "Why only seven?" he asked. "Why not eight or more?"

"It is not simply a matter of piling more rock on top to make another level, my lord. The higher you go, the wider must be the base or else the whole thing becomes unstable. It would be a disaster if it was nearly built and it collapsed."

"Very well, if you say it cannot be more. I will issue a draft for the treasury, enabling you to draw whatever you need, but Imhotep; I rely on you to make my tomb as much a wonder as you did my father's."

"It shall be done, my lord. There is now just the place to be decided. I recommend we build in Sekera again."

"I thought somewhere else," Sekhemkhet said. "Sekera will always be associated with my father's tomb. I should have mine elsewhere, so that it stands out."

"There are advantages to Sekera, my lord. First, there is a thriving workers' village on the site, so it will save greatly on costs if we do not have to duplicate it elsewhere." Imhotep smiled, recognising that the king's greatest concern was not the cost. "Your tomb will be larger and more magnificent than that of your father, but people will not know that if they are in different areas. Build yours close to your father's and everyone will be able to see at a glance that your tomb is bigger and better."

Armed with the king's permission, Imhotep collected Den and several scribes and set sail for the building site at Sekera. They were there in less than a day, and made their way up from the river to where the village lay. Crowds of workers came out to greet them, asking if there was more work. It pleased Imhotep to be able to reassure them that he had been commissioned to build another tomb close by, and that there would shortly be work for all.

Imhotep and Den ventured out onto the plateau to search for a suitable site for the king's tomb. Sheets of limestone rock capped the plateau, but desert sand lay in drifts, obscuring some of the rock layers. Cracks, hollows and humps marred the rock surfaces, so it was not just about building anywhere. A suitable place would have to be found. There were places to the north where level limestone beckoned, but faults in the rock warned them off. To the southwest, several hundred paces from Djoser's city of the dead, lay a sheet of rock sufficiently big to accommodate the planned structures, but it was far from level.

"We cannot build here," Den said. "The whole thing would be tilted, or one side would be higher than the other."

"Unless we levelled it first," Imhotep said. "Build up the sunken areas, so that we have a flat base, and then construct the tomb on top of that."

"It would be simpler to find a level piece of rock. We have not looked farther to the west."

"Any farther, and you would not be able to compare the two tombs. The king is adamant that people must be able to see both tombs together so they know his is bigger."

"And I thought that we had already made a city as large as we could," Den grumbled. "Now we have to build a bigger one, so what comes next? A bigger one still? Where will it end?"

"One step at a time, Den. Our job is to build this one, and by the time Sekhemkhet's son is ready to build his, it will be someone else's problem."

"Then let us hope for the sake of our sons who follow us, that future kings lose interest in having such large tombs."

Deciding on the place, Imhotep sent a runner back to the village to bring up masons with surveying equipment to start marking out the boundaries of the city. Within an hour, they were busy setting up lines, pacing out distances, and making sightings between stakes to work out the rise and fall of the rock surfaces. Scribes accompanied them, making copious notes that Den would later compile into a detailed plan of the area. Two days later, he had the first sketches ready and he and Imhotep started planning where the various structures would fit and which areas needed to be built up.

"That is a lot of terracing work just to make the site level," Den said. "It might be better to look for somewhere else."

"There is nothing else close enough to Djoser's tomb," Imhotep said. "The king made it plain that he wants his close to his father's. Anything else is too far away."

"Yes, but the amount of rock we need to build the terraces..."

"We have rock already. There are piles of it we never got to use."

They paced out the limits of the sheet of limestone, following the guidelines the masons had laid out with their red ochre markings and string, checking the distances and making fresh compilations. Then they looked at the stockpiled rock, quickly determining that there was enough there to make a start on the terracing.

"Enough for half a month," Imhotep estimated. "If we order more from the Troyu quarry immediately, the first deliveries of casing stone will be here by the time the builders need it."

Den nodded, consulting his plans once more. "I will get the teams organised at once, and appoint overseers. Once the terraces are under way, we can start marking out the placement of the *mer* and the vertical shaft down to the underground tomb." Imhotep grimaced, looking uncomfortable, and Den frowned, and asking him what was the matter. "You disagree with what I said."

"No...no, not exactly. The actions are correct. It is just that...well, I want you to spend more time on the planning and calculations, rather than on overseeing the site."

"I can do both. I did before."

"Yes, and you did a good job, Den. Nobody disputes that."

"Then what is the problem, sir?"

"My son Rahotep will act as my deputy on site. He will be the overall Overseer of Sekhemkhet's city of the dead."

Den frowned, but said nothing. There was little he could say. Occupations in Kemet tended to follow along family lines; son succeeded father, from the king through the Tjaty, nobility, the ranks of officialdom down to the lowliest street sweeper or dung carrier. It was just the way things were organised, and Den knew that his own experience of breaking away from being a simple scribe like his father to become personal assistant to the Tjaty was unusual. Now, the King's Architect was setting his own son on the first rung of the ladder that would lead to him taking up his father's responsibilities one day. It was to be expected, even though it was personally disappointing.

"Of course, sir," Den murmured.

"He needs the responsibility," Imhotep went on. "He is a grown man and although he is a priest of Re, I want him to get into government..."

"I understand, sir."

"This is not a criticism of you, Den. I am fully cognisant of your years of service as my personal assistant and you will continue to hold a favoured position with me."

"Thank you, sir."

"I would give Rahotep a position under you as he lacks experience, but he is nearly the same age as you and he...uh...is of higher rank."

Den wished to spare the Tjaty further embarrassment when it was not really needed. "I understand, sir, I really do. Your son is a member of the king's household and such oversight is only his due. Will your other son also take on responsibilities?"

Imhotep looked relieved that the subject had been steered away from the Sekera site. "Yes, I will put Sekhemre in charge of the Troyu quarry. He has been working there already, and he shows enthusiasm for the task."

"I am glad, sir, that both of your sons will have the opportunity to rise in the world. It is their due."

Imhotep had not yet broken the news to his sons, the decision having just been made in his own mind, so he called his sons back to Inebu-hedj to tell them about their futures. Rahotep had to come from Iunu, where he was a priest of Re, but Sekhemre was only at Troyu, across the river, so he learnt of his father's decision first.

"Overseer? Of the whole quarry? I mean, I know you intended this, but are you sure, father? It is a big responsibility."

"One that I feel you are ready for," Imhotep said. "Nebra agrees. He has been watching you, assessing you, and it is his considered opinion that you have matured in the last several months. He thinks you are ready to take over the supervision..." Imhotep smiled at his son, "...and so do I. What do you say?"

Sekhemre fell to his knees and grasped his father's legs. "Father, I am honoured beyond measure. I will not let you down."

Somewhat embarrassed, Imhotep raised his son to his feet and embraced him. "It is no more than your due, my son, and you deserve this position. It need only be the start, you know. I have the king's ear, and he will heed my recommendations."

Sekhemre grinned. "There is something else, father. I hesitated to raise the subject while I was only an apprentice, but now that I am supervisor of the quarry, I can afford to get married."

"I was not aware you were thinking of that," Imhotep said. "You have a woman in mind?"

"Yes, father."

"Well, do not keep me in suspense. Who is she? Of good family, I trust?"

"She is Perimset, the daughter of Ipysankh."

Imhotep frowned. "I don't think I know this Ipysankh. Where is he from?"

"Per-Bast, father. He is a trader of some note there. He owns ships which trade with the cities of Kanaan and..."

"A trader? He is not of the nobility?"

14

Now Sekhemre frowned, sensing his father was troubled. "No, father. Does it matter? I wish to marry his daughter, not enter into business with him."

"You are son of the Tjaty, cousin to the king. You have a high rank in Kemetu society, whereas your intended wife is merely the daughter of a trader."

"I love her, father."

Imhotep sighed. "Why could you not fall in love with someone of suitable rank? Are you sure it is love and not just a desire to lie with her? I am sure she would deem it an honour to have the son of the Tjaty sow his seed in her."

"I am no longer a callow youth, father. I know my own mind. I love Perimset and she loves me. If...if you will not give me your blessing, I will marry her without it."

"I did not say I would not give my blessing. If you have given the matter due consideration and this is what you truly desire, then I will not stand in your way."

"Thank you, father."

"To show that I support you in this, I will cause to be built a fine house of limestone for you both near the Troyu quarries. Here, you may oversee the work and raise a family."

Sekhemre went off happily to tell Perimset the welcome news and to make the necessary arrangements for transferring her abode from that of her father to her husband's house.

Rahotep arrived in Inebu-hedj a few days later, apologising to his father for the delay, telling him that his duties as a priest of Re precluded his immediate departure.

"Well, you will not have to worry about that anymore," Imhotep said. "As Hem-netjer of Re at the Iunu temple, I release you from your vows and your duties there."

Rahotep went pale. "How have I displeased you, father...Hem-netjer?"

"You have not displeased me," Imhotep reassured him. "In fact, I have new duties that will please you, I am sure. You were always interested in architecture; I remember the enthusiasm with which you assisted in the building of the temple."

"That is true, father. Fashioning a temple out of stone is akin to being a god. It is an act of creation that excites me."

"Then you will like your next task. King Sekhemkhet desires a tomb that excels that of his father. I am putting you in charge of it."

Rahotep gaped. "I... I am h...honoured, but, father, that is too great a responsibility. I had a hand in the creation of the temple of Re, but it was already planned out and... and..."

"The tomb will be planned out too. I have been doing this with Den...you remember him? My personal assistant? He is a skilled scribe and architect, and will be working under you. I strongly recommend that you consult with him in all things, but of course, that will be your decision."

"I am truly honoured by your faith in me, father, but...forgive me if I appear ungrateful, but why do you not just assign this task to Den? If he is so skilled and knows the site and plans so well, wouldn't he be the best man for the job?"

"Den is a good man, but he is a commoner. The position of Overseer of the king's city of the dead should be the purview of nobility. I cannot think of a man more suited to the position than my own son."

"Then I gladly accept, father."

Chapter 2

S ekhemkhet was delighted with his accession to the double throne of Kemet. He had always lived in luxury, with virtually every whim catered to, but he had been conscious that everything depended on the continuing goodwill of his father. His future life had never been in doubt--he was the only son and sole heir to the throne--but it rankled that his life was dictated to rather than being under his control. Now it was. He was the king, reigning under the name of Hor-Sekhemkhet, and his word was the law of the land. The king owned every property, be it land or house; every part of Kemet belonged to him. It was a heady feeling. For the first time in his life he could do as he pleased, without regard for other people's wishes.

Immediately after coming to the throne, he took his sister Inetkawes in marriage. There was no lust and little desire involved, though she was a beautiful young woman of nineteen, but it was expected of a king. The ruler of Kemet guarded his power jealously, and allowing a man from outside the family to marry into it was foolish. Such a man might claim the throne and even if his attempt failed, it would still disrupt the *ma'at* of the realm. Better that brother should marry sister and keep the power within the ruling family. Inetkawes had not objected to the union. It was expected and though it seemed strange to lie with her brother, having known him since they both ran naked around their father's palace, she was able to put aside her feelings.

"It is what we do," her grandmother Nimaathap told her just after the official announcement of the marriage. The old queen was stooped and wrinkled, mumbling through a mouth almost bereft of teeth. About the only pleasure left in her life was taking an interest in her granddaughters.

"You did not have to," Inetkawes said.

"No, but I had no choice either. My sister and I were daughters of a defeated king and were taken as wives by Khasekhemwy. I bore Djoser and his sister Hetephernebti, and in due course they married as was expected of them. Do you imagine your mother was unhappy with the arrangement?"

"She has never said anything about it."

"Nor will she," Nimaathap mumbled. "She knows her duty to her family is more important than personal pleasure. Mind you," Nimaathap cackled, "there is nothing wrong with having pleasure mixed with duty. Your brother is virile, and if half of what is said by the gossips of the palace is true, his member will give you much enjoyment."

Inetkawes grimaced. "Every time I look at him I see that grubby little child who used to annoy me when we were children."

"Drive that thought from your mind," Nimaathap said sharply. "He is the king now, and you will be his queen, bearing his sons."

"Will I be his queen though? He married that Djeser-Ti girl and seems happy with her."

"He has not made her queen though, and he will not. Sekhemkhet is young, but he can see sense. Djeser-Ti ranks far below you, and though she is expecting a child already, you will be the one to produce an heir."

"What if she bears a son?"

19

"Pray she does not, but if she does, well..." The old queen shrugged her shoulders. "It still has to live long enough to become king."

Inetkawes looked shocked. "You would not wish harm on the child?"

"Of course not, but more children die than live to become adults. It is just the way of the world. If Djeser-Ti bears a son and he lives, then Sekhemkhet may well make him his heir."

"And make Djeser-Ti his queen."

"That does not follow. You are a royal princess. He will make you queen."

"When?"

"When it pleases him; he is the king."

The lack of ceremony involved in a Kemetu marriage was even more pronounced on the day Inetkawes married the king. Normally, the woman was brought to her husband by her father, while servants carried traditional gifts of fire and water, along with a portion of the father's wealth. This time, of course, there was even less. Her father the king was dead, and she already lived in the palace, so all that could take place was a parading of the princess through the halls of the palace, followed by the king visiting her rooms to consummate the marriage. Officials and nobility gathered to witness the king taking his sister in marriage, lining the hallways and rooms as the couple walked through them, bowing to the king and his consort.

Djeser-Ti was there, her face twisted in a mix of emotions as she faced her husband's sister. She bowed to the king, and then to Inetkawes, though her obeisance to the princess bordered on insult.

"Greetings, husband. I congratulate you on your marriage, and pray that it will be as fruitful as your marriage to me." She flashed a look of triumph at Inetkawes, and ostentatiously stroked her swollen belly.

"Djeser-Ti," Inetkawes said, inclining her head politely. "You are well?"

"I carry the king's son and heir in my belly."

"A daughter, I think. I wish you and your daughter joy," Inetkawes said. She turned her face from Djeser-Ti and walked toward the marital chamber, with Sekhemkhet a step behind.

Djeser-Ti took the comment to be a curse on the gender of her child and quickly muttered words that would turn the curse aside, while adding a few phrases of her own that might visit ill upon the princess. Magic was an imprecise art at the best of times, and Djeser-Ti took comfort in the absence of any magical charms that might strengthen the princess's curse. Still, it would do no harm to take precautions. She hurried away to seek a purification spell that would protect the gender of her unborn child, though only time would tell is the spell was efficacious.

Inetkawes now faced the performance of a duty that she could no longer avoid. When she was younger, she had toyed with the idea of gaining sexual experience as most Kemetu youths did. Her father had forbidden it with any man except her brother, so she had refrained. Well, almost. She smiled as she recollected the fumbling of a young girl and boy as they sought to make sense of an adult pastime. The act had given her no pleasure, and it was not repeated, but at least she knew what to expect when she lay with her husband-brother.

It was over quickly. Sekhemkhet stayed for a while, making polite conversation and sharing a cup of wine, but he excused himself and left Inetkawes to the ministrations of her ladies, retiring to his own rooms. Inetkawes washed herself thoroughly and donned fresh apparel, before going to her bed. She lay awake for a time, exploring her thoughts, remembering sensations, and concluded she could live with being her brother's wife as long as she became queen.

"I will talk to him about it tomorrow," she murmured to herself.

Djeser-Ti, in the meantime, spent the night awake. She could not keep from imagining the scene in the royal chambers. It was not that she resented the king having relations with another woman--that happened all the time. Sekhemkhet was young and virile, and he often lay with one or other of the palace women. It was expected of a king and meant little. What did anger Djeser-Ti was the king taking another wife, and especially one of higher rank than herself. Inetkawes had the advantage of her birth, but perhaps she could negate that by producing a son and heir.

Lying awake all night did nothing for her looks, so as soon as the sun's rays lit up the palace she washed and applied fresh makeup, dressed in garments that increased her beauty, and presented herself at the king's suite of rooms just after he rose. Sekhemkhet welcomed her and asked after her health before sitting and calling for food and drink, which he shared with his wife.

"How was your evening, my lord?" Djeser-Ti asked. "Inetkawes is a beautiful young woman. I hope she brought you much pleasure."

Sekhemkhet nodded, reaching for another slice of roast goose. He licked his fingers before replying. "My sister fulfilled her duty quite pleasantly," he said.

"And I warrant you were as virile as you always are, my lord. Even now she will be with child."

"That is in the hands of the gods."

Sekhemkhet wiped his hands on clean linen and took a drink of cool river water. He smiled at Djeser-Ti. "The gods looked favourably upon our union from the first day, Ti. I thank them daily for the child in your belly."

"A son, my lord, I am sure of it. A son and heir."

"I pray it is so."

"My lord, I hesitate to bring it up, but I must speak with you earnestly on a related matter..."

"I think I know what it is," Sekhemkhet said. "Perhaps it would be better if it remained unsaid."

"I must, my lord," Djeser-Ti said. "If not for my sake, then for the sake of our unborn son."

The young king frowned, and signed to a servant to bring him the plate of figs. "Speak then, if you must." He selected a ripe piece of fruit and bit into it with enjoyment.

"My lord, it is only proper that the mother of your heir bears the title of Queen."

"My own mother did not," Sekhemkhet pointed out.

"She should have," Djeser-Ti said. "It was an injustice that she did not."

"Are you accusing King Netjerikhet of being unjust?"

Djeser-Ti realised she had gone too far, and hurried to correct her mistake. "Forgive me, my lord, if I misspoke. My words were those of a woman, feeling the hurt of your mother at being denied a richly deserved title. I intended no criticism of your father."

"It is as well that you do not. The king's word is law."

"In the days of your father, his word was indeed the law, my lord, but you are king now. That means your word is the law and if you speak of your own will rather than that of your father, who can dispute it?"

Sekhemkhet was pleased to be reminded of his absolute power, but less so that his wife was attempting to influence him. He threw the remains of the fig he had been eating onto the floor and stood up. "I have work to do," he announced.

Djeser-Ti also rose and bowed to her husband. "You will think about my words?" she asked.

"I have heard your words," the king said noncommittally.

He took up his duties in the law courts, but his mind was not on the cases before him. After he made two dubious decisions, the chief scribe tactfully suggested that the king might like to pursue other interests while leaving the drudgery of the law to a lesser judge. Nodding, Sekhemkhet left the throne room and summoned Imhotep.

"Congratulations on your marriage, my lord," the Tjaty said as he entered the room. "With two such notable wives, your dynastic future is assured."

"Yes, I shall have many sons."

The king frowned and walked to the window, looking out toward the city. He stayed silent for several minutes and Imhotep waited patiently. Sekhemkhet would make his wishes known in due course, and it was not up to him to hurry the king.

"Are women more troublesome with the passage of time, Imhotep, or is it just that I have become king?"

"In what way, my lord?"

"Djeser-Ti seeks to importune me constantly. When we first got married, she was pleasant and amenable in all things, deferring to me and never disagreeing. Now, however..."

"I have only ever had one wife, my lord," Imhotep said. "Nefertsen has always been agreeable. How...ah...has Djeser-Ti changed?"

"She dins my ears on the question of becoming Queen."

Imhotep nodded slowly. "It is natural that a wife seeks to know her station in life, especially the wife of a king. In addition, you have just taken another wife, and that must be unsettling for her. She will accept your decision as king, my lord."

"What is my decision?"

"There can only be one, my lord. Your sister Inetkawes is daughter of the king and must be made your queen."

"Djeser-Ti believes the mother of my son and heir should be queen."

Imhotep hesitated, treading delicately on treacherous ground. "As yet, you have no son and heir, Hor-Sekhemkhet."

"No, but Djeser-Ti will shortly be brought to the birthing chamber. If that child is a son, then doesn't she deserve to be queen?"

"Djeser-Ti is a beautiful young woman, and worthy of being your wife, my lord, but she is not descended from royalty. Her father, Asarhotep, is of the nobility, but only for three generations. Inetkawes, on the other hand, has the same illustrious ancestry as you."

"So she cannot be queen?"

"I would advise against it, my lord," Imhotep said.

"But if she bears a son? He would be my heir."

"One does not necessarily follow the other. Your own mother was not queen."

"I have used that argument with Djeser-Ti already."

"It is a good argument, my lord. Inetkawes is a royal princess and should be made queen. The Crown prince could come from her or Djeser-Ti. If they both bear sons who live to become men, then you can choose your heir. Otherwise, let the gods decide. They will give sons as they see fit."

"That is why you are my Tjaty, Imhotep, as you were for my father. Great is your wisdom."

Sekhemkhet immediately set about preparing for his sister-wife Inetkawes to assume the position of queen, but this immediately led to veiled recriminations from Djeser-Ti. She attended the coronation, but glowered darkly and excused herself at the earliest opportunity.

Djeser-Ti soon had other things to distract her, as her labour pains started. It was a hard birth, and the young woman was exhausted by the time the child made its way into the world. She was elated that she had brought forth a son for the king, but concerned that the baby's first cries were weak. A healthy child was expected to cry lustily, exhibiting rage when denied the wet-nurse's breast, but this boy whimpered, or grizzled weakly.

Hesy-Ra, the court physician, examined the infant, but could find nothing explicitly wrong. He hesitated to give the parents bad news, but neither could he be unduly optimistic about the child's chances.

"His life is in the hands of the gods," he said. "Let him suckle, keep him warm and clean, and we shall see."

While the health of the royal child still hung in the balance, there was nothing wrong with the king's virility. Djeser-Ti spent some time recovering from her ordeal, and the king paid greater attention to Inetkawes, and before long her *hesmen* failed, much to the satisfaction of Sekhemkhet.

"It will be another son," he exclaimed.

Another son would be a welcome addition to the royal family as the infant boy became steadily weaker. He had trouble feeding, and often vomited up his latest meal. His eyes grew dull, his limbs listless, and his cries became no more than faint moans. Hesy-Ra prescribed tonics, but the baby could not keep them down. Prayers written on scraps of papyrus and bound to the baby's body held out the only hope now. In an effort to gain strength through the magic of names, Sekhemkhet named the child Khasekhem after his grandfather.

"Khasekhem was a strong king, uniting the two kingdoms," he declared. "Let his strength flow into this child named for him."

If the gods were listening, they turned their backs. Barely two months old, Khasekhem faded away and died. Djeser-Ti's cries of anguish were heart-rending, both for the lost baby and also for her own ambitions. Inetkawes commiserated with the king, but gently insinuated the idea that her own child would be the longed-for heir. Sekhemkhet was philosophical, grieving for a lost son, but also recognising that he was still a young man and would undoubtedly father many more sons.

"I will prepare a place in my city of the dead for my first son. He shall enjoy the afterlife with all his brothers and sisters yet to be born."

He gave the necessary instructions to Imhotep, who incorporated them into his plans for the South Tomb within the king's enclosure. Having arranged for the burial, Hor-Sekhemkhet's attention turned to the living. Inetkawes's pregnancy continued without problems, but Djeser-Ti lost her child through an early miscarriage. As soon as was decent, Sekhemkhet lay with Djeser-Ti again, determined to sow another son. He also started looking elsewhere, and sent for his younger sister.

"Meresankh, I am minded to take you as a wife also, alongside Inetkawes. You, too, shall bear sons for me."

She made no reply, knowing her brother could do what he liked, but lacking any desire to be married. Instead, she excused herself and hurried away, her mind in turmoil. When she calmed down, she thought about what she could do, and decided to take her problem to her uncle Imhotep.

"Help me, Uncle. I don't know who else to turn to."

"If I can. What is the problem?"

"The problem is my brother. He is talking about marrying me and I have no desire to do so. How can I dissuade him?"

"Wait, Meresankh. This is something new. Your brother has just married Inetkawes, and he has another wife whom he loves very much. Why should he want to marry you?"

"He is obsessed with having sons."

"Everyone needs sons to be his heirs," Imhotep said. "Kings even more so."

"I know, but he has two wives already and he can have whatever woman he pleases. Why does he have to turn to me?"

"You are a royal princess, daughter of a king, and whoever marries you has a claim to the throne of Kemet. It makes sense for the king to marry his sisters."

"I thought you would support me," Meresankh said bitterly.

"I do support you, but we must also obey our king, and if he desires you as a wife, then it is your duty to agree."

"Never."

Imhotep frowned at Meresankh's vehemence. "Would it be so bad?" he asked gently. "You know Sekhemkhet; you grew up together. He loves Djeser-Ti; you can see it in his every look, touch or word. He would be a gentle and caring husband."

"Let him be a gentle and caring husband to Djeser-Ti then. He can be a brother to me."

A thought occurred to Imhotep, and he smiled. "You are in love with some other man? Who is this paragon for whom you would reject the king?"

"There is no man," Meresankh said firmly. "I have no interest in men."

"You have not yet fallen in love, and are inexperienced in the intimacies that are shared by a man and a woman. I understand, Meresankh..."

"No, you do not understand, Uncle. I am not completely inexperienced. How could I be in Kemetu society? I just have no interest whatsoever in doing what men and women do together."

"You will fall in love one day..."

"Never with a man."

Imhotep smiled condescendingly. "You say that now, but one day you will meet the right man and be happy with him, want to marry him..."

"Uncle, that will not happen," Meresankh interrupted. "I will never fall in love with a man because...because I love a woman."

"I don't see why that should preclude love and marriage. It is good for young women to have close friendships with other women."

"Not friendship, Uncle; love. I would live with her as if I was married."

Imhotep stared at his niece. "Am I missing something here? You seem to be saying you want to lie with a woman as if with a man."

"Not as if with a man. I care nothing for the sowing of seed in my belly, but I value instead companionship and intimacy with another woman. Men think in terms of ruling their woman, of sowing their seed, while true friendship they limit to their male comrades. I have met a woman who, like me, seeks true friendship and intimacy with a woman who can return it in equal measure."

"I did not think such things happened," Imhotep said.

"Probably more than you might think, Uncle, but most women believe they must marry and have children, so they put aside their love for other women."

"Who is this woman?"

Meresankh hesitated. "I would rather not say. I do not wish to visit trouble upon her."

"I would not do that," Imhotep said.

"Perhaps not, but others might, if they knew."

"If you live with her, others will know soon enough."

"I would still rather not reveal her name yet. It would be proper to ask her permission first."

"I can understand that, at least." Imhotep nodded. "Very well, Meresankh, what do you want me to do?"

"Persuade my brother not to marry me."

Imhotep grimaced at the thought of trying to turn the king's desires aside. If he was to succeed he would need a better argument than the truth. He went away to consider how he might do this.

The king was in an expansive mood when Imhotep came to see him. He greeted his uncle with a grin despite the recent death of his infant son, telling him that Inetkawes was with child, as well as several palace women.

"I will populate Inebu-hedj with my progeny."

"My congratulations on your virility, my lord, but if I must speak to you on an important matter..."

"And I have it in mind to take another wife. Can you guess who, Uncle?"

Imhotep had a very good idea and knew he had to speak first if he was to turn the king's intentions aside.

"I pray it is not who I think it might be, my lord, for I have had a dream."

"A dream? A true dream? One that foretells the future? Have you consulted the priests to decipher the meaning?"

"My lord, you forget that I am the Hem-netjer of Re at Iunu. The interpretation of dreams is part of my duties. In this case, the gods sent it directly to me, knowing I had the ear of the king."

"Yes...yes, I can see that," Sekhemkhet said. "What was the dream?"

"My lord, I saw a funeral procession with mourners lining the streets."

Sekhemkhet went pale. "Whose funeral was it?"

"That was hidden from my sight. The whole scene appeared as if seen through smoke. Only one thing stood clear, my lord, and that was your sister Meresankh. She stood mourning her husband."

"Her husband?"

"Indeed, my lord. The meaning of this dream is clear. Whoever marries Meresankh faces the certainty of a premature death."

Sekhemkhet's right hand sketched out the lines of the Eye of Horu, seeking to turn aside fate.

"There can be no other interpretation?" the king asked.

"No, my lord. If Meresankh marries a man, he will swiftly die."

Sekhemkhet sat down, looking pale. "I had intended to marry her myself. That is what I was going to tell you."

"I would strongly advise against it, my lord. The will of the gods could not be plainer."

"A pity. Marriage to both of my sisters would be a kingly thing to do." His worried look suddenly cleared. "What if she got married to someone else...someone expendable...and then when he died, I could marry her?"

"I do not believe the gods can be cheated, my lord. Besides, even if your ruse worked, a son born to her afterward would be of suspect parentage."

"The man need not lie with her."

"An unconsummated marriage is no marriage, my lord. There is one other aspect that must be considered too. The dream did not indicate which husband of Meresankh would die. It is entirely possible that it was a second husband. The identity was obscured."

"But if the dream is a warning from the gods, why would they obscure the identity?"

"That is plain, my lord, to one skilled in the interpretation of dreams. The identity of the dead husband is hidden so that you might make a choice. If you choose to marry Meresankh anyway, you know your fate; but if you choose not to, then some other man will have that fate. The future is not yet written."

"Then I cannot marry Meresankh," Sekhemkhet declared. "Though I pity her, knowing that her husband must swiftly die."

"I will counsel her, my lord," Imhotep said. "It may be that if she puts off marriage for a time, the gods will relent and allow her the marital happiness that we enjoy."

Chapter 3

Den faced the choice of hiring a woman to look after his children after the death of his wife Khasenet, but as this would necessitate leaving them in Inebu-hedj while he worked at Sekera, he decided he would like to take them with him. Financially, he drew a good wage from the treasury as Imhotep's assistant, but even that was in doubt now that Rahotep had been promoted over him. He might lose the use of the house at Sekera too, and that would prevent him caring for his children. There was only one thing to do, and that was to apply to the Tjaty for an increased wage.

"I am not paying you enough already?" Imhotep asked, looking up from his papers.

Den stood awkwardly in front of the Tjaty's worktable. Imhotep had not asked him to sit, or otherwise put him at his ease, another disturbing sign of their worsening relationship. Perhaps this was not a good time to ask for a better wage, he thought.

"I have a family of five...four children, my lord, and must maintain a house in Inebu-hedj for them and also one in Sekera. I no longer have a wife to care for them but must hire a woman. These things are a severe drain on my income."

Imhotep did not comment on Den's slip of the tongue, claiming five children for a moment before changing it to four. He assumed that Den had been referring to his wife, so recently deceased, as a dependent.

"Sell your house in the city and take your children to Sekera," he said. "That way you will have only one household to maintain."

"Overseer Rahotep has taken over my house at Sekera."

Imhotep grunted, seeing where this was going. "That house was built with treasury funds, Den. It does not belong to you, so Rahotep has a right to live there."

"Yes, my lord, but where then am I to live? My children too?"

"Move back to Inebu-hedj then. You are still my assistant, and you can work for me in the city. Your main duties now are planning and calculations anyway."

"Yes, my lord, but those duties entail having ready access to the building site, so I can ensure that the plans are being accurately translated."

"So take trips to Sekera as needed. I really don't see what the problem is."

"If I take regular trips to Sekera, I will be away for days at a time. Therefore, I need to hire a woman to look after my family, and I cannot afford that."

It was on the tip of Imhotep's tongue to suggest Den get married again as a solution to his problem, but caught himself in time. Not enough time had passed to assuage the pain of Khasenet's passing. Instead, he sighed and sat thinking for a few moments. Den was a valuable member of his staff, and it was only his need to foster Rahotep's career that had led to Den being pushed aside. Imhotep did not want to lose Den's service, so he had to do something to ensure his continued loyalty.

"Very well, I appreciate your problem. Find a woman to look after your household in Inebu-hedj for three months." He held up a hand as Den opened his mouth to once more protest his poverty. "I will pay her wages for that time. You will go to Sekera and build another house for you and your family. Thereafter, you will live at Sekera permanently."

"I... I cannot afford to build a house out of my own purse, my lord."

"The treasury will pay for it. Does that meet your needs, Den?"

"You are most generous, my lord. Thank you."

Imhotep told Den to write out the necessary permits to draw on treasury funds for the housekeeper and the new building, leaving the latter sufficiently open-ended so he could build whatever he needed, and Imhotep put his seal to the documents. Then Den went away rejoicing. Selling the house in Inebuhedj and moving his family to Sekera, to a house built to his specifications without cost to himself, was all that he needed.

He hired a housekeeper, and took stock of his financial situation, drawing up the plans for his new house. With the treasury to draw upon, he intended to make it large enough to cater for any future additions to his family, as well as his present four children.

"I could marry again," he murmured, as he drew up his building plans. "A fine, new house and the favour of the Tjaty will attract the interest of women."

How can you think of bringing a new woman into your life so soon? Khasenet is barely in her tomb.

"I need someone...and the children need a mother rather than a housekeeper."

What would Khasenet think? You were not a good husband while you were alive. Will you now compound your error by marrying again so soon?

"I did not want to hurt her... it was just that I was in love with Ranefert."

Nevertheless, you were married to Khasenet. Does your word mean nothing?

Den groaned, pushing aside his plans. He could not help but feel guilty over Khasenet's death. She was probably...possibly...unaware of his infidelity, but she had become pregnant in an effort to win Den back, and that pregnancy had killed her. Dying in childbirth, their daughter had survived, and was a daily reminder to Den of his crime.

"Not a crime in the legal sense," he muttered.

A crime, nonetheless, he thought. *You betrayed her and she died because of it.*

"I cannot turn back the days. I would if I could, but I cannot. What is, is."

Would he though? he wondered. He had only married Khasenet in the first place because he was barred from marrying Ranefert. His later infidelity with Ranefert was proof of his abiding obsession with the Tjaty's daughter. Khasenet had been happy enough, Den told himself, and childbirth was often dangerous for women. Her death had not been his fault. The gods had ordained it for some reason known only to them.

"I am free to seek another wife," Den murmured. "Life moves on."

Are you thinking of yourself or your children?

"Why cannot it be both? My children are young and need a mother's influence, while I am still young and lustful. We all need a woman in our lives."

You can satisfy your lust with a woman off the streets.

"I am a man of position and responsibility. A wife would be better, and with my new house in Sekera I can afford one."

Ranefert?

The thought gave Den pause. He was unmarried and so was she. Moreover, they had a child together, a young boy called Khamose who lived with her, and he would benefit from being raised with his other children.

"Why not? I will go and see her. I am sure she will see the sense of such a mutually advantageous arrangement."

Den dressed in his best clothes, donning jewellery as befitted his station in life, and selected gifts for Ranefert and his son Khamose. A fine onyx ring would appeal to her, he thought, and a wooden soldier, carved and armed with a shield and spear, would be welcomed by any small boy. He left his house and made his way to Ranefert's home bearing the gifts. A servant opened the door and showed him into the courtyard of the house, saying he would inform the mistress of his arrival, and after several minutes Ranefert appeared, though she did not look as if she welcomed the visit.

"Why are you here, Den?"

"I cannot call on a friend?"

"Is that what we are? You should have requested an audience; I might have been entertaining an invited guest."

This was not going according to Den's plan. "I would also like to see Khamose. I brought gifts. For you too, Ranefert. See?" He brought out the onyx ring and the toy soldier.

Ranefert examined the setting of the ring and the sheen of the stone, slipped it onto her finger and admired it for a few moments. "It is nice...thank you."

"Is Khamose here? I would like to give him his gift."

"What will you tell him about who you are?"

"What do you mean? I am his father."

"He believes Nubsekhem is his father, and that his parents are estranged. I will not have him told otherwise."

"Why would you do that?" Den demanded. "He should know who his real father is."

"And that his mother committed an act of infidelity with her father's scribe? I think not. Nubsekhem may not acknowledge him publicly, but that is better for him than being a by-blow of adultery."

"You are ashamed of me?"

"I do not think of you at all. You have your life to live, and I have mine. As for Khamose, you are not really his father, and if you say otherwise I will make trouble for you. I am sure my father will want to protect the good name of his grandson."

Den wanted to weep with frustration at the turn the conversation had taken. Did she not realise his situation?

"You are unmarried, Ranefert, and raising our child. I, too, am unmarried, and...and I thought that..."

"That I would fall into your arms, grateful that any man would want me?"

"We loved each other..."

"You might have." Ranefert shrugged. "I was bored."

Den stared at her. "You do not mean that. You seduced me..."

Ranefert laughed. "And you were only too willing to forget your wife in favour of someone more exciting. To enjoy ploughing a field outside of marriage. Face up to the facts, Den. We both enjoyed a few months together. If it gives you any consolation, you are a better lover than Nubsekhem ever was..." She paused, a smile on her lips, "...but then again, there is a farm labourer whose name I forget that was better than either of you."

"You are cruel," Den whispered. "I must bear the guilt of betraying Khasenet, knowing that my behaviour might have led to her death, but I genuinely loved you. I still do."

Ranefert sighed. "I do not mean to hurt you, Den, but I have to make you understand that whatever we had is over. It was a passing thing and we must both move on from there."

"And Khamose?"

"Khamose is a constant reminder of my mistake, but he is also my son, and I will raise him properly."

"He is also my son," Den said.

"You cannot prove that, and I will continue to aver that he is Nubsekhem's son, even though he denies him."

"Wouldn't it be better for him if he lived with both his parent? You and I could give him a real home. He has brothers and sisters who would welcome him."

"You offer marriage?"

"Yes."

"I must decline."

"How can I persuade you? I love you; I cannot just walk away."

"And yet that is what you must do, Den. Leave now and do not return. There is nothing for you here."

Ranefert called her servants to escort Den from her house and bade them refuse him entry should he ever call on her again. Den left, sorrowing and wondering how he could return to Ranefert's house, but his duties called to him and soon he left his family in the care of a housekeeper and went to Sekera, where he reported to Rahotep.

Overseer Rahotep consulted with Den on the plans drawn up for Hor-Sekhemkhet's city of the dead, marvelling at the size and complexity of the planned structures.

"I have walked through the enclosure of Netjerikhet's city and was amazed at what I saw there. Now you plan a *mer* and city of greater size. Is it really possible?"

"It is, sir," Den said. "I have experience with these things."

Rahotep scowled at Den's comment, taking it as a criticism of his own lack of experience. He gave Den his orders and dismissed him. Den went off to set things in motion among the masons and labourers, making sure each of them understood the part they were to play in the proposed structures. The terraces that levelled the building site were almost complete, so Den walked the boundaries once more, checking the measurements against his own calculations. Everything seemed to be in order, so he left the various overseers to organise the work teams and went scouting elsewhere on the plateau.

His previous house, now taken over by Rahotep, had commanded an outcrop that gave a wonderful view of the river and the approaches to the building site. At the time it had been built, Den thought that it was the best place for his purposes, but now he was looking for something different. It still had to be close to the site, but it also had to serve as a home for his family. Climbing up and down the approaches to the plateau, wandering along the riverbank and the rim of the high ground, he found a place where the early morning light poured in, but by the time the heat of the day set in, the cliffs and trees shaded it. Furthermore, the prevailing north wind in the valley cooled the site, and would make the house pleasant to live in.

Den paced off the boundaries of a large house and grounds, making sketches on a scrap of papyrus, which he drew up later into detailed plans. There was ample mud brick and limestone associated with the old building site to use on his new house, so he called a team of builders away from the king's tomb and set them to work on his own behalf.

Work progressed rapidly on the house, as the builders were all experienced men and all the materials were to hand. Scores of labourers worked to lay the foundations, erect the walls and fashion wooden beams to hold the roof in place. Soon, they turned their attentions to smoothing down the interior walls with mortar and applying lime to freshen the atmosphere. Furniture from the finest carpenters of Inebu-hedj who willingly sent their wares to Sekera, filled the new house. Den brought servants in to clean the house, to cook and launder the clothing, while others would care for the grounds. A small fortune was spent on his new home, far more than he could afford, but Den presented all the bills to the treasury, where Imhotep's writ took care of every payment.

Within two months, the house was ready and Den brought his family from the city, together with Init, the housekeeper paid for by Imhotep. She would continue her service. The new house completely overshadowed Rahotep's house on the plateau, and he wrote a letter of complaint to his father, protesting that his subordinate lived in greater luxury than he did. His language was intemperate, and Imhotep arrived within days to see for himself. He stalked through Den's new house, wincing at the cost of the building and its furnishings, before accosting his scribe.

"I gave permission for you to build a new house at Sekera at the treasury's cost, but I did not imagine you would spend this amount." Imhotep waved a piece of paper under Den's nose. "When I heard of your supposed extravagance, I pulled out the treasury records, and I am appalled. This house of yours is more expensive than my own in Inebu-hedj, and I am the Tjaty. You are only my assistant and my scribe; why do you live in more luxury than half than nobles in the court?"

"My lord, I told you my circumstances and you most generously offered to help me. At no time did you put limits on my spending, so I created a home that would cater for my needs and those of my family."

"Catering for your needs or catering for your desires, Den?"

"My needs, my lord. If I might point out one aspect you seem to be overlooking, it is that this house was built at treasury expense, and using labour drawn from the workforce here at Sekera. It does not belong to me, but is the king's house, lent to me and my family while I am employed as his architect."

"That employment could easily come to an end," Imhotep said. "One word from me and you would be looking for other work."

"I pray you do not utter that word, my lord, as I believe my skills are useful to you."

Imhotep grunted, and looked out at the vista of the river visible from the main veranda of the house.

"You live in greater luxury than my son Rahotep, who is the Overseer of this entire site. He is your overseer too."

"My lord, your son Rahotep is unmarried, whereas I have four children to take care of. I need a larger house for them and the necessary servants to look after the household. If Rahotep deserves more, then what is to prevent him from using the labourers on the site to refurbish his house? I have no desire to live above my station, my lord, and I was only doing what I deemed necessary under the circumstances."

Imhotep grimaced. "It is my own fault," he said. "I did not set adequate boundaries. Well, this is an end to it. The treasury writ is at an end, and the servants with which you have stocked your house are dismissed. Find other servants at your own expense."

"Of course, my lord," Den said.

Imhotep went and spoke to his son, telling him that he had curtailed Den's spending and that he should look at expanding his own house at Sekera.

"You are the Overseer and should live according to your station. Do whatever is necessary to ensure your comfort."

"Including dismissing Den?"

"No. Den is my assistant, not yours, and he serves me well. He is yours to command however, so work him as you will." Imhotep noted the look of satisfaction on Rahotep's face, so added, "Do not abuse your authority over him. I value Den highly; otherwise, I would have dismissed him myself. I do not want him seeking employment elsewhere because you make his life here miserable."

Den was not particularly concerned about the dismissal of his servants, as there were plenty of other men and women associated with the building site. Some of them would be happy to exchange their onerous jobs for the relative ease of looking after a household. He switched duties for a number of promising men and women, and added Init to the payroll so she could continue as housekeeper. None of these appointments was at his own expense as they were already employed by the king. He was merely reassigning them.

Den's household was a busy one. His eldest son Khawy was nine years old and already starting to put away his childhood toys, swapping them for the tools of his father's trade. He could write in the common script, and haltingly read the priestly language, was taking the first uncertain steps into mathematical calculations, and could recognise one rock from another. Den had assured him that when he was older, there was a place for him on the building site.

"If we are still building tombs by then," Den said. "If not, there is always work for a competent scribe."

His younger son Khepankh, only seven years old, had only the rudiments of reading and writing, but his interests lay elsewhere. Khepankh loved the physical aspects of construction and had prevailed upon his father to make hundreds of little clay blocks, no longer than a man's finger joint. These he guided and manipulated into copies of the buildings his father erected, and even experimented with new creations, some of which caused Den to smile and shake his head.

"I can see that you too will follow me into the building profession," Den told him, delighting the young boy.

Merit, his oldest daughter, was six, but her interests lay with her young sister Khasenet. She doted over the baby, ably assisting Init the housekeeper, who also acted as a wet-nurse. The young girl watched every aspect of the infant's upbringing avidly, and listened to every tale Init spun. Her avowed intent was to become a mother and have lots of babies, and this too, Den supported, buying her cloth dolls as presents.

Den enjoyed the company of his three eldest children and spent time with him whenever he could. The only one he consciously avoided was Khasenet, as her little face reminded him of his dead wife, and he felt his heart pierced with renewed guilt every time he saw her. Khamose, his son with Ranefert, was a child he wanted to see more of, but his mother refused him access.

"I will work on her," he swore. "The day will come when she will accept me, and she and Khamose will live in my household."

Chapter 4

General Khaba increasingly felt his age, particularly on the colder mornings of the winter months, or whenever the north wind blew strongly. His joints stiffened, his muscles were less inclined to drive him with the same strength an intensity of his youth, and his teeth hurt when he bit into anything sweet. One thing remained for him; his mind was as active at sixty as it had been in his youth, and he was still capable of commanding Kemet's small army of the north. He was ably assisted by his First Officer, his son Nubsekhem, and his newly appointed grandson Huni.

His men were at Hut-waret in the far northeast of Kemet, close to the border with Kanaan and its warlike tribes. The fortress there was their base of operations as any threat to the lands of Kemet was most likely to come from Kanaan or the adjacent Land of Sin, a great wedge of mountains and desert to the east. These lands were sources of copper and turquoise and valuable possessions of the king of Kemet.

The borders were at peace now, but that situation would not last. Khaba knew that his men had to be in a constant state of readiness, and that was expensive. Throughout the reign of Netjerikhet Djoser, letters had come from the king and treasury, complaining about the gold being spent on a permanent army. Djoser had even sent for Khaba, demanding the general report in person.

"You have said it yourself, Khaba. The border tribes are at peace. Why do you insist on spending my gold on five hundred men who would be better employed elsewhere?"

"My lord king, the border is at peace because those five hundred men, and five hundred others, beat back the warring tribes."

"Yes, but they are not fighting now. Let them go back to being farmers and fishermen, labourers and artisans. That way they can contribute to the treasury rather than being a drain on it."

"I could do that, my lord king, but when a tribe invades our land, I must then round up my men or train new ones. That takes time, and while I do so, the enemy plunders our land. It is better to keep an army trained and ready for anything. Cheaper too, in the long run."

Djoser consulted with Imhotep, who supported the idea of a permanent army, and he reluctantly agreed to the extra expenditure.

"If we are only talking about tribes invading us, then five hundred men is extravagant. Two hundred should be more than enough."

"I was contemplating a thousand men," Khaba said.

"A thousand? I cannot afford to keep that many men idle."

"Can you afford not to?" Khaba asked. "What do you say, Imhotep?"

"A thousand men will be expensive," the Tjaty said. "General Khaba is right, though, my lord king. Delay in meeting and expelling a foreign invader may be even more expensive. Perhaps we could entertain a compromise?"

"What sort of compromise?" the king asked.

"An army of five hundred men, kept under arms and trained in that profession. The treasury can afford that. Then, in a few years we can judge whether more men are needed...or fewer."

"Even five hundred is too many," Djoser complained. "Two hundred men permanently, rising to five hundred if a threat presents itself."

So Khaba had got his permanent army of two hundred men, and as the years passed, he had been able to expand the size to close on a five hundred men. However, the soldiers guarding the forts near the copper and turquoise mines, numbering several hundred more, diverted funds from the treasury that Khaba believed should have gone to his army. The problem rose from the fact that these men came under a different commander and a different accounting, over which Khaba had no control. He petitioned the king for overall control, but was refused, being told that a man called Neben, a Commander who had risen through the ranks, had overall command of the king's forts in the Land of Sin. There was nothing Khaba could do except make the best of the situation.

Despite his age, Khaba liked to take the men out on exercises as much as he could, and often arranged mock battles between his men and others commanded by his son Nubsekhem. He made these exercises as realistic as possible, though he limited the use of edged weapons. Wooden staffs and cudgels were still capable of inflicting painful bruises or breaking bones, but deaths were uncommon. For half a month at a time, the units under father and son manoeuvred through the desert, setting ambushes, tracking each other, and launching sudden attacks with the aim of capturing the opposing banners. Eventually, limping and bruised, the army units returned to Hut-waret, and much-needed rest, while the officers went over the notes they had made, deciding where they had succeeded or failed, and how they could improve.

Khaba, his son and grandson, retired to the general's quarters, where servants took their sweat-stained and dirty clothing, whisking them away to be laundered, while others brought jars of clean river water so they could wash the filth from their skins and hair. Then they sat in clean clothing, sipping on refreshing cups of beer, and eating a light meal, and discussed the recent exercises.

Much laughter ensued as each generation made fun of the others, and what they saw as each other's military failings. Dishes and cups were cleared from the table and sand scattered over its surface as the three of them stood around, tracing patterns in the sand with their fingers. Battles were refought, skirmishes reinvented, and their voices rose in volume as they argued. Khaba drew on his many years of experience, while Nubsekhem revealed his coldly calculating mind, and Huni, lacking in experience as well as years, could only rely on imagination and daring to challenge his elders.

A messenger came in, saluted his general and passed him a scroll which bore the Tjaty's seal. Khaba broke the clay seal, unrolled the scroll and read, frowning as the import of the words sank in. Dismissing the messenger with thanks, he ordered the guards outside the door to withdraw.

"I think you had better leave us too, Huni," Khaba said grimly.

"What has happened, father?" Nubsekhem asked. "What was in the Tjaty's message?"

"Leave us, Huni. These words are not for your ears."

"Grandfather, I am an officer in your army, and a member of your family besides. Do not send me away as if I am untrustworthy. Anything that reflects on you reflects on the whole family, including me."

"He is right, father," Nubsekhem said. "Whatever you have to say can be said in front of Huni."

Khaba frowned, but then nodded abruptly. "He will hear it soon enough, and it might be better if he knows the background." He flicked the scroll with his finger. "The king's son is dead."

"He cannot have been more than a few months old," Nubsekhem said with a shrug. "Children die all the time. What is one more?"

"Father, he is...was the prince," Huni protested. "It is a sad day for all Kemet."

"I have no doubt the king will enjoy making another one," Nubsekhem said. "He has two young wives to lie with." He looked at the general. "Why is this news so important you send the guards away and would exclude Huni?"

"I have to ask you something," Khaba said, "and you might prefer it was done in private."

"I cannot imagine what you might want to ask me, father. Just go ahead."

"As you wish. Nubsekhem, did you have anything to do with the prince's death?"

Huni's mouth fell open and he looked from his grandfather to his father and back again. Nubsekhem scowled but said nothing.

"Well, it is not so hard a question, is it?" Khaba said.

"Why would you even ask me such a thing?"

"Have you told Huni what you did a few years back? No? Do you think he deserves to know?"

"I can see no good reason to tell him," Nubsekhem said. "It is all in the past."

"You don't think he deserves to know why the king's men might drag him from his house to be tortured and executed, just because you made a miscalculation?"

"What is he talking about, father?" Huni asked, going pale.

"Nothing. It will never happen."

"Do not deceive yourself," Khaba said. "You risked everything before and only luck prevented disaster."

"It was a risk, but I thought the rewards worth it."

"Will someone please tell me what you are talking about?" Huni asked. "What risk?"

"Are you going to tell him, or will I?" Khaba asked.

Nubsekhem grimaced, but faced his son. "A few years ago, I saw the possibility of replacing the royal family with our own. I was careful, despite what your grandfather believes, and made sure that nothing could lead back to us."

"What did you do?" Huni looked pale, but his expression was avid.

"I introduced a poison into the king's wine." Nubsekhem shrugged. "It was a crude poison, but it could have worked. The king recovered, and I thought about how I could improve on the technique. I improved the poison, making it more effective, and poisoned the king again."

"But it did not work?"

"Oh, it worked, but I only gave him enough to make him sick, rather than kill him."

"Why?"

"We were not ready to take over the kingdoms. I know how to do it now, so when your grandfather gives the word, I will kill the king and anyone else who stands in our way, and make General Khaba, King Khaba."

"Grandfather? Could this happen? You could be king?"

"It is nonsense," Khaba growled. "Dangerous nonsense. It is much more likely that we would all end up being impaled and our bodies burnt."

"It could happen," Nubsekhem insisted.

"But it will not," Khaba stated. "So I return to the question I asked you before, Nubsekhem. Did you have anything to do with the prince's death?"

"You told me before not to attempt anything without your permission."

"You are evading the question. Did you kill the prince?"

"No."

"Did you attempt to kill him? Was he weakened by your poison?"

"No."

"Then there is no reason for the king to suspect anything? No trail that leads back to us?"

"I cannot answer for what might be in the king's mind, father, but I have given him no grounds for suspicion."

Khaba sighed. "Good. You can call the guards back now."

"Before I do, please consider the possibility, father. We have the means to remove the king and any heir he might have, the whole family if need be. You would be King of Kemet. Does that thought not excite you?"

"You would be king, and my father would be your heir?" Huni asked. A vision of himself sitting on the throne made his heart beat faster.

"It will not happen," Khaba said. "I am loyal to the king. The gods have placed him on the throne and I will not dispute their choice."

"Sekhemkhet is only the king because he is Djoser's son, and Djoser because his father was Khasekhemwy--who was your cousin. You have royal blood, father."

"We do?" Huni asked.

"Not really," Khaba said. "My father and Khasekhemwy's father were brothers, but when I was born, Khasekhemwy was still only a general. He did not seize the throne until later, so no, we do not."

"But you have a claim to the throne," Nubsekhem persisted. "Marry one of the princesses and your claim is all but certain."

"You insist on forgetting I am loyal to Sekhemkhet, even as I was loyal to his father."

"Even loyalty has its price," Nubsekhem muttered. Louder, he said, "Father, answer me honestly, if you were offered the throne because it was vacant, and you had taken no action to secure that vacancy, would you take it?"

"I am not going to answer such a ridiculous notion."

"It is not impossible, father. Say a plague swept through Kemet and killed the king and his heirs. The kingdoms are in turmoil and a firm hand is needed. You are that firm hand. Would you act to save Kemet then?"

"You seem to think that I only have to stretch out my hand and the throne is in my grasp. If by some mischance the throne became vacant, many would seek to take advantage of the situation. What makes you think I could succeed?"

Nubsekhem smiled to himself. His father had progressed from a categorical denial to a tentative affirmation. "You have nearly a thousand men under your command. Nobody would dare to question your claim."

"They are the king's men."

"Under your command, father."

Khaba frowned. "This is a pointless conversation. The king is alive and well, and I will make no move against him. If the throne was vacant and neither I nor any of my family had a hand in that situation, then I might consider it. However, you would be much mistaken if you thought that these soldiers would follow me if there was even a hint of blame attached to our family."

"Who knows what the future holds?" Nubsekhem said. "I only ask that you consider the possibility should circumstances change."

"You will not act against the king or his heirs," Khaba said. "Is that understood?"

"I understand, father."

Nubsekhem bowed to his father and left the general's quarters, calling for the guards to take up their duties once more. Huni excused himself and hurried after his father, catching up with him in the open ground outside the fortified enclosure of Hut-waret. He walked beside him in silence for a time, sensing his father was deep in thought. After a while, though, he ventured a question.

"What was the poison you used, father?"

Nubsekhem raised his eyebrows in surprise. "I did not expect that question. It does not have a name, as far as I know. Some rocks associated with copper ores contain something that poisons people."

"So you add rocks to their drink?"

"Ground up rocks. Steeped in wine, the rocks release their poison into the liquid. Then I add a few other things, extracts of plants. A few drops added to a cup of wine or beer will make you sick; more will kill you."

"Nasty. I do not like poison." Huni hesitated. "Forgive me, father, but poison seems...well...unmanly."

"I agree, but it is not always possible to kill a man face to face. If I tried that with the king, I would probably be killed for my trouble by his guards, and there would be no benefit to anyone. Better to find a way to achieve the same thing without too much risk."

"I would face the king," Huni said boldly.

"I am sure you would," Nubsekhem said, "but I would rather you survived to enjoy the fruits of your actions."

"I would find a way to survive."

"Yes, I believe you are clever enough."

Huni preened himself with his father's words of praise.

"So it comes down to this," Nubsekhem went on. "Would you like to make your grandfather the king?"

Huni hesitated, searching his father's face. He nodded slowly. "The throne would be yours to inherit, and mine afterward. Such a prize is worth great risk."

Now it was Nubsekhem's turn to gaze at his son, taking the measure of his bravery and determination. "Then let us take that risk," he said after a few moments.

"What about grandfather?" Huni asked. "He does not favour such action."

"He is an old man, and old men are cautious," Nubsekhem said. "We will not tell him unless we have to. I am quite sure that when we hand him the throne, he will take it."

"You have a plan, father?"

"I am working on one. It will be good to be able to discuss things with a trusted person. It is not just a simple matter of striking down the king, you know. We must plan who else dies, how we seize control of the court, the army, the law courts... everything."

"We already have the army," Huni said with a grin.

"I would not count on that. Not just yet, anyway."

"But the men will follow us, won't they? They obey us willingly."

"It is one matter to give them a command during training or when fighting Kemet's enemies, but quite another to order a man to attack his king."

"I had not thought of that. There are ways to change his loyalty?"

"I believe so; and that is what we will work on."

Nubsekhem did not tell his son, but he had already started on those ways. Loyalty can be bought with gold, but bought loyalty cannot be relied upon. If a man will change his allegiance in exchange for material benefit, there is always the likelihood that he will change it back for a further inducement. The common men could be bought, but the officers who commanded them were more important. For them, gold would not be enough. Nubsekhem would have to find another way to change and hold their loyalty.

His endeavours were aided by the king, in that first Netjerikhet, and then Sekhemkhet, did not favour a large permanent army. It was cheaper to maintain the bare minimum needed to act as a trained nucleus and, when a foreign threat presented itself, raise levies from the nearby provinces as needed. The duration of a threat and the size of the levy were never strictly defined, however, and both Khaba and Nubsekhem managed to slowly build up a sizable army. Quality of the officers concerned both general and commander, though for different reasons. Khaba looked for tough individuals who could command obedience and respect, showing loyalty to the throne, while Nubsekhem looked mainly for men who would offer him personal loyalty.

Gradually, as levies were returned to their homes, and re-enlisted for the next threat, Nubsekhem was able to get rid of the overly competent men who were too loyal to the throne, and replace them with men who were prepared to swear loyalty to anyone who paid them. Over a period of several years, Nubsekhem built up a cadre of men he could count on.

Chapter 5

The sorrow that had enveloped the palace at Inebu-hedj the previous year at the loss of the king's heir and the subsequent loss through miscarriage of another child dissipated with the birth of a son to Inetkawes. Holding the young prince in her arms, she paraded before everyone, but especially before Djeser-Ti. If anyone thought it cruel to show a living son to a woman who had lost two children so recently, they turned their faces away without comment. Sekhemkhet was overjoyed, swiftly putting aside his grief, and proclaimed the new child his heir, naming him Nub-Re, or 'Golden One of Re'.

Djeser-Ti was brought to the birthing chair not long after, full of hope that she could produce another son that could at least be a rival for Nub-Re.

"Why not?" she declared. "I birthed a son first, and though I lost my next child before it was possible to determine its sex, I feel confident it was a son, too. This child I carry within me is also a boy; I feel it in my bones. He will grow up tall and strong, and inherit all that is good in Kemet."

The labour was long and hard, but the child eventually greeted the outside world with an outraged cry. Djeser-Ti, thankful her ordeal was over, could only weep when the patient midwives revealed she had given birth to a girl. She lay with the child in her arms, hoping that the king would tear himself away from his newborn son long enough to greet his new daughter, and thought about what it meant for her ambition to become a queen. Sekhemkhet put in an appearance eventually, but he was matter-of-fact about the whole business, dismissing her feelings.

"What is one girl-child here or there?" the king said. "You are young and have shown yourself capable of bearing children. There will be plenty of opportunities to give me a son."

This did not satisfy Djeser-Ti and she was offended that her husband dismissed her so readily. She had loved him even before she knew his identity, and afterward, he had promised her they would always be together. They still were, of course, but now he had taken another wife and raised her up to be queen. Compounding the hurt, the heir she had borne was dead, replaced by the new prince Nub-Re. Her anger rose, and a determination to do something to return the king's favour to her children. She sent for her father, Asarhotep.

"Do not lose hope," was her father's advice. "You have a healthy daughter."

"Of what use is a daughter?" Djeser-Ti demanded. "Only a man sits upon the throne of Kemet."

"Have you forgotten what lies in front of your eyes?" Asarhotep asked mildly. "The king's sister became his wife and queen, and now has given him an heir."

"You twist the knife that pierces my belly," Djeser-Ti said bitterly. "I think of little else."

"Then do you not see that this Nub-Re, when he becomes king, will marry his sister, your daughter, and father an heir on her?"

"I want my son to be king."

"At least your grandson will be king," Asarhotep pointed out. "Is that not enough?"

Djeser-Ti grimaced. "It will have to be enough for my daughter. Even the gods are powerless to turn her into a boy. However, I want to bear a son of my own...another son. I do not care that the other woman has a son; children die, after all; but I must have another son to take Nub-Re's place."

"Then you must have the king sow his seed in you again. As often as is needed."

"What can I do to be sure I have a boy?"

"Why do you ask me? That is with the gods."

"The midwives and women of the palace prattle behind my back, hinting at ways to make it happen, but none will admit to my face that they know how. Will you find out for me, father? It is in your interests too, that I bear a son."

"I am unaware of anything like that but I will make enquiries."

Asarhotep took his leave of his daughter and made his way to the rented room he used when visiting Inebu-hedj. He missed the comfort of his home in Abdju, and was starting to think about relocating to the capital city. It made sense now that the court, and his only surviving child, was in the north. In the meantime, he had a pleasant enough room above one of the higher-class taverns, and a problem that he could see was going to occupy his mind.

Picking up a jug of wine and a loaf of bread from the tavern, he ascended the outside steps to his upstairs room and sat down to eat and drink. The problem he faced was not something he had ever thought about. He had always assumed that when you lay with a woman and sowed your seed, then the child that ensued was an accident--it was either a boy or girl. The thought that one could actually influence the sex of the child was a new one, but perhaps it was not unreasonable. Gods controlled everything from the rising of the sun each morning to the falling of sand grains. If that was so, then why not the sex of a child?

So, Asarhotep thought, if the gods could control the birth of a boy or girl, then how to influence them? Prayer was the obvious answer, but the ears of the gods must be dinned by millions of prayers every day, so how could he be sure one specific prayer got through. Even if it did, there was no guarantee that it would be granted, so something more was needed-- something that would bend a god's will to his own. Asarhotep shivered at the thought. How did one coerce a god?

First things first, he told himself. Prayer with persuasion. He had done it often enough in his life, petitioning the gods for a favourable outcome by making a contribution to a temple, supplying the priests with food or incense or gold. Sometimes it worked and sometimes it did not. Asarhotep remembered praying for a child when he first got married. It worked, and Djeser-Ti was the proof of it. Praying for a son--not granted. Petitioning for a business deal to show a profit--granted. Pleading for his wife to survive the growth in her belly--not granted. The memory of that loss so many years before still brought tears to his eyes.

"It is still worth trying though. I am not rich, but I am wealthy; I can afford gifts of gold to some temples, at least. It is just a matter of selecting the gods most likely to look favourably on my petition."

Asarhotep smiled ruefully and poured himself another cup of wine. The selection of relevant gods did not help much; there were so many gods and goddesses who had the subject of fertility as one of their aspects. Still, some were more important than others. Mesenet, the goddess of childbirth, was an obvious choice, as was Auset, the goddess of motherhood. Taweret, who oversaw childbirth, and Min, the god of fertility and reproduction, were also important. Heqet, the frog-goddess perhaps, and Renenutet. Asarhotep started working out how much he could afford to give each temple, and grimaced. Giving generously to them all would bankrupt him.

"Can I afford not to, though," he muttered. "If I neglect one god, he might work against me. Besides, having a grandson who is heir to the throne of Kemet is worth much gold."

Having settled the most obvious action, Asarhotep looked outside and saw that the evening was close. He went for a walk through the city, looking through the stalls in the marketplace as the heat of the day receded. The odours of frying fish and onions pervaded the air, reminding him that they would soon be serving the evening meal in the tavern. Wine and bread staved off hunger for a while, but he looked forward to a satisfying cooked meal. In the meantime, his feet guided him down to the broad expanse of the river, and the docks, still bustling with activity despite the lateness of the hour. He sat on a bale of wool and watched the boats, his mind turning back to his problem. As he sat in thought, a young woman in flimsy attire that left little to the imagination accosted him.

"You look lonely," she said. "My name is Nef. Come with me and for a little copper you can enjoy my body all night."

Asarhotep felt himself stir with desire, but the woman was young enough to be his daughter, so he thrust aside his inclination, thanking her but refusing her offer. She looked a little annoyed at the refusal, but persisted.

"Are you sure? If my body does not attract you, perhaps one of my sisters can make you stand up. Or perhaps my young brother, if you are so inclined. We can negotiate the price, too."

"You are kind," Asarhotep said, "but my mind is elsewhere."

Nef snorted indignantly and started to walk off. She turned back, though, curiosity written on her face.

"What is so interesting that a healthy man like you would turn down the offer of a willing field?"

"Nothing that need concern you," Asarhotep snapped. Regretting his harsh tone almost immediately, he added, "My daughter has given me an impossible task. She wants a son, but that is only something the gods can provide."

Nef shrugged. "Gods listen but only respond to expensive gifts. Luckily, there are other ways for common people."

"Really? What ways?"

Nef smiled coquettishly. "A scrap of copper and I will tell you."

Asarhotep shook his head. "You do not know. This is just your first proposition presented another way."

Nef laughed. "Oh, I know things. Women have knowledge men dismiss. Come with me, and for a copper bracelet and a fish supper I will tell you what you need to know. If you don't believe what I say, then for no extra cost I will open my legs for you." She saw the hesitation in Asarhotep's face and smiled, laying a hand on his arm. "Come, sir, I offer you knowledge and comfort for the cost of a copper bracelet. How can you refuse?"

Asarhotep did not refuse. He told himself that it was solely so he could learn what Nef knew, but after they had eaten and he handed over the copper bracelet, listening to her words, he could not resist the offer of her body.

The next day, recovering after a night filled with much exercise and little sleep, he mulled over the words Nef had spoken, remembering the events of the night. She spoke of several possibilities, but at the time, he had been too distracted by her company to pay them full attention. Now, however, he could weigh the import of her ideas.

Her first idea had been a matter of diet, assuring him that what a woman ate while pregnant influenced the sex of the child. Similarly, potions could have the same effect. Asarhotep knew nothing about the inner workings of the body, but he reasoned that a woman's belly could be approached in two ways. Food went to the belly through the mouth, but a man's seed went there by another route. It seemed reasonable to suppose that one could influence the other. The problem was to identify foods that engendered maleness in the unborn baby. Most people did not care one way or the other--all children were valued in most families. It was only when a man required a male heir that people looked for a solution.

Nef had not been very helpful in this regard, though she had two possible treatments. Men's blood burned hotter, she said, which was why men became warriors. Anything that heated the blood would encourage a baby to become male. She suggested mustard seeds and other plants that produced a burning sensation in the mouth.

"Putting them closer to the woman's belly might work better," Nef said with a smile, "but I cannot imagine a woman wanting a boy that badly." She had gone on to speak of how a woman's urine could be used to predict the sex of a baby. "If the barley sprouts first, the child will be a boy."

"How does that help?" Asarhotep asked. "I want to change the sex, not just know what it is going to be."

"I have heard it said that the application of urine from a woman who is having a male child is efficacious," Nef said.

Asarhotep had not paid great attention at the time, as Nef sat cross-legged and naked, preparing a mixture of crocodile dung, honey and wool. When she had prepared it to her satisfaction she inserted it in front of a bemused Asarhotep.

"That takes care of preventing your seed from reaching my belly," she said. "Shall we test it?"

It was only much later, while Asarhotep recovered his strength, that she spoke of other ways of influencing a baby's sex.

"Magic," she whispered. "The gods work through magic, and some men employ the same methods. It is said that the High Priests of Ptah can work magic."

"You know this for sure?" Asarhotep asked.

Nef's answer was evasive, but she reiterated her belief that some men had the power. "Everyone knows magicians exist." She could not name one, though, or even claim she knew anyone who knew a magician, so when Asarhotep pressed her to say more, she distracted him into more pleasurable pastimes.

They had lain together in the pre-dawn darkness, Asarhotep exhausted from his exertions, and Nef pleasantly fulfilled. She had twirled the copper bracelets on her wrist, Asarhotep having given her another one, and murmured that there was a method of last resort.

"Eh?" Asarhotep struggled to focus his attention on his companion. "What do you mean by 'last resort'?"

"If prayer does not work, if magic and potions prove ineffectual, you can always switch the child."

"I don't understand."

"If your daughter truly desires to raise a boy, then if a girl is born to her, have one of the midwives take the girl-child away before your daughter sees it, and substitute a boy-child. She will never know the difference."

"I... I couldn't do that," Asarhotep said. "The boy would not truly be my son-in-law's heir, but a stranger."

Nef yawned and stretched, and then got up to find a pot and perched on it, relieving her bladder. "One child is much like another," she said. "Rich people have been known to adopt a boy to be their heir, so why not your daughter?"

Asarhotep thought about Nef's words the next day. The urine and magic seemed worth following up, but swapping children defeated the purpose of the whole thing, he thought. Besides, it was unlikely any mother, especially his daughter, would agree. Urine was the first of his tasks, so employing a woman to act for him, approached pregnant women and asked if they had taken the test to determine the sex of their unborn child. Several had, and then it was a matter of offering a fee for the supply of their water.

Djeser-Ti was less than enthusiastic about applying the urine to her belly, and she flatly refused even to think about drinking it. It was only the urgent need to produce a son that made her agree to try it. Sekhemkhet had lain with her in the meantime, and she believed his seed had sprouted in her belly. She applied the urine, letting it dry on her as long as she could stand it, before washing it off, repeating the process as her belly slowly swelled. Nine months later, when she gave birth, she eagerly awaited the midwives' smiles to let her know she had a son, but it was another girl.

The disappointment Asarhotep felt was compounded by the revelation that the woman he had bought the urine off in the first place either lied or was mistaken in her belief that she was going to have a boy. She had a girl. Asarhotep wondered whether that proved the method worked--after all, urine from a girl-producer had produced a girl in Djeser-Ti. He wanted to try again, but his daughter refused.

"Find some other way," she told her father.

The magical realm was next, but finding a reputable magician was harder than it seemed. There were many men in the city who claimed magical powers, but all they could actually do were a variety of common tricks to fool people in the street, earning themselves a living. After a great deal of searching, Asarhotep tracked down an imposing looking Kushite who had the reputation of being a successful magician. The man was tall, his black-skinned body covered in scars and cicatrices, a completely bald head and eyes that gleamed brightly.

"I am Psartu. My magical arts are second to none," the man rumbled, his voice so deep it sounded like distant thunder. "I was initiated into the arts as a child in Kush, and no other magician has ever bested me. Who do you want to kill?"

"Kill? I do not want to kill anyone. I want..."

"Are you sure? My death spells are particularly effective."

"I want my daughter to give birth to a boy. It is imperative that she gives her husband an heir."

"Have they tried to have children normally? With what result?"

"They have had three children. First, a son who died after a month or so, then two daughters."

Psartu nodded, looking thoughtful. "You are willing to pay? These things can be expensive."

"I am willing to pay for results," Asarhotep said.

"For a finger of copper, I will approach my spirits and see if it is even possible."

Asarhotep handed over the copper, and Psartu took out a small leather bag, tipping the contents onto the ground. Several small bones were mixed in with shiny pebbles and gaudy feathers. He poked at them with a finger, scrutinising the patterns they made.

"My spirits say it is still possible for you daughter to bear a son, but that the door of her belly is closing. It must happen within the next three months or not at all."

Asarhotep grimaced. "What do you need?"

Psartu sat back on his haunches as he gathered up his spirit items and put them back in the leather bag, pulling the drawstrings tight.

"I will need her *hesmen* blood, the father's seed, and..." Psartu looked at Asarhotep calculatingly, "...five fingers of gold." He held up a hand as Asarhotep opened his mouth to object to the cost. "There are other items I must buy that will account for most of that. You need to ask yourself if an heir is worth the price."

"I will consider it," Asarhotep said, getting up.

"Do not take too long. Remember the door of her belly is closing."

Asarhotep stalked away from the magician's house, sure that Psartu was a charlatan. Five fingers of gold for a magical spell? It was a huge sum, and not one he could afford. By the time he got back to his lodgings though, he knew that he could not afford to ignore the possibility. To have a grandson sitting on the throne of Kemet was worth any price. He turned around and retraced his steps, telling Psartu that he agreed to his terms.

"Seven days," Psartu said. "My spirits are strongest at the time of the new moon. Have the ingredients and the gold ready by then."

"I do not know if my daughter's *hesmen* falls within that time," Asarhotep said.

Psartu frowned. "*Hesmen* blood is most effective, but ordinary blood will do. I would say to delay until the next new moon, but there is only a small gap of opportunity here. The father's seed is essential, though."

"How will I get the king to spill his seed into a jar?" Djeser-Ti demanded when her father told her about the magical spell. "I can prick my finger to get blood, but if I ask him to spill his seed he will think I have gone mad. Or worse, he will believe I weave a magical spell to do him harm."

"Did I say that? Have him spill his seed in you, and remove as much as you can afterward. Try and accomplish this on the fifth or sixth day, so everything is ready for the new moon."

Djeser-Ti said she would try, and Asarhotep waited anxiously for word from her. It came on the morning of the seventh day, and she handed her father two tiny unguent jars, tightly stoppered.

"My blood and the king's seed," she said.

Asarhotep took the jars, together with five fingers of gold, to the house of Psartu that evening. The magician led him into a secluded courtyard when a small fire burned and several items were laid out on a black cloth. Only a few of the items were recognisable--a dagger, a few small carved statues of hideous looking beings, a scroll of papyrus and a bowl. Four small pots filled with unidentifiable substances completed the magician's paraphernalia.

"You have the items?" Psartu asked.

Asarhotep handed over the blood and seed, and then the gold. The metal quickly disappeared into the magician's purse. Then he told Asarhotep to sit on the ground to one side of the fire.

"Conjuring my spirits will take time. Say nothing unless I ask you to speak. Some of the spirits are dangerous, and they will concentrate their attention on the one speaking. I have ways of protecting myself; you do not."

Psartu hunkered down and scattered a few grains of incense in the fire, releasing wisps of sweet-smelling smoke. He took up each carved beings in turn, passing it through the smoke and muttering phrases in a tongue that Asarhotep could not understand. It might have been his imagination, but Asarhotep could feel the night drawing down around him, and felt flutterings of fear as the unintelligible phrases fell upon his ears.

"They are here," Psartu said. "Speak now your desire."

Asarhotep licked lips that were suddenly dry. "I... I desire my daughter Djeser-Ti to bear a healthy son to her husband."

Psartu held up his hand to prevent any more words, though fear had closed up Asarhotep's throat. He unstoppered the two unguent jars and tipped a few drops from each into a bowl. To this, he added a pinch of the contents from each of the four pots.

"The dried, embalmed flesh of a dead man," he said as he added the first. "The man was virile and had seven sons, no daughters." A pinch from the second pot. "The dried lifeblood of a bull, taken as the animal expired," The third followed. "Slime from the sacred frog of the goddess Heqet." Psartu reached into the fourth pot and sprinkled a black powder into the bowl. "I will not name this last one, as even the mention of it would make you cry out in fear."

The magician mixed the contents of the bowl, then dipped a strip of papyrus into it, drying it in front of the fire. He then took another piece of papyrus and wrote a phrase on it, handing both to Asarhotep.

"Have your daughter bind this one close to her body when she next lies with her husband, and utter the phrase on this other one as he spills his seed in her." Psartu smiled at the stricken look on Asarhotep's face, "The spirits have left us; you may speak freely."

"Wh...what does the phrase mean? I do not recognise it."

"It is an invocation to draw down maleness. Only your daughter must say it, and only at the moment of release."

"It will work?"

"I have never known it to fail."

Asarhotep passed on the instructions to Djeser-Ti and she carried them out. If Sekhemkhet wondered at the spoken phrase at the moment of climax, he did not remark on it, and half a month later, Djeser-Ti was delighted to learn that once more she was with child.

"This time it will be a boy," she told her father. "Once he is born, we shall find a way to make him the king's heir.

Chapter 6

Den was up before dawn every day. A quick wash, then packing a flask of water and a crust of bread, he walked toward the building site in the cool air, appreciating the first flush of light from the rising sun. The site itself had been cleared of sand, the irregular surface of the limestone base levelled off, and the brick terraces taking form to lift the low-lying areas to the same height as the rest of it. By the time he arrived, the first workers were making their way there from the workers' village, overseers starting to direct them to their daily tasks. Den would walk the boundaries of the site, pacing off the distances that he knew off by heart, seeking to put himself in touch with the spirit of the area. He had tried to explain this feeling to Imhotep.

"It is as if the structure we build there already exists," he said. "I can see it in my mind's eye, and I try to connect with it every time I am there. It guides me in what I do."

Imhotep nodded solemnly. "It confirms my belief that you are the right man to guide this project, Den."

"But not to be Overseer."

"Have you told Rahotep of your vision?"

"No. He would dismiss my notions."

Rahotep was seldom on site, preferring to deal with the project through a score or more supervisors, who reported to him daily. Den, on the other hand, was everywhere, watching as the masons drew their lines in red ochre, the workers carried the small limestone blocks for the terraces, and other labourers started chipping away at the entrance to the underground tomb. He talked to the supervisors, making suggestions but never ordering them to do something as he knew such orders would find their way back to Rahotep. The site Overseer might then forbid him from interacting with the supervisors and workers, and Den did not want to take that risk. Sekhemkhet's City of the Dead was going to be greater than that of Netjerikhet, and Den was determined to have a part in its construction as well as the planning.

One of the major differences in the planning of this *mer* was the positioning of the vertical shaft that would give access to the underground burial chamber. With Netjerikhet's tomb, the shaft had been central, but as the structure rose above two *per-djet* layers, it had become necessary to seal it off and dig out another access tunnel from the north. This time, although there would still be an access corridor to the north, the vertical shaft was situated far off centre, in the gap between the first and second layers. It would be accessible during the whole construction period. A descending passage would lead deep under the rising *mer* so the actual burial chamber would still be centrally placed.

Discussions were still taking place about the sarcophagus that would hold the king's body, but with the shaft still open right up until the completion of the tomb, it would be as simple matter to lower it down to the descending passage. Initially, they had considered a limestone sarcophagus, like the facings of the passages and the planned outer casing, but Sekhemre had vetoed the idea, saying the rock was too soft to allow a secure holding for the king's body. Den suggested granite from the Abu quarries, having some small experience with the cutting and transport of granite blocks, but Rahotep had overruled him at the discussion meeting.

"Granite is too hard," Rahotep said, "and too expensive."

"Should not the decision of cost be left up to the king?" Den asked.

"I am the Overseer of the City of the Dead," Rahotep said dismissively. "I will make that decision, and I have decided we will use limestone after all."

Sekhemre shook his head. "Limestone is too soft. We should use a harder, more durable rock like granite."

"I have made my decision," Rahotep said. "Limestone."

So it was decided. Den quickly realised that if he suggested something, Rahotep would find fault with it, so he started making his suggestions to the site overseers, letting them take it to Rahotep and encouraging them to present it as their own ideas. Aware that he ran the risk of being completely sidelined and cast as useless to the project, he wrote down the suggestion every time, dated it, and sent it to Imhotep. That way, his ideas were made available to the Tjaty who had ultimate oversight of the project, before they could be reported on by Rahotep. Imhotep soon became aware of what was going on, but said nothing, content to let Den record the ideas while letting his son take the official credit for them.

Den was thankful at least that the overall dimensions of the structures had been decided before Rahotep was promoted over him. His discussions with Imhotep when the king had first given them the assignment had led to the boundaries being set. Rahotep would have to have a very good reason for changing the plans now, and Den did not think he would as the Overseer had little planning expertise. The Overseer would follow the existing plans, which he thought of as having come from the mind of his father.

The first of the limestone blocks lay in a heap near the building site. Masons managed teams of workers, drawing on the lines along which they would chip away at the soft rock, roughly shaping the blocks before raising them into position. Inner blocks were more roughly cut, the rubble and chips from their shaping being used as filler between them, packed down with sand. Blocks selected for the outer layers were shaped more accurately, the sides flattened and smoothed, but even here, there were gaps. It would not matter, as casing stones of finer quality limestone would cover the whole *mer*. Den took some measurements of the blocks. The bottom layer of the *mer* would be two hundred and twenty *mehi* on a side, and with each block measuring only one *mehi* in length, more or less, that added up to many thousands of blocks. He knew he had the numbers written down somewhere in his office, so he did not trouble himself calculating the number again. Instead, he just shook his head as he contemplated the enormous effort involved and wondered, not for the first time, whether it was really worth the cost.

He heard voices and looked up to see Rahotep approaching with two of the lesser overseers. It was too late to avoid them, so Den stood and waited.

"What are you doing here?" Rahotep demanded. "Your job is in the planning and calculation of costs."

"I know what my job entails, Overseer Rahotep," Den replied mildly. "I like to come out to the site each day to view the progress."

"Finding fault with the blocks, are we?" Rahotep gestured at the pile of blocks and the masons and labourers chipping away at them. "Nobody listens to what you have to say, Scribe Den, so I suggest you get out of here and let us get on with the real work."

Not wanting to argue, Den inclined his head politely and departed, though he did not return to his office. Instead, he went to walk the outer limits of the site, farther out than the limits of the *mer*, out to where the enclosure wall would eventually surround the burial complex. It was a long walk; the planned circumference was nearly three thousand *mehi* in length, and as he walked, Den tried to imagine what the finished product would look like. Twenty *mehi* high, crenelated, with false doors and niches, the complexity of its construction would confuse and amaze anyone who viewed it.

By the time Den completed his perambulation, it was mid-morning and the heat of the day was starting to make the desert air ripple. Rahotep had long since retired to his house, so Den took another quick tour of the building site, watching the workers laying the *mer* stones on an inclined angle like that of Netjerikhet's stepped structure, before going back to his office. Something about the stones stirred his interest and he decided to do some more calculations.

His older children were at their lessons when he returned home, the younger ones playing with their nurses, so he stopped off to have a few words with them, give them a hug or play a quick game. Then he went to his office and opened the large chest of scrolls in which he kept copies of the plans. He pulled out the plan of Netjerikhet's *mer*, briefly marvelling again at the image of the greatest building ever seen. No man had built higher, and may never again. Sekhemkhet's *mer* was supposed to be one more layer than his father's was, but Den's plan was to fulfil his word to the king while saving time. Each layer would be slightly less than those of Netjerikhet, with the result that the summit of the present king's *mer* would be slightly lower. The two structures were not close enough together to be able to directly compare them, so unless somebody showed the king his plans, Sekhemkhet would never know. As a result, Den calculated they would save at least a year on the construction time, and a concomitant saving for the treasury.

He took out the detailed plans he had made, examining the details of how the many different parts had come together, wondering, not for the first time, whether it could have been done differently.

"Differently," he muttered, "but better?"

Den took out the earliest sketches of the original *per-djet*, paying attention to the arrangement of the mud bricks, and later the limestone blocks. The blocks had been laid in horizontal layers, and it was only when they started putting another *per-djet* on top of the first that they had gone for a different arrangement. It had seemed reasonable enough at the time--the pressure of the overlying structure would push the lower layers outward. That was when they started inclining the blocks so they tilted inward toward the core. The inclination would prevent the downward forces of the towering *mer* from pushing the base out and collapsing it. He looked up as a scratch came on the door of his office.

"Khawy. I thought you were at your lessons?"

Den's eldest child entered the room. "I told Nekh I could learn more from watching you, father."

"I do not pay your tutor for him to sit around doing nothing."

Khawy grinned. "I have done all my work to his satisfaction, and he still has Khepankh and Merit." He gestured toward the scrolls on the table. "What wonderful building are you planning now?"

Den beckoned his son to come and look. "Nothing new. I am just going over the original plans for Netjerikhet's City of the Dead."

"I still find it hard to believe you built that, father. It is one of the wonders of the world."

"I had a bit of help," Den said with a smile. "Thousands of men on the workforce, and as for the planning, most of it was put together by Tjaty Imhotep; I was just his assistant and scribe."

"And architect."

"Imhotep was the architect. I was just his assistant."

"You were more than that, father. Everyone says you were an architect. You followed Imhotep's direction, but most of the ideas were yours."

Den preened, enjoying the praise of his eldest son. "Well, I have to admit that many of the innovations were mine."

"So why are you looking at old plans, father? Shouldn't you be drawing up new ones for Hor-Sekhemkhet's city?"

"He wants one bigger and better than the one we built for his father."

"I am sure you can do it."

Den nodded. "Yes, I know we can, but sometimes it is useful to look at what we did back then. There might be another way of doing things that is better...or faster...or more economical."

"Have you found anything?"

"Not yet."

Den showed Khawy the plans and told him of the decision to incline the blocks inward against the core of the *mer*, so the weight of the completed structure would not crumble the lower layers. Khawy frowned in concentration as he listened and looked.

"I can see the way you have drawn the inclined blocks on the outside, father, but what is in here?" Khawy tapped the central core of the *mer*. "Why haven't you drawn the arrangement there?"

"That is because the core has no special arrangement," Den said. "It does not need one. It is just rough-cut stones, rubble and sand packed tight. We lean the limestone blocks against it."

"Wouldn't it be stronger if the core was also made of inclined blocks?"

"It does not need to be. Besides, doing that would use thousands more blocks, adding to the cost and time taken. Nobody can see the core when the *mer* is finished, so it does not matter if it is less than perfect."

Khawy stared at the drawings for several minutes, and Den watched him. The boy was only ten years old, but he seemed to have inherited Den's language and mathematical abilities, and he was curious to see what he would make of the drawings.

"What happens if you want to build rooms inside the core?" Khawy asked at last.

"Why would we want to do that? The burial chamber and corridors are underground."

"The vertical shaft is not."

"We built up around it with limestone blocks as we went. Besides, we only went up two layers before capping it off and digging a new access tunnel to the north."

"But if you did want to have rooms inside the *mer*?" Khawy persisted.

"Well, obviously you cannot if the core is rubble," Den said. He tapped the drawing with his finger. "You would have to build them in the outer layers."

"Hmm. Would you build them as you went, or tunnel through afterward?"

"You have a lot of questions, Khawy. Is there a point to them?"

His son shrugged. "I want to be an architect like you, but you have already built the greatest building in the world. If I want to make a name for myself, I must think of something new."

"Like putting rooms in a *mer*?"

"Maybe."

"So would you build the rooms into the structure as you went, or tunnel through the stonework after?"

"I would have a plan and build the rooms and passages as I went."

"What would be the purpose of these rooms?" Den asked.

"I don't know," Khawy admitted. "The burial chamber perhaps?"

"The safest and most secure place for that is deep underground. That is why the king and his treasure are buried there."

"But there are passages leading to it, and everyone knows he is buried there."

Den said nothing but smiled enigmatically, knowing the truth.

"If you built secret rooms in the *mer*, you could seal them off and nobody would ever get in," Khawy said.

"It is worth considering," Den agreed. He was impressed by his ten-year-old son's thoughts. "What other ideas do you have?"

Khawy shrugged. "That is all I can think of."

"It is a good start," Den said. "Tell you what, why don't you draw up some plans for a new mer. Draw it as you think it should be; just as an exercise."

"Be an architect? Can I?"

"Consider it your next school exercise. I will talk to Nekh about it."

Khawy worked hard on his project, making full use of the materials in his father's office. He made many sketches before settling down to draw with a shaky hand what he considered was the ultimate stepped *mer*, twice as high as Netjerikhet's, its boundary dimensions dwarfing the one being built for Sekhemkhet, and filled with little rooms. When he was satisfied with it, he unveiled it in front of his family and tutor.

Khepankh laughed at his brother's efforts or more particularly the little stick figures around its base that he had drawn to indicate the scale. Merit wandered off with her little sister Khasenet, but Den and Nekh studied it intently. They asked questions, and Khawy, his chest swelling with pride, answered them all seriously.

"So what is your opinion, Nekh?" Den asked. "Has my son completed his project to your satisfaction?"

"Indeed, he has, Scribe Den. If I did not know better, I would say this was the work of a renowned architect."

Khepankh laughed, but Den motioned him to be quiet.

"You do not think the angle of the steps too great? The number of layers too many?"

"My lord, I must defer to you in that regard," Nekh said. "You are the architect, while I am but a lowly tutor of small boys and girls."

"Then I will address some issues that I have with your design, my son." Khawy looked crestfallen, so Den smiled and put a fatherly hand on the boy's shoulder. "No criticisms, only questions."

"With respect, then, my lord, I will leave you and Khawy to discuss technical issues that will only perplex me," Nekh said. "Come, Khepankh, let us practice your numbers."

"Do I have to?"

"There will be a treat if you get them right. I believe the cook has made some honey cakes."

"What questions do you have, father?" Khawy asked after the others had left.

"I have three," Den said. "The first one is about the core. You do not appear to have one."

"I forgot," Khawy admitted, "and then I thought, 'why bother?'. It will be just as strong without one...stronger even."

"And a lot more expensive."

"This is a *mer* for a really great king; one who rules the world. He will want a great tomb and he will be rich enough to afford one like this."

Den laughed. "A rich and powerful king. Why not? All right, so you have done away with a rubble core, but you have included many rooms in it...how many? Twenty, thirty?"

"More, father."

"The trouble with that is that open spaces as you have drawn them will weaken the whole thing. You need good, solid beams to support the weight of rock above them. Otherwise they will collapse and bring the whole thing down."

Khawy scowled, "Is that why you did not have rooms in the one you designed?"

"In part. The other reason was that I could see no good reason to include them. The burial and storage chambers were all below ground."

Khawy nodded. "Your third question, father?"

"I do not know if you intended this or whether it is just an error in the drawing, but none of your blocks are inclined. They are all in horizontal layers. I told you what would happen if that happened... the weight of the structure would push the lower levels out and collapse them."

Khawy frowned. "I thought that was only with mud bricks."

"With limestone too. I made some very careful calculations when we first thought about raising the height."

Khawy stared at his drawing. "You only had small blocks, didn't you, father? What if I made my blocks larger?"

"Larger blocks weigh more," Den pointed out. "You would have difficulty moving them into place, and even if you did, you would multiply the weight pressing down on the lower levels."

"What if the higher levels were made of smaller blocks?"

"Then it might work," Den conceded, not wanting to crush his son's spirit entirely. "I am very pleased with your work, my son. Study hard and you will be a famous architect like Tjaty Imhotep one day."

"I would rather be a famous architect like you, father."

Den laughed. "That too, then." He started to leave the room, but Khawy asked another question.

"If the bottom layers were much larger, and the upper ones smaller, could you lay the blocks flat?"

Den considered the question carefully. "I would have to make careful calculations, but I suppose it is possible."

"Then why not do so, father. It would be much quicker to lay horizontal layers."

"You are forgetting the weight of the blocks. The ones we used in Netjerikhet's *mer* could be carried by a single man, two if needed. The blocks you have drawn are many times larger in every direction. You would have great difficulty moving them into position."

"But if I could find a way of moving them easily?" Khawy asked.

"Then perhaps you could lay blocks in flat layers," Den said. "That is something you can work toward when you become an architect. For me, I will stick with what I know; small blocks set at an inclined angle."

Chapter 7

When Djeser-Ti was brought to the birthing chamber, both she and her father Asarhotep were confident the child would be a boy, a prince to contend with the boy born to Queen Inetkawes for the title of Crown Prince. The birth was protracted; something Djeser-Ti took heart from, believing a boy was more likely to fight the birth process, but in this she was disappointed once more. A sickly baby girl was placed in her arms, and she wept as she nursed it.

Disbelief and anger overcame Asarhotep. He had spent five fingers of fine gold to get a favourable outcome, and the Kushite magician had all but guaranteed this child would be male. He stormed round to Psartu's house, but the man was not there. Neighbours told Asarhotep that he had departed for an unknown destination several months before. Asarhotep ground his teeth, knowing he had been cheated by a charlatan. None of the methods he had researched had proved efficacious, so that only left one way of securing a boy child for his daughter.

"It is the only way left open to us," Asarhotep told his daughter. "You must lie with the king again and get with child. Then, if the baby should prove to be a girl once more, we will change it for a newly born boy."

"Are you mad, father? Do you truly advocate pretending a boy is the son of the king? We would be found guilty of treason and be put to death."

"Only if we were found out...and we won't be."

"How could we possibly keep something like that secret? The midwives would know, for a start."

"Midwives can be bought."

Djeser-Ti shook her head. "Even if you could exchange a child, why would you want to? The boy would be a stranger, neither my son nor your grandson. Would you endanger us all to put a stranger's son on the throne of Kemet?"

Asarhotep sat down and took his daughter's hands in his own, looking earnestly into her eyes. "Daughter, you gave birth to a son once, and you can do that again, but your recent children have all been girls. I am worried that the king will put you aside and take another wife in the hope that she will give him sons. This scheme buys us time. Present the king with a son and he will keep you close in the hope of fathering more sons on you. If that happens, then we can put the stranger's son aside in favour of your new one."

"You mean you would kill him?"

"The boy would be a stranger's son, not yours. Why should you care what happens to him?"

"He would still have been raised as my son."

"But he would not be," Asarhotep said. "Wouldn't your natural son be more important?" He shrugged. "If you balk at the obvious solution, we can no doubt find another."

"I do not want him killed," Djeser-Ti insisted.

"Very well, I will think of something else. That apart, though, you agree with the idea."

"It is dangerous..."

"But the rewards are very great," Asarhotep said.

It was as her father had said; the king's desire for Djeser-Ti was falling away. Queen Inetkawes had given him a son and heir, and there were plenty of palace women prepared to open their legs for the king in the hope of finding favour. Djeser-Ti knew that unless she could secure Sekhemkhet's affection once more, she would be put aside. She paid special attention to her clothing, her perfumes and make-up, and petitioned the king for his attention. He responded favourably and once more he vigorously ploughed his young wife, planting his seed once more in her fertile field.

Sekhemkhet enjoyed being with Djeser-Ti, but had almost given up expecting a healthy son from her. Her conversation was increasingly pedestrian, he thought. She was no longer the lively young woman he had fallen in love with and married. He supposed that at least some of that had to do with his enthronement. Being a king involved many more responsibilities than being a mere prince, but at least he had an experienced Tjaty to lift most of the burden from his shoulders. The problem with the women in his life was that they had little conception of the things that interested and concerned him.

Inetkawes knew, of course. As a royal princess and his full sister, she had been reared knowing what it meant to be a member of the royal family. She knew the burdens that lay on her brother, and she behaved in ways that reflected such knowledge; not at all like his young wife or the many palace women.

Well, Djeser-Ti would always have a place within his palace, even if other women produced the sons he needed. He had lain with her again, giving in to her pleas, but without any real hope of a son. Inetkawes had given birth to his heir and would likely produce others, and the bellies of a score of palace women would birth the many officials he would need to govern Kemet and hand the throne to his successor.

Thinking about it all irritated Sekhemkhet. His life as a king should be free of the worry of producing an heir. He sent for Imhotep and demanded to know the situation within the women's quarters.

"You have a healthy son and heir in the person of Nub-Re, my lord king," Imhotep said. "Two other sons have been born to palace women, but neither woman has the required status to have you acknowledge the children as yours. I regret to say that both of them have had somewhat dubious careers."

"They might not be mine, you mean?" the king asked sourly.

"There is doubt, my lord king."

"Do I have any that are indisputably mine?"

"Prince Nub-re, of course, and a handful of daughters, including two with your wife, the Lady Djeser-Ti."

"I need sons," Sekhemkhet grumbled. "One is not enough."

"The solution is...ah...obvious, my lord. You must sow your seed widely."

"I do that already. Half the women in the palace have spread themselves to receive my royal seed. I daresay I will get around to the other half."

"If you will forgive my saying so, my lord, that is a lot of activity for very little result."

Sekhemkhet smiled. "Enjoyable, though."

"No doubt, my lord, but in terms of getting yourself more than one son, not very productive. I have been keeping track of the women you lie with..."

"Have you been spying on me?"

"Of course, my lord king, but only in your interests." Imhotep unfolded a piece of papyrus and consulted the cryptic notations on it. "You have one queen, one wife, and thirty-seven women you have lain with more than once. For all this activity, you have one living son and three daughters that are indisputably yours, and another two boys and five girls born to women you have lain with. If you will forgive my remarks, my lord, that is not many for three years and more of diligent ploughing."

"Are you implying I am impotent?" the king said, scowling.

"Far from it, my lord, but your greatest success lies among those women who are your official consorts, Queen Inetkawes and Lady Djeser-Ti. You must take more wives."

"More women to harangue me. At least with casual women I can dismiss them. Yes, yes, I know, I can do the same with my wives, Imhotep, but they give me such hurt looks. If I give in, then I have to put up with complaints and grumblings."

"If you had more official wives, you would have to spend time with them all. Less time with any one of them."

Sekhemkhet pondered this for several minutes. "I would not be averse to that," he said. "Perhaps it is time I took my sister Meresankh as wife."

"Alas, my lord, the gods still frown upon such a course. I will let you know as soon as they change their minds."

"Who then, if not my sister?"

"I will prepare a list of suitable young women of high birth."

The wives of Netjerikhet, Hetephernebti and Khemtet, had also been thinking about the succession. Both women had changed in status since the death of the old king and enthronement of the new one. Hetephernebti, as sister of the old king and Queen, still retained her rank, but her status had now slipped beneath that of her own daughter, Inetkawes, the new Queen. Khemtet, on the other hand, who had previously been a secondary wife, was now elevated to the status of King's Mother, a position that sometimes gave her precedence over Hetephernebti. They had adapted to changed circumstances as there was nothing they could do about it. The future of the family now concerned them more.

"You know I love Sekhemkhet as if he was my own son," Hetephernebti said.

Khemtet did not believe that, but was not going to reveal it. "And I love your daughter Inetkawes as my own."

"That being said, our beloved son has a problem."

"I am sure I do not know what you mean," Khemtet bristled.

"He has been married for three years, king for nearly two, yet he has only one son by my daughter and some sickly girls. That is not much on which to base a dynasty."

"He is still a young man, and reputedly virile," his mother said. "Palace women have given him many children."

"Not that many," Hetephernebti said. "Two boys and five girls out of how many? Twenty or thirty he has lain with."

"He is young," Khemtet repeated. "He will have more."

"I sincerely hope so, but if I was to be a little more critical I would point out that none of the children are strong and healthy. Some have already died..."

"Young children often die."

"That is true, but show me one of the king's children who is healthy."

"Your daughter's son."

"He is perhaps the strongest of them," Hetephernebti conceded. "But he is the exception. And now Sekhemkhet is producing only daughters."

"That is the fault of the women," Khemtet said, bridling. "Not my son. I blame that woman from Abdju most of all."

"Djeser-Ti? She is just a slip of a girl who has wrapped the king round her fingers. How is it her fault?"

"I have heard things."

"What sort of things?" Hetephernebti asked.

"Dark things."

"Can you be a little more explicit? Or are these things just unfounded rumours?"

Khemtet frowned. "You must make up your own mind on that, but her father Asarhotep was seen consulting a magician last year."

Hetephernebti went pale. "A magician? Asarhotep is casting a spell on the king? Do you have any proof of this?"

"One of the servants of the bedchamber reported a strange occurrence when my son lay with Djeser-Ti this last time before she became pregnant. She uttered a strange phrase when coupling with the king."

"Probably just an utterance of joy," Hetephernebti said. "I would not think too much about it."

"If that was all, I would not," Khemtet replied. "We all say things in the throes of ecstasy, and my son must often induce that. No, the servant reported something else. When she was changing the linen, she found a scrap of papyrus stained with strange and evil-smelling fluids."

Hetephernebti sketched the sign of the eye of Horu with one hand. "You have seen this papyrus? What was it?"

"The servant threw it away, but taken with the strange utterance and Asarhotep's visit to a magician, what can we think?"

"But why? What would he hope to gain? Or Djeser-Ti for that matter?"

"I cannot think why either of them would wish the king harm. Djeser-Ti only has status because she is the wife of the king, and Asarhotep as her father. If anything happened to the king..." Both women made the sign now, "...they would lose everything."

"Unless they are part of a plot to kill the king," Hetephernebti said. She thought for a few moments and shook her head. "That cannot be the case. Only one man stands high enough to rule Kemet, and I trust Imhotep implicitly."

"There is no one else?" Khemtet asked. "Presumably, it would have to be a family member. You would know; being descended from kings. Are there any other relatives?"

"Only General Khaba, who was cousin to Netjerikhet's father. He is old, though, and completely loyal."

Khemtet considered Hetephernebti's words. "Then if there is no plot to usurp the throne, what else could it be? Some slight? Would a man throw away everything he had to avenge some wrong? Would Djeser-Ti? She has even more to lose."

"If not revenge, then what?"

Khemtet shook her head. "Perhaps we are looking for ill feeling when there is none. There are good spells as well as bad ones."

"A good spell? One that benefits the king? What sort of thing?"

Khemtet smiled. "Something I did not need, but that you might have employed once upon a time. Inetkawes does not need it, but Djeser-Ti might see the need for it."

"A son?"

"Can you think of anything more important?"

Hetephernebti nodded slowly. "Djeser-Ti's first-born son died, and then Nub-Re, the son born to Inetkawes, became the king's heir. A son would be very important to Djeser-Ti...no...her son would still be younger, and unlikely to become the heir."

"Unless Nub-Re died. Children do...I am not suggesting anything more. Besides, Sekhemkhet is a young man, who can say what might happen in the next twenty or thirty years of his rule. Nub-Re may fall into disfavour and another son be raised up. I would say the need to have a son is very great, and it is no surprise that Djeser-Ti and Asarhotep might resort to magical means to achieve one."

"If that is all it was--a spell to ensure a son--then there is no great harm done," Hetephernebti said. "Still, I do not like the idea of magical spells being cast on the king for any reason. Unscrupulous people could use them for nefarious purposes."

"Then we should investigate Asarhotep," Khemtet said. "If only to be sure in our own minds that the spell, if there was one, was innocent in its nature and has not been misused."

"And Djeser-Ti."

Khemtet shook her head. "No need. Any spell cast must have come through the father. As wife of the king, she will be watched closely and will not have had any opportunity of consulting a magician. No, it is Asarhotep we must investigate."

"How will we do that? We also lack opportunities to leave the palace. I cannot imagine Asarhotep willingly divulging his scheme if we asked him directly."

Khemtet thought for a while. "My father was Hem-netjer of Wesir in Abdju, and though he has passed into the West, there are others among his confraternity who will help me if I ask. I have the authority as King's Mother to order these things."

"Be circumspect though," Hetephernebti cautioned. "If Sekhemkhet was to hear of it, he might react precipitately against Djeser-Ti, and she may be innocent."

Khemtet set her agents on the task and they made discreet inquiries in the palace and city, tracking down the neighbours of the reputed magician. When they found that he had departed for places unknown, they interviewed Asarhotep, who swore, weeping, that he intended no harm.

"I knew that the king sought another son, so I engaged a magician to cast an innocent spell to ensure the sex of my daughter's next child. No harm was intended, none done, and the spell did not work either. The child was a girl."

No action would be taken against Asarhotep, though he was warned against doing anything like that again. Eventually, Khemtet's agents tracked down Psartu the magician in the city of Nekhen. Questioned, he indignantly rejected any notion that he would cast a spell involving the king, even for such an innocent purpose.

"I was happy to relieve the man of his gold, but all I gave him was a piece of paper steeped in harmless herbs, and a meaningless phrase for his daughter to utter. There never was a spell, so I cannot be guilty of any crime against the king."

The agents agreed with Psartu and released him, reporting back to Khemtet that the whole affair had been meaningless, and that no spell had been cast, for good or ill.

What Psartu had never told them was that he still had a small amount of the king's seed in a small jar, and that there were potent spells that could be cast using such an intimate fluid. The reward would have to be much more than five fingers of gold, though, so he would bide his time.

Chapter 8

D en tried to lose himself in his work at Sekera, spending as many waking moments as possible on the building site, or recalculating the quantities of stone needed, and how the giant *mer* and associated structures would be constructed. Rahotep would take the credit for the success of the project, but Den would take the blame if it failed. He was determined that would not happen. However, there were just so many hours of the day he could devote to work. When the sun set, he would light oil lamps and continue his work until his head ached, and then collapse exhausted into his bed. His health suffered, and his children made demands upon his time, so eventually he had to sit down and take stock of his situation.

"What matters most?" he asked himself. "Approach this as you would one of your mathematical problems."

My career as personal assistant to Imhotep, he thought. *I desire to be an architect of great fame.*

"You will never achieve that while Rahotep is the Overseer."

What I have is enough.

"Is that all? What about your family?"

Well, of course my family, but unless I have a suitable career, my children suffer.

90

"What of love? Your wife has been dead for a year."

I do not want to think of Khasenet.

"Because you feel guilt. You believe you killed her."

I did not; she died in childbirth. I loved her.

Den groaned. "She would not have tried for another child if you had been faithful. She wanted to give her husband--you--a reason to stay with her."

I do not know that; not for certain. Anyway, it does not matter any longer. Khasenet is dead and buried, while I live. My children need a mother.

"Do not hide behind your children," den scoffed. "You just want a woman."

All right, so I want a woman. What is wrong with that?

"Not just any woman though. You want Ranefert."

So?

"So she has rejected you. You cannot have...have...her." Den broke down into sobs of self-pity, knowing that he still loved Ranefert. "What am I to do? I love her and want her, but she does not want me."

By degrees, Den's thoughts turned to the child he had had with Ranefert. She denied the child was his, but he knew, as had her husband Nubsekhem, when he threw her and the child out of the house.

"His name is Khamose. He is not just a child, but your child. He should be here, in your household, being reared with your other children."

So go and claim him. Demand that he be turned over to your care.

"She would refuse to allow it..." A thought occurred to Den, so he relinquished his internal argument while he considered the idea that had popped into his mind. "Her father is Tjaty Imhotep, my master. If anyone can convince her to relinquish my child, it is him. I must go to him and ask him to intervene, to command his daughter to give up my son."

Nothing would do but for Den to cease all work at Sekera, to leave his children in the care of tutors and nurses, and make the short journey to Inebu-hedj, where he petitioned Imhotep for an audience. The Tjaty believed that Den had run into some problem that needed his opinion, so he disposed of the rest of his duties as quickly as possible and sent for his assistant.

"What problem have you encountered that the Overseer of the site cannot solve?" he asked as soon as Den entered the room.

"My lord, it is nothing like that. I have overcome any problems associated with the building. It is on a more personal matter that I come to see you."

"Oh...well, tell me why you have come."

"I ask you to intervene on my behalf with Ranefert, persuading her to give up Khamose into my care."

Imhotep stared at his assistant. "You are talking about my daughter Ranefert? And Khamose, my grandson? Why would you imagine she would ever give up her child, or that I would help you to do so?"

"Because Khamose is my son."

If Den thought that his words might have an effect on Imhotep, he was rewarded with an incredulous look.

"Have you taken leave of your senses? Khamose is the son of my daughter and Nubsekhem."

"Then why does Nubsekhem deny it, my lord? He sent Ranefert and her child from his household, didn't he? Why do you suppose he did that if not because she had borne a child to another man?"

"You?"

"Yes, my lord."

Imhotep shook his head and sat down, trying to comprehend why Den should say such a thing. "I do not believe it. Ranefert would not behave like..." His voice trailed off as he recalled that his daughter had, in fact, behaved just like that ever since she had become a woman. "When is this...this infidelity supposed to have taken place?"

"You recall when Ranefert declared a passion for her husband and journeyed north to lie with him? Khamose was born six months later, and though she claimed the child was born before his time, it was obvious to everyone that the child was full term. Nubsekhem saw it immediately, and threw her out of his household."

"I... I heard rumours, of course," Imhotep said. He stared at Den. "The child is yours? When...when did you...?"

"Nine months before the birth, my lord," Den said with a faint smile upon his lips. "I am a man like any other."

"Not quite like any other," Imhotep said. "Not only was my daughter married, but so were you. Who instigated this infidelity?"

Den remembered it as a seduction by Ranefert, but in truth he knew he had not needed much persuasion. "We are adults, my lord, capable of making our own decisions. I do not think blame should be apportioned."

"A man and a woman who decide on an action that disrupts two families and hurts many other people," Imhotep said. "I think there is blame enough for both of you."

"Yes, my lord, but that is all in the past. Ranefert and I are both unmarried, and Khamose needs to grow up in a family. Where better than in mine?" Den drew himself up, determined to put on a good face. "I wish to take Ranefert as my wife."

"Do you, by the gods?" Imhotep snapped. "I do not see much to recommend you as a suitable husband for my daughter and father for my grandson."

"My lord, I am your personal assistant and can provide for her and my family."

"I can dismiss you from my service with a word. You could not even provide for your children by your wife Khasenet. Gods, what did she think of all this?"

"I believe she was unaware of my indiscretion."

"That gives you comfort?"

"No, my lord. If I could, I would unwind the years and never stray, but what's done is done. I cannot change what has happened, but I can do the right thing in the future. I want to marry Ranefert and raise Khamose openly as my own son."

"What does Ranefert say to all this?"

"A year ago, she refused me and forbade me all contact with my son. I hope she has changed her mind, but if she has not, I ask your help in persuading her."

Imhotep snorted. "Has any man ever been successful in changing my daughter's mind?" He thought for a few moments. "I am not convinced that your marriage would be the best thing for my daughter. What happens a few years later when you tire of her? Will you then be unfaithful to her?"

"I have always loved Ranefert, my lord. I wanted to marry her before, if you remember, before I met Khasenet. You prevented our marriage then, but if you had not, none of this would have happened. We would be happily married now."

Imhotep shook his head, stifling a wry laugh. "You delude yourself, Den. If you had married then, she would still have been unfaithful." He sighed. "I have refused to believe these things of my only daughter, but I can see now she has always been this way."

"She has changed, my lord, and so have I. The only thing that has remained constant is my love for her. If I could persuade her, I know that I could make her happy."

"So go and persuade her."

"She will not see me. That is why I ask you to speak to her first and persuade her of my love."

"I am not going to persuade her to do any such thing," Imhotep said. He saw the stricken look on Den's face and relented. "I will speak to her and gauge her mood. The most I will do is ask her to speak with you. What happens then is up to you."

"Thank you, my lord."

"Return to your work at Sekera. I will tell you in due course of her decision."

"My lord, could you not talk to her this very day? I am eager to know and my mind would be distracted by not knowing."

"Would you have me leap into such a discussion and risk failure? I will judge the most opportune time to talk with my daughter."

Den returned to Sekera, where he could not settle to any work but spent his time staring down toward the river, waiting for a messenger to arrive from Imhotep.

Imhotep, meanwhile, considered Den's request, and how best to present his assistant's request to her. He went to see her at her house, and was admitted to her presence as she played with her little son. She embraced her father and asked why he had called upon her.

"Do I need a reason to see my daughter and grandson?"

"You are very welcome, father. I do not see much of you these days, nor of mother."

"I have no doubt she will call upon you soon," Imhotep said. "You are well? Khamose certainly seems full of life."

"Well enough for one cast aside by Kemetu society," Ranefert said, a trace of bitterness in her voice. "It is fortunate that Khamose is too young to appreciate how we are shunned."

Servants brought wine for the Tjaty, and served both him and their mistress, placing a bowl of dates beside them. Imhotep bit into a date and chewed as he thought about how to broach the subject he had come to discuss.

"At least your status as daughter of the Tjaty is unaffected. That should count for something."

Ranefert shrugged. "I suppose it protects me from the worst of the comments, but apart from that I have no standing in society."

"I would never have guessed that the family of Khaba held such sway. People seem to have sided with Nubsekhem, though you did yourself no favours with your behaviour."

"Do not start that again, father. I made mistakes when I was younger, I admit, but am I to be castigated for those errors of judgment for the rest of my life?"

"And now?"

"I am a modest, well behaved young woman trying to raise her infant son."

"That would not prevent you from entertaining men in the privacy of your own home."

"No, it would not, but I don't. I have no desire for casual assignations."

"How about marriage? Your status could still secure you a reasonable husband, and Khamose would benefit by having a father that cared for him."

Ranefert laughed bitterly. "You obviously do not mix much in society, father. No decent man spares me a second look. If I wanted a husband I would have to look among the artisan class or even lower. However, I can live without a man in my life."

"What about Khamose? He needs a man in his life. What about asking Nubsekhem to take him back? Perhaps that might elevate your status too."

"Haven't you been listening to the gossip, father? Nubsekhem denies being the boy's father and will have nothing to do with him."

"Is he?" Imhotep asked bluntly.

"You too, father?"

"He was born six months after your visit to Nubsekhem in the north, but he looked like a full term baby. What did you expect people to think? Is Nubsekhem the father?"

"What does it matter?"

"Who is the real father? One of the men whose company you enjoyed while your husband was away?"

"As you say."

"Then who is the father?"

"If a score of men sow their seed in a field, to whom does the crop belong? I know that in your eyes and those of Kemetu society I am no more than a whore who opens her legs for any man."

Imhotep sighed. "You are my daughter whom I love very much. I greatly desire your happiness, and would see Khamose live a fulfilling life. I do not believe you are a whore, but you must know who his father is."

"Perhaps I do. It does not matter."

"Is he married?"

"No."

"Then why not speak to him about raising Khamose together?"

Ranefert shook her head. "No."

"You must have had some feeling for him once, otherwise you would not have lain with him. Has that feeling vanished entirely without hope of resurrection?"

She shrugged. "I might have loved him once."

"Did he love you?"

"He protested long and loud that he did, but men say many things to women in the hope of parting their legs."

"Did he speak of love after you lay with him?"

Ranefert nodded reluctantly.

"That tells me that he might very well love you. Love is a greater prize than the act of sowing the seed. You should examine your heart and see whether the love you felt for him once might yet be nurtured. Love between two people is something to be grasped avidly."

"What if the man is of lower status?"

"Love is love. Daughter, you say society shuns you. Would they shun you more if you married beneath you? What would you care if you loved your husband and he loved you? And you would always have the love of your family."

Ranefert played with Khamose for a time after her father left her house, and then put him in his bed to sleep, while she stayed up with a cup of cool river water and considered her father's words. She admitted to herself that she had once loved Den, and still harboured feelings for him, so why had she rejected him so adamantly? It was not something she cared to dwell upon, but she suspected guilt had hardened her heart.

"It was not my fault that his wife died," she mused. "Death in childbirth happens."

No, she decided, that was not the guilt that eroded her peace of mind. It was seducing a married man for her own pleasure and then casting him away when she lost interest.

"Did I lose interest though? Or was it just that I was already married and could not truly have him for my own?"

That was not the case now. Neither of them was married, and the product of their love lay asleep in another room. What was to prevent them getting together now?

"Pride," she muttered. "I rejected him out of hand, and must I now go begging on my knees to him? Never may that happen!" She drank again from her cup, thinking back to her days with Den. "And yet," she murmured, "if those days could come again, I would be content."

Ranefert shook her head, thinking that it was a vain thought. After her rejection, Den had moved on, taking his family to live in a new house at Sekera.

"He will no longer be interested in me, but I would still like to see him. Is that foolish? To gaze upon that which I cannot have? I do not care; I will invite him to come and see his son. He will scarcely refuse that, and who knows what may then happen."

She told herself firmly that she would not relinquish her pride by asking him to take her back. That would be too much.

Den accepted the written invitation and joyfully sped back from Sekera, bringing gifts for her and for Khamose. Once in the house and in the company of Ranefert though, he seemed to lose all his daring, hardly able to look at the woman he loved. Instead, he spent his time playing with his son.

Ranefert watched the two of them together, thinking that Khamose was very like his father. She was a little disappointed that Den paid her no attention and wondered whether she had misspoken in the letter inviting him to call. Perhaps he still believed she rejected him beyond hope of recall...or perhaps he no longer loved her.

Khamose tripped and fell, bursting into tears. Ranefert started forward, but stopped when Den swept the boy into his arms, kissing him and reassuring him. His tears vanished and soon the two were once more playing on the tiled floor. Ranefert's heart warmed toward Den, and before she fully realised what she was doing, she was on her knees beside him.

"Forgive me, Den," she blurted.

Den looked surprised. "For what, Lady Ranefert?"

"You professed your love for me and I turned you away. It was wicked of me, but I felt hurt and was sure you could not really love me."

Den got to his feet and helped Ranefert up too. "How did I hurt you, my lady? I never intended to."

"I know that. I felt guilty at having broken up your marriage and mine, at your wife dying, and...and everything. I could not bear the burden of my guilt and turned everything around; telling myself it was all your fault. Can you ever forgive me?"

"All those things are in the past," Den said. He hesitated. "Does...does that mean you have feelings for me?"

Ranefert could not look at him. He had not confessed his love at the present time, and perhaps he no longer felt that way, but he deserved to know how she truly felt. "I love you, Den," she said softly. "I always have, even when I sent you away. I know I do not deserve your love, but you deserve to know my heart."

Silence greeted her words, and she felt her heart break, tears welling in her eyes.

"I love you too, Ranefert. I always have, from the first time I saw you, when you were just a child. I was so happy when we came together. It was so natural, and Khamose is a child of the love I felt. I love you now, and I always will."

Ranefert wept openly, and Khamose howled until Den picked him up and they all embraced, murmuring words of tenderness and love.

"Does this mean you will marry me?" Den asked.

"You will only find out if you ask me," Ranefert said, wiping away tears that were now tears of joy.

Den asked her, and she accepted.

Imhotep was happy that his daughter was getting married again, this time to someone she loved. He hoped that this marriage would last. The only slight misgiving he had was that Ranefert, daughter of the Tjaty, one of the highest rank of nobles in the kingdoms, was marrying a mere scribe, even if he was a talented assistant. Imhotep knew he would have to find a way to elevate Den's status, if only for his daughter's sake.

Hard on the heels of this news, came more. His youngest son, Sekhemre, Overseer of Stone at the Troyu quarries, married Perimset, daughter of Khensankh, a wealthy trader from Waset. The trader had come north on a business venture and brought his only unmarried daughter with him, hoping to find her a husband. He succeeded, and was very happy that Perimset would be marrying into the family of the Tjaty, to a skilled mason and Overseer in the employ of the king.

Both marriages took place within the space of a month, and before the summer flood, both women were with child.

Far to the south, in the city of Abdju, a family argument happened at about that time, which had far-reaching consequences. Kagemni, the fourteen-year-old son of Hor (the brother of Den) and Khetnesu, in an injudicious moment, remarked that he could think of no greater honour than to work as a scribe under the authority of Den, personal assistant to Tjaty Imhotep.

Hor was furious, and bade Kagemni say no more on the subject. Being a dutiful son, he begged his father's forgiveness, and obeyed him. He said no more, but he did not stop thinking about it, and resolved that one day he would make his dream come true.

Chapter 9

Hor-Sekhemkhet was bored. He had a competent Tjaty who took care of the everyday duties of managing the kingdoms, from presiding in the law courts to judging complaints and punishing miscreants. His tomb construction was in good hands, Imhotep also being in charge of construction. Apart from these things, the only duty expected of the king was to act as intermediary with the gods, conducting ceremonies and chants of praise, but the priests of every god could perform even these.

There was always hunting. The reed beds along the river abounded in wildfowl of every sort, and the king spent many pleasant hours standing in a punt while men beat the reeds to send flocks of birds clattering from their shelter. Swift arrows struck them down in their scores, and other men would leap into the water to retrieve dead and wounded birds. If hunting birds palled, there was always bigger game. A hunt for the great *pehe-mau* was dangerous; the great beasts could erupt from beneath the water, smashing small boats and killing men. Although his heart beat faster and he felt the urge to flee, Sekhemkhet controlled his fear and sent arrows into the gaping maw of the bellowing beasts. Crocodiles, too, fell to his arrows, though their scaly skin resisted all but the most accurately placed shafts.

When the king became tired of water sports, he took to the scrublands and desert, his hunters tracking down the wild bull and ass, ostrich and antelope, or even lion and leopard. Risking their lives, the hunters would drive the game toward the king, so he could dispatch them in relative safety. Every kill was celebrated as a victory by the king, though he was seldom in any danger. At last, even hunting no longer interested him, and he looked to that most dangerous of all sports, the hunting of men in war.

"The kings of Kemet are warlords," Sekhemkhet told Imhotep. "Every king before me has waged war against the enemy, gaining wealth and glory. I am minded to do the same."

"All Kemet will praise your name, my lord king," Imhotep said. "But what enemy threatens our lands? The tribes of Wawat are at peace, and even the tribes of Ta Mefkat no longer cause us trouble."

"There must be somebody. Find me an enemy worthy of my prowess, Tjaty. I thirst to make war and prove myself in battle."

Imhotep went away to consult with military men, with counsellors and to examine reports from the governors of far-flung *sepats*. As he suspected, the south and west was at peace, the tribes there accepting Kemet's sway over their lands. A few small tribes in the wasteland of Ta Mefkat sometimes caused trouble, but it was nothing the local garrisons could not handle. None of them would provide an enemy worthy of a king's attention. Faced with peace on every border, he sent a letter by fast boat to General Khaba in his fortress at Hut-waret, bidding him find a worthy foe for the king to fight.

A letter arrived only days later, in which Khaba said that though the border was at peace, an incident could be manufactured with one of the tribes if that was considered necessary.

"Do so," was Imhotep's reply.

Half a month later, Khaba sent a report south to the court, telling of an insurrection by the Wahabi tribe of the hills of southern Kanaan. Sekhemkhet immediately declared that he would lead an army against them, and dispatched letters to Khaba and the governors of northern *sepats* to muster men for the campaign. They were to raise and arm five hundred men and send them to Hut-waret under their own officers. These men, together with the soldiers under Khaba's command, would be enough to conquer any rebellious tribe.

Sekhemkhet boarded a ship together with a score of his palace guards and set sail for Hut-waret, arriving there three days later to find his army waiting for him. Upon the advice of Imhotep, he made Khaba and his son Nubsekhem commanders of the army under his own authority, and set out only days later for the border of Kanaan. They soon came upon the remains of burnt-out villages and trampled crops, which Khaba pointed out as the work of the Wahabi.

"Where are they to be found?" Sekhemkhet demanded. "They will suffer for the harm they have inflicted."

"In the hills, my lord king," Khaba replied, waving his hands toward the eastern horizon where the land rose up to meet the sky. "Their village is two day's march; though they will flee if they have word of our presence."

"Cowards," the king said. "We must make sure they do not learn we are near."

"If I might make a suggestion, lord king. We should divide our force in two, with half taking a circuitous route to block off their retreat into the hills, while the other half makes a direct approach. Then, if they flee, we can catch them in a trap."

Sekhemkhet nodded. "An excellent suggestion. I shall lead the half that goes around, and you can drive them onto my spears."

"With respect, my lord, the commander of the blockading army should be somebody who is familiar with the terrain, like my son Nubsekhem. Let him take our own men, who know this country well. The main army of conscripts will engage the enemy, my lord, and that honour is rightly yours as king."

The king scowled at being corrected, but allowed Khaba to make the necessary dispositions. Khaba took his son aside to give him his instructions.

"You know what to do. Just make sure that no men are left alive to deny having rebelled."

Nubsekhem nodded. "And the women and children?"

"The king will want captives, and they will make useful slaves."

Nubsekhem led his men off a day before the others, angling to the north to bypass the supposed Wahabi village and approach it from the east. A day later, Sekhemkhet, with Khaba beside him, advanced slowly from the west. Late on the second day of their march, they saw smoke rising in a column far ahead of them, in the foothills of the high ground. The king wanted to immediately advance with all haste as obviously battle had been joined, but Khaba counselled against it.

"Better to advance in battle order, my lord king. We do not know if the smoke we see is from the Wahabi village, and even if it is, whether another tribe is responsible. Rushing in without scouting the situation could be disastrous."

Sekhemkhet allowed himself to be persuaded and the army of four hundred men advanced in battle order, ready to engage the enemy or retreat depending on what force they encountered. The Wahabi village came in sight, or rather, the remains of it. Most of the huts were smouldering sticks, and Nubsekhem's soldiers were camped outside it, waiting for the king. Nubsekhem came hurrying toward the king and his father as they drew near, and he dropped to his knees to give his report.

"My lord king, the enemy tribesmen were warned by shepherds of our presence and attacked in force. We beat them off and pursued as they fell back on their village, whereupon we engaged them and burnt the village around them, killing and capturing as we did so."

Sekhemkhet scowled at being deprived of his victory. "How many Wahabi men have you captured? I can, at least, make an example of them as a warning to others not to break the peace."

"None, my lord king," Nubsekhem said, glancing at his father. "They fought bitterly, and we could do little else but kill them all. We captured the women and children too small to bear arms."

"How many of your men were killed?" the king asked.

"None, my lord."

"None? What about your wounded?"

"A few minor injuries, my lord. The men fought well and gave the enemy no opportunity to strike back."

Sekhemkhet frowned. "You captured the women? I will inspect them."

The king strode off toward the village, to where sobbing women and children were under guard. Khaba and Nubsekhem followed and spoke together in a low voice.

"You encountered no difficulties?" Khaba asked.

"No, father. We surprised the village at dawn and swiftly slaughtered the men, and a few women. They were not expecting us."

"Why would they?" Khaba remarked with a smile. "They have been at peace with us and their neighbours for several years."

"The only thing that worries me is if the king finds out it was not the Wahabi who burnt the other villages."

"Well, I would tell him that if it was not the Wahabi, then it was another tribe, but that the Wahabi were guilty of something otherwise they would not have attacked our men. Personally, I think the tribesmen all look the same. Anyway, the men who actually did it have been posted elsewhere, and will not be encountering the king or his guards on this expedition." Khaba clapped his son on the shoulder. "Stop worrying; the king has had his victory and can return to Inebu-hedj in the belief that he is a great Kemetu king."

Sekhemkhet selected some of the captive women to be sent down to his palace to work there, and allowed the others, and the children, to be sent as labourers on the farms and estates in the north of Kemet. He led the army back down to Hut-waret, and ordered a triumphant procession through the town to celebrate his victory over the enemies of Kemet. This triumphal procession was to take place in every city throughout the kingdoms so that all who witnessed it might acclaim his greatness. The king did one other thing before leaving Hut-waret. He called Khaba into his presence and castigated him for his excessive caution in the approach to the Wahabi village.

"Had it not been for your excessive caution, bordering on cowardice, I would have been the first into the Wahabi stronghold, and it would have been my force of arms that subjugated them rather than just that of the men under my command. It does not lessen my victory, Khaba, but it makes me reconsider my trust in your judgment."

Khaba knew that anything he said in mitigation might precipitate the king's anger, so he said nothing.

"You have served me well as Kemet's General in the North, so I will not humiliate you, though you deserve it. Instead, I will relieve you of your command and send you back to your estates where you can practice such harmless pursuits as tending your vines and breeding your cattle. You are an old man and likely to die soon, so you will no doubt be grateful for this retirement from public life."

"I would rather continue to serve you, my lord king."

"That will now be the duty of others."

Sekhemkhet dismissed Khaba from his presence and called for Nubsekhem briefly before boarding his ship to sail upriver to Inebu-hedj. After the king left, Khaba and his son spoke together.

"You heard?" Khaba asked bitterly. "I am dismissed from service and ordered into retirement on my estates. And for what? All I did was try to get the king into a position where he could complete our plan; to achieve a victory without Sekhemkhet finding out there had been no rebellion."

"It was unfortunate, father. He took it harder than I thought he would. Perhaps now you appreciate why I think you would make a better king."

"Whatever anger and resentment I feel over my dismissal is still outweighed by my loyalty," Khaba said. "He is still the legitimate king."

"Will nothing sway you, father? How much more indignity must be heaped on you before you realise you owe him nothing?"

"Enough," Khaba said, waving his hand dismissively. "I suppose I should find the man to whom he has given my command, and arrange a seemly handover of authority."

"The king promoted me to the rank of general," Nubsekhem said. "I am now in command of the Northern Army."

"You?" Khaba stared at his son for a moment and then nodded slowly. "That makes sense. You were the ranking officer under me and you acquitted yourself well at the Wahabi village. At least our family retains our status in the north."

"It will continue," Nubsekhem agreed. "I will raise up Huni to be my second and...and father, I would have you stay as my advisor."

"No. The king has dismissed me to my estates and if I do not obey him, I risk his suspicions. Unwarranted suspicions, but I do not desire the king's scrutiny to fall on our family. Rather, Imhotep's. I fear your past actions still have his attention."

"There is nothing to find, father. I told you that I will do nothing further without your permission. You are my father and general and of course I obey you."

"And now that I am no longer your general?"

"You are still my father. I will do nothing that will cause Sekhemkhet or Imhotep to look upon our family with distrust."

Khaba took his leave of Hut-waret a few days later and took a ship down to his estates near Per-Bast, where he sat and contemplated his future. He could foresee that time would hang heavily upon him in enforced retirement as neither tending his vineyards or overseeing the breeding of more cattle was anything more than a passing interest. His real interest lay in the management of an army, and using it to safeguard his beloved Kemet. Contemplating his abbreviated future, he wondered how long it would be before he lost the will to live and passed into the West to join those who had gone before. It was a depressing thought.

Meanwhile, Nubsekhem now had a free hand with the Northern Army, and set about modelling it as his own private force. He used the change in command to retire other officers loyal to the king, and bring in his own men. His son Huni became his second in command, though at the age of seventeen, he was young for the post.

"I am delighted for you, father, though I sorrow for grandfather's fate," Huni said. "I know he did not seek this...nor did you...so I have mixed feelings."

"Do not be dispirited," Nubsekhem countered. "The gods have spoken through the king."

Huni looked puzzled. "How so?"

"Your grandfather has long countered the idea that our family belongs on the throne of Kemet. As you know, I have tried to influence him over the years, but without success. Now, at long last, I have the opportunity to put my plans in motion and, ironically, it is the king who has brought this about. That is what I mean about the gods speaking to me."

"We march against the king?" Huni asked, frowning.

"Not yet; we are not ready. However, as General of the Northern Army, with full powers over the soldiers and officers in my command, I can, at last, mould this army as I see fit. By the time I am ready, every man in it will be loyal to me."

"You really mean to overthrow the king?"

"Have I not said so already? I thought you understood this."

"Yes, father, I do," Huni said. "I... I suppose I thought it something of a dream."

"Not a dream, but reality. Get used to the idea of being the heir to the throne when I claim it for my own."

"What about grandfather? I thought he was going to be king."

Nubsekhem snorted. "The old man has lost his nerve entirely. I thought when the king dismissed him that he might seriously look at taking over, but he is content to tend his vineyards and milk his cows. Well, let him do so. I will become king and you will be my heir."

Nubsekhem set to work, fashioning his little army into an efficient fighting unit. He knew that he would stand a better chance of victory with a few hundred utterly loyal men than leading a thousand of doubtful loyalty. It was no small thing to overthrow a king, especially when the king was regarded as being chosen by the gods. Fighting such a chosen king could be viewed as opposing the gods, and few men would choose that. Instead, he had to devise ways of lessening Sekhemkhet's divine status, showing him to be just a man, and not the best leader for Kemet.

He already had a score of junior officers he had bought for gold, and with the promise of better things in the future, but men bought with gold might not stay loyal when faced with the reality of challenging the king.

Nubsekhem knew he would have to think of a surer way. In the meantime, he needed to train up his men to be a formidable fighting force, and he thought he knew how he might do that at the same time as instilling loyalty.

Organising his men into groups of five soldiers under the command of a junior officer, he put them through exercises in the desert where their survival depended on teamwork. The officers were encouraged to get rid of any man who thought more of himself than of his comrades, and in the early days of the program, many soldiers quietly disappeared into desert graves. The ones that survived were brought together by bonds of common hardship, fostering friendships that bound them together on and off duty. These units of six men--five soldiers and one officer--gave themselves names that distinguished them from other units. As they trained and became competent in the use of weapons, learning to fight together as a unit, Nubsekhem and the senior officers bound the units together under a mid-level officer, so ten groups learned to subjugate their unit pride to that of the larger unit. They vied for the praise of the senior officers by competing one with another to be the best. All the time, Nubsekhem weeded out the officers and men who owed their primary loyalty to the king, replacing them with men who saw honour in being a member of General Nubsekhem's Northern Army.

The training and comradeship of the New Northern Army paid off the next time they marched out of Hut-waret to confront a rebellious tribe. One of the tribes of the northern triangle of mountains and desert that made up the Land of Sin, started raiding the copper mines. It had been years since the last trouble in the area, so the soldiers guarding the mine had grown lax. Tribesmen poured out of the hills, overran the mine and associated fort, stripping it of anything useful, but leaving behind the heaps of rich copper ore. The ruddy-hued metal would have been welcome, but the tribe lacked the means to smelt it from the ore. A single soldier fled the scene to report the raid.

Nubsekhem marched one hundred and twenty men of his New Army in pursuit of the tribe, confident that the spirit of comradeship engendered by his new methods would overcome the enemy. They caught up with them as they straggled back to their mountain fastness, and the new methods of teamwork paid off. Groups of sixty soldiers assaulted the tribesmen from both sides, shattering their loose ranks, whereupon each group of sixty split into ten groups of six and fought separate actions. Used to fighting one-on-one, the tribesmen were confronted by units of six men who guarded each other's backs, advanced and withdrew together and proved almost unassailable. Despite outnumbering the Kemetu almost two to one, the discipline of the tribesmen disintegrated in the face of men fighting as a unit. Breaking off the engagement as best they could, they fled for the shelter of the mountains, leaving their spoils and their dead behind them.

Nubsekhem counted up the dead. Forty tribesmen had died and another twenty were captured. These he put to death on the spot. His own losses were seven dead. These men he lauded as heroes and gave them a decent burial where they had fallen, and the wounded were helped back to Hut-waret. Here, he rewarded every man of the expedition with gold, praising them in front of the whole army. They cheered their general, swearing loyalty and clamouring for the opportunity to serve him as the others had done.

"You have done it, father," Huni said. "You have an army loyal to you."

"It is a start," Nubsekhem replied. "However, I will need more than two or three hundred men if I am to wrest the throne from Sekhemkhet."

Chapter 10

Tjaty Imhotep celebrated the marriages of two of his children with citywide festivities. The king gave his permission and contributed to the occasion by releasing quantities of grain from the city granaries. Bakers and beer makers worked hard to turn the grain into great conical loaves of bread and vats of foaming beer, while Imhotep's men scoured the countryside for onions, lettuce and garlic, as well as buying up many cattle. Public kitchens produced dishes of meat and vegetables, bread and beer, which was handed out free to all comers. Crowds of men and women cheered Imhotep and the marriage partners as all work stopped for three days. Every Kemetu man and woman loves a festival, and they welcomed the opportunity of feasting and drinking at someone else's expense. Soon, the city streets were full of drunken people and inevitably, fights broke out. Soldiers from the city garrison curbed the worst of it, allowing the celebrations to continue unabated.

None of this affected the private feasting that went on in the Tjaty's house. Though neither Sekhemre nor Den had an actual physical house in Inebu-hedj, Imhotep leased two small dwellings near his own for the duration of the festivities. As no formal ceremony of marriage took place under Kemetu law or custom, the only public recognition involved the woman leaving her father's house and taking up residence in her new husband's home.

Perimset set out in a joyful procession from where her father lodged in the best tavern in the city, scores of well-wishers accompanying her, with musicians playing and entertainers dancing, as the crowds cheered. Sekhemre, in his temporary home, formally welcomed her, with her closest friends and relatives carrying in furniture and kitchen equipment to set up the new house.

Ranefert's procession was more subdued. She left her father's house, crossing to Den's temporary residence with only a few friends keeping her company. She was estranged from many of her former friends and acquaintances because of her former behaviour, but others were happy to see her finally settling down.

Both couples, now effectively married, returned to Imhotep's home, where a wedding feast was set out in the courtyard as the sun set. Tables groaning under the weight of food greeted the guests, while beer and wine sat cooling in vats of river water. A large fig tree covered one end of the courtyard and under it were set chairs for the Tjaty's family and his new relatives.

Sparrows swarmed twittering in the branches of the leafy fig as dusk set in, but the pattering of their droppings did not disturb the guests. Imhotep had foreseen this problem and his servants had erected awnings to cover people and tables. Musicians played, and tumblers entertained the guests, while servants brought round perfumed oils to anoint each man and woman, while others served food and drink. Over the course of the evening, the conversation increased in volume, calls became more raucous, and many of the guests got up to dance and sing in time with the music. Drunkenness overtook many men, but Imhotep turned his face away from their conduct, only caring if the guests became too boisterous and started annoying others. When that happened, he had servants quietly conduct them away from the main party, giving them time to sober up a little before re-joining the festivities.

There was a separate party for the younger children, though Khawy insisted he was old enough to join the adults. He was overruled. Shrugging philosophically, he proceeded to lord it over the younger children in a separate room. Their fare was similar to that of the adults, except wine was excluded and milk was more freely available. The older children were allowed a little beer when the time came to praise the married couples and listen to the speeches. Their fare avoided the spicier dishes and focussed more on fruits, sweetened pastes and honey cakes, and some of the children made themselves sick gorging on an excess of sweet things.

Well into the evening, when most of the guests were replete with food and drink, and the married couples were contemplating their marital beds, a servant discreetly whispered in Den's ear that someone requested an audience with him.

"Tell him to come back in a few days' time," Den said. "This is my wedding day and I grant no interviews tonight."

The servant went away to convey his message but returned a few minutes later. "Forgive me, sir, but the young man is most insistent. He says he is a family member."

"Family? I have no family member who is a young man." Den had a moment's qualm, trying to remember if he had ever had a physical liaison with a girl that might have resulted in a child, but could not recall one. "Ask him for a name, and that of his father."

The servant returned to say that the young man had replied, "Kagemni, son of Hor."

Frowning, Den made his excuses to Imhotep and Ranefert, saying he had a bit of family business to attend to, but that he would be back in a few minutes. Then he accompanied the servant to an inner room.

The young man dropped to his knees when Den entered the room and held out his hands in supplication. "Lord Den, hear my request, I beg."

"I am no lord that you should kneel before me. Get up. Your name is Kagemni, son of Hor? My brother Hor?"

Kagemni got to his feet and bowed. "I am your nephew, sir, and I have come to serve you."

Den told the servant to bring food and drink, and then sat the young man on a bench and told him to speak plainly and explain himself.

"Yes, sir. My name is Kagemni, son of Hor the scribe and Khetnesu, of Abdju. I was born fifteen years ago, and since childhood I have trained in the ways of a scribe. A year ago, I told my father that I wished to come to Inebu-hedj and work for you."

Kagemni ate hungrily when the servant brought food and beer, and Den waited until his first pangs were assuaged before questioning him.

"What was my brother's reaction to that?"

Kagemni grimaced. "He forbade me to even contemplate such a thing."

"But you came anyway?"

"I could do nothing else, sir. Your name is famous throughout Kemet and it is my heart's wish to serve you."

"You disobeyed your father..."

"Sir, I am fifteen years old and I know my own mind. Will you take me on as one of your scribes? It is all I have ever wanted to do."

"If your father forbade it a year ago, how do you think he will react to you running away?"

"I do not care, sir. This is all I want; to be a scribe in your service."

Den sighed. "I could wish for a better relationship with my brother, and I fear this will not improve matters. He will order you home, Kagemni. Will you disobey him again?"

"He cannot order me home if I have a position with the king."

"I am not the king," Den pointed out.

"You work for the Tjaty, who works for the king. You are but two steps removed and in a position of influence within the court."

"I think you overrate my importance," Den said mildly.

Kagemni smiled and looked toward the sound of revelry in the courtyard outside. "The servants tell me you have married the Tjaty's daughter, so you must be important."

"I have no desire to come between my brother and his son..." Den held up his hand as Kagemni started to protest, "but I may be able to forestall his anger. I will ask the Tjaty if he will offer you a position on his staff. Your father can scarcely object to you working for the Tjaty."

"I want to work for you, sir," Kagemni said.

"I work on the Tjaty's staff; are you too full of your own importance to do so?"

"Of course not, sir."

"Then let me try to get you this position. If you do well, he may let you join me in Sekera."

"Thank you, sir."

Before he could stop him, Kagemni fell to his knees and clasped his uncle's legs, thanking him profusely. Den freed himself and raised his nephew up. He called a servant and bade him find a bed for the young man.

Then he went in search of Imhotep. He found him presiding over the last gasps of the party. Sekhemre and Perimset had already left for their temporary home, and many of the guests had drifted away. Den drew his father-in-law aside and explained the situation.

"He says he is a trained scribe, my lord. It will cause a disturbance within my family, but I cannot just turn away a request from my nephew. My brother will block his progress solely to spite me."

Imhotep nodded thoughtfully, trying to clear his head of wine fumes. "I took a chance on you, Den, and I have never regretted it, so I will take a chance with your brother's son too. Let him turn up for work tomorrow and I will set him tasks that will examine his ability. If he proves worthy, I will notify your brother that Kagemni is in my employ."

Rahotep, Overseer of Works at Sekera, had come to celebrate his brother's wedding and, to a lesser extent, that of his sister. His duties were piled high on his shoulders, and he knew in his heart that he was unequal to the task. He had spent many sleepless nights agonising over the path that lay before him and how he might avoid it. Only one thing occurred to him, but he was fearful that it would not be allowed. The realisation made him bitter, and he had, over the last few months, descended into a well where nothing seemed to please him and he often struck out against those weaker than him. He was aware of his weakness and hated himself for it.

At last, he could bear his burdens no longer and resolved to speak to his father. By good fortune, his siblings were getting married and he had a good excuse to leave his duties behind and come to Inebu-hedj.

He loved his brother Sekhemre and wished him well, congratulating him on finding such a jewel of a girl, but his words with Ranefert were scarcely polite.

"Is this marriage going to be any more meaningful than your last?" he asked.

"Have you no kind word for me, brother? I am no longer the young girl I once was, led astray by men."

"Your memory is at fault if you believe you were the one led astray. You led men around by their members to the shame of your family."

"I have changed," Ranefert insisted. "I married once for duty; now I marry for love."

Rahotep snorted derisively. "You lower the status of the Tjaty's family by marrying the paid help."

"You have changed, brother. Once, you had kind words for me."

"Den is nothing more than a servant, and you are just infatuated with his coarse aspect."

"Den is more than a servant...but even if he was, I love him. I do not care what you say, and if you cannot find it in your heart to wish me well, then go away."

Rahotep laughed. "I wish you well, sister. I will be most interested to see if this marriage lasts any longer than the last. Personally, I give it a year."

He kissed Ranefert on her forehead and went in search of strong drink to blot out the bitterness and loathing welling up in him. The party swirled about him, but although he drank deeply of unwatered wine and ate of the choicest viands, he could find no satisfaction in the wedding feast. Watching his parents making merry with their other two children and their partners soured his mood so he sought to enjoy himself with one of the female entertainers.

Rahotep watched her as she played a flute with the other musicians. Tossing her flute aside, she hitched up her skirts and executed a series of tumbles that elicited cheers from the audience. Flushed, and breathing hard, she straightened her dress where it had parted, revealing firm young breasts and sat down near Rahotep.

"A wonderful display," Rahotep said, his voice slurring from the drink. "Have some wine?"

The girl accepted a cup of wine, but closed the gap in her dress with her other hand, unsure whether the man's praise had been for her tumbling or for her youthful anatomy.

"My name is Anit," she said, sipping her wine. "What's yours?"

"I am Rahotep, eldest son of the Tjaty, our host."

Anit raised an eyebrow. "Really? Why aren't you sitting with the others?"

"Because my sister's new husband sits among them and he is a mere scribe seeking to better himself by marrying above his station."

"A scribe is hardly a lowly station," Anit protested. "It is far above mine."

"Everyone's is far above your own," Rahotep said, leering at the young girl. He felt a strong desire to belittle her, hoping it would relieve his own feelings of inadequacy. "What do you do when you are not showing off your private parts in your tumbling routine?"

Anit edged a little farther from Rahotep. "I am a musician and tumbler, both respectable professions. I am not a whore."

Rahotep drank deeply and filled both their cups with more wine from a jug on a table. "I'll warrant you have shown off your parts in private for copper, though, haven't you? Be honest, now."

Anit shrugged. "A girl has to make a living."

Rahotep slipped a copper bracelet from his arm and held it up. "Does this buy me a private showing? More perhaps?"

"Here?" Anit asked, looking around at the crowded courtyard.

"This is my father's house. I know a private room where we can get to know each other."

Anit licked her lips, her eyes fastened on the bracelet which was worth several of her usual assignations. "I am unprepared," she said. "If you come to my room, I have honey, wool, and other things so I can prepare myself."

"Why do you need those things?"

121

"I do not want to find myself with child. I cannot tumble if I am pregnant."

Rahotep yawned and looked away, slipping the bracelet back onto his arm. "I am losing interest," he said. "If you want payment then let me plough your field now." He shrugged. "Who knows, perhaps your field is barren and my seed will not sprout."

Anit grimaced, and nodded. "Very well. Give me the bracelet."

"When we are in the room." Rahotep stood. "Come, then, Anit, let us make sport."

The two of them emerged from the private room an hour later, though only one of them was satisfied with the transaction. Anit rejoined her musician companions and continued to entertain the guests, while Rahotep, his mind still unsettled, sought out his father. He had something to say, and his belligerence toward his sister and lust toward the girl tumbler had only delayed his conversation.

"Rahotep, my son," Imhotep cried out jovially, embracing him. "Is this not a glorious day? Perhaps one day soon it will be your own marriage day...you must have young women queuing up for your attention."

Rahotep wondered briefly whether someone had seen him with the tumbler and reported it to his father. Not that it mattered; both men understood the need to relieve lust. "I have no such plans, father," he said. "There is something I wish to discuss, though."

"By all means. Let us get ourselves some more wine."

He accepted a cup from his father, but asked if they could talk in private, away from the noise and bustle of the party. Imhotep led his son to a small room adjoining the courtyard. It was marginally quieter, but at least they would not be overheard.

"So, tell me what this is about."

"Father, you know I am appreciative of the great honour you do me by raising me to the position of Overseer of the King's Works in Sekera..."

"I was not thinking just of you, my son," Imhotep admitted. "I am getting old, and while I believe my mind is as sharp as ever, my body increasingly lets me down. I need a man I can rely on totally to help me with the king's work, and I can think of nobody better than my eldest son." He smiled and tapped the side of his nose. "When I get too old to manage my office, I intend to recommend to the king that you take my place as Tjaty."

Rahotep grimaced. "Do not think I am ungrateful, Father, but I do not aim that high."

"You always told me, when you were growing up, that you wanted to follow where I led. You are a skilled scribe like me, you have become a priest of Re like me, and you are now but a step or two below me as Overseer of the King's Works. The final step to Tjaty is yours for the taking...when I retire, of course," Imhotep added with a smile.

"I know what I said, Father, and there was a time when I wanted to be everything you were...and more." Rahotep shrugged. "I was a child then, but I see things more clearly as an adult. I do not want to be Tjaty...I do not even want to be Overseer at Sekera."

"What are you talking about? Those are both great honours."

"I know, but I know now that both tasks are beyond my capabilities. I would not even know where to start as Tjaty."

Imhotep frowned, trying to make sense of his son's words. "And that of Overseer? I thought that was what you wanted to be."

"I cannot do it, and my inability eats at my liver."

"I did not ask whether you could do it, but whether you wanted it. Ability comes with continuing practice."

"I did want it, Father, but I soon realised it was for the power and status it gave me, rather than the opportunity to serve the king. Such a life does not suit me. Father, forgive me, but remove this weight from my shoulders and let me seek out another career."

"What life do you seek, Rahotep? I hoped you would follow my path of service, but I will not try and force you to do so. Do you want a position within the palace, perhaps? You are a trained scribe and such men are always needed."

"I would be a priest, Father."

Imhotep looked puzzled. "You already are a priest."

"A priest of Re, but I want to be a priest of Inpu. I want to serve at the temple that exists beside the great statue you created."

"That is not a position of great status."

"Yet it will be enough for me."

"You seek an easy path in life?"

"Do you really think I want this?" Rahotep asked, tears in his eyes. "I want to be a son you will be proud of, but I cannot be Overseer. I do not like ordering men around; men who know more about building work than I do. I am all but useless, and it eats at me. That cursed man Den, for instance, knows more about building than I ever will. If I cannot be a man of importance worthy to be your son, then let me be a humble priest caring for the temple set up beside your great creation near Djesa."

"You really think that will be enough for you?" Imhotep asked. "Life as a priest can be full of drudgery, menial tasks serving the Prophets of the God. I suppose I could arrange to have you installed as a Sem priest at least."

"No, father. I seek a simple life. Let me toil as an ordinary priest for a while at least. If the life suits me, I can look for advancement on my own abilities."

Imhotep sighed and embraced his eldest son. "Very well, Rahotep. If that is your wish, then I shall grant it. Give me a few days to make the necessary arrangements, so stay here in my house."

"Thank you, father."

"Now I shall have to find another Overseer for Sekera," Imhotep said, grimacing.

"You have one who stands ready and able, father. I do not like Den personally, and I pity him as husband to my sister, but I respect his capabilities. I do not think you will find a better Overseer."

"I will think about it."

Rahotep smiled wryly. "For better or worse, he is part of the family now."

The day after the wedding, while still nursing a slight queasiness in his stomach, Imhotep set about facilitating his son's transfer from the position of Overseer of the King's Works to that of a simple priest at the temple of Inpu at Djesa. He wrote to the Hem-netjer of the temple, requesting he take on Rahotep, though he knew a request from the Tjaty ranked as an order to lesser men. It was no more than his due; if he could not use his position to further the ambitions of those close to him, then what was the point?

Someone had to take over the position of Overseer, and here he had to decide whether to give an unofficial post to a qualified man just to tide things over, or to petition the king to make a more formal announcement. It depended on whether there were several suitable candidates. If there were, then the king might want a court favourite in such an important and lucrative position. If not, then his recommendation would secure the post. He drew up a list of men, but quickly found it was a very short one, and that Den sat at the top of it.

Imhotep went to the king, slipping the notice of a replacement for the position of Overseer in amongst a host of other things requiring the king's attention. Sekhemkhet had no objection, being quite content to leave such appointments to someone else.

"Just make sure the man you appoint knows how to get things done," the king said. "My agents report there does not appear to be much happening in my City of the Dead."

"We are on schedule, my lord. The early work is largely underground and invisible to casual scrutiny. Proper preparation is very important."

The king dismissed Imhotep, so he decided to take the time to travel to Sekera himself to tell Den the good news. He found him on the site, watching the master masons as they dug down into the limestone bedrock, creating the passages to the tomb. When Den heard that the Tjaty was looking for him, he hurried to the surface, a worried look on his face.

"I realise I have a subsidiary position on site, my lord, but for some reason Overseer Rahotep is not here, so I thought I had better keep an eye on progress."

"Rahotep has been assigned other duties," Imhotep said. "I am happy to see you have stepped in as an overseer without being asked to."

"Who will be replacing him, my lord?"

"It is my intention to make you Overseer, Den."

"My lord...I don't know what to say."

"Say yes. Do not view this as an appointment based on your status as my new son-in-law. I have carefully examined the qualifications of a number of people, and I cannot think of anyone more suited to the position. The king concurs."

Den's mouth fell open. "He does? I did not think he would notice a lowly scribe."

"No longer a lowly scribe, but rather Overseer of the King's Works at Sekera, Keeper of the City of the Dead. You already have a new house on site, but your salary will be commensurate with your new position."

"Thank you, my lord. I...I am overwhelmed."

"Do not let me down, Den; that is all I ask. The king has his eyes on us, and it would not be wise to fail him. Now, onto more pleasant matters...Ranefert is well?"

"Indeed she is, my lord..."

Imhotep glanced around and saw that they were alone. "There is no need for honorifics when we are alone. You are my son-in-law now, so you may call me by my given name." He chuckled and added, "I would probably answer to 'Father', when with the family."

"Yes, my lord...sir...Imhotep. Thank you for so honouring me."

Imhotep waved a hand dismissively. "Well, Overseer Den, why don't you show me the progress that has been made on the site?"

The year drew to a close, and as the days of the annual Flood approached, both Ranefert and Perimset were brought to the birthing chamber. The course of their pregnancies had been remarkably similar, and both women's bellies were swollen, the midwives being of the opinion that the most favoured outcome--twins--would bless both families. Imhotep was concerned for the lives of both women and insisted that they leave Troyu and Sekera as their time approached and take up residence in Inebu-hedj.

Perimset went into labour first, and her pains were fierce. The midwives cared for her well, having been instructed by Imhotep to spare no expense in bringing mother and child safely through the ordeal. It was long and drawn out, and Ranefert joined her in the chamber. Ranefert had gone through this before, having already borne two children, so her labour was mercifully swift. Both mothers delivered their first child almost simultaneously, bellows of outrage arising from two sets of lungs at opposite ends of the room. A few minutes later, the second children arrived, and the midwives were busy caring for four children and two exhausted mothers. All the babies were healthy.

Imhotep and Nefertsen rejoiced at the birth of so many grandchildren, and insisted on bringing the fathers back to the capital, along with other relatives, to celebrate the births. Ranefert's children were twin girls, both beautiful in her eyes and those of Den, so they were named Neferka and Senefer. They appeared to be identical, and many jokes were voiced about being unable to tell them apart when they got older, but Den pointed out that Neferka, the elder by a few minutes, had a small red blemish behind her right knee.

"Not that I regard it as any sort of blemish," Den said. "They are both my beautiful girls and I adore them."

Perimset also had twins, but these were easier to tell apart than Ranefert's children--one was a boy and the other a girl. Sekhemre desired that his children's names reflect the fame of his family, so named his daughter Neithotep after Khasekhemwy's junior wife, the mother of Imhotep.

"I am naming the boy Imhotep," Sekhemre declared. "I could not be prouder of being a son of the elder Imhotep, and I pray to the gods that the younger one will live up to his illustrious grandfather and namesake."

"I am honoured," Tjaty Imhotep said, lifting up the infant and kissing him. He then picked up and kissed his other grandchildren, declaring that they were all beautiful and he did not want to favour one above another.

The occasion proved to be a celebration for the whole family. Rahotep returned from Djesa to introduce his new wife Neit, who was the daughter of the Hem-netjer of Inpu. He had settled into his new position as a simple priest in the temple, where he made the acquaintance of Neit. One thing followed another, and they were married three months earlier. Neit was already with child and only one thing spoiled her complete happiness.

"I do not want to be the wife of a simple priest of Inpu," she told her husband the night they got married. "You must become the Hem-netjer."

"But your father is Hem-netjer," Rahotep pointed out.

"He will not always be. In fact, he contemplates retirement. The king will not appoint a simple priest to succeed him, so you must think of some way to put yourself forward."

The only thing Rahotep could imagine was to ask his father for a favour, and he did not want to do that. He wanted a quiet life, but there was no possibility of that as long as Neit's ambitions for her husband went unfulfilled. Rahotep promised to speak to his father, and with the arrival of his nephew and nieces, that opportunity arrived.

"I wondered how long it would be before you tired of the quiet life," Imhotep said when Rahotep broached the subject.

"It is not that at all, father," he replied. "I am content to be a simple priest, but my wife seeks my advancement and already makes my life miserable."

"You want your old position back?"

"No, not at all. I like it where I am."

"That is a relief, as Den is very good at his job and I would hate to dispossess him of it. So what is it you want?"

"Neit wants me to become Hem-netjer when her father retires."

Imhotep frowned. "High Priests are appointed by the king."

"That is what I told her. She says you have the ear of the king, so I must ask you to approach Hor-Sekhemkhet. I am sorry, father. I would not ask this of you of my own accord."

"I understand," Imhotep said. He thought for a few moments. "The king will never raise a junior priest to such a rank, so you must advance swiftly within the temple hierarchy. You are a *wab*-priest now, but I have it in my power to make you a *sem*-priest, and in six months, I may be able to elevate you to *hery-heb*. Then it will need the king's intervention, but I may be able to influence him."

"Thank you, father. I did not want to ask you, but..." Rahotep shrugged.

"That is what family is for," Imhotep replied. "One of the perquisites of power. You may tell your wife that if you do not become Hem-netjer after her father, you will likely be the next one. Your advancement is assured."

Chapter 11

D en spent the first month of his expanded duties as Overseer becoming reacquainted with the site. He frowned when he first walked the boundaries of the proposed *mer* and enclosure, because it seemed to him that the original poles and markings on the rock had been altered. Before he could order a new survey of the site, a host of other small problems came crowding in, and he forgot to follow up. Walking and talking with the overseers and masons, he went over the plans they had, making corrections as he saw fit. It appeared that Rahotep had made a number of changes to the original plans. Most were small and apparently inconsequential, but he needed to be sure, so he went over every aspect with the men in charge of that area.

Rahotep had cut back the food allowance to the labourers, nearly halving their daily bread, so Den immediately returned it to the former levels. Onions, garlic, melons, fish and meat allocations were also increased. The former Overseer had also altered work schedules haphazardly, resulting in work teams getting in each other's way. Den drew up new schedules, increasing the hours of some teams, cutting back on others. A few of the overseers and supervisors had taken advantage of Rahotep's mismanagement to steal resources, and these men Den dismissed on the spot. When one man remonstrated, Den told him that he was fortunate he did not report the theft to the king.

"The only reason I am lenient is that the man in charge of you let you get away with it. That stops now."

Den descended into the vertical shaft to examine the progress of the excavations. At the bottom of the shaft, three teams of masons were at work, one burrowing south toward the burial chamber, another angling upward toward the north where the access passage would lead, and a third one had gone west for a few paces before turning to the north. The team digging out the west and north passage had started to angle it upward, paralleling the access passage, so Den took the head mason aside and showed him on the plans where he had gone wrong.

"This passage will end in store rooms to east and west, and unless you cease the upward slant, you will break into the access passage."

The other aspect that required Den's attention was the *mer* itself. Ahtep had been placed in charge of getting it started and he worried that Den was going to replace him. He had delayed setting the first stones in the courses, amassing quantities of them from local quarries, as well as casing stones of Troyu limestone.

"Why the delay?" Den asked. "The limits of the *mer* have been set out, and the terraces constructed that make the boundaries level. I would have expected more progress than this."

"It is true, Overseer Den, that Rahotep gave me the order to start building, but I delayed. Sir, I am concerned that the first course will be unstable unless precautions are taken."

"You have good reasons for these concerns?"

"I believe so, sir. I have no problem with the central core of rubble, and stacking limestone blocks against it at an angle..."

"What angle are you working with?"

"I have a *seked* of six-tenths."

Den consulted his notes. "That appears to be correct. What is the problem?"

"Nothing in close to the core, sir, but on the outer edges, there is nothing to prevent the sloping stones from sliding outward. They are stable enough at the moment, but when we start on the second course, the pressure will be too much, leading the whole structure to collapse."

"The *mer* was planned carefully," Den said. "I was responsible for the initial calculations, and I have checked them since. Are you telling me I am wrong?"

"No sir," Ahtep said unhappily. "It is just that...well...the outer layers need a proper footing."

"They have one; it is in the original plans."

Ahtep looked uncertain. "I did not see one, sir. I suppose I could have missed it."

Den glared at the building supervisor. "If it is on the plans and you have missed it, you are plainly incompetent and I must replace you. Come with me; we shall examine the original plans ourselves."

Den led the way to the main site office, where scribes copied out orders for the many overseers and supervisors, while others accounted for the many other items relating to the maintenance of the whole place.

"Fetch me the plans for the *mer*," Den instructed the head scribe.

The plans were on several scrolls, each detailing a small portion of the whole. Den pored over them and found the one showing the footings of the outer layers of the mer. Or rather, it was the one showing the lack of a footing.

"This cannot be right," he declared. "I distinctly remember a footing designed to stabilise the base."

"You see, Overseer Den?" Ahtep ventured. "This is why I hesitated to put the outer layers in place."

Den called the head scribe over. "Are there other plans?" he asked.

"No current ones," the scribe said. "When Overseer Rahotep had these copied out, the others were scrapped. There might be a few that have been saved."

Den asked that all the existing ones be brought to him, and started going through the score of scrolls set before him. The twelfth one gave him what he was looking for.

"There, you see, Ahtep. These are my original plans and they show, quite plainly, a footing beneath the outer layers."

Drawn on the papyrus were the outermost stones of the *mer*, inclined inward slightly, with a stone pavement dug into the bedrock perpendicular to the angle of the building blocks.

"The pavement spreads the load," Den explained. "You will need to make sure it surrounds the whole structure." He pointed this out to the head scribe too, telling him he would have to revise the drawings. "I will examine all of those created by Rahotep and if any of them have been changed from the originals they will have to be redrawn."

Sending Ahtep off to get started on the excavations to take the stone footings, Den took baskets of scrolls back to his own office, resigned to the idea that every single one of them would have to be checked. Hours later, by the flickering light of an oil lamp, he finished, stretching and yawning. Innumerable small corrections had been made, as well as several larger ones that if ignored, might have brought the whole project into chaos.

"I cannot decide if this is just incompetence on Rahotep's part," Den told Ranefert, "or whether it is something worse. I should tell your father."

"Either way, he is my brother," Ranefert said. "It would hurt my father if he had to chastise Rahotep, whether he deserved it or not."

"You think I should just let it go?"

"Has any harm been done?"

"Very little," Den admitted. "I think I have found everything."

"Then is anything to be gained by heaping blame on him? He told us that he did not like being Overseer, and it was his decision to stand down. Perhaps he knew he was making mistakes and wanted to stop."

Den decided to agree with his wife for the sake of domestic peace, but privately wondered if the 'mistakes' had not been deliberate attempts to undermine Den's authority. Rahotep had always seemed to resent Den's presence on site, regarding him as a commoner, even though trained as a scribe. Perhaps he was jealous of the relationship Den had enjoyed with the Tjaty. Whatever the reason, if the *mer* had collapsed later, Den would have taken the blame.

Several of his original scrolls were missing, so Den had nothing to compare with Rahotep's revisions. He went over these carefully, making complicated calculations, but could find nothing that had been deliberately changed. Thankful that catastrophe was unlikely to be visited upon the City of the Dead; Den destroyed Rahotep's revisions and applied his own seal as Overseer to the existing scrolls.

One of the scribes he assigned to making new copies of the plans was his nephew Kagemni. Imhotep had employed the youth in his palace offices, writing to Hor in Abdju, explaining where Kagemni was. Hor had replied tersely that although he appreciated the honour shown to his family, he thought that Kagemni was too young and inexperienced to hold down such a responsible position. He asked him to send Kagemni home. Instead, Imhotep had sent him to work for Den.

The young man expressed his gratitude at being allowed to work with his uncle and Den, in an effort to appear impartial, scrutinised Kagemni's work carefully, looking for any errors. His penmanship was superb, and he had a good grasp of language. If he had a fault, it was that he had an erratic relationship with the art of calculation. This could be corrected with time and a good tutor, and Den resolved to teach his nephew himself.

Khawy raised an objection, though it was scarcely a reasoned one. Den's eldest son was only twelve years old and not yet ready to take up scribing duties, but he scowled when told that Kagemni would be joining the household.

"I do not like him," Khawy declared. "He is also the son of your brother, and Hor bears no love for you. How do you know Kagemni is not here to spy on you?"

Den smiled indulgently. "He wants to work for me, and Hor does not want him to. I do not think that makes him a spy."

"Perhaps he is just very clever. He is going to worm his way into our home and dispossess me. I am your eldest son and I am supposed to be your personal scribe."

"And you will be when you are older," Den assured him. "You are still a year or two from being ready, but when you have completed your studies, you will come and work for me."

"Instead of Kagemni?"

"How about as well as? He has excellent penmanship, while you are better at calculations. I have use for both abilities in my office."

Khawy allowed himself to be persuaded, and although he still resented Kagemni's presence in his father's household, he was polite for his father's sake.

Things were just settling down at Sekera when Hor arrived. He had taken a boat down from Abdju, determined to fetch his son home. He stormed up from the dock to Den's house, but only found his brother's family there. Finding his brother living in such luxury further enraged him and he forgot himself to the extent of shouting at Ranefert. She restrained herself from replying in kind, and left it to her servants to remind him of her status as daughter of the Tjaty. Den and Kagemni had gone up to the building site, so Hor followed them there. He saw them both talking to a group of masons and shouted out, breaking into a run.

Kagemni saw his father approaching and went pale, stepping behind Den. The Overseer waited calmly until his brother arrived, red-faced and shaking with anger, before dismissing the masons, who looked grateful. Den tried to calm his brother's anger.

"It is good to see you, my brother. You should have told me you were coming. I would have laid on a feast in your honour."

"Never mind that, I am here to fetch my son home," Hor shouted. "Kagemni, come here now."

"N...no, father," Kagemni stuttered, sidling sideways to stay behind his uncle.

"Hor, he wants to stay," Den said. "He is safe here."

"Leave him with you?" Hor yelled. "I'll die before I let that happen."

"Let us all sit down and discuss this over a cool cup of water," Den said. "There is nothing to be gained by standing around shouting at each other in the hot sun."

"There is nothing to discuss. Kagemni is coming home with me."

"I am staying here, father," Kagemni said. "Uncle, don't I have a choice in all this?"

"Yes, you do," Den confirmed. "Look, brother, you cannot physically force your son to go with you, so why don't we talk about it. Maybe you can convince him."

Still angry, Hor allowed himself to be persuaded and the three men went to the site office, where a servant poured cool river water for them before absenting himself. Den gestured to chairs and took a long drink.

"Ahh, that is just what I need after standing in the hot sun. What about you, Hor? Are you hungry? I can send for beer if you would prefer that."

Hor gulped his water and set the cup aside. "The only thing I need is my son. He came here without my permission, and I intend taking him back to Abdju."

"I do not need your permission, father," Kagemni said. "I am sixteen years old and I am an adult. I can make my own decisions."

"You are just a child in the ways of the world," Hor said. "If you had asked my advice I would have told you to seek good, honest work in Abdju, rather than seek out your uncle. You do not know him as I do. He does not have your best interests at heart."

"Brother, when have I ever done you harm?" Den asked.

"You harm me by your very existence," Hor said. "You take all that is good in the world and leave nothing for the rest of us. You lord it over everyone as the chosen one of the Tjaty, while I must fight for scraps in the provinces."

"I do not follow your reasoning, brother. I have been favoured by Imhotep, I admit, but I have had to work hard over many years to achieve what I have. You could do the same if you apply yourself."

"You are calling me lazy now?"

"Of course not, but you choose to remain in Abdju when the court has moved to Inebu-hedj. If you want advancement as a scribe, you must follow the court and find yourself a patron. That is what I did, and that is what Kagemni is doing. He wants more than what Abdju has to offer."

"He spurns me, his father, and follows you," Hor said bitterly.

"That is not true," Kagemni said. "You are my father and I honour you, but I have dreamt of this since I was a child. I want to be a scribe of the royal court and help create such wonderful structures as the king's *mer*. To do that, I must work for the Tjaty and my uncle."

"You are merely a scribe and you would do well to remember that," Hor said.

Kagemni looked crestfallen, but Den spoke up for him. "He is more than just a mere scribe, brother, which you should know. He has the ability to make a name for himself."

"Then he can make a name for himself in Abdju. You cannot keep him here, Den. You have no authority over him, and if he tries to object, saying he is too old to be treated like a wayward child, then he should think again. I am his father, and until he gains proper employment, he comes under my authority. And before you make objection, you cannot employ my son because you are employed yourself."

"But I am working down here, father," Kagemni said. "Uncle Den has taken me into his home, and gives me satisfying work to do."

"There would be something in what you say if I was trying to employ your son," Den told Hor. "I can employ labourers, but I do not have the authority to hire skilled workmen. However, I am not the one giving him work. Kagemni is employed by Tjaty Imhotep. If you want to dispute his right to be here, you must argue your case with the Tjaty."

"Who just happens to be the father of your wife," Hor said bitterly. "You conspire against me."

"Not so, brother. I only want what is good for all my family, you included, but you must see that I can, through my influence, give Kagemni a better life than he can get in Abdju."

"I have given him everything; a home, an education..."

"And I am grateful, father," Kagemni said quietly. "I honour you and my mother, but there comes a time in everyone's life when they must follow their heart. Mine leads me to the court and a Tjaty famous throughout the kingdoms as an architect, scribe, and priest, as well as being second only to the king. He has accepted me into his service and I hope to rise in the world through my efforts. Can you not be happy for me, father?"

Hor looked extremely unhappy. He had quietened down from his earlier outrage, and Den recognised that his brother was now concerned about appearing weak in front of him.

"I appreciate your concern for your son, Hor. I would feel exactly the same if he was my own child. You might like to go and argue your case with the Tjaty; if you do, I will do my best to get you a hearing. Otherwise, you might consider accepting the Tjaty's decision to use Kagemni where he believes he would be most use to the king. Kagemni is Tjaty Imhotep's scribe, not mine. He was employed in Inebu-hedj by the Tjaty, and the Tjaty sent him to Sekera as he knew I needed skilled scribes. From what I have seen of him, he could well be the most successful scribe to come out of our family."

Hor looked sceptical. "My son?"

Den nodded. "Your son. He will always be your son, raised by you and trained by you. What he makes of himself he will owe to you, his father. I know you do not like me, brother, but I only want what is good for you and for Kagemni. Let him work for the Tjaty here at Sekera, and I will do my utmost to guide him in ways that will bring credit on you."

Hor muttered under his breath, and then sat in silence for a few moments. "I suppose it would do no harm to let him to let him work here for a while. He will soon see that work as a scribe is much the same no matter where you are." He frowned and then nodded slowly. "Very well, I will allow Kagemni to work for the Tjaty in this place for a year, but if he wants to return home before the year is up, you will make sure he is relieved of his service to the Tjaty. Agreed?"

"I agree, brother," Den said.

"I agree too," Kagemni said with a grin.

Hor waved his hand dismissively at his son, as if discounting his opinion. "I will hold you personally responsible for his well-being, Den. If any harm befalls him, you will answer to me."

"He will be as if he was my own son," Den said.

Hor would not stay any longer, refusing Den's offers of hospitality. He stiffly embraced his son, nodded toward his brother, and took his leave of both of them. Kagemni watched his father trudging along the road that led to the river and shook his head.

"He actually has concern for me," he said wonderingly. "I never knew he thought that way about me."

Den knew Hor's mind was more concerned with hatred for his brother, rather than genuine concern for his son, but was not going to mention something so negative. "Your father loves you," he said instead.

Kagemni smiled at his uncle. "I am truly blessed to have such a loving family. I will work hard and make you and my father proud of me."

"I would expect nothing less of you, Kagemni. Now let us return to our work and our interrupted discussion with the masons."

Chapter 12

Disease ran through the palace at Inebu-hedj. As diseases went it was not especially virulent, but it seemed selective in its effect. It swept through the city, laying low young and old, men and women, but most recovered within a few days. Some died, but it was hard to distinguish between those deaths and the ones that normally afflicted the people of Kemet. They came down with a fever and a cough, mucus streaming from noses. If they worsened with diarrhoea or shortness of breath, they died, but if their sickness grew no worse after five days, they usually recovered.

Half a score died in the palace, three adults and seven children, of which three were daughters of the king. Great lamentations arose from all quarters, but especially from Queen Inetkawes who lost one daughter, and Djeser-Ti, who lost two. It was some consolation that though Prince Nub-Re sickened, he recovered quickly. King Hor-Sekhemkhet took the loss of three of his four children as a personal affront. He sought advice from his counsellors, including Tjaty Imhotep, sure that he had offended the gods of Kemet in some way. No one was prepared to accuse the king of any impropriety though, so Sekhemkhet could only believe that he had to try harder to fill the palace with his children.

"I need to take another wife," Sekhemkhet told Imhotep. "Do the gods at last look favourably on taking my sister Meresankh as my wife?"

"They have not spoken to me on this subject," Imhotep said evasively. "With your permission, I will approach them so I may learn their will."

Imhotep knew the gods had nothing to do with preventing the marriage. Meresankh herself had entreated Imhotep to find a way out of the issue, and he had invented a warning dream. The king would keep asking, though, so he needed to find out if his niece was still rejecting marriage with her brother.

"Gods, yes," Meresankh said. "I have no interest in any man, let alone my brother. Please continue to act on my behalf, Uncle."

"I will do what I can," Imhotep assured her. "May I ask where your interests do lie, Meresankh? You say you have no interest in men...is that lack of interest to do with sex in general, or is it distaste for men in particular?"

Meresankh laughed. "You are asking if my taste runs to women?" She shrugged. "Perhaps. Do you have any objections?"

"None at all, dear Meresankh. What you do is your own business. Have you...ah...found a partner?"

"If I have and you do not know, then I am being suitably discreet. Do not worry, Uncle, I will not do anything to engender gossip."

Imhotep pretended to have another dream, and informed the king that the gods still did not look favourably on any union with his younger sister.

"Well, I need another wife," Sekhemkhet said. "This sickness that has claimed the lives of my children shows how tenuous is my hold on a dynasty. I have a single son born to my Queen, and now not even daughters with Djeser-Ti."

"I am sure that you will have more, my lord. You are still young."

"I have had others on common women, but they cannot inherit. I need a son from another wife. I am allowed more wives, aren't I?"

"Of course, my lord. The king can have as many women as he wants."

"Then I shall marry again."

"Have you selected the fortunate young woman, my lord?"

"Her name is Seshen."

"Named for the sacred lotus? That is a good omen, my lord. Whose daughter is she?"

"I do not know. She is one of the chambermaids in the Queen's apartments."

"A common girl, then. What makes her suitable as a wife, my lord, when you could simply enjoy her any time you choose?"

"I told you, I need a son, and I know she is fertile, having borne me a son already."

"Indeed, my lord? May I offer my congratulations?" Imhotep hesitated, picking his words with care. "My lord does realise that a son borne to a concubine cannot inherit?"

"I know that. It is why I want to marry her."

"Even so, my lord. Marriage after the fact..."

"Will not legitimise him. I realise that," Sekhemkhet said impatiently. "But I know she can bear sons, so if I marry her and sow another son; that one could inherit."

"You have Nub-Re, my lord."

"Who is my heir," the king said. "I know that, but I do not seem to be very fortunate with my children. It seems I must have many, if any are to survive long enough to inherit."

Hetephernebti, as mother to Queen Inetkawes, objected to the new marriage, but was limited in what she could say. She tried to get her daughter to speak to the king, but she was unexpectedly reluctant.

"My son Nub-Re is the heir," she said complacently. "Why should I care how many women the king lies with?"

"He has married this one," Hetephernebti said. "What if she bears him a son?"

"He cannot be the heir; that honour belongs to Nub-Re alone."

"A king can do whatever he wants. If Sekhemkhet decides to make someone else the heir, who will say he cannot?"

"I will tell him he cannot," Inetkawes said. "He will always listen to me, because I am his sister and his Queen."

When Hetephernebti saw that her daughter was going to pay no attention to the dangers presented by Seshen, she took her concerns to Khemtet, but as the king's mother, her priorities were different.

"The king is my son, and any son he has is my grandson. I appreciate your feelings, Hetephernebti, but while Nub-Re is my grandson, so will be any boy born to this Sheshen girl."

Hetephernebti sniffed. "Does it not matter to you that your grandson by Sheshen will have the blood of commoners? At least Nub-Re is royal on both sides."

Khemtet shrugged. "I would prefer Nub-Re inherited, of course, but who am I to tell the king what he can or cannot do. If he wants to marry half the women in Kemet, I am not going to raise an objection." She smiled. "My son could do that, you know. He is virile."

Hetephernebti saw that she had no allies in this regard, so went to her apartments to think through her options. The easiest was to just wait and see. Sheshen might not bear another son, and even if she did, the boy might not live. Even if the child proved to be healthy, there was little likelihood of him being made the heir--as long as Nub-Re survived. Put that way, she realised, the potential son of Sheshen posed very little threat to her daughter's child.

"But very little threat is still a threat," she muttered. "If I am to protect my daughter and ensure that my grandson Nub-Re ascends the throne of Kemet, I must take action."

The question was what action? It was hard to determine the most effective action against an unborn child, against one who might not even have been sown in Sheshen's belly. There were two possibilities she could see--either she prevented the seed from reaching the field, or she removed the field altogether.

"What am I thinking? I cannot prevent the king from sowing his seed where he wills."

No, but you can remove the field, she thought. *Without Sheshen, there can be no male child.*

"He will only take another wife."

Almost certainly, but maybe not one proven to bear sons.

"What am I talking about when I say 'remove'?" she muttered. "Do I mean...?"

Do not say the word; who knows who might be listening. Think it, if you must, but do not say it. You are contemplating murder; the murder of an innocent young woman.

"What do I care? She is a commoner, and I will be protecting the future of my daughter and grandson. That is worth any risk."

There would be little risk if she were careful, she knew. She would not be attempting an act of violence, a physical assault with a weapon. Such a thing would be too obvious. No, any murder she committed would have to be subtle. No one must suspect. They might believe she had been killed, but there must be no outward evidence of it. Nothing that might get someone wondering who might be guilty. Such things were possible, she knew, if one knew where to look. And she did. Years before, she had talked to a foreigner from one of the northern nations and he had in his possession something that looked like a gemstone, but was not. It was a substance, a hard, clear, slippery-looking substance that came from the nations of the north, something that she had been told was a by-product of metal smelting. It was hard to come by, but not impossible. The same foreigner who had shown her the substance had warned her about one of its deadly properties. It could shatter under a blow and the tiny fragments were very sharp. If taken with food or drink, they could cut the intestines and the person inevitably died within a few days. There was no known antidote or cure.

Hetephernebti went to the chest in her apartment that held her sandals and, taking them out, revealed a small wooden box inlaid with lapis and onyx. Within this lay her most precious jewels and, in the bottom, lying unseen save to the most diligent searcher, lay a greenish bead of this dangerous substance, the size of her thumbnail. She took it out and held it up to the light, marvelling once more at its beautiful translucence.

"It could be a gemstone," she murmured, "but it is worth far more than mere gems."

Was she really going to do this? Commit a murder on behalf of her daughter and grandson? Or should she wait and see if it was necessary? The woman might not even bear the king a son, the as yet unborn child might pose no threat to her grandson. All this might be unnecessary. Perhaps she should wait...it was a serious step to take, and possibly a dangerous one.

Hetephernebti almost dropped the bead back into her box when another thought occurred to her. At the moment, Sheshen was just another palace woman, even if she was the king's new wife, but what would happen if she bore a son? The same thing that had happened to Inetkawes after Nub-Re had been born--increased security, ever-present nurses and tutors, servants coming and going. If she attempted to kill Sheshen then, she would have to kill the son as well, and somehow bring it about under the scrutiny of others. No, if it was going to be done, it had to be now. One victim rather than two, subtly instead of openly.

"Very well, it must be now, but how to do it? How do I administer the sharp fragments? I cannot just persuade her to swallow them, so I must disguise them; put them in food or drink."

She searched through her belongings and found a small stone mortar and pestle she sometimes used to grind up herbs for tonics, or ochres for her makeup. Dropping the bead into the mortar, she hesitated for a moment and then brought the pestle down onto it, fracturing the translucent bead. A fragment flew out of the mortar onto the table. She picked it up and cursed as it pricked her finger. Dropping the fragment, she sucked the drop of blood on her finger, but nodded with satisfaction. If it would do that to her finger, it would do the same to Sheshen's intestines.

Hetephernebti poured a cup of wine from the jar on her table and added the bead fragments, leaving behind the powder. Peering into the wine, the pieces had disappeared. She swirled the wine and carefully poured it into another cup in small amounts, imagining it was as if a person drank from the cup. At the bottom lay the bead fragments; they had not been drunk along with the wine, but had stayed behind. She frowned, realising that wine would not be the best method.

"What else? Food? If the pieces are in food, it will be chewed and she will bite down on them."

Grain was ground in large stone mortars, and sometimes chips of stone broke off and became baked into the bread. People encountered chips of stone in their bread all the time, sometimes even cracking a tooth on them. Hetephernebti had spat out her share of stone chips over the years.

"Soft food," she murmured. "Something she really likes but that does not need much chewing. She must swallow it before she realises the fragments are there."

Carefully retrieving the fragments from the wine cup, Hetephernebti locked them away in her chest and went to find out Sheshen's favourite foods. Despite being a commoner, Sheshen had developed a taste for spicy and sugary foods since becoming one of the king's women. Morsels of ripe date flesh, already sweet, had honey added to them, together with sesame oil. Providing Sheshen with a bowl of these dessert treats, she would devour them one after the other until sated.

Hetephernebti decided these were the very things, and ordered a bowl of them from the kitchens. She sat at a table with a bowl of the sweetmeats and contemplated them. They were sticky and very sweet, and did not need much chewing, but she knew she could not eat more than one or two without feeling nauseous. Sheshen was different, it seemed, and had been known to eat a score of them at a sitting. Hetephernebti had no doubt that she could tempt Sheshen with the sweetmeats, but it would look suspicious if she offered them and refused to eat them herself. The answer was to put the fragments of bead in only one or two and make sure she did not eat any of them herself.

"Sesame seeds," Hetephernebti murmured. "She loves sesame."

She sent for some from the kitchen and when it arrived, experimented with rolling the sticky date balls in a dish of the seeds. They stuck easily and looked very different from the unadorned sweetmeats.

"Good, I can tell them apart."

Pressing the fragments of bead deep into the sesame seed coated morsels, no more than one large piece and some of the powder into each one, she sent an invitation to Sheshen to call upon her for an informal meeting. She came, as Hetephernebti knew she would, and was ushered into the room. Sheshen had brought a companion with her, which did not please Hetephernebti, but it would look suspicious if she sent her away.

"You are most welcome," Hetephernebti said, taking Sheshen's hands, drawing her close and kissing her on the cheek. "You have become part of a very select group of royal women devoted to the king. As soon as I heard that Sekhemkhet had married again, I wanted to meet you."

Sheshen seemed surprised and relieved by the warm welcome. Despite the embrace, she bobbed into an awkward bow. "I...I am most happy to meet you, Queen Hetephernebti. I have heard so much about you." She gestured toward her companion. "This is Ansut, one of my ladies. I hope you do not mind that I invited her along."

"Of course not. I am delighted to meet you, Ansut. Now please, will you all sit? We shall take refreshment and you can tell me all about yourself, Sheshen."

The conversation was a little stilted at first, but Hetephernebti served strong wine that soon lowered inhibitions, and promoted loquaciousness. She soon had Sheshen talking about her background and how she found herself attracting the attention of the king.

"I could hardly believe it, my lady," Sheshen said. "I know your son..."

"My son-in-law," Hetephernebti corrected. "Queen Inetkawes is my daughter."

"Your pardon, my lady," Sheshen frowned, picking up the thread of the conversation. "The king has a reputation as being a veritable bull among the palace women, so I was happy to spread my legs for him. I was blessed with a son, but then he sent for me scarcely half a month back and said he wanted to marry me. I was...well, I was amazed."

"I am sure you will make the king very happy," Hetephernebti said. "That is all that we royal ladies desire from life, after all."

"I think it was because Sheshen had a son," Ansut said boldly. "It is no secret that the king desires more sons, and as Sheshen had already borne a son..."

"That is Lady Sheshen now," Hetephernebti pointed out. "She is your Lady now."

Ansut grimaced. "Of course. I meant to say Lady Sheshen. The fact that she has already had a son augurs well for the future, don't you think. She will have another son, I think, and he may well become the heir."

"The heir is the son of Queen Inetkawes," Hetephernebti said coolly. "My daughter."

Ansut shrugged. "He is the heir now," she murmured, slightly emphasising the last word.

Hetephernebti tamped down her anger at the slight, and clapped her hands for a servant. "I have heard you have a liking for date sweetmeats, so I had some prepared for you." The bowl arrived, and Hetephernebti insisted on serving Sheshen with her own hand, a gesture she saw pleased the young woman.

"I was not sure whether you liked sesame seeds, so I had some made with them, some without."

"Oh, definitely with them," Sheshen said. She took one of the seeded sweetmeats and popped it into her mouth, chewed once or twice and swallowed. "Delicious," she said, taking another one.

Ansut reached over and took a plain sweetmeat, swallowing it quickly and taking another one.

Sheshen devoured her second and reached for another one. "I can see I am going to have to eat quickly," she said, around a mouthful of date. "Ansut likes them almost as much as I do."

Hetephernebti took a plain sweetmeat and nibbled on it, watching as the two women steadily ate their way through the bowl of desserts.

Ansut grimaced once, her mouth working. "Something hard," she complained.

"Probably a piece of date kernel, or perhaps a toasted sesame seed," Hetephernebti said. "Don't eat any more if it concerns you."

"Not that much," Ansut replied. She swallowed and took a sip of wine to wash it down.

Sheshen seemed to have no problems with her sweetmeats. She devoured over half of them, sesame coated ones first, and then whatever was left, and Ansut ate most of the others. Hetephernebti only ate one unseeded treat, and watched the other women with great curiosity. Her knowledge of the internal effects of the bead fragments was almost non-existent, so she was not sure whether anything would happen immediately, or only after a delay.

Sheshen got to her feet and Ansut followed, wiping her mouth. "Thank you for your hospitality, Queen Hetephernebti," Sheshen said. "Perhaps I could entertain you when my next son is born."

The two women left and Hetephernebti sank back onto her couch in perplexity. According to everything she had heard, the bead fragments should be doing their work, but neither woman had shown any signs of distress. Perhaps she did not eat enough of it, she thought. After all, Ansut had eaten many of the sweetmeats and she had not allowed for someone else eating them. Frowning, Hetephernebti had the dishes cleared away and washed, and then she checked that all the powder remaining in her mortar was washed out and the water poured away. If her plan worked, there must be no connection with her.

Then it was just a matter of waiting for something to happen. Hetephernebti quickly found that sitting around doing nothing, waiting for the first signs of a successful plan was more nerve-wracking than actually feeding someone the harmful substance. She could not ask after the health of Sheshen, lest anyone wonder why she was asking, but she had to know if the court physician had been called to treat her. The only thing she could think to do was to ask after the general health of the palace people.

"I have heard there is sickness in the city," she mentioned to one of her ladies. "I hope that has not spread to the palace."

"I have not heard anything, my lady, nor of any general sickness. Who told you this?"

"I forget," Hetephernebti said vaguely. "So no one is sick? That is good."

"You are feeling well, my lady?"

"Yes, I am...perhaps a little tired." Another possibility occurred to her, so she added, "Ask the court physician to attend on me."

Hesy-Ra still held that position and he arrived with his bag of instruments and an assistant within the hour. "My lady, you are not feeling well?" he asked solicitously.

"Just a bit tired."

Hesy-Ra smelled her breath, listened to the sound of her breathing, and examined her eyes. "I can prescribe a simple tonic," he said. "My assistant will make it up and deliver it to you."

"I was concerned that my tiredness might be part of a more widespread sickness within the palace and city," she said. "I have heard rumours."

"Put your mind at rest, my lady. There is no general sickness; only the usual ills that befall any group of people--toothache, bellyache, headache, cuts and sprains. Certainly nothing for you to worry about."

"So nothing out of the ordinary?"

"No, my lady."

Rather than reassuring her, Hesy-Ra's words dismayed her. Had she worked to remove Sheshen without success? Evidently, the sharp pieces of the fractured bead had not injured her intestines and, if the bead had not worked, she would have to find something else.

Two days later, the palace buzzed with talk of a woman with severe stomach pain who had taken to her bed with a high fever and nausea. Ominously, fresh blood stained her vomitus and her wits had started to wander.

"Who is it?" she demanded of her attendant ladies.

"Ansut, who attends upon Lady Sheshen, my lady."

The bead had worked, Hetephernebti realised, but it had struck down the wrong person. By attending the meeting, Ansut had saved her mistress from death, but at the cost of her own. Hetephernebti felt a pang of guilt, but quickly thrust it aside. The woman had been rude.

Ansut died three days later, in considerable agony, but Sheshen seemed to have escaped without ill effects. Nobody suspected anything, though Hesy-Ra was of the opinion it was something the woman had eaten. Neither Sheshen nor Hetephernebti had suffered even a moment's pain, so the sweetmeats they had shared were obviously no more than a passing consideration.

Hetephernebti's failure was brought home to her a month later when Sheshen missed her *hesmen*, and two months later her pregnancy was confirmed. She had missed her chance to remove the king's wife, and now she would be a lot more careful about what she ate or drank. Sheshen was brought to the birthing chamber in due course, but the gods denied the king what he most desired. A daughter was born, and Hetephernebti smiled with satisfaction. She had a breathing space in which to guard the future of her daughter's son, Nub-Re.

Chapter 13

There was plenty to keep Den busy at Sekera. The king's City of the Dead started to take shape as thousands of rough-cut blocks arrived on site from local limestone quarries, and hundreds of casing stones of fine, white limestone arrived by ship from the Troyu quarries. As Overseer of the King's Works, Den was conversant with every aspect of the site, and had a hundred lesser overseers and as many scribes kept busy recording every facet of the construction.

Den often stayed up late at night, a single oil lamp casting a pool of yellow light over his worktable as he pored over the latest figures supplied by his overseers. Sometimes, Kagemni worked with him, taking down notes as Den dictated them. Den wished the whole process was as simple as quarrying the stone, bringing it to the site, and raising one block upon another. Few people had oversight of the whole process and only those few appreciated the work that went into fulfilling the king's exacting demands. Supplies that went directly into the construction of the *mer*, the tomb and associated structures was only one aspect of the work.

"Do you think the king truly appreciates the drain on his treasury that his tomb entails?" Den asked one evening. He leaned back stretching. "No, do not answer that. He may know, but he has no real concept of what is involved. Luckily, Imhotep knows and even appreciates it."

"I had no idea of all this," Kagemni replied, gesturing at the tables and lists they had been going through that evening. "I thought stone was the greatest expense...perhaps transport costs...but all this?"

"These are just the costs in keeping it all together," Den went on. "If we included the cost to the previous king when we set up the workers' village, the king would howl with despair."

"How much can a those hovels cost though? They are just mud brick."

"Mud brick has to be made. Look, first, hundreds of men are employed digging up clay, moistening it, cutting and adding straw, moulding the bricks and drying them in the sun. Not just scores or hundreds of them, but thousands. They are carried on men's backs to the planned village and built into houses. The village is planned...you have seen it...a main street with scores of little houses opening onto it, roofed over with timber cut from woodlands and brought here. Furniture has to be supplied, whitewash made for the houses of the overseers. Some of them want brightly coloured columns or door surrounds, so paint must be brought in..."

"Is all that really necessary?" Kagemni asked. "I mean, whitewash, coloured paint?"

"It is if you want to keep your workforce happy," Den replied. "A happy workforce works harder. Making the houses is the least of it, though every time we get more labourers coming in, the more houses we have to build. No, the real expense now is supplying the men with food and drink, cloth, baskets, pots, straw, firewood...a hundred other things."

Kagemni nodded slowly. "I think I start to see what you mean, sir."

"How much does a man eat when he is working hard? How much does his woman eat, or his children? How much grain, how many onions, melons, garlic, lettuce? What area of land is necessary to grow all this food, just for the workers at Sekera? What does it cost to transport it all here?"

"A lot?"

"You have no idea," Den said. "We can cut costs by setting up bakeries in the village, next door to brewers. As long as the average worker gets his bread and beer every day, he is content."

"I had not thought even something as simple and basic as bread involved so much."

Den laughed. "I have not gone into detail, but think about this. The grain is delivered, many sacks of it every day. It must be ground into flour by other workers, made up into dough, and then baked in conical pots over open fires. Where do the pots come from? Every single one of them must be made new because more often than not the only way to get the bread out of them is to break the pot. Have you never wondered why the ground is so often littered with pottery sherds? Then there is firewood...it all has to be cut, transported and dried." Den shook his head. "Endless details, Kagemni."

"I had not considered any of this," Kagemni said. "I do not know where I thought it all came from."

"Of course, beer and bread is not enough to sustain a working man. He needs fish most days--easily supplied with the river within the throw of a stone, providing you have fishermen to catch them--but he also needs meat from time to time. Cattle are valuable, as are sheep and goats, geese, wildfowl. All this has to be reared or caught, slaughtered and cut up and brought here. None of it is free."

Den got up and stretched, pacing the room. "I am honoured to be Overseer of the King's Works. I could not have imagined being so important when I was your age, Kagemni, but I had the backing of a powerful man. Imhotep is second only to the king..."

"And you are married to his daughter," Kagemni said.

"Do not imagine that relationship has anything to do with my position," Den said sharply. "I was his personal assistant long before that, and that was because of my ability."

"I am sorry, sir, I did not mean to belittle you or play down your achievements."

Den nodded. "I know you did not. You are a good lad, Kagemni, with natural ability. I can see you going far if you apply yourself."

"Thank you, sir. I want to make you proud."

"Both I, and your father, are already proud."

"My father does not really believe in me," Kagemni said sadly. "When the year was up, he ordered me home again, but I refused to go." He sighed. "I should have, if only to bid farewell to grandfather Djer. I loved him and now he is gone...I am sorry, sir. I was forgetting he was your father as well as my grandfather..."

"No need," Den said. "I have grieved for him and he is in his own House of Eternity, enjoying himself with whatever I and your father could provide."

"Which has made my father head of the family," Kagemni said. "He cannot order you around--you are too high for him now--but I worry he has the authority to order me home against my wishes."

"He cannot go against the wishes of the Tjaty," Den pointed out. "And Imhotep will listen to my counsel. If you want to remain with me, that is exactly what you will do."

"Thank you, sir. I appreciate your support."

Den smiled. "It is in my own interest to keep you close. I am going to give you some real responsibility...if you want it, of course."

"I do, sir," Kagemni said eagerly.

"Then I will put you in charge of the accounting for the workers' village. All the reports will come into you, and you will collate them, calculate overall costs, and submit those figures to me. Still want to do it?"

Kagemni gulped, but nodded. "Yes, sir."

After Kagemni had gone to bed, Den poured himself the dregs of the beer jug and sat outside on a stool, looking out over the darkened river and the thin strip of vegetation on either side of the rippling water. The moon was not up yet, but the night sky, the body of the goddess Nut, blazed with stars in the clear air. Calls of night creatures, both from the woodlands along the river, and the desert behind him, accentuated the loneliness of the burial plateau, though he knew that thousands of sleeping men lay nearby. The dichotomy of the situation impressed itself on him once more, the two-fold nature of Kemet that overshadowed every aspect of life. Two kingdoms, black land and red land, life and death, man and woman, being alone in the midst of many, day and night, gods and men. It all meant something profound, Den knew, but he could not think what it was.

"I am too tired to think," he murmured, "and possibly I have drunk too much too." He poured the dregs of his beer out onto the ground by his stool and contemplated going to his bed.

The moon rose over the eastern hills, washing the land in a silvery light and casting a shimmering road over the waters of the river. Turning his head, Den looked at the great stepped structure of King Netjerikhet that he had helped build. In the moonlight, the white limestone encased steps gleamed and Den could imagine the spirit of the king ascending by means of them to the undying polar stars in the north.

"What must it be like to be a king and know that you live forevermore in the abode of the gods, ascending to the heavens to live in glory," Den murmured. "And what do I have to look forward to? If I am judged worthy, I may live in the Field of Reeds, living much as I do here in Kemet." For a few moments he contemplated the ordinary afterlife that awaited everyone except the king, and a new thought struck him. "I wonder if I will find work to do in the afterlife? I have built great things for the king in life, but in the afterlife he will be in the heavens, so for whom would I build things?" The thought troubled him, so he relieved himself against a rock and went to bed, falling asleep quickly.

Den slept in the next morning, only waking with the first rays of the sun. He washed and dressed, taking a small meal with his family. Life with Ranefert was everything he hoped it might be; a loving woman to care for his family, providing companionship and exciting intimate moments. She had settled into married life, taking care of their twin daughters Neferka and Senefer, their shared illegitimate son Khamose, and Den's children by his dead wife--Khawy, Khepankh, Merit and Khasenet. Den enjoyed his new expanded family and grasped any moments he might have in their presence.

"Where is Kagemni?" he asked.

"He rose early and left the house," Ranefert said. She spooned a mixture of pounded grain, milk and honey into the mouths of their small daughters.

"Gone to the building site, of course," Khawy said. "He will do anything to prove himself your greatest helper."

"He is hardworking," Den conceded, "and I gave him added responsibility yesterday. He will be putting in extra time to get a grasp of the details."

"What did you give him?" Khepankh asked.

"The accounting of the workers' village."

"Prepare for chaos," Khawy muttered.

"I disagree," Den said. "He is aware of the complexity of the task and he will come to me if he has any problems."

"And he is handsome," Merit murmured.

"What has that got to do with anything?" Khawy jeered. "You think any new man who comes to work for father is handsome."

"No, I do not," Merit said. "You work for father and I do not think you are handsome."

"Then it is just as well we are not of the royal family, otherwise you and I would have to get married."

Merit stuck her tongue out at her brother.

Den smiled at the bickering, and decided it was time for Khawy to join the workforce. His eldest son was thirteen summers, had done well under his tutor, and obviously thirsted to become a proper scribe.

"How would you like to join me on the site today, Khawy?"

"Me too?" Khepankh asked eagerly.

"You are too young," Khawy said. "You mean it, father?"

"Why not? Your tutor tells me you are a credit to his teaching, and I think it is about time you see what the real world of scribing is like."

Khawy got up from the table, grinning broadly. He strutted up and down with his chest thrust out. "I am a scribe today," he declared. "Soon, I will be building Cities of the Dead and great temples for all the kings."

"We only have one king," Merit objected, "and father builds the king's buildings."

"There will be other kings," Khawy said. "Hor-Sekhemkhet will not live forever."

"Nor will you if such words should reach the king's ears," Den said sharply. "Have I made a mistake in elevating you, Khawy? Perhaps the tutor can teach you discretion and humility."

"I am sorry, father," Khawy said. "I am just excited at the prospect of becoming a scribe and an architect like you."

Den did not want to squash the enthusiasm out of his son, but he knew that Khawy's expectations were unrealistic. He tried to let him down gently on the walk from the house to the mud brick site office.

"It took me twenty years of hard work to reach my present position as Overseer," Den said. "Even now, having reached that as a relatively young

161

man, I am unlikely to progress much further. We are not nobility, Khawy, and we cannot expect to be treated as such."

"Tjaty Imhotep is a noble," Khawy said. "He is uncle to the king, and you are married to his daughter. I would say that gives us certain expectations."

"You would be wrong. I may be Overseer and married to his daughter, but I am still a commoner and a scribe in his eyes, and more importantly, in the eyes of the king. Do not get ideas above your station, my son. That way lies only disappointment and despair."

Khawy thought his father was being unnecessarily cautious. As far as he was concerned, he intended to inherit the title of Overseer of the King's Works from his father, and then add to it. In his youthful mind, he saw himself one day as Tjaty of Kemet, ruling in the king's name and being the owner of a magnificent tomb that would rival the ones of the kings.

His daydreaming lasted all the way to the site office, where he saw Kagemni sitting in his father's chair with papers and scrolls spread out in front of him. His father, instead of being angry at Kagemni, merely nodded in his direction, took a scroll and a tablet, and walked out of the door, beckoning to his son.

"You let him sit in your place, father?" Khawy asked indignantly.

"Where would you have him sit?" Den asked. "The floor?"

"The floor is appropriate for a lowly scribe."

"So when you work for me as a scribe, you will expect to sit on the floor?"

"I am your son, so I will have a stool."

Den stopped and looked into the distance for a few moments and then turned to his son. "Khawy, I do not have sons or nephews on the building site; only scribes. If you want to be just my son, then return home and resume your lessons, but if you want to be a scribe, then your rank, your duties and your privileges are what I say they are. Is that understood?"

Khawy scowled but nodded. "Yes, father."

"Good." Den smiled. "Then let us go about our work."

Den took his son to the place where the underground tomb was being excavated, and started his daily round of questioning the masons and lesser overseers. Every now and then, he would turn to Khawy and tell him to record a particular measurement or make a note of something to be investigated later.

They entered the northern shaft, at first hardly having to bend at all, but as they neared the workface, the tunnel became more cramped, the walls rougher, and the air more foul. Khawy coughed and spat rock dust, complaining of the heat and dirt.

"You will get used to it," Den said. "Though I have to admit that after twenty years I still do not enjoy these passages."

"Then why are we here at all?" Khawy asked. He turned and directed an angry gaze at a labourer who jostled him while hauling a basket of stone chips to the surface. "We are scribes and you are the Overseer of the whole site. You can surely delegate someone to perform this filthy task."

"Of course I could," Den replied calmly. Another labourer stumbled and he reached out to steady the man. "If I refused to come down here, though, I would have to rely on the honesty of the overseers and I am sorry to say they sometimes tell you what you want to hear."

"You don't trust them? Dismiss them and raise up others."

"The new overseers would be just as lazy as the old ones," Den said with a laugh. "Isn't that so, Ratep?" The question was directed at the overseer in charge of the workface.

Ratep was a burly man with the whip of his office tucked into his kilt. He had obviously been listening to the conversation and now he turned and grinned at Den, sweat carving runnels in his dust-begrimed face and body.

"As lazy as we can get away with, sir," he said.

"And do you tell me only what I want to hear?"

"Hard to do that, sir, seeing as how you are always down here and can see for yourself. Wouldn't be any point in lying, sir."

"This is my son, Khawy," Den said. "He is a scribe and I am training him. You will likely see more of him in future."

"A chip off the old rock face is he, sir?"

"That remains to be seen. I hope so."

"Pleased to meet you, young sir," Ratep said. "You have a lot to live up to if you hope to be like your father." The overseer nodded to them both and turned back to his work, bellowing at a labourer who had taken advantage of Ratep's distraction to ease his aching muscles.

Den led the way out of the underground passage, and they both availed themselves of a bucket of water to wash the dust from their faces and mouths.

"I make a point of inspecting every aspect of the work as often as I can," Den said. "Never rely on what people tell you if you can possibly see for yourself."

They continued their inspection of the building site, paying attention to the limestone blocks being brought up and fitted into place on the *mer*. Den pointed out the footings on the boundaries of the planned edifice, shallow trenches dug out of the bedrock into which specially carved slabs were laid, angled inward.

They completed their rounds of the building site, and made sure that enough water was being brought to the workers. It was hot and thirsty work, and Den believed in making conditions as pleasant as possible given the arduous and uncomfortable labour. Towards noon, as the sun blazed down, rippling the air and almost physically beating down on them, they made their way back to the site office. Den turned aside just before they got there, to have a word with a runner from the port.

Kagemni had moved outside under a linen awning, the mud brick building proving stifling in the heat. Merit and Khepankh had brought food and drink for them all from the house, and Merit waited on Kagemni personally, pouring his water and selecting the best bread and fruit for his plate. The young man accepted it with an embarrassed smile, prompting Khawy to make fun of his little sister.

"Don't you think you are too young to be offering yourself to him?" he jeered. "You won't be old enough to marry for years yet, and by then he will have a family of his own."

Merit went bright red and threw of piece of fruit at Khawy, who dodged and laughed.

"Pay no attention to him," Khepankh advised. "He is just jealous."

"Me? Jealous? Of my little sister who only a couple of years ago was running around naked and peeing on the floor?"

Merit burst into tears, and Khepankh turned on his older brother indignantly. "You are jealous because Kagemni is getting her attention. She can see he's better than you, and so can I."

Khawy snarled with rage and pushed his brother. Kagemni tried to pull the brothers apart and was punched by Khawy for his trouble. Merit howled with rage and anguish, screaming at her brothers to leave Kagemni alone, and Den ran up, alarmed by the raised voices. He quickly restored order, expressing his disappointment at his sons for fighting, and apologising to Kagemni.

"There will be no more of these displays," he said. "We are scribes and overseers and above such things. Khawy, you are the eldest and should be setting an example. You will spend the afternoon transcribing the notes you took this morning, while your brother and sister will return to their lessons." Den waited until the younger children had left and Khawy stamped off into the hut before apologising to Kagemni once more.

"There is no need, sir," Kagemni said. "It was just youthful squabbles."

"Well, it disturbed the *ma'at* of the workplace, and I am unhappy about that."

"May I ask you some questions about the material I am working on, sir?"

"Later. I have just received word that Tjaty Imhotep has arrived at the port and wants to see me."

"I hope it is nothing serious, sir."

"He probably just wants to visit his daughter and grandchildren," Den said. He hurried off so as not to keep his father-in-law waiting.

When he reached his house, he found Imhotep sitting and chatting with Ranefert, while Khamose played on the floor, and the twins tottered unsteadily on their feet. Den greeted them, kissed his wife and children, and accepted a cup of water from a servant.

"How may I serve you, my lord?" Den asked.

"Firstly, by dropping that form of address," Imhotep said with a smile. "In private, I am just the father of your wife."

"And as such, worthy of respect, my...sir."

"I was sorry to hear of the death of your father."

"Thank you, sir. He was an old man, and I am sure he will have looked forward to joining my mother in the afterlife."

"I am sure he was proud of you."

"He was prouder of my brother Hor, sir, though my father accepted me toward the end."

"I am very sure he was proud of you both. You became scribes and followed his profession." Imhotep looked pensive. "I have two sons, both trained as scribes. I had hoped that one, at least, would follow me in government or as an architect."

"You have two fine sons, sir, skilled at what they do."

"I do not dispute that, Den, but one is content to be a priest, and the other has a fascination with rocks, and wants nothing more than to supervise a quarry. Both are worthy professions, but neither of them follows the path I have set out."

Den could not think of anything encouraging to say, so said nothing.

"I have many titles," Imhotep said. "I am Tjaty of the King of Kemet of the North, First after the King of Kemet of the South, Administrator of the Great Palace, Hereditary Nobleman, Hem-netjer of Iunu, Builder, Sculptor, Maker of Vases in Chief, Director of Works, Controller of the King's City of the Dead, Lord of Stone Buildings, Governor of the King's Quarries, and Commander of the King's Ships. Is it too much to want a son who will follow me?"

"Of course not, sir," Den said, wondering where the conversation was leading.

"Such a son must be a skilled scribe, a talented mathematician, and a man who is conversant with every aspect of the king's City of the Dead and all the things associated with it. Such men are uncommon."

"I can think of one, father," Ranefert said.

"As can I," Imhotep said.

They both looked expectantly at Den, who first stared back in perplexity, and then blushed deeply. "I...I am your son-in-law, sir, and naturally I follow you in everything to the best of my ability..."

"There is precedence, Den, and I would never have broached this subject while your father lived. Please consider it now."

"Wh...what exactly am I considering, sir?"

"I want to adopt you as my son, Den," Imhotep said.

Den had wondered what the Tjaty was getting at, but had never considered that possibility. It just seemed too outrageous to be contemplated. He looked dazed, and sat down. "I am married to your daughter, sir. How can I be your son?"

"There is precedence for both estates," Imhotep said with a smile. "Legally, you would be my son, but no one would ever consider you a natural brother to Ranefert."

"For which I am truly thankful," Ranefert said. "I have done many things in my life, some of which I regret, but I have never felt the least desire to lie with my brothers. You and I will continue as husband and wife, Den, but now you will be Lord Den, son of Imhotep, and a very important man in Kemet."

"So do you accept?" Imhotep demanded.

Den shook his head, frowning. "Are you sure this is what you want, sir?"

"I would not have mentioned it had I not been completely sure. Come, Den, join my family as an honoured son. If there is one man in Kemet able to live up to my exacting standards it is you. What do you say?"

"I...I say...yes, father."

Chapter 14

Prince Nub-Re, only son and heir of Hor-Sekhemkhet and Queen Inetkawes was sick. Barely two years old, the little boy cried incessantly, complaining of a 'hurt tummy'. Court physician Hesy-Ra was in close attendance, moving a pallet into the prince's room so he could watch over the child day and night. He prescribed potions and tonics, but the only effect was to make his tiny patient cry harder and vomit up the often nauseous concoctions. Prayers seemed to have no effect, though the king spent a great deal on burning incense in the temples, and gifts of gold and land to temple coffers. The only thing that worked, at least temporarily, was controlling the boy's diet.

The prince was fond of sweet things, particularly honey cakes, and complained when Hesy-Ra put the child on a basic diet of raw vegetables and fruits, a little bread and meat broth prepared under his supervision. However, Nub-Re's health improved. As soon as he stopped the regime, though, the symptoms reappeared. This troubled Hesy-Ra, as he had seen something similar before, so he took his concerns to the Tjaty.

"This happened before, if you recall, my lord," the physician said.

"The sickness of Netjerikhet?" Imhotep asked. "Are you sure it is the same thing?"

"How can I be?" Hesy-Ra asked, a trifle testily. "There are many sicknesses that involve stomach pain, nausea, and general malaise. It might just be something in his diet, as he gets better when I supervise the preparation of his food."

"Which is what happened with Netjerikhet, I seem to remember."

"That is why I brought it to you, my lord," Hesy-Ra said. "There was the possibility then of the king being poisoned. If it is the same sickness, then we must face the possibility that the person or persons who wanted the king dead, want this little boy's death also."

Imhotep considered the physician's words. The idea that an enemy was striking at the royal house in such a terrible and cowardly way appalled him.

"What does such a person, if he even exists, gain from killing the child?" Imhotep asked. "If there is a foe determined to kill a king, it can only be so he can replace him on the throne, but what does he gain from killing an infant?"

"He is the heir."

"Yes, but Sekhemkhet is the king. If a man meant to kill him, I could understand it, but it is pointless killing the child first. With the army behind him, he could ignore the child until after he had taken power."

"You mention the army, my lord. Does this mean you suspect Khaba once more?"

"I am not convinced that anyone is trying to take over the throne."

"I am sure you know best, my lord, but if someone was, Khaba would be suspect."

"Khaba has retired," Imhotep pointed out.

"That need not end the man's ambition. Besides, his son Nubsekhem now commands the Northern Army. Is he any less ambitious?"

Imhotep conceded the point, but counselled taking a wait and see attitude. "You cannot identify the poisonous principle, so we do not know for sure whether the boy is even being poisoned. Continue to treat him as you would for a flux or other digestive sickness, and I will make some discreet enquiries."

It was not something that Imhotep talked about, or even intimated the presence of, but he deployed a large unofficial army of informants and agents throughout Kemet. Managing and safeguarding the king and the kingdom was his primary duty, and he took it seriously. Despite his seeming lack of interest in ex-general Khaba as a possible conspirator, that possibility had crossed his mind as soon as Hesy-Ra mentioned the illness. He called in his agents and spies, and set them the task of tracking the presence and movement of Khaba, his son Nubsekhem, and any of the men known to be under their influence. Reports flowed in within days, and reading them, Imhotep felt disappointed. A finger pointed clearly at Khaba would, in some ways, make his job easier. He would be able to strike at the head of the serpent and remove a threat to the *ma'at* of the kingdom. There was no indication that Khaba was involved, however. Nobody connected to the Northern Army and its officers had been in Inebu-hedj during the prince's sickness. It was possible that his spies had missed someone, Imhotep knew, but an investigation of the palace servants involved in food preparation turned up nothing of interest.

"So if not Khaba, then who?" Imhotep asked himself. "Or is the sickness just that? Something sent by the gods that does not have the hand of man in it?"

Under Hesy-Ra's care, Prince Nub-Re's health slowly improved, but the sickness alarmed both the king and his wife's mother Hetephernebti, though for different reasons. The king worried once more about the fragile link that he had to the future, resting the hopes of his dynasty on a single son who had almost been snatched from him. It was ridiculous to think that a young virile king like him had but a single son. His wife Djeser-Ti had borne a son, but he died; his latest wife had birthed a son outside of marriage, but only a daughter within it; while his sister-wife was the only one to have given him a living son.

"What am I to think?" Sekhemkhet asked his Tjaty. "Only my sister-wife has given me a son who still lives, so I must once more look to my other sister, Meresankh. I have to marry her and have another son."

"My lord king, I can only repeat that the gods prohibit this marriage. Great misfortune would descend on Kemet if you took her as wife."

"Great misfortune has already descended on me...and I am Kemet," Sekhemkhet grumbled. "A curse on all those who would work against me, Imhotep. I am the king; surely I can do as I please?"

"Of course you can, my lord king. Nobody would dispute your right to act in any way you chose, but as well as your rights, you have responsibilities."

"You dare to lecture me on my rights and responsibilities?"

"Not lecture, my lord king. Neither can any man tell you what to do. You made me Tjaty so that I might advise you, and my advice is that you pay heed to the will of the gods. If they deny you this marriage, then there must be a good reason for it. Perhaps they see a greater good for you and Kemet elsewhere."

Sekhemkhet grunted. "Why must the gods be so opaque? Let them speak plainly."

"They do," Imhotep replied, "if you have ears to listen. My lord king, I am the Hem-netjer of Re, and the god has spoken categorically to me in a dream. I realise this is not what you want to hear, but you must trust that the gods of Kemet know what is best for the king of Kemet. If I might offer my own advice, lie with your wives again, and maybe the gods will relent and let you have another son."

Imhotep shivered in the privacy of his own rooms after advising the king. He knew that he had invented the voice of the gods through his supposed dream as a device to prevent the marriage between Sekhemkhet and Meresankh, and it concerned him that he might be denying the will of the gods. A man risked disaster by misrepresenting the gods, but he consoled himself with the thought that the gods could give a son to any woman if they so chose. They did not need Meresankh's belly for that; the king had plenty of fertile fields in which to sow his seed.

The other person alarmed by the sickness of Nub-Re was Queen Hetephernebti. Her daughter Inetkawes was the mother, and both women had a big stake in being the mother and grandmother of the next king of Kemet. Sickness was an ever-present reality of life, and never more so than in the early years. If anyone had bothered to record the number of deaths at all stages of life, they would have found more young children dying than at any other time; more even than during war or famine.

Hetephernebti was unaware of the actual numbers involved, but she knew as well as anyone, that death lurked on the threshold for any young child. The only factors favouring Nub-Re's survival were adequate supplies of food and the presence of a capable physician. Hesy-Ra had been court physician for many years, though many credited Tjaty Imhotep with the cures that came from Hesy-Ra's hand. Whoever had kept Nub-Re alive, Hetephernebti knew, might not succeed should there be a recurrence of the sickness.

Hesy-Ra and Imhotep had attempted to keep the notion of poison a secret, but secrets tended to leak out of any container. Soon, the idea that some man or woman had raised a hand against the king's heir became known throughout the palace. Physician and Tjaty might have suspected Khaba, but the mother of the queen was in no doubt about the guilty party.

"Sheshen," Hetephernebti murmured, when she first heard the news. "That whore has dared to lift her hand against the king's heir."

Talking to Hesy-Ra, she learned how sick the child had been, and how close to death. Such a thing could not be allowed to happen again. She had acted alone against Sheshen, but now she would have an ally in the person of Khemtet, mother of the king. Khemtet's concern was only for the king, rather than Hetephernebti's daughter, but both shared in young Nub-Re's continued health and welfare.

"What were you thinking?" Khemtet asked, when Hetephernebti told her what she had done. "You attempted to kill a wife of the king...my son, if you remember."

"Sheshen is a low-born whore and not at all suited to be a wife of the king."

"In that, at least, we are agreed," Khemtet said. "Still, you acted rashly...and unsuccessfully."

"I might have succeeded. It was an untried method, but I had been assured of its efficacy." Hetephernebti described the bead and how she had used it.

"Cutting the intestines from the inside? That is something new."

"One of her ladies ate a lot of the sweetmeats meant for Sheshen. The bitch died because of her greed."

Khemtet waved her hand dismissively. "All right, you tried and you failed, but it did not matter anyway; she had a girl. Why have you told me all this now?"

"Because Sheshen has tried to kill Prince Nub-Re. I know that another son born to one of his other wives benefits the king rather than my daughter, but this act is greater than that. Nub-Re is descended from us both, and any harm done to him harms both of us. I hoped you would help me."

"Help you how?"

"Help me kill Sheshen."

"You have proof that she tried to kill our grandson?"

"What proof do I need? She benefits if he dies."

Khemtet considered Hetephernebti's words. "Djeser-Ti would also benefit if she bore a son and Nub-Re was dead."

"Djeser-Ti has not got the fortitude for such an act," Hetephernebti scoffed. "Besides, she loves the king and would not do anything to hurt him, even if it hurt her."

"There is truth in what you say," Khemtet conceded. "However, I do not like the idea of killing someone just because she would benefit. What if she is not guilty?"

"You would rather wait until she establishes her guilt beyond all doubt by killing our grandson?"

"No...no, of course not, but I do not like it."

"You think I relish the idea? Yet I would do so if it meant Nub-Re became the king after his father."

"In that case, I will help you," Khemtet said. "How is it to be done?"

"I hoped you might have some ideas. Neither of us is capable of using overt violence, nor would I want to involve others in our act."

"That leaves poison," Khemtet said. "Could you get another bead?"

"It did not harm Sheshen last time, so it may not if we tried again. I think we need a more potent poison, and for that I must make some enquiries."

"Discreet enquiries," Khemtet said.

175

It was not easy to ask about poisons without revealing their purpose, so the matter was still unresolved a month later when the king suddenly announced that he wanted to hunt wildfowl in the reed beds of the delta. Rather than just take a hunting party, he decided he wanted others to view his hunting prowess, especially the women of the court. He would also take his son and heir, Nub-Re, now fully recovered. It was about time the prince was introduced to the manly pursuit of hunting. The palace was thrown into a flurry of activity, with servants scurrying to put together great lists of what would be needed.

While the king and his huntsmen were prepared to forego comfort for the thrill of the hunt, the women flatly refused to go if it meant leaving behind their fine clothes, cushions and awnings against the sun's fierce rays. What started as a simple hunting trip to the local reed beds turned into an expedition reminiscent of a war against foreign invaders.

People and equipment poured aboard a small fleet of boats and headed out in the current, the watermen on board guiding the little craft to a suitable grassy knoll that boasted a few small trees. Reed beds spread out like a cloak between the low-lying land and the sluggish branches of the river. Servants hurried to erect awnings, spreading out cloth and plumping cushions for the court women and the young heir, while others unpacked food and drink in abundance.

The king organised his hunters and examined his equipment. He would hunt from a low punt poled into position by one of the guides, while other small boats would hold other members of his entourage and small boys whose main duty was to collect the anticipated drifts of ducks, geese and other waterfowl the king killed. Nobody else would be hunting until Sekhemkhet had slaked his blood lust. He made a big show of setting off on the first foray into the reeds, calling out to the women and greeting by name and title his Queen, other wives, his mother and mother-in-law.

"Watch me, my son," the king called out. "Hunting is training for war, and I shall smite down hundreds of enemies of Kemet."

The little boy, delighted to be the centre of attention, squealed with excitement and jumped up and down, brandishing his own little toy bow.

Sekhemkhet's punt was poled to a small lily-covered lagoon almost surrounded by reeds, the other boats hanging back out of deference, while other hunters circled round the beds and started beating the reeds and shouting. Birds erupted from cover, beating wings creating a rushing noise like a storm wind, and as they wheeled above the lagoon, the king took aim and loosed arrow after arrow into the flocks. Ducks started falling, either killed outright or wounded, and the small boys leapt overboard, swimming out to retrieve them. Wounded birds were quickly dispatched by wringing their necks, and the bodies thrown onto the boats.

The wheeling flocks dispersed, the fallen ones were collected, and the king moved onto the next lagoon and fresh reed beds. Servants retrieved a few score of the waterfowl and started plucking and gutting them, while others prepared fires for cooking.

The women lost interest in the hunting after the first hour, and were content to lie back with cups of watered wine and gossip. Inetkawes kept an eye on her young son, though her ladies were diligent in their tasks. Others wandered the grassy shores of the little knoll, excitedly exclaiming as they saw a shoal of tiny silver fish, a white egret engaged in a hunt of its own, iridescent dragonflies darting above the reeds, and the occasional leap and splash of a frog. Sheshen was one of these women, and two of her ladies accompanied her.

Hetephernebti watched the young woman from the shade of the awning, and if her thoughts had had substance, Sheshen would have been writhing in agony in the shallows.

"A pity Nub-Re's bow is only a toy," she murmured to Khemtet. "I could put an arrow through her from where I sit."

"Have you ever used a bow?" Khemtet asked. "I am told it is not as easy as it looks, despite my son making it look so."

"Yes, your son the king is a mighty hunter. Could he be persuaded to send a stray arrow into his latest wife?"

"He would not think it to be in his interests to do so," Khemtet said.

"But we are still resolved to remove the threat she represents, aren't we?"

"Of course." Khemtet watched the three young women paddling in the shallow water. "Perhaps a crocodile will take her."

"I shall pray to Sobek so that he might send one," Hetephernebti said. "Who else can we pray to?"

The old queen shrugged. "Wadjet, perhaps. She is the protector of kings, and we seek to protect a future king."

"Ugh, I hate snakes."

Their attention was distracted by the sound of a slap, a cry and a shout of outrage. Close to where the other wives of the king sat and talked, Prince Nub-Re sat on the grass bawling his eyes out, while one of the Queen's maidservants knelt beside him with an expression of fear. Inetkawes was on her feet, standing over the maidservant.

"How dare you strike the prince?" Inetkawes said. "I will have you beaten."

"Forgive me, my lady, I meant no harm." The woman grovelled at the Queen's feet. "There was a mosquito on his arm and I slapped the insect without considering my action."

Inetkawes scowled, still outraged that anyone had dared lay a hand on her son, but also glad that the offending insect was now just a smear of blood on the little boy's arm.

"You should have rubbed garlic over him to keep away the mosquitoes. Do so now and if you commit no more crimes against the prince today, I will reconsider your beating."

"Yes, my lady. Thank you, my lady."

A clove of garlic was produced and the juice from it was rubbed liberally over the protesting prince. The juice stung two bites on the boy, but the maidservant distracted him with a honey cake, and Nub-re soon forgot his discomfort.

The king returned from his hunt at midday, to the accolades of the other hunters. Dead birds were piled up on the grass and the women marvelled at the number, praising the king effusively, while he postured and boasted of his hunting prowess. They sat down in the shade of the awnings, cooled by a gentle northerly breeze, and feasted on the food brought from the city, together with the freshly roasted birds from the hunt. Afterward, Sekhemkhet wanted to resume the hunt a little farther afield, so the hunters set off again, leaving the servants to clean up and the women to doze or walk around the grassy knoll.

One of the women produced a cloth ball filled with straw and a number of them hitched up their skirts and threw it from one to another, making a game of it. Once or twice it landed in the river's edge, the straw soaking in the water, and the added weight hindered their efforts to throw it straight. Sheshen, in particular, delighted in throwing the ball so hard that others often missed it, and there was some argument over her tactics.

"If it lands in the water or reeds, the person who threw it must retrieve it," Djeser-Ti said.

As she was the most highly ranked young lady playing, (Inetkawes being asleep with her son), her word became the rule thereafter. The game continued, with people laughing at Sheshen's wild throws. She became so agitated by the laughter that she aimed at Djeser-Ti's head and threw. It missed, though it plucked at her dress as it sailed past and splashed into the reeds several paces offshore.

"Go and get that for me," Sheshen told one of her ladies, but Djeser-Ti stopped the young woman.

"The one who throws it has to get it. That means you, Sheshen."

Grumbling loudly, Sheshen hitched up her skirts even higher and waded into the reed bed, the water quickly mounting up to her thighs.

"It's too deep," she called. She started to turn back.

"Go on," Djeser-Ti commanded. "You are nearly there."

Stifling a curse, Sheshen waded deeper, tripped and fell headlong with a shriek. She emerged from the water with weed clinging to her, her dress askew, and her hair straggling over her shoulders. The laughter of the women did not improve her mood as she splashed and stumbled her way the extra few paces to where the ball lay half submerged in the water. Reaching for it, she shrieked again.

"Stop screaming and just pick it up," called one of the ladies, emboldened by Djeser-Ti's treatment of Sheshen.

"I've been bitten!" screamed Sheshen, stumbling back toward shore. She clasped her right hand to her, and after a few moments, her ladies ran to her assistance as she fell in the shallows. Their cries joined Sheshen's.

Hetephernebti looked up as the yells and screams increased in volume. "What's happening?" she asked.

"I think Sheshen has been bitten," Khemtet said.

"What by? It would be too much to hope a crocodile was responsible."

Khemtet stood so she could get a better look at the gaggle of women at the water's edge, clustered around Sheshen. "I don't think it was a crocodile."

Male servants were called upon, and they carried Sheshen, moaning, up to the camp, where the expedition physician examined her.

"Snakebite," he pronounced. "Did anyone see it?"

"Cobra," Sheshen whispered. "Am I going to die?"

The physician frowned, but said nothing. He had Sheshen made comfortable and took one of the servants aside.

"I need the snake that bit her," he said. "Its blood may yet save her life."

The servant looked at the reed bed where the cloth ball still marked the spot and shook his head. "I'm not going in there," he said.

Nobody else was prepared to do so, and the physician said he could do nothing for her. Over the course of the next two hours, Sheshen's hand swelled and bruised, while she complained of a headache and dizziness. The physician gave her something for the pain, but he shook his head when anyone asked after her.

She died, convulsing and struggling to draw breath, just before the king returned from his afternoon hunt. He rushed to her side but, when he saw that he was too late, withdrew. Hetephernebti remarked that he looked more annoyed that attention had been drawn away from his successful hunt than concern for his dead wife.

"My son feels grief," Khemtet said. "He just does not show it as other men would. Anyway, what do you care? You wanted her dead."

"As did you," Hetephernebti pointed out. "It seems like our prayers were answered after all. I must make a handsome donation to the temple of Wadjet."

Chapter 15

"**I** am still head of this family," Khaba thundered. "I expect to be obeyed."

While Khakhet quailed, close to tears in the face of his grandfather's anger, and Huni looked worried, Nubsekhem merely bowed politely.

"Nobody disputes your right to rule the family, father," he said. "How do you imagine you have been disobeyed?"

Khaba dismissed all the servants, telling them to completely vacate the house, and waited until they had done so.

"There was an attempt on the life of the heir, the prince Nub-Re. Is it coincidence that he suffered the same sickness that plagued Netjerikhet?"

"Inebu-hedj can be an unhealthy place during the inundation," Nubsekhem said.

"Enough!" Khaba roared. "Your flippancy is insubordinate. You know very well that I am referring to the sickness you induced in the last king, not some flux caused by standing water and stenches."

"In that case, I have no idea what you are talking about."

"I am not a fool," Khaba growled. "A single case of sickness striking the royal family could just be an act of the gods, twice is suspicious, but three times is almost a declaration of war. Do you want the king to move against our family? Do you seriously have a desire for an early death?"

"I have no such desire, father," Nubsekhem said, "and though I know about the first two events, that was some time ago. I do not know of a third time."

"You deny it?" Khaba demanded.

"I imagine I would if I knew what you meant. Has someone been poisoned?"

"You know very well Prince Nub-Re fell sick with something that sounds suspiciously like the poison that afflicted Netjerikhet."

"Now that you mention it, I seem to remember hearing something, but I do not listen to every barrack room rumour. Nub-Re was sick, you say? Did he recover?"

Huni looked from his father to grandfather and back again. "My father would not poison a child," he told Khaba forcefully. "We do not make war on children."

"There, you see?" Nubsekhem asked, smiling smugly.

"So you did not try to kill the prince two months ago?" Khaba asked.

"Grandfather, is this something we should be discussing in front of Khakhet?" Huni asked. "He is only eleven years old."

"Khakhet knows my mind. You can say anything in front of him," Khaba growled. "So, answer my question, Nubsekhem."

"Really, father, I cannot be held accountable for every little sniffle or bellyache in the royal family."

"You swear that?"

"It pains me that my spoken word is no longer good enough for you," Nubsekhem said.

Khaba scowled and harrumphed. "What about the prince's current sickness? Did you have anything to do with that?"

Nubsekhem looked genuinely surprised. "He is sick again? What with this time?"

"A fever that peaks and recedes..."

"Like the river?" Huni interrupted.

"What?"

"The fever rises and falls, like the river does at flood time."

"Not in the least like the river," Khaba said tersely. "And do not interrupt your elders."

"There might be something in what the lad says," Nubsekhem mused. "Maybe the fever is tied in some way to the river."

Khaba shrugged. "It appeared shortly after they all returned from a hunting trip in the reed beds. That commoner wife of the king died of snakebite, and the boy came down with a fever. I do not see a connection-- one to the other, or to the river."

"Either way, I had nothing to do with it," Nubsekhem said. "I have better things to do with my time than to murder children."

"What are you doing with your time?" Khaba asked.

"That is not really any of your concern now, father. You retired from the army."

"No, I was forcibly retired. There is a difference."

Nubsekhem shrugged. "I am performing my duties."

"Which involves?"

Nubsekhem stared at his father and sighed. "You know very well what my duties entail. I train the men and I patrol the north-eastern borders, ready to repel invaders and defend Kemet."

"Then why do I receive reports that men loyal to the king are being replaced by men with a loyalty to you alone? Officers first and now common soldiers?"

"I do not know where you get those ideas from, father. Do you know, Huni?"

"No, sir," Huni said, though he frowned and looked down at the floor.

"You are being fed false information, father," Nubsekhem went on. "You might wonder why. Could it be that someone is trying to divide our family? Drive a wedge between you and me?"

"To what purpose?"

"A family divided against itself is weakened. Perhaps somebody like Imhotep seeks to safeguard the king by removing any perceived threat."

"Are you a threat, Nubsekhem?" Khaba asked. "To Hor-Sekhemkhet and the *ma'at* of the kingdoms?"

Nubsekhem looked his father in the eyes. "I swear I am completely loyal to the king."

Khaba stared back at his son, wanting to believe but not quite trusting his words. He opened his mouth to speak, but closed it again, shaking his head.

"I am tired. Leave me."

Nubsekhem and Huni bowed and left Khaba's presence, but Khakhet stayed, sitting unobtrusively to one side. After his father and brother had gone, he got up and poured Khaba a cup of wine, offering it to him.

"My father really tried to assassinate the last king?" Khakhet asked.

"Against my wishes and advice," Khaba said, sipping the rich wine that came from his own vineyards. "My loyalty lies solely with the king, for to do otherwise risks civil war, with man turned against man, kingdom against kingdom, as in the days of Seth-Peribsen. I will not bring that fate upon Kemet, and I will hand my son over to Imhotep before I allow that to happen."

Khakhet looked unhappy at the thought of his own father betrayed. "Imhotep hates us?"

"He is loyal to the king. In that, we are agreed, though there is much in which we disagree. I do not trust him, though I will work with him to maintain *ma'at*."

"My mother is Imhotep's daughter," Khakhet said slowly. "Does that mean you do not trust me?"

"You are your father's son, not your mother's, Khakhet. I would not speak like this or let you listen to family confidences if I did not trust you implicitly."

Nubsekhem and Huni walked in silence as they left the family estate, joining with a small detachment of soldiers for the journey back to Hut-waret and the garrison there. They crossed the eastern branch of the river by ferry, landing north of Iunu and taking the road of beaten earth that followed the edge of the farmlands toward the northeast. Secure within the borders of Kemet, they ordered their men ahead, lagging behind so they could talk without being overheard.

"I am saddened that my grandfather should believe our enemies rather than you, sir," Huni said. "He talks about family loyalty, but other things rank higher in his mind."

"How does he believe our enemies?" Nubsekhem asked mildly.

"By accusing you of trying to kill Netjerikhet, and now Sekhemkhet's heir. Even when you swore loyalty to the king, I do not think he believed you."

Nubsekhem laughed. "My father could always tell when I was lying."

"You were, sir?"

"Well, not completely. I am loyal to the king, but I did not specify which king. You know I think Sekhemkhet is not the true king of Kemet, so I would be a fool to swear allegiance to him. No, my loyalty belongs to King Khaba if he will take the throne, and if not, then to King Nubsekhem."

Huni gaped at his father until a fly landed on his lips, causing him to spit and wipe his mouth. "You would dare take the throne?"

"Have you learnt nothing these past months? To what end have I been gathering men loyal to me rather than to the king?"

"I...well, what commander would not want men loyal to him? I thought..."

"I have talked of this before, Huni. Was I wasting my breath?"

"I thought it was just that, father--talk. You really mean to gather an army to challenge the king and take the throne?"

"Now you know the truth of it," Nubsekhem said. "You join a select few...your grandfather and your brother...who are aware, if not of my plans, at least of my desires." He glanced sideways at Huni. "Are you with me?"

"Of course, father."

The lack of even the slightest hesitation warmed Nubsekhem's heart. He had thought his son fully understood his ambition, but it seemed he had not. Huni was aware now, though, and he would watch him carefully in case he was as good at dissembling as his father.

"So you did try to kill Netjerikhet?" Huni asked after a few minutes.

"I did."

"How?"

"Without going into details, which are unimportant, I tried to poison him. You could say I failed, but then I was not really trying to kill him. I only wanted to see if it could be done. Your grandfather found out and it angered him."

Some farm workers, laden with the tools of their trade, came toward them, edging to the side of the road to let the armed men past. Nubsekhem waited until they were well past before continuing.

"I think your grandfather was more angry that I had not asked his permission than that I had made the attempt."

Huni nodded. "So you obeyed him?"

"No, but I was more circumspect. I found a better way of delivering the poison, but only enough to make him sick. The same with the young prince a few months ago. I had no real interest in killing him as I was not ready."

"And his present sickness?" Huni asked. "After the river trip? That was you also?"

"Actually, no. I do not know the cause of his sickness, only that I had nothing to do with it."

Huni pondered his father's words as they marched on. He kicked a small stone, sending it skittering across the packed earth until it ended up in the soft sand by the side of the road. "I am glad," he said at length. "I do not think we should wage war against children."

"When I am ready to wage war against the king of Kemet, I will kill anyone who stands in my way," Nubsekhem said. "At that time, should Nub-Re still be alive, he will be the heir and to succeed, I must eliminate him as well as his father."

"In that day, I will stand beside you, father," Huni said, "but how will you do it?"

"I have not decided."

The two men, father and son, continued on their way, conscious of the twenty men of their guard marching a hundred paces or so in front of them. Huni, being less experienced, saw the men as a fine body of soldiers trained in the arts of war, but Nubsekhem saw them solely as a means to an end.

"We have five hundred men in the Northern Army," Huni said. "From what I know of the troops available to the king, they should be more than enough. He has less than half that if he stripped the garrisons of any of the forts near Inebu-hedj."

"True, but what would result from pitting Kemetu against Kemetu? A civil war benefits no one."

"Then what is the point of training up an army, father, if not to use them?"

"A civil war will result if we challenge the king and give him time to respond. If we do that, we have lost before we start. Most of our men, even those who profess loyalty to us, will balk at openly facing the king in rebellion. To succeed, we must somehow remove or seriously weaken the king before we strike."

"Ah...so that is why you tried poison," Huni said.

"It was an experiment. I learned from it, even if I never use it."

"It would be better never to use it, father. Poison is not the honourable way."

"Would you rather be a success or an honourable failure?" Nubsekhem asked.

"A success, but I would hope to retain my honour."

"Then let us find a way."

Chapter 16

Overseer Den was pleased with the building progress at Sekera. The basic blocks that made up the core of the *mer* came from local quarries that yielded low or medium quality limestone. Structurally, it was strong enough to bear the downward forces of the weight of the upper layers, even though it was discoloured and not aesthetically pleasing. The whole edifice would eventually be covered with polished white limestone from Troyu, so the underlying blocks could be composed of imperfect stone.

Blocks of white limestone arrived from the eastern quarries, but Den had these stored well away from the main building site so as not to interfere with the main construction. The vertical shaft lay on the north side of the proposed *mer* and would open on the second layer, remaining open and accessible during the whole of construction, before being finally sealed when the casing stones were fitted. Now, Den had masons constructing a sturdy surround for the shaft so that the internal stones could continue to be leant against each other from the centre outward, without collapsing into the open shaft.

Below ground, masons continued burrowing through the limestone bedrock, carving out the burial chamber itself, driving north to connect with the long passage that led down from where the mortuary chapel would be built, and starting on a myriad of underground galleries that would store the king's wealth. Some would be developed into spacious apartments that mirrored the king's suites in the Inebu-hedj palace. They would be decorated and furnished to provide salubrious surroundings in which the king's spirit could relax.

On this topic, the king had much to say. He insisted on meeting with Imhotep and Den on a regular basis, poring over sketches of the proposed galleries, peering closely at delicate and intricate models created out of clay, wood and paper by Khawy and Khepankh. Den always made sure the king realised that his young sons had made the models and were as dedicated to the king's eternal welfare as was he.

"I want blue faience wall tiles like those of my father," Sekhemkhet declared. "They are cool and remind me of the waters of the Great River. Also, the stone should be carved to look like bundles of reeds and wall panels to look like reed mats, painted in bright colours."

"All this can be done, my lord king," Den said, scribbling notes on his tablet.

"What will my sarcophagus be made of?"

Den looked at Imhotep questioningly, and the Tjaty shrugged.

"I don't think any decision has been made of that," Imhotep said.

"It is early," Den added.

"How long does it take to make one?" Sekhemkhet asked.

"I believe that will depend on what material is used," Imhotep said cautiously. "If we use limestone, then perhaps a year; if granite, then five years or more."

"Why so much longer?"

"Granite is a very hard stone, my lord king. Copper tools have very little effect on it."

"That cannot be right. You used granite blocks in my father's burial chamber. How were they cut?"

Imhotep looked at Den. "Perhaps you could answer that. You were present during at least part of the process."

Den nodded, marshalling his thoughts. "I am not a mason, lord king, but although granite is too hard to be worked by copper tools, the stone can be worn away by pounding it with a harder rock like diorite. For the finer work, copper saws are used, but sand is the actual cutting material that eats through the granite. It is very labour intensive, requiring many men and long hours."

"We have men, and we have the time if we start immediately," Sekhemkhet said. "I have no intention of dying before my tomb is finished."

"Rose granite would make a kingly sarcophagus," Imhotep said. "Is that what you desire, my lord?"

Sekhemkhet nodded his assent, and Den made the necessary notation. The cutting of the block for the sarcophagus would need his personal attention, so after securing permission from Imhotep, Den made the arrangements for a swift visit to the granite quarries at Abu. He had been there before to oversee the cutting of slabs for Netjerikhet's burial chamber, and had selected and started the cutting after consultation with Nebra the mason and Aha, a local stoneworker.

Nebra accompanied Den south once more, and though Aha had retired, he said he was honoured to work on the king's sarcophagus. Once more, the three men toured the granite quarries, looking for a flawless piece of rock.

"It must not only be without even the finest of cracks that might compromise the strength of the sarcophagus, but also be pleasing to look at," Nebra said. "It would be better to spend a year looking for the best piece than to rush to cut the first block we see. Haste makes men careless, and if a mistake is made, we must start again."

It did not take a year, as there were quarries that yielded fine, blemish-free rose granite. Nebra identified two pieces of rock, and could not choose between them, so Den ordered both pieces cut from the bedrock.

"We can decide later which one we select, and I am sure the other one will not go to waste."

Work started, and although Den had been absent for nearly two months, he stayed longer to see the cutting commence. Holes were laboriously drilled, the central cores snapped off and the holes drilled deeper. Then dry wooden wedges were rammed home and water poured over to expand them, the resulting pressure fracturing the stone in a more or less straight line.

"How will you hollow out the sarcophagus?" Den asked.

"Carefully," Aha said. "Pounding with diorite stones will wear away some, drilling will define the edges, and polishing with sand will smooth down the sides. It is a similar procedure to the way we make bowls, but so much larger. I do not anticipate any problems."

Den came away from the workshops at Abu, content that the king's sarcophagus was in good hands. He looked forward to being able to report on it to the king, but was content to relax aboard the ship carrying him north with the current. It was almost like celebrating the holy day of one of the gods, when work ceased and one had the luxury of spending the days in blissful lassitude. In a way, it was a holy day, for the Great River was a god, Hapi, who brought life to the fertile lands on the borders of its waters. Den lay on the deck of the small ship, watching the land of the southern kingdom slide past, its farms and orchards, pastures and forests. The barren desert pressed close to the life-giving waters in places, receding far from them in others, while above the burgeoning life and rocky desert, the great faded blue dome of the sky with its fiercely glowing sun, enclosed the world. He arrived back at Inebu-hedj, rested and ready to start work again, to find a city in mourning. While he had been away, Prince Nub-Re had died.

The fever that assailed the small boy ever since the king's hunting trip returned at regular intervals. A month had passed from the ill-fated trip until Nub-Re broke out in a fever, sweating and crying, followed by complaints of cold, and then sweating again. The court physician prescribed cooling when the fever gripped him and bundling him up in wool when he started shivering. Hesy-Ra was at a loss what to do; and nothing he prescribed reduced the symptoms or offered relief. Headaches followed, but the painkillers he coaxed the prince to drink induced vomiting.

Every few days, the cycle repeated itself, with the prince becoming weaker, his cries breaking the hearts of all who heard them. One of the servants on the hunting trip also sickened, displaying similar symptoms, but she seemed to shake the disease off and never really became ill, though the fever and chills returned at intervals. The servant's recovery gave hope to the king and queen that their son would also prevail, but it was not to be. Two months after the trip, the child fell into a deep sleep and never regained consciousness.

Grief racked the royal family, and the palace took it up, then the city and surrounding countryside, until it seemed that all of Kemet mourned the prince's death. Inetkawes was inconsolable, and Djeser-Ti was reminded of the loss of her own son. Despite her sympathy for the queen, she felt a guilty satisfaction that the gods were not angry with just her. Their anger seemed directed at the king, denying him a male heir from any of his wives.

Sekhemkhet ordered a sumptuous funeral for his young son and until his tomb was sufficiently complete, had the ornate coffin stored within the House of Embalming. He called Imhotep and Den into his presence and ordered that his tomb be completed immediately.

"It is not fitting that the bodies of my children remain unburied in the Place of Embalming. Prepare my tomb at once so they may be buried and enjoy the afterlife."

"My lord king," Imhotep said, "that is impossible."

"Did you not hear me? Get it done now. I do not care how much gold you spend or how many men you employ, but I want my tomb finished this year. I will not make my dead children wait."

Imhotep tried again, but the king grew angry, seeing his inability to agree as wilful refusal. The king was on the point of dismissing Imhotep as Tjaty and appointing someone who would obey him, when Den made a suggestion.

"Forgive my presumption, my lord king, but there is a solution. There are rooms within the tomb, galleries that are being prepared as we speak, that we could use. If I put our masons and artists to work on that alone, we could prepare a small room that the children could occupy in comfort until such time as the whole City of the Dead is finished."

"How long?"

"A few days, my lord king."

Sekhemkhet pondered for a few minutes. "Let it be so," he said at last. "I want my children to be with me in the afterlife, but I do not want them to have to wait years before I join them. It is only right that they enjoy a proper burial now."

Den rushed back to Sekera and had the masons, sculptors and artists turn their attentions to a small suite of rooms carved from the bedrock beneath the *mer*, close to where the king would one day lie. Despite giving the skilled artisans their detailed instructions and impressed on them the need for haste, Den could not relax. He stayed close by from dawn to dusk, neglecting his other duties, and making a nuisance of himself with his continual demands. Masons and artists alike complained to one of their overseers.

"Prevail upon Overseer Den to stay away from where we are working. He demands that we work faster, but it is his repeated interruptions that slow us down."

The overseers found excuses to draw Den away from the underground rooms, inventing problems and even, once, setting fire to a storeroom. Den cursed, but remembered his duty long enough to find solutions for the problems and arrange for the repair of damaged goods. They distracted him long enough for the rooms to be finished, complete with carvings and wall paintings. The king came to inspect the tomb of his children and expressed himself satisfied, though he did not think to thank Den or any of the men who had worked so hard to prepare it.

The bodies of the embalmed children of Sekhemkhet were laid to rest within the special rooms of the tomb, with all due ceremony by the priests. Wives Inetkawes and Djeser-Ti, together with Hetephernebti and Khemtet, laid toys beside the carved and painted coffins, so that the spirits of the children would have something to play with in the afterlife. Then masons sealed the chambers, plastering over the walls so it was impossible to see that the brickwork concealed hidden rooms. Work in the rest of the tomb complex would continue around the resting place of the children of the king.

Hardly had the children been interred than the king changed his mind, and gave Den other orders.

"My father had a South Tomb built within his enclosure. I want the same, and in it you will place my children."

"It will take time to construct, my lord king," Den said.

"As long as it takes. My children are safe where they are, and when the South Tomb is ready I will order the priests to bury them there."

A month later, the king ordered Imhotep and Den back into his presence, and they found a master stoneworker, an artisan of some note there. Sekhemkhet revealed the man was a worker of vessels of the goddess Bast, and demanded to know why Imhotep had not recommended the use of this stone for the royal sarcophagus.

"It is akin to limestone, but is sacred to Bast."

"My lord king," Imhotep replied, "I am unfamiliar with the stone you refer to."

"This man, Bastmose, has dedicated his life to working it. Tell the Tjaty, Bastmose. Speak of the qualities of this stone."

Bastmose bowed deeply. "My lord king, noble Tjaty, Overseer Den...this is a sample of the stone with which I work." He held out a small statuette of Bast, a translucent white carving of the cat goddess, every line beautifully delineated and the whole thing polished so it appeared to glow as if there was a light inside it.

"Beautiful," Den breathed. "What is it called...this rock?"

"It is sometimes called ala-Bast, Overseer Den."

"Tell us about it," Imhotep said.

"It is a soft rock, easily carved, and as you can see it can be polished so that light makes it glow. I know of no other rock that does this."

"You are to be commended for your artistry, Bastmose," Imhotep said. "I have never seen its like." He took the statue and rubbed his fingers over its smooth surface wonderingly. "Could it be made into a sarcophagus?"

"I have never worked with such a large block, noble Tjaty," Bastmose admitted, "but in principle I do not see why not."

"Can you imagine a sarcophagus made of this Bast stone?" Sekhemkhet asked. "Truly it would be a sarcophagus made for a king. You will take charge of this, Imhotep, and order it made for me."

"Yes, my lord king." Imhotep left the presence of the king with Bastmose and Den, and made arrangements for the stoneworker to have a suitably sized block carved from the ala-Bast quarry many *iteru* south of the capital.

"I will journey down there with you in a day or two," Den said. "Together we will find a suitable piece of stone."

One other thing concerned Den, and he spoke of it with Imhotep. "The granite sarcophagus that Nebra and Aha are creating in Abu...what shall I do about that, now that the king has changed his mind?"

"Continue its production," Imhotep advised. "This ala-Bast sarcophagus may come to nothing, and we must use the granite one after all. On the other hand, it may be that we shall find some other use for it later. Kings will always need sarcophagi."

Den made the arrangements, sending for one of the ships that had transported the granite slabs for Netjerikhet's burial chamber. They were to meet them near the quarry at Hatnub. Then he asked Overseer Sekhemre, Imhotep's son, to accompany Bastmose and him down to the ala-Bast quarry, as he had experience in extracting rock. Imhotep gave his permission and the three of them sailed south for six days before landing on the eastern shore and journeying inland to find the quarry. It was a small excavation, and only a score of men working the stone, supplying a scattering of stoneworkers that carved the special stone.

"Who are you?" a man said truculently as they approached the mine workings.

Den produced a scroll displaying the seal of Hor-Sekhemkhet and Imhotep. He held it up in front of the man.

"I cannot read that," the man said. "It could be anything. Who are you and what do you want?"

"I am Overseer of the King's Works, Den." He introduced the men with him. "Who are you?"

The man picked at one nostril while he looked at his visitors. "My name is Sed. I am the supervisor here."

"Well, Sed, the king has ordered us to excavate a suitable block of ala-Bast rock. Direct us to the best quality stone you have."

"What does he want it for?"

"That is none of your business."

Sed shrugged. "You are right. I don't pry into the king's business and he don't pry into mine." He turned and walked over to the rock face, where some of his workers were chipping away with copper chisels and wooden mallets. "This is the best rock. How much do you need?"

"Ten *mehi* in length, by five by five."

Sed whistled. "How big a statue are you making? Never mind; I don't want to know." He cleared his men away from the rock face and with Sekhemre, examined the rock for flaws, meticulously scrutinising the stones and chalking out rough measurements in red ochre. They allowed extra on every dimension, even though Bastmose had already been generous in his allowance. Then the quarry workers started chipping away at the soft rock with their copper chisels, digging a deep trench. After a while, the trench became too deep to work with ease, so they had to widen it considerably at the expense of the surrounding rock. A day later, the team of quarrymen had separated the required block on all sides and started chipping away underneath. They had to work more carefully here, propping up the weight of the slab as they excavated more deeply.

They heard a sharp crack and the workers leapt back. Sed and Sekhemre examined the block closely, noting how a hairline fissure had opened up through the last section holding the mass to the rock face.

"Time to knock the props out," the quarry overseer said.

Positioning Sekhemre with a mallet at the far end, Sed readied himself, and at a signal, both men swung their mallets, knocking out the props. The massive block groaned and, with another sharp cracking sound, slumped down.

"Perfect," Sed crowed.

He ordered his men to prise the block free with long poles and after much effort the massive piece of ala-Bast tumbled to the ground, sending up a cloud of dust as several chunks broke off it.

Den worried that the broken pieces had marred the overall dimensions, but a quick check with a measuring string revealed the damage would not affect the integrity of the whole.

"How are you going to transport the block, sirs?" Sed asked.

"We build a sled and your men will pull it to the river's edge where a ship will be waiting."

"That is all the same to me, sir. My men get paid no matter what work they do."

Timber for the sled was readily to hand, and several of the quarry workers had experience in shaping wood. A sturdy sled was constructed and the block of ala-Bast rolled onto it. Then, with the aid of ropes attached to the sled and the block, the men set about hauling it across sand and soil to the distant river. It took them three days, and Den was happy to see a ship waiting for them at the designated place, and even happier when he saw that the captain of the ship was Bennu. He greeted him warmly, introducing him to Sekhemre and Bastmose.

"I hoped it would be you," Den said. "You managed the blocks of granite so well, I knew this ala-Bast would be no problem for you."

Bennu walked around the block, examining it and, with an effort, rocked it on its cradle of wood. "Larger than the granite slabs, but not as heavy," he said. "How strong is it?"

"About as strong as limestone," Sekhemre said.

"Then we do not want to deal it any heavy blows, do we?"

Bennu gave it some thought, walked down to his ship and stared at it for a few minutes, before walking along the river's edge, testing the solidity of the ground. He found, and inspected, a shelf of sandstone a few paces from the water, then straightening, he came across to Den.

"How many of these blocks are you transporting?"

"This is the only one for now," Den replied. "It has a special purpose."

"Then it is not worth digging out a special harbour like we did for the granite slabs," Bennu said. "Even so, I think we are going to need something like that." He quickly outlined his thoughts with regard to the sandstone shelf and the river.

"It seems like a lot of work," Sekhemre said, "but it is up to you, Den."

"And I will be guided by your expertise, Bennu," Den said.

"Then let us get to work."

The plan involved digging out a small inlet to the shelf of sandstone, and backing the ship into it. Bennu organised the removal of the ship's stern post, and the sinking of two strong wooden posts into the ground near the river, one on either side of the ship. While this was going on, Den had his team drag the block on its sled to the edge of the shelf. Then, when all was ready, ropes from the sled were passed around the upright posts and teams of men, by hauling back on the ropes, pulled the sled in the opposite direction.

Slowly, carefully, the sled moved over the edge of the shelf, tilted, dipped, and with a groan of timbers, eased onto the ship. The vessel responded by settling in place, tilting slightly to the left, and Bennu yelled at his men to pull more on one side than the other, easing the heavy block into the middle of the boat.

Bennu had wedges knocked into place beneath the runners of the sled to prevent it moving when they got underway, but then they found the inlet had not been dug deep enough and the weight of the block pressed the flat bottom of the boat into the mud. Cursing, Bennu rigged the ropes and posts so the teams of men could now haul the ship forward, while his own men tried to pole it out of the inlet. For several minutes it looked as if nothing was happening, and then with a great sucking noise, the ship slid forward and floated.

Den thanked Sed and his team of quarry workers, before joining Bennu aboard the vessel. They poled it out into the current and managed its course with broad-bladed oars as the river carried them north.

"Where to, sir?" Bennu asked. "Sekera, like the others?"

Bastmose indicated he was happy to work anywhere providing facilities were made available, so Den promised him all he would need.

"Sekera it is, Bennu," Den said.

Chapter 17

Court physician Hesy-Ra was getting old and looking forward to retirement. Long years of service had earned him gold and land, and he had long since had a small mud brick *per-djet* constructed for himself and his wife. Now he was training up his assistant Khentu to take over from him, and introduced him to Imhotep.

"Pay attention to whatever this man says," Hesy-Ra advised his assistant. "Not just because he is Tjaty, and second only to the king, but because he is a physician of superlative skill. In fact, there is little he cannot do."

"Your master exaggerates," Imhotep said mildly. "However, I look forward to working with you." He turned to Hesy-Ra. "Do you have a few minutes to spare? There is something I must discuss."

Hesy-Ra gave instructions to Khenti to attend to the stocks of herbs and other materials necessary for their art. "In particular, we need more bat dung. You will find a small colony of bats in the temple of Ptah. If you ask the priests they will let you clean out a sackful." He winked at Imhotep as Khenti bowed and went off to do his master's bidding. "A beastly job, and one I am glad to hand over to someone else. Now, what did you want to talk to me about?"

"You remember the sicknesses of Netjerikhet?"

"I do, but I thought we had decided those were natural occurrences, sickness sent by the gods."

"Yes, we did," Imhotep agreed, "but I have been thinking about them again."

Hesy-Ra settled himself comfortably on a chair and leaned back against the wall. "Speak to me of your thoughts then, my friend."

"Do you remember the symptoms?"

Hesy-Ra nodded. "Headaches, sweating, cramps, vomiting, diarrhoea, blood in the urine. Only the first illness was serious, though. The second involved vomiting and pain, but he recovered swiftly."

"I said at the time that I considered poison a possibility," Imhotep said.

"And I seem to remember that you could find no real evidence."

"That is true, but considering who would benefit from the untimely death of the king, there was only one main suspect. Do you remember who he was?"

"Refresh my memory," Hesy-Ra said.

"General Khaba."

"Ah, yes. But there must have been many people in Inebu-hedj at the time, and just being in the city at the time is not enough to accuse someone."

"Khaba was not in the city at the time," Imhotep said.

"Then how was he a suspect?"

"His son Nubsekhem was here."

"So he is the real suspect?"

"Khaba is the head of the household. Nubsekhem would not take such an important step without his father's consent." Imhotep shook his head. "I would have staked my life on Khaba's loyalty."

"You are raking over the same sand, my friend," Hesy-Ra said. "If it was not enough to accuse Khaba then, it will not be enough now. Or do you have some new evidence?"

"Not evidence exactly. If I had, I would have gone straight to the king and had Khaba and his family arrested."

"But you have something?" Hesy-Ra queried.

"I found the wine jar that the poisoned wine came in, and it bore the mark of Khaba's vineyards in the north."

"What? All this time later? How can you be sure?"

"Well, I can't. Not really." Imhotep frowned, collecting his thoughts. "The possibility of poisoning always worried me, because if there was an enemy trying to kill the king, he would likely try again. I have agents who work for me throughout Kemet, including a few in the palace. At the time of the king's sickness, I considered wine as a suitable means of delivering a poison, particularly as the king favoured wine from Khaba's vineyards, and he usually tried to keep it all for himself."

"I remember you advanced that argument at the time," Hesy-Ra said.

"I am sorry if I am repeating myself," Imhotep said, "but I need to get this straight in my own mind. The wine jar went missing at the time, and I assumed it had just been thrown out, but it turned up a few days ago."

"Intriguing. How do you know it is the same one?"

"Ansekh, the overseer of the kitchens, took it. It was empty, but he wanted it for his own tomb. He thought he would put cheap wine in it and the mark of Khaba's vineyard on the jar would transform it into fine wine. Well, he died a month ago, but before it was put into Ansekh's tomb, his son decided to sample the wine, thinking it was good wine. He broke the seal and poured himself a cup." Imhotep's lips quirked in a wry smile. "Not only was he disappointed with the vintage, but he came down with a sickness that stomach-ache, vomiting and diarrhoea. Similar to Netjerikhet's sickness. I treated him myself...you were away at the time, Hesy-Ra...and learned the story. I secured the jar, saw that it had Khaba's mark, poured out the wine and found a sludge at the bottom of the jar."

"Most wines have sludge," Hesy-Ra said, "but I am guessing that is not the end of the story."

"I took some of the sludge, mixed it meat, and fed it to a dog. The dog died in agony a few hours later. The poison was in the sludge found at the bottom of a jar of wine that came from Khaba's vineyard."

"Then you have the proof you need," Hesy-Ra exclaimed.

"No, because years elapsed between the king drinking the original wine and Ansekh's son stealing a little from the refilled jar. Who knows what happened in the meantime? Perhaps the sludge was always there, perhaps it was added later. All I can really say is that Netjerikhet really was poisoned at the time of his first sickness."

"Then you are no closer to finding the poisoner."

"At least I now know, to my own satisfaction, that it was a deliberate attempt to kill the king. If I could now tie in evidence from the second and third attempts, I might have absolute proof I could take to the king."

"I know about the second attempt," Hesy-Ra said frowning, "but what was the third attempt? It cannot have been the death of the king, because that resulted from a fall."

"The third attempt was on Nub-Re, heir to Sekhemkhet."

"But that was from the shivering fever," Hesy-Ra said. "I know, because I treated him."

"I am not talking about the sickness that killed him, but about the thing that afflicted him a month or so before. Stomachache, a desire to vomit, sweating. Does that sound familiar?"

Hesy-Ra grimaced. "Yes, but a score of sicknesses have those symptoms. If it was the poison, how was it administered?"

"In his food somehow. When his diet changed, he got better."

"Then it could just be bad food," Hesy-Ra said.

"Perhaps," Imhotep agreed, "but I feel it in my liver. Someone seeks to harm the king's family."

"Then you must take your suspicions to the king. It is better that an innocent man suffers than a killer escapes punishment."

"If Khaba falls, then so does his whole family...and one of his grandsons is Khakhet, the son of my daughter." Imhotep groaned. "I cannot condemn him without more proof."

"Then what will you do, my friend?" Hesy-Ra asked sympathetically.

"Continue my investigations," Imhotep replied. "What else can I do?"

Despite his reluctance to implicate his own grandson, Imhotep still considered taking his suspicions to the king. The only thing that stopped his was his realisation that the king was still a young man and one likely to act before giving the matter proper consideration. A few days later, Sekhemkhet called for him, and it was still on his mind when he bowed to the king. After a few moments, he realised the king had spoken to him, but he could not recollect what he had just said.

"Your pardon, my lord king, my mind was still on my last problem."

"Oh? What was it?"

"Nothing of any importance, my lord king." Imhotep hesitated a moment, not wanting to ask the king to repeat himself. "May I ask what concerns you?"

"I am going to war again."

"What unlucky people will face your might, my lord king?"

"One of the Wawat tribes; I cannot remember their name, but they have raided our southern lands and must be taught a lesson."

"I have no doubt you will give them salutary instruction, my lord king. When do you leave?"

"In five days. I will sail south, visiting cities and temples on the way, so all my people may see me. Governor Seth-Aha of Abu will have five hundred soldiers waiting for me."

"You will command the soldiers yourself?"

"Who better?"

The king took an honour guard with him made up of palace guards, and priests of every temple he would be dedicating in the south. Imhotep stayed behind to govern the kingdoms in the king's absence, which was likely to be lengthy. It would take time to visit the cities of the south and officiate at the half score of new temples dedicated there. Then the punitive expedition into Wawat would occupy at least another two months, so Imhotep reckoned that at least six months would pass before the king returned to Inebu-hedj. At least he had left his wives and most favoured concubines something by which to remember him--all had been vigorously ploughed and half of them believed they were pregnant.

Sekhemkhet took his time on his journey south, letting the gentle northerly winds push them upriver against the current, and he stopped often to hunt. Wildfowl died by the hundreds, *pehe-mau* and crocodiles too, and if the landscape looked promising, he took the time to hunt lion and wild dog, antelope and ostrich. As a result, his men ate well, and the king remained in a good mood.

When they reached a city or town with a temple to be dedicated, the king spent time there, enjoying the adulation of the crowds for their youthful king. Governors, mayors and Hem-netjers vied for the opportunity of entertaining the king and he enjoyed the attentions of many young women. The ones he favoured most were sent to Inebu-hedj to join the wives and concubines in the Women's Quarters. At Tjenu, he went inland to see the royal cities of the dead at Abdju, noting how unimpressive the *per-djet* tombs were when compared to his father's massive *mer* and enclosure.

"My own City of the Dead will be far more impressive even than that of my father," he told the Governor of Abdju.

Sekhemkhet made brief stops at Waset, Ta-senet, and Behdet, but now seemed eager to press on to Abu and the start of his expedition into Wawat. The river narrowed and split up into separate channels, and the rounded grey boulders that gave Abu its name appeared. Governor Seth-Aha turned out an honour guard to greet his king, and hundreds of inhabitants of the southern city cheered them as they walked through the streets to the governor's palace.

"You have my men for me?" Sekhemkhet asked.

"Five hundred trained and equipped soldiers drawn from the garrison here and the surrounding countryside," Seth-Aha replied.

"Excellent. I will inspect them tomorrow and leave the following day."

"As my lord king wishes," the Governor said, "but I had hoped you would enjoy my hospitality for a few days."

"Perhaps on the way back. I am eager to get to grips with the enemy. Who is the enemy, by the way? The information I had just said it was a Wawat tribe."

"The tribe is called Merana, my lord king, after its chief. Merana the man led his tribe in rebellion, killing some Kemetu traders. He raids up and down a section of the river."

"There is a man who can guide me? A man familiar with the territory?"

"Yes, my lord king. His name is Pantusa, a member of the Merana tribe fled for his life from the present chief. I have attached him to your army."

Sekhemkhet enjoyed an evening's entertainment with Seth-Aha, and was up early the next morning to inspect his troops and meet the senior officers. He was struck by the number of Kushites among the soldiers, and he asked the senior officer, Ankhre, a Kemetu, about this.

"They are loyal to Kemet, my lord king, if that is what you are asking," Ankhre said.

"Can you be sure of that? It seems to me they are just as likely to join forces with their Wawat brethren."

"Every Kushite man here has sworn their oaths of fealty, and are drawn from the more southern tribes or ones that have an enmity with the Merana. They will remain loyal, my lord king."

Ankhre introduced him to Pantusa, and Sekhemkhet asked the guide many questions concerning Merana the man and tribe. He learned that they numbered close to two hundred fighting men and came from three villages on the western shore of the river. Chief Merana had only recently taken over the tribe, killing the previous chief who had been at peace with Kemet.

"How is it that Chief Merana holds the same name as his tribe if he has just seized power?" Sekhemkhet asked.

"The name 'Merana' is as much a title as a name," Pantusa said. "My uncle was the previous 'Merana', but any man can challenge for leadership."

"How much loyalty will the men of Merana show him, if the chief took control by force?"

"They will follow him loyally, as he took control by legitimate means." Pantusa grinned. "Given the opportunity, I will challenge him and become 'Merana' in his place."

In consultation with Ankhre and Pantusa, the king worked out a plan of attack for the expedition. Pantusa pointed out that previous forays into Wawat territory had taken place along the course of the river, pushing through the first cataract on the eastern shore before fording the river.

"They will be expecting this, Great King," the tribesman said. "There are only a few good places to ford the river and it will be easy for them to contest our crossing."

"We outnumber them two to one," Sekhemkhet said.

"They fight on ground familiar to them. Your numbers mean you will likely prevail, but at what cost? Do you want to lose a hundred men, two hundred?"

"How then?" Ankhre asked. "You must have a way of countering their defences."

"I have," Pantusa said, "but it means splitting your forces."

"Divide, so the Merana can defeat us one at a time?" Ankhre said. "Find another way."

"Wait," Sekhemkhet said. "Explain your plan, Pantusa."

"We send a hundred men up the eastern bank of the river to the first ford, and there they set up camp, preparing defences as if for hundreds more to join them. This will draw the enemy's attention. In the meantime, the other four hundred men strike west through the desert, swing round and descend upon the Merana villages from the west while they are unprepared."

Ankhre did not like the plan, but could not offer a better one, so the king ordered detailed plans be drawn up along those lines.

"You will take the hundred men, Ankhre," Sekhemkhet said. "I will take the desert route with Pantusa."

"My lord, no," Ankhre remonstrated. "It is too dangerous. You should..."

"Do not lecture me on what I must or must not do," Sekhemkhet said coldly. "I am the king and I will decide."

Ankhre could only submit, but took Pantusa aside later and explained forcefully to him that he had a responsibility toward the king.

"He is a young man and young men are often hot-headed. Furthermore, he is the king and will believe he knows best. Do not expose him to more danger than is necessary, and make sure he returns safely. You will have me to answer to if any harm befalls him."

"I hear you, Ankhre," Pantusa said mildly. "No harm will come to him while I live."

Ankhre set off with his hundred men and a train of donkeys carrying everything that was needed to set up a fortified camp with a hundred five-man tents. They passed through the gorge of the cataract, emerging onto the Wawat plain. Shadowing them on the western shore were patrols of the rebel tribe, and as Ankhre brought his men to the first ford and started constructing an apparently permanent camp, the enemy swelled his numbers until over a hundred armed men faced them across the shallow water.

"Of course, we did not discuss what I would do if they attack my position," Ankhre muttered to himself.

He need not have worried; the Merana tribesmen seemed content to watch him with the river between them.

Meanwhile, Sekhemkhet let his men westward into the desert, travelling light and fast. Pantusa led them well away from the river, bringing them round in a broad circle before striking eastward on the third day. They saw no sign of human life and little enough in the way of animals, which perhaps had something to do with the lack of water. Their guide had brought them to a small soak in the lee of a rocky hill on the first day, but there was barely enough to quench thirsts and refill water skins. The second night was dry, and now water supplies were low as they caught sight of thin spirals of smoke to the east.

"The Merana villages," Pantusa explained.

Kushite scouts pressed close to the three villages and reported back to Pantusa and the king that very few men had been left behind, and these were mostly older ones. The warriors had moved toward the river and there was talk of crossing the water before the men in the Kemetu camp were reinforced.

Sekhemkhet wanted to attack the villages immediately, but Pantusa counselled against it, saying that victory over women and children was no victory.

"The villages contain some wealth, lord king, but it would be difficult to capture all three villages without giving warning. Then we lay ourselves open to attack by the men of Merana. I recommend we bypass the villages and fall upon the rear of the men at the river. Once we have won that battle, we can return and enjoy the fruits of the villages."

Sekhemkhet, though he thirsted to fight the enemy, saw the sense of Pantusa's plan. There was little glory in seizing undefended villages, particularly when to do so would allow the real enemy, the men of the tribe, to attack or escape. He agreed, turning the words of Pantusa so that it looked as if it had been his decision to do so all along.

The men turned aside from the villages, moving first north and then east, moving slowly while the Kushite scouts made sure they would be unobserved. As they neared the river, they were nearly taken by surprise as three warriors trotted out of the scrub, heading back toward the Merana villages. They saw the Kemetu army at the same time they were spotted, and with cries of alarm, sped off, two toward the river, the third toward the villages. An arrow took the third man, but the others ducked and dodged, and would have escaped to give warning, had not a Kushite, fleet of foot, given chase and killed them both with his stone axe.

"Take that man's name," Sekhemkhet said. "He has earned gold for his feat."

"Gold is meaningless to a Kushite," Pantusa said. "Cattle on the other hand..."

"Then he shall have fifty cattle from the Merana herds."

Pantusa did not look too happy at that as he was hoping to take over the tribe and its cattle once the king's army was victorious, but he realised fifty head of cattle was a small price to pay for gaining the chieftain's position.

Another few minutes brought the army to the river, where they saw the Merana tribesmen milling on the water's edge, shouting insults at Ankhre and his men on the other side. Some were knee-deep or more in the river, trying to goad Ankhre's men into crossing. Sekhemkhet grinned and swiftly deployed his men, making sure that the wings of his little army overlapped the main mass of the enemy.

"That is Chief Merana," Pantusa said, pointing to a tall man with ostrich feather plumes rising from a cowhide helmet. "He is mine."

Sekhemkhet frowned. "It is customary for the enemy commander to fall beneath the king's blade," he said. "I should be the one to kill him."

Pantusa shrugged. "You want to become chief of a small tribe instead of king of Kemet? The chieftainship passes by right of combat. Let me avenge my uncle and when I am chief, you will have no more trouble from the Merana."

"Take him then," Sekhemkhet said.

The Kemetu swept down upon the unsuspecting Merana tribesmen, pinning them between the river and copper weapons. They turned to fight and did so bravely, but they could not hope to stand against a foe superior in numbers and weaponry. A score or so braved the river crossing, but Ankhre's men waited for them and slew them mercilessly, their blood discolouring the river's edge for several minutes.

Sekhemkhet and a few men close to him saw a small group break away from the fighting and flee to the south, seeking refuge in a swampy area. The Kemetu pursued and killed them, the king striking down the last of them as he waded waist deep in the murky water.

Pantusa called out Merana as the tribesmen died around him, and the two men withdrew a few paces to decide the leadership of a very much depleted tribe. Merana was a seasoned warrior, but defeat weakened him, whereas his opponent was young, vengeful, and his spirit was lifted by the victory of the king's men. Merana died, struck down by Pantusa's stone axe, and Pantusa lifted his weapon and cried out in a loud voice that he had avenged his uncle.

"I claim leadership of the Merana tribe by right of combat. Men of Merana, surrender now and your lives will be spared."

The tribesmen, demoralised by the swift and successful attack, and the death of their chief, threw down their weapons and fell to their knees. For a few moments, the Kemetu continued their attack and several more men fell before first Sekhemkhet, and then his officers, ordered the killing to stop.

Seventy tribesmen survived, though some of those would undoubtedly die of wounds sustained in the battle. Each man knelt in submission to Sekhemkhet, and then to Pantusa, who ordered them to return to their villages and announce that a new chief ruled over them.

"I suppose I will have to call you Merana now," Sekhemkhet said to Pantusa as his tribesmen walked and limped home.

"It is the custom, Great King, but I think I shall change it. I desire all men to know that I, Pantusa, am their rightful chief. I shall be known by that name."

Sekhemkhet and his men crossed the river to Ankhre's camp to rest the men and provide medical attention for the wounded, burial for the dead. Pantusa said he would go back to the villages.

"Alone? Are you mad? They will kill you. Stay with me for a day or so and we will march on the villages together. That way we can enforce your authority."

215

"No, my lord king," Pantusa replied. "How can I command the tribe if they see me depend on a foreign army. If they kill me, so be it, but I do not believe they will. They accepted me as chief by right of combat, and they will keep their word."

"Very well, but if they turn on you I will kill them all."

"Follow me in three days, Great King, and I will feast you and your men."

Sekhemkhet did just that, against the advice of Commander Ankhre, advancing in battle order toward the Merana villages. A thousand paces or so before, as they emerged from the scrub into an open space, the women of the tribe, waving leafy branches and singing, met them. Staring nonplussed at the spectacle, Sekhemkhet called a halt, and Pantusa came out to meet them, grinning broadly with his arms held wide.

"Welcome, King Hor-Sekhemkhet of Kemet, to the lands of the Merana. All here are your friends, and in their name I offer my fealty and swear an oath never to invade Kemet or engage in hostile actions against you or your descendants."

The remaining men of the tribe came out, all unarmed, and bowed to Sekhemkhet, ushering him inside the largest village, together with his guards. Pantusa had organised a feast in honour of the king, slaughtering cattle, baking bread, and brewing up great stone vessels of foaming millet beer, together with a wide range of vegetables, fruits, and spicy dessert dishes.

Entertainment was also laid on, with musicians and dancers raising cheers from the Kemetu. One young girl, a dancer of extraordinary beauty, caught the eye of Sekhemkhet, and his gaze followed her everywhere. Pantusa noticed, and beckoned her over to the royal dais.

"King Hor-Sekhemkhet, may I present my uncle's daughter, Tetimene? She was the daughter of my uncle who was Merana before the last one. In keeping with our custom, she is untouched by any man, and I offer her to you as a wife, so that your kingdoms and my tribe may be joined in bonds of peace."

"Marriage, you say? Remember I am king of a powerful nation. I could take her as a concubine."

"My lord king, you would take a concubine from a conquered enemy, but this tribe is a friendly people. Tetimene is as close to a royal princess as we have, and deserves marriage to a man of high status." Pantusa saw Sekhemkhet hesitate and quickly went on. "She is the only woman in her line as her family produces sons."

"Sons..." Sekhemkhet murmured.

Tetimene bent her head submissively, but looked up at Sekhemkhet from long-lashed eyes, a bold smile on her lips. "My lord king," she whispered.

Sekhemkhet felt his heart surge in his chest, and other parts of his anatomy followed suit. "This meets with your approval?" he asked.

"Yes, my lord."

Sekhemkhet looked at Tetimene with evident lust. He turned to Pantusa. "Very well, arrange for the marriage."

"It shall take place this very day," Pantusa exclaimed.

The women of the tribe whisked Tetimene off to prepare her for the nuptials, while the rest of the tribe shouted out with joy and threw themselves into the other arrangements. The feast of welcome became a feast of celebration. Drums were brought out and a pulsing rhythm soon put everyone in mind of the occasion, and as night fell and huge bonfires were lit, Sekhemkhet took Tetimene as his latest wife.

He stayed in Wawat for half a month, before starting for home, and made his way slowly through the southern kingdom, showing off his wealth and power to Tetimene, and enjoying her company every night. By the time they arrived in Inebu-hedj, she was with child.

Sekhemkhet returned from Wawat with something else, though he was not aware of it for some time. It would prove to have an even greater effect on the future of Kemet than the child that grew in Tetimene's fecund belly.

Chapter 18

Nubsekhem usually sent in his reports on the Northern Army and its interactions with the tribes of Kanaan and the Land of Sin every three months, but this time he chose to deliver it himself. He knew that the king had made a successful foray into the land of Wawat to punish a rebellious tribe, and he wanted to gauge the mood of the city toward its king. Huni came down with him and they were on hand when Sekhemkhet's ship docked at the wharves of Inebu-hedj.

Small boats had brought the news of the approach of the king's ship, so a great crowd turned out to cheer their king. The people had heard of the latest marriage, and there was curiosity concerning the young woman who was reputed to be a beauty. Nubsekhem and his son joined the crowd near the docks, staying out of sight as much as possible. It was intention to see without being seen.

The king's ship came in sight, its oars beating the waters of the river into foam as it cut across the current to reach the city docks. A large flag bearing the symbol of a hawk in gold on a black background flew from the ship's bare mast. As the ship drew near, the captain's shouted commands could be heard, oars being withdrawn and coiled ropes hurled ashore with dock workers scrambling to tie up the ship.

Sekhemkhet stepped out of the wickerwork cabin in the stern of the ship, his lithe young body wearing gold and the finest clothing, and a pace behind stood a short dark-skinned girl similarly dressed in finery. The ship bumped alongside the wharf and a gangplank fitted. Then, to the acclaim of the waiting dignitaries of the city, the king stepped ashore, followed by his young bride. The crowds and size of the city seemed to overawe the girl as she openly gaped, looking all around with wide eyes at the colour and spectacle.

Tjaty Imhotep bowed to the king, greeting him and welcoming him back from Wawat.

"The news of your glorious success precedes you, my lord king. Your deeds bring glory upon your name and make Kemet foremost among the nations."

"Yes, I did rather well, didn't I," Sekhemkhet said. He looked around and passed a hand over his face, smearing the make-up around his eyes. "I have a headache," he muttered.

"Then perhaps we should go to the palace as quickly as possible," Imhotep said. "I can clear the streets and send for a chair."

Sekhemkhet shook his head, wincing at the motion. "I will walk. The people have come to see me...and my new wife, I suppose. Imhotep, this is Tetimene, my new Wawat wife. I think she is with child already."

Imhotep smiled at the young girl and welcomed her to Inebu-hedj. The king's soldiers, and the palace guards Imhotep had brought with him, formed a cordon around the king and his wife, and the procession set off for the palace along the main roads of the city. Crowds of people pushed in close, forcing the soldiers to use their staffs to beat them back. The men and women did not seem to mind, bearing their bruises with good cheer, and following the procession as it made its way from the docks.

Nubsekhem and Huni moved along the outside of the milling populace, pushing their way through to keep pace with the king. They noted the mood of the people, listening to muttered words and excited conversations, while watching the expressions on faces.

"She is beautiful," Huni remarked, "though I do not think I have ever seen skin so dark."

"You have not been paying attention, then," Nubsekhem said. "There are several Kushites in the army who are as dark."

"Yes, you are right, come to think of it, father. Perhaps it is just that her skin is so glossy and firm, rather than weather-beaten like our soldiers..."

"Enough of the girl, Huni. If you are in need of one, we will find you one this evening. In the meantime, look at the king. What do you see?"

Huni quickened his pace to get ahead of the king, and pressed close to look at him, but shrugged his shoulders after he had passed. "What am I supposed to be looking at?"

"Does he look sick to you?"

"Perhaps," Huni said doubtfully.

"See how he rubs his head. His eyes are listless and his movements lack energy."

"He might just be tired after his voyage."

The crowds thinned as the procession approached the temple of Ptah and then the royal palace that, despite Imhotep's efforts, still looked like an adjunct to the temple. With a last wave at the remnants of the crowd, the king entered the dim recesses of the palace, followed by Imhotep and Tetimene. Nubsekhem and Huni waited outside until the crowd had dispersed and the palace settled down.

"What do we do now, father?" Huni asked. "You have already submitted your report, so there is no good excuse for us to stay."

"I am not leaving until I find out whether the king is sick."

"How will you do that? You do not have the authority to demand such information from the court physician, and I doubt Imhotep will tell you."

"We will find lodgings in the city and make discreet enquiries," Nubsekhem said. "Have you ever known a secret kept by a number of people?"

Nubsekhem took them down into the lower city and rented a room close to a tavern, and a woman to cook and clean for them. He caught his son eyeing the woman speculatively and laughed.

"We must find you a decent young woman," he said. "Our cleaning woman is too old for you."

Both men enjoyed some female companionship that night, but after that they concentrated on finding out what they could from the palace. Nubsekhem was too well known to ask questions in the main part of the palace, so he confined his enquiries to the servants' quarters, while Huni made friends with young men and women among the servants close to the king. Each evening, they compared notes, and it quickly became obvious that not all was well within the royal suites.

"The king is not a well man at the best of times," Huni said. "Before the expedition to Wawat, he had aches and pains despite being a young man."

Nubsekhem nodded. "Talk in the kitchens is of the king's liking for sweet things, but several servants have heard him cry out in pain when eating honeyed dishes."

"Toothache?"

"It would seem reasonable to suppose so."

"That is not uncommon. Many people suffer that."

Nubsekhem grimaced. "I have cause to rue the day I cracked a tooth on a chip of stone. Now I cannot eat anything sweet without a throb of pain."

"Servants also speak of boils," Huni went on. "Hesy-Ra, the court physician has successfully treated those, though, with blade and poultices."

"No digestive upsets?" Nubsekhem asked. "The kitchen staff sometimes says he returns dishes untasted."

"Nothing more serious than discomfort, though a servant of the bedchamber reports a pot stinking most foully a few days ago."

"Shit stinks," Nubsekhem said. "Is there nothing else?"

"There is one other thing," Huni said slowly, "though I do not know if it is serious. The king came back from Wawat complaining of an itch in his legs and a few small blisters."

"A lot of people get itches; usually people who go swimming in ponds, though it is hard to imagine the king doing that." Nubsekhem pondered for a few moments. "See if you can find out more...if there is more to know, of course. It might be something we can exploit."

Huni said he would do so, and then asked after Tetimene. "I hear she is with child."

"That seems to be common knowledge in the palace," Nubsekhem confirmed. He smiled at his son. "You seem to be unusually interested in the girl. Attracted to her, are you?"

Huni coloured and looked away. "No."

"Well, a pregnancy there will unsettle the other wives. With the deaths of the previous princes there is a lot of competition to produce an heir. If Tetimene bears a son, we can expect plots and counterplots within the palace, which may be to our advantage."

"So there is nothing more for us here?" Huni asked. "Do we go home?"

"I think we stay a bit longer. At the least, we need to know if the king's itch continues. Normally, that only lasts a few days and should have disappeared by the time he returned. If it is still there, it may be something more serious."

They stayed, sending word north to Hut-waret that they would be delayed. There was no serious incursions or unrest on the northern borders, so they felt justified in pursuing other information. Nubsekhem, working through friends within the kitchen staff of the palace, struck up an acquaintance with the court physician's assistant, a man called Khentu, and over a cup of wine or two, learned that the king was afflicted with something a little more serious than an itch.

"Do you know anything about medicine?" Khentu asked.

"Only what an army commander might know," Nubsekhem said. "Wounds mostly, a flux after drinking foul water or rotten food. A few sundry ailments."

"An itch is common if a person bathes in ponds or slow water, though why this should be is unknown. The king fought in still water in Wawat, but his itch has lasted longer and developed into a rash."

"Is it serious?"

Khentu shrugged. "Of itself, perhaps not. There are poultices and ointments that will ease a rash, but he has other things now... I should not really speak of these things."

"Has the king told you not to?"

"No."

"Or Imhotep, or Hesy-Ra?"

"No."

"Perhaps that is because it is not a matter of state security," Nubsekhem said. "He is the king, and every man and woman in the kingdoms prays for his health and recovery. Besides, how many people in the palace already know? I am sure his body servants know and those who serve in his bedchamber, as well as his wives and concubines and their servants." He smiled and poured more wine into Khentu's cup. "I am probably the only man in the palace who does not know."

"There is probably truth in what you say," Khentu said. He sipped his wine and pondered the situation for a few minutes. "The king has a fever," the assistant physician admitted. "His muscles ache, he has chills, a cough, and his bowels are loose."

"None of those sound particularly life threatening," Nubsekhem said. "We have all suffered those complaints at one time or another and recovered. I am sure the king will get better soon."

Khentu nodded. "With Hesy-Ra and me to look after him, how could he not?"

Nubsekhem found it difficult to contain his excitement when he spoke to Huni that evening, reporting on Khentu's revelation of the king's affliction.

"But you said yourself these things were not life threatening," Huni said. "So why are you in such good spirits?"

"Nothing he has in dangerous by itself, but taken together..."

"But you said Khentu is not very concerned."

"He did not say he was, but he must be. Anyway, the fact of the matter is that the king is sick. Now, we must ask ourselves, will he die from it or recover? If he dies, then are we ready to strike with our army, and if he starts to recover, should we act in other ways?"

Huni frowned. "What other ways?"

"Administer my rock poison."

"Please, father, no. Poison is a foul way of killing."

"It can be efficient, though, and is safest for the administrator. Whoever slips the poison into his cup can just walk away."

"I would rather face him with a blade in my hand."

Nubsekhem waved his hands dismissively. "It might never come to that, anyway. What we must consider is what we do to prepare in case the king becomes seriously ill or dies. It is imperative that we are ready to strike fast and hard, removing anyone who might oppose us." He looked quizzically at his son. "I presume you are not averse to that?" he asked.

"No, father, only to poison."

"I ask because some might say that rebellion against the anointed king is as heinous a crime as slipping poison into his drink."

"I do not believe that the gods look with favour upon Hor-Sekhemkhet any longer," Huni said. "If a king angers the gods, then removing him is in the interests of the kingdoms."

Nubsekhem nodded in satisfaction. His son might display a strange reluctance to killing the king by any means to hand, but at least he grasped the necessity of acting in the interests of the nation. It helped that the interests of the nation matched those of his family. The gods had shown their displeasure with Sekhemkhet by denying him an heir, whereas they had blessed the other line within the royal family--his own. Khaba was the natural choice of the replacement king, but he was already an old man. Nubsekhem smiled at the thought that Khaba's heir was him, and after him, Huni would reign. Sekhemkhet could not even extend his dynasty by a single generation, whereas his own family held three generations before Huni even started a family.

"Tell me then, my son," Nubsekhem said. "You are my captain and know the mood of the men. Is the Northern Army ready to march with us to take over the kingdoms?"

Huni stared at his father. He knew what his father wanted to hear, but he shook his head. "No, sir. The officers will join us, but the men will be reluctant." He saw his father's frown and added, "The reluctance will be to attack the throne. If, however, the king was to attack us, the men would rally behind us if we could show ourselves unjustly persecuted. Then our defence could be turned to attack."

"And how are we to do that?" Nubsekhem asked.

"I do not know, sir. Perhaps if the king believed he was about to be attacked, he might move first, but I confess I do not know how to make him believe it without our men also believing it."

Nubsekhem nodded thoughtfully. "Aside from that, how is our readiness?"

"I think that you as commander would know better than me, sir."

"Indulge me."

"Very well. Our Northern Army is well equipped, well trained, and motivated to fight Kemet's enemies. Considering Kemet is not supposed to have a standing army of more than two or three hundred men, we have five hundred ready to go...providing we can convince them to follow us."

"So if we can convince them of the rightness of our cause, we could beat any army the king might raise to confront us?"

"Yes, sir."

"Then that is what we must do," Nubsekhem said.

Dismissing his son, Nubsekhem considered whether there was any advantage to staying in Inebu-hedj and looking for a way to poison the king. Reluctantly, he realised that he was not prepared for what would follow. Unless he could immediately step in and assume the throne--whether for himself or for his father he was undecided--there would be other contenders. Imhotep would have a claim; he was the king's uncle and was likewise descended from Khasekhemwy and a daughter of Seth-Peribsen. The Tjaty swore he was loyal to his brother's line, but Nubsekhem was certain he would not draw back from the throne if he saw it within his grasp.

"The man is ambitious as any of us," he murmured. "No, Sekhemkhet must stay alive until I am ready for him."

Nubsekhem and Huni returned to their duties at Hut-waret, thinking of ways to ready themselves should an opportunity for rebellion present itself. In the days and months following their return, the king's household experienced further evidence of the gods' displeasure when Inetkawes was delivered early of a daughter who died within days of being born. The queen took it hard, her anguish tearing at the hearts of all who heard her grief. Even Sekhemkhet and her mother Hetephernebti could not console her.

The news was a little better following the birth of a son to Djeser-Ti, but the boy was sickly from birth and was not expected to live long. Sekhemkhet made much of the child, burning a fortune in incense on the altars of the gods in the hope that the sweet aroma would placate their anger. He named the boy Hor-Re.

The only unadulterated good news came with the birth of a son to Tetimene. She had invoked her Wawat gods continually through her pregnancy, and credited them with having had her deliver a healthy boy. Sekhemkhet was delighted and named the son Hor-Nubkhet. He clearly wanted to name the son his heir, but Inetkawes and Djeser-Ti united in their opposition, prevailing upon the king to wait until it was clear that Kemet's gods were in favour of a half-Kushite heir to the throne.

"Her gods are not our gods," Inetkawes declared. "We must be sure that our gods favour his elevation."

"And my son was born before hers," Djeser-Ti said. "Hor-Re should be your heir before the Wawat child."

Desirous of keeping peace within the palace, Sekhemkhet acceded to their wishes, refraining from naming an heir. The palace polarised into camps supporting either Djeser-Ti and Hor-Re on the one hand, or Tetimene and Hor-Nubkhet on the other. As palace servants and nobles gathered around the two wives and their male offspring, Inetkawes felt increasingly isolated, pushed aside from the succession, and she started to question her place in life.

"My babies are all dead," Inetkawes wept in the presence of her mother. "My life has no meaning anymore."

"You are still Sekhemkhet's Queen," Hetephernebti reminded her.

"What use is a queen who cannot produce an heir for her king?"

"You are still a young woman," her mother pointed out. "There will be opportunities to have more children."

"And have them die as well? How much more heartbreak do you think I can take?"

"You will do your duty to the king and the kingdoms," Hetephernebti said firmly. "Lie with your husband and have him sow his seed in you. Give birth to another child...and another...as many as may be needed. The gods will relent, daughter, and give you a living child. I pray it will be a son, but even daughters are valuable." She reached out and stroked Inetkawes' hair gently. "I should know, because I had two beautiful daughters who delight my heart."

"I cannot even do that," Inetkawes sobbed. "Even my daughters die."

"I was twenty-six years old when I gave birth to you," Hetephernebti said, "and you are only twenty-four now. You will have other children."

Inetkawes shook her head sadly. "To have children, my husband must sow his seed in me but he is reluctant to lie with me. He spends all his time with Djeser-Ti and Tetimene, who have borne him sons. I am no use to him."

"That is not true. Sekhemkhet loves you."

"No, mother. He honours me still as his sister and his queen, but his love for me has fled. If I could bear a living child for him, he might look upon me with favour, but I cannot even do that for him."

"Do not give up," her mother urged.

Inetkawes sighed and brushed away tears. "My babies have gone ahead of me into the afterlife, and even there I have failed in my love and my duty. Who will care for them in the afterlife while both their parents live?"

"That is foolishness. Your babies will await your arrival in the fullness of time. What is more, you will be able to present them with brothers and sisters yet to be born."

"I wish I could believe that, mother."

"Believe it, daughter. Go to your husband and bid him lie with you. Have him fill your belly so you may both rejoice in your children. Give me grandchildren so I might hold them on my knee and tell them stories."

Hetephernebti embraced her daughter and departed. Inetkawes sat and stared at the closed door for some time before getting up and walking to her own rooms. She lay on her bed for a time, her mind dwelling on her lost children and then, despite the lateness of the hour, called her ladies to bathe her and attend to her make-up. After she had dressed in her finest clothes, she dismissed her women, telling them that she did not wish to be disturbed, and sat, with a single oil lamp to give her light, beside the window that looked out upon the palace gardens.

Night fell, and the few people who frequented the gardens disappeared inside. Now only the bats flittered across the darkening sky, and the sparrows twittered sleepily in the palm trees. A lion roared in the menagerie, dogs in the city barking a response, and then silence fell over the city and the palace.

Inetkawes sighed and got up, crossing to a wooden chest in a corner of her room. She knelt beside it, opening the lid, and took out a small copper knife. Going back to her chair, she sat and stared out at the night, absently running a thumb over the blade, back and forth. The glow of torches in other parts of the palace flickered and went out, and a soft knocking sounded on the door of her inner room.

"My lady, it is Init. Do you need anything?"

"No, Init. There is nothing I need. Go to bed."

"Yes, my lady."

Inetkawes listened, and heard soft footfalls outside her door, and then silence. She looked at her left wrist, marking the presence of the tendons and veins beneath her tender skin and smiled. Lifting the copper blade of the knife, she positioned the tip on her skin, wincing as the blade sliced through her soft flesh. Blood welled, trickling over her wrist and pattering onto the tiled floor. Gritting her teeth against the pain, she pushed the knife deeper, pulling it up her arm and opening a wound that gushed blood.

She stared at the blood cascading over her arm and thought the pain was bearable. The knife clattered to the floor and she leaned back with her arm dangling, feeling the warm blood pour over her hand in a sticky flood. She smiled as it pooled on the floor.

"Soon, my darling children," she whispered. "I will be with you soon."

Inetkawes closed her eyes as a great lassitude swept over her, her thoughts starting to wander. A lion roared again from the menagerie and she opened her eyes, looking at the night through her window, thinking how dark it had become. The lamp beside her cast only a small pool of light and the shadows in the corners of the room crept inward as her vision narrowed. She closed her eyes again and sighed.

"I am coming, my babies. Wait for me. Soon we shall be together."

Chapter 19

After the burial of two children in a walled-up section of the galleries beneath his *mer,* Sekhemkhet ordered progress be made on the South Tomb. It was always his intention that wives and children be interred there, and increasingly there was a need for a finished tomb. As well as his children, Queen Inetkawes had died, scandalously taking her own life. Some argued that having committed suicide, Inetkawes should not be embalmed and buried as befitted her station in life, but never in the king's hearing. He was insistent that she be buried together with the dead children she had borne, in the South Tomb.

Den pushed his workers to complete the *per-djet* structure to the west of the king's *mer,* and although it was by no means finished when the Queen's embalmed body was ready for interment, it would suffice. The underground chamber was carved out and decorated, and then her body and those of her children were laid to rest in carved, ornately painted and gold-decorated wooden coffins. Jewellery that she had loved in life were laid there for her use in the afterlife, as well as the usual grave offerings of food and drink.

"She will be forever young and ready to welcome me with open arms when I ascend to the gods," Sekhemkhet said.

Though the queen and her children lay underground, work on the *per-djet* continued, its construction taking longer than the available time before the burial.

Grief had torn the palace apart, though not all of it was heartfelt. People like Djeser-Ti and Tetimene openly wailed and cried, rubbing onion juice in their eyes to stimulate tears, but secretly they rejoiced. The queen was dead and the king would be looking to raise another woman to that status. Both of Sekhemkhet's wives lusted after the title, and both had sons by the king. They eyed each other suspiciously and factions within the palace, already existing, became more pronounced. Supporters of either wife would gain favour when their lady gained the king's blessing by becoming queen. Tensions within the palace reached such a pitch that Imhotep felt he had to broach the subject to the king.

"I grieve with you for the loss of our queen, Inetkawes, my lord king, but we must focus our attention on the future rather than dwelling on the past. The palace has become almost an armed camp with people choosing sides, supporting one or other of your wives. Will you not make a decision, so we can restore the *ma'at* of the palace?"

"Why should I make either of my wives the queen?" Sekhemkhet asked. "Djeser-Ti comes from common stock, and while it could be argued that Tetimene is cousin to a Wawat chieftain, she owes her status in Kemet to her marriage."

"It would calm things down, my lord king. Choose one, so we can have peace once more."

Sekhemkhet shook his head. "I love both my wives, but neither is suitable queenly material. Inetkawes was perfect, being my sister and the daughter of a king. That is why I chose her, but with her gone, who is left? Have the gods relented? Will they let me marry my other sister Meresankh?"

"You would make her your queen?"

"If I could marry her, then certainly. She is also my sister and daughter of a king."

Imhotep pursed his lips as he thought. Meresankh had made it very clear to him that she did not want to marry her brother, preferring the company of women to that of men, but would she change her mind? Elevation to the throne of Kemet was a big incentive. He knew he could not make the decision on her behalf.

"I will sacrifice to the gods and petition them for an answer," he told the king.

Imhotep made a point of visiting the temples and offering incense on the king's behalf, but that was just for show. Later that day, he called upon Meresankh, seeking a private audience with her. He told her of the king's desires and the promise he had made.

"Queen? He actually said that?"

"There is no other woman with the right qualifications."

Meresankh shook her head. "I would have to marry him though, and my heart rebels at the thought of being married to my brother."

"You told me before that you loved a woman. Are you still in love with her?"

"Yes, I am, and she with me. We are very discreet. There is no provision in law for a woman to marry another, but if there was, we would be married."

"The thought of being Queen does not entice you?"

"My sister Inetkawes was queen, and in my mind she will always be queen. I could not replace her."

"You are sister to the king every bit as much as was your sister," Imhotep said. "I have no doubt that if you had married the king when he first wanted to, you would have been queen alongside your sister. Do you think she would have begrudged you the title?"

"No, of course not, we loved each other."

"Do you think she would begrudge you the title now, after her death?"

Meresankh shook her head again. "No, she would probably welcome it, but that is beside the point, Uncle. I do not want to lie with my brother...or any man...even for the queenly crown."

Imhotep sighed. "I thought that might be the case, but I had to ask, not just for the king's sake but for the sake of peace."

"Peace? What do you mean?"

"You must have noticed the tensions within the palace. There are two factions centred around Djeser-Ti and Tetimene, both wanting the crown.

How is the king to decide when both women are commoners? They make good wives, and can bear a son and heir, but neither can rightly be his queen. That is why he wants you. If you were queen, he would disappoint both factions, but as neither would have gained the ascendancy, peace would be restored. If you refuse, then he might choose one or other wife and tension could dissolve into open warfare."

"You seek to put the blame on me," Meresankh said bitterly. "If I refuse, any harm that comes to the kingdoms is my fault."

"No, my dear, not at all," Imhotep said. "I am just telling you the situation within the palace. You have made it clear that you detest both men and the crown, and I will make your excuses to the king as usual. The gods will still withhold their blessing on such a union."

"It is a pity that marriage and the crown are inseparable," Meresankh said.

Imhotep thought there was a touch of wistfulness in her voice, and pursued it like a hawk after a sparrow.

"You are not against the crown in principle, then?"

"How could I be? My mother was queen, my sister was queen, my father was king, and my brother is king. I would like to be a queen too, but the price is too high. I will not let any man lie with me, sowing his seed in my belly."

Imhotep went away, wondering how the king would take the news that the 'gods' had once more refused to let him marry his other sister and plant sons in her. It was not something he looked forward to, and his approach to the gods in prayer that night was for help in breaking the news to Sekhemkhet. The next day, he delayed attending upon the king until Sekhemkhet sent for him.

"Well? What do the gods say? They must look upon me with favour now that my queen has died."

"My lord king, the gods will not let you lie with your sister Meresankh."

Sekhemkhet scowled and so forgot his dignity as to stamp his foot in frustration. "What do they want of me?" he demanded. "Have I not honoured the gods of Kemet in every way? Am I not my father's son, the legitimate successor of Netjerikhet on the throne of the Two Kingdoms? Why then, do they refuse to let me take another queen?"

Imhotep did not immediately answer as he was thinking about what Meresankh had said. He tried to recall her exact words, wondering if there was a way out of this dilemma to be found in them. *I would like to be a queen too, but the price is too high. I will not let any man lie with me.*

"Well? What do the gods want of me, Imhotep?"

Imhotep thought hard, trying to pick his words with care. "My lord king, your virility is famed throughout Kemet. You have lain with many women, sowing sons and daughters within their bellies in the same way that that a farmer sows seed in his fields and harvests a bountiful crop from his fertile fields..."

"Yes, yes, what is your point?"

"My lord, you have been the successful and prosperous farmer in all ways but one. Sometimes, particularly in years when the flood falls below the required levels, the farmer will allow a field to remain fallow, unplanted with seed, so that it might bear bountifully at another time."

Sekhemkhet frowned. "What are you saying?"

"My lord, I do not know if this is in the minds of the gods as I have not thought to ask them this particular question, but it may be that they require the fertile field of Princess Meresankh to remain unsown for a purpose." Imhotep hesitated. "It is possible...that they would allow you to marry her, raising her to the status of queen...if you did not lie with her."

"What would be the point of that? I need to raise sons with her as I did with her sister Inetkawes."

"I believe it would be in the nature of a sacrifice, my lord. You have proven your virility beyond question in the eyes of men; maybe it is time to show your restraint in the eyes of the gods."

"I would be laughed at," Sekhemkhet grumbled. "Men would say I was no longer able to impregnate my wives..."

"None would dare, my lord," Imhotep interrupted. "Besides, you would prove that a lie by your continued attention to your many other women. Let Meresankh rule the Women's Quarters and restore the *ma'at* of the palace. You would have your marriage, your queen, and peace among your women." He smiled confidingly. "My lord, one woman is much like another if all you consider is her field. You are the farmer whose lands encompass the whole of Kemet. Please the gods by leaving one field unsown."

Sekhemkhet looked thoughtful. "That is an interesting idea, Imhotep. Is that really what the gods want?"

"Let me petition them and seek to know their mind, my lord. If, that is, the idea has merit."

Sekhemkhet nodded slowly.

"If the gods allow the marriage of Meresankh, would you make her queen yet put her aside, never sowing your seed in her? Before you answer, my lord, know that this would be an unbreakable vow to the gods. Disaster would befall you and Kemet if you broke your vow."

"My word is holy," Sekhemkhet said stiffly. "I do not go back on it."

"Then I will approach the gods on your behalf, my lord king."

Rather than going to the gods, Imhotep went straight back to Meresankh.

"No! Uncle, how can you betray me like this?"

Imhotep tried to explain his thinking; in the face of the king's determination to marry her, but for some time he was not sure whether his words were getting through to her. After a while, he stopped talking and waited for his niece to calm down. She cried a bit more, wiped her face on a piece of linen, and called for her women to attend to her make-up. Imhotep waited patiently until they had finished and been dismissed.

"You do not bring welcome news, Uncle," she said calmly. "I thought you were on my side."

"Meresankh, I am on your side. Have I not lied for you to the king, pretending it was the gods who forbade your marriage? I have striven to give you the freedom you desire, but the king will no longer be denied. I fear that if I cannot tell him the gods favour your marriage, he will force the issue. That is why I have tried to reach a compromise solution."

"Some compromise," Meresankh said bitterly. "The king wants to marry me, I do not want to marry him, and your compromise is that he marries me."

"Have you not been listening? The marriage would be one of form only, no substance. You are not required to lie with him."

Meresankh snorted delicately. "How long do you imagine that would last? Once I am ensconced in the palace as his wife, he will demand that of me and I will be unable to refuse."

"He has sworn not to, on his word as the king," Imhotep said. "I believe him."

"Then what is the point...for either of us? Just let me remain at home as an unmarried woman, enjoying my lover, and let the king do as he pleases with other women."

"He needs a queen to settle the factions in the palace and restore *ma'at* to the Women's Quarters."

Meresankh stared at Imhotep. "What has that need got to do with me?"

"Have you even been listening to me?" Imhotep demanded. "Sekhemkhet wants to marry you and make you his Queen. I have impressed on him that he must not touch you sexually. He does not like the idea, but

238

he will do it because he believes the injunction comes from the gods." He shook his head and sighed. "I am misrepresenting the gods and I have no doubt I will be called to account for it one day."

"I would be Queen Meresankh?"

"Yes."

"Married to my brother?"

"Yes."

"But not have to endure his intimate attentions?"

"No."

"Nor have him sow his seed in me?"

"The king has sworn this and declares he will not break his word."

"I...I do not know what to say," Meresankh whispered.

"Say yes," Imhotep urged. "You have said you want to be a queen; well, here is your opportunity. Your duties do not include having sons for the king; he will rely on other women for that. All you have to do is be seen with the king, appearing as his queen, and reigning over the other wives and concubines."

"I think I might enjoy that last part," Meresankh said with a smile. The smile disappeared quickly. "But what about An...what about my lover? She does not deserve to be discarded because of my ambition."

"You could always make her one of your ladies. She would be with you continually and I am sure you would find opportunities to be alone with her."

Meresankh turned away to consider the offer the king had made through his Tjaty. She knew Sekhemkhet would never stop trying to make her his wife, and if she accepted this offer, he would have won that particular campaign.

But does it actually matter? she thought. *He has sworn never to lie with me, so I lose nothing by agreeing...but look at what I gain. I would be a queen like my mother and*

239

sister before me, and that is no empty title. I will never produce an heir...I will never be King's Mother...I will never have children at all...but I would hold real power within the palace.

She was tempted, even though she did not fully trust the king to keep his word.

"How can I be sure the king will keep his word?" she asked.

"He has sworn to do so."

"I want him to swear that publicly."

"He will never do that," Imhotep said. "His initial reluctance to swear was because he would be perceived to be impotent. I persuaded him that his continued attentions to his women would prove that a lie, but a public declaration would be too much. He will imagine people are laughing at him." He shook his head. "The agreement must be private."

"Then how can I trust him not to break his word? And broken once, it will be broken for evermore. Before I know it, I will be bearing children and I tell you, Uncle, I will not allow that. I will kill myself first."

"Do not even think that, child," Imhotep said, horror in his voice.

"For me, it would be preferable to having children with my brother."

Imhotep thought hard, his forehead wrinkling and a frown making his expression grim. "There must be a way," he muttered. "Wait...what if he swore his oath before the gods in person, witnessed by the Hem-netjers? I think he would agree to that, and having sworn in the presence of the gods he could not go back on his word."

"That...that would be acceptable," Meresankh said.

"I will see what I can do."

Imhotep went first to see the Hem-netjers of the principal gods in Inebu-hedj--Ptah, Djehuti, Horu, Re, and because the subject was a marriage, Auset. The priests were disturbed at his request, but he spent time talking to each, convincing them that it was necessary to restore *ma'at* to the king's affairs. One of the principal objections was voiced by the Hem-netjer of Ptah.

"If the gods are truly against the consummation of this proposed marriage, then why has Ptah not made his wishes known to me? It is strange that he would manifest to you in a dream, rather than to his dedicated servant."

"I cannot speak to that," Imhotep said, "but remember that I, too, am a servant of the gods, being Hem-netjer of Re in Iunu. It is possible that the gods selected me as I was close to the king, being of his family. I am his Tjaty, and I serve him in all things."

"No man doubts your loyalty and abilities," the priest of Ptah said. "The construction of the *mer* of Netjerikhet is an act worthy of the gods, and now you are constructing one for Sekhemkhet. Forgive me if I seemed suspicious, Tjaty Imhotep, but I have given my life to the service of the god and yet he chose another to proclaim his will."

Imhotep nodded sombrely, wondering what the priest would think if he knew the truth. "It may be that you stand too high in the god's estimation. Each god desired the message be delivered to the king, but how could they choose just one Hem-netjer without incurring jealousy among the others. If that is the case, they chose me because I was insufficiently high in their estimation and could be a useful compromise."

That argument seemed to please the priest of Ptah, and the other priests concurred with his decision. If the gods sought marriage between the king and his younger sister without physical intimacy, then who were they to disagree?

"We will witness the king's oath in the presence of the gods," they said.

The king was less pleased with the arrangements, and Imhotep suspected he had thought to find some excuse to go back on his word once he and Meresankh were married. He grumbled and tried to put off the swearing until after the marriage, asking whether Imhotep doubted his word. Imhotep assured him that he trusted the king implicitly, but that the gods had given him the terms.

"As before, my lord king, the gods came to me in a dream, insisting on you swearing in their presence. I cannot imagine why they would want that; they did not tell me."

Sekhemkhet sent for his sister, and greeted her warmly, sitting her down and having food and wine brought. They dined together, talking about innocent things of their childhood and avoiding the contentious issue before them until after their meal.

"You are prepared to marry me?" Sekhemkhet asked.

Meresankh hesitated. "And?"

"And be my queen," he added.

"Yes, I am, brother."

"Then let us proceed immediately. Why should we wait?"

"There is something that must happen first. Imhotep told me."

Sekhemkhet scowled. "He did, did he? You do not trust me?"

"My lord king," Meresankh said meekly, "it is not a matter of mistrusting you, but rather of obeying the gods. They desire your oath, and who are we to question them?"

"Oh, very well, if I must, though I cannot see why you refuse to bear my children. You might even have a son who would be king after me. Wouldn't you like that?"

"Who would not be honoured by that, brother? However, it is not up to me. The gods have said I must not have children by you, so I shall obey them."

Sekhemkhet shrugged his shoulders and had Imhotep arrange the swearing. By turns, the Hem-netjers of the selected gods received the king, Meresankh, and Imhotep into their presence and, after cleansing ceremonies, led them into the holiest part of the temple. The statue of the god, clothed in the finest linen garments, anointed with precious oils and perfumes, loomed in the darkness of the inner sanctuary, the single flickering torch making the shadows dance and sway, bringing life to the carved and gilded wood.

Meresankh gasped and shrank back, and the king trembled as he mastered his fear. Even Imhotep, knowing the statues were just representations of the gods, and having seen the gods many times before, was impressed. The priest made offerings to his god and then signed the young man and woman to step forward. They did so, reluctantly, gazing up at the imposing height of the god.

"I, Meresankh, daughter of Netjerikhet and Hetephernebti, do swear in the presence of the god, that I will be a faithful wife to my lord king, Hor-Sekhemkhet, acting as his Queen and obeying him in all things save one, which the gods have forbidden. I shall not lie with the king or bear children to him."

The priest nudged the torch, and the shadows lurched and fled, making it look as if the god inclined its head.

"The god assents," the priest intoned.

"I am King Hor-Sekhemkhet, son of Netjerikhet. I take Meresankh my sister as my wife and my Queen. She shall be my wife in all things except that which is forbidden by the gods at this time. I shall not lie with her and beget children on her. This I swear in the presence of the god."

Again the shadows moved and the priest averred the god's assent. He looked toward Imhotep and beckoned him forward.

This was the moment that Imhotep dreaded. The dream forbidden sexual relations had been his invention, and he was not sure what the gods thought of his actions. He had taken upon himself the authority of the gods and now he had to face them in their inner sanctuary and answer for his deeds.

I may be struck dead in an instant, he thought, *but at least the king and Meresankh have already sworn their oaths and cannot take them back.*

"I, Imhotep, son of Khasekhemwy, Tjaty to my lord king Hor-Sekhemkhet, do witness the oaths of the king and his new queen."

The shadows moved again, and for a moment, Imhotep thought the statue of the god was falling upon him, but it was only a momentary illusion.

"The god assents," the priest said.

The ceremonies were repeated in the temples of all the gods, and it was with some relief that Imhotep conducted the king and his new queen back into the palace. Here, Meresankh was presented to the assembled court and Imhotep, acting both as Tjaty and Hem-netjer of Re, placed the crown on Meresankh's head. Most of the court seemed pleased that the succession had been resolved, but he noted sour expressions on the faces of Djeser-Ti and Tetimene. One other woman looked stricken too, and Imhotep had to struggle to recall her name.

Ansenet? Yes, that is it...daughter of Maya. Is she the lover of Meresankh?

He put his thought aside for later consideration. The king insisted on a small celebratory feast so that he could show off his new queen to everybody. He made sure that people regarded the marriage as a normal one, hinting at the possibility of future sons, and Meresankh smiled weakly at ribald comments that drifted around the room. Then it was time for the royal couple to retire, and even Imhotep could no longer be there to inhibit the king's desires. The servants left the two alone. Meresankh looked nervous, but Sekhemkhet smiled and gestured to the next room.

"There is a bed in there," he said. "I suggest you get some sleep. I will stay out here and do some work. As far as anyone will be able to tell, we have consummated our union, but the gods are watching and I will not disobey their commands."

Chapter 20

Overseer Sekhemre was aware of what went on in Inebu-hedj and the royal palace as his father, the Tjaty, kept him apprised of the news, but he did not really care about any of it. All he cared about were his rocks and his workers. He lived as much in the quarry as he did in his house with his wife and children, the odour of rock dust was as pleasing to his nose as the perfume of the lotus flower, and the gleaming white limestone was as beautiful in his eyes as the limbs of his young wife. Not that he told Perimset that, of course.

The quarry workers loved and respected him, having all learned that Sekhemre would not ask a man to perform any task he was not willing to do himself. He was a skilled mason, but if a block needed hauling out of one of the underground galleries, he was there to lend a hand. When the rock dust and rubble started accumulating in the deep passages, no one was surprised to see him grab a wicker basket and start hauling the chips out alongside the common labourers. He sat down to the midday meal with the workers, using with them the tubs of water to wash dust from faces and mouths, and then sharing the plain but plentiful food he supplied.

It was on one of those days when he trudged out of the quarry with his workers, tired and with aching muscles, that the ground trembled beneath his feet. He stopped and looked around.

"Did you feel that?" he asked the men near him.

"Yes, sir. What was it?" asked one.

"Look there, sir," said another, pointing toward the entrance to the underground workings.

A cloud of dust billowed from the doorway, and workmen stumbled out, coughing.

"It's a cave in," shouted another man.

Sekhemre ran back, seeking out the work overseers. "Is everyone out? Asen, how many are still underground? Katem, make a count of those outside already."

The work overseers set about organising the men into their work teams, counting off each man as they called their names. Meanwhile, Sekhemre ventured into the entrance with a cloth tied over his face. The dust was too thick and only slowly clearing; he could not see anything or anyone. He stumbled out again, coughing and spluttering as the acrid dust bit deep into his throat.

"How is the count going?" Sekhemre yelled. "Katem, Asen, your reports, if you please."

"The only men underground are Mentep's team, sir," Asen said. "They were working in the 'Glory of Geb' shaft."

"Mentep is here, sir," Katem added. "Most of his team are here too. The only ones missing are a labourer and two water boys."

"Mentep, get over here," Sekhemre ordered. "Why were three members of your team still underground?"

"Someone had to bring up the empty buckets, sir. Pen left them near the workface, and the others were fooling around for half the shift, so it only seemed fair to send back to get the buckets."

"Pen is one of the missing?"

"Yes, sir, a water boy. The other one is Horem, and the labourer is Ramose."

Telling Mentep and Asen to follow him, Sekhemre entered the quarry shaft again, now that the dust was settling, though their feet stirred it up afresh as they moved. They dipped cloths in water and tied them around their faces to give them some relief, and lit oil lamps to give them light as all the lamps lining the shafts and galleries had been extinguished. Moving cautiously, they made their way along the wide carved corridors to where the galleries descended to lower levels. Sekhemre called out as they descended, hoping to hear one of the missing persons calling back, but not even echoes sounded, the dust muffling all sounds.

"I think they must be dead, sir," Mentep said.

"I will not accept that until I see their bodies," Sekhemre snapped back.

Asen stumbled and nearly dropped his oil lamp. He turned back and shuffled his feet in the darkness, exclaiming as his bare feet met a low ridge of rock traversing the gallery.

"That should not be there," he said. "These gallery floors are supposed to be smooth."

Sekhemre knelt and examined the floor and the ridge. "It is sharp-edged and fresh." He lifted his lamp high, staring around him. "I think this is where the ground caved in. What is below us?"

"'Glory of Geb' rock face," Mentep said. "If this lot fell on them, they are certainly dead."

"I told you I would not accept that until I see their bodies, so lead us down there," Sekhemre ordered.

Mentep took the lead, taking them another hundred paces to where a cross-gallery angled downward to another level, then back toward where the 'Geb' rock face lay. They had not gone far when they came across boulders littering the floor and then rubble filling the passage from ceiling to floor.

"The work face is behind here?" Sekhemre asked.

"Yes, sir. They lie buried beneath this lot," Mentep said.

Sekhemre contemplated the pile of rubble before starting to pull rocks out of it, tossing them aside, but after only a few had been shifted, the mass shifted and dust cascaded down from the roof of the tunnel. He stopped immediately and retreated.

"Organise a team of workers, Mentep. Have them bring timbers to shore up the roof as well. Otherwise we risk another collapse."

"This will have to be reported," Asen said gloomily.

"I know. That is my responsibility."

Sekhemre waited until Mentep returned with a team of twenty men who formed a chain passing rocks from the rubble slope back into a clear part of the gallery. Other men brought in stout timbers and eased them into position, but the rock continued to groan and release drifts of dust from the roof. Every time that happened, work would stop, and the men would look fearfully at the roof, before beginning again when nothing further happened.

Leaving Asen in charge, Sekhemre made his way back up through the galleries and shafts, passing into the great excavated halls and out into the open. The hot sun and fresh air was a huge relief after the dusty confines of the mine. He noted that the other overseers were organising the workers into teams, some to relieve the men underground, and others to work on surface quarries instead of risking another collapse in the lower levels. Hurrying home, he told his wife what was happening and then took himself down to the quarry wharf.

249

Commandeering a fast fishing boat, he sailed for the capital, taking advantage of a lull in the northerly breeze. They made good time, but it seemed to Sekhemre that the boat dawdled as his anxiety increased. Leaping ashore as soon as they touched at the docks, he raced up through the streets to the palace and breathlessly demanded to see the Tjaty.

"There has been a cave-in on one of the lower levels of the mine, father. Three men are trapped."

"I am sorry to hear it," Imhotep said, "but what do you expect me to do? I would have thought your presence at the quarry more valuable than anything I can do."

"I have a team working on the blocked gallery, but the roof is unstable. I would like to organise the workforce to drive another gallery alongside the blocked one to reach the trapped men that way."

"How many men would you need?"

"All of them for now."

"So production of rock from the quarry would cease?"

"Inevitably, father."

Imhotep shook his head. "That is not something under my authority. I must ask the king for permission."

"He will give it though, won't he?" Sekhemre asked anxiously.

"That is up to the king, but I do not see why not."

In this, Imhotep was wrong. He took the news to the king, laying out the plan for rescuing the trapped men, and explaining that production from the quarry would cease while they dug out a new gallery.

"No, I will not allow production to cease," Sekhemkhet said.

"It would only be for a few days," Imhotep pointed out.

"I am not going to have my *mer* put in jeopardy by a few careless men. I do not give permission for work at the quarry to stop."

"Two of them are mere boys, my lord."

"If they are working in the quarry, they are men."

"My lord, I beg you to reconsider. With a break in the work, we can save their lives."

"They are probably dead already."

"Maybe not..."

"No. I have spoken," Sekhemkhet said firmly. "I will not stop work at the quarry to find these men who are already dead and buried. That is final. If I find that work has ceased, the overseers there will feel my wrath."

Imhotep had to carry the bad news to his son, enjoining him to get the quarry working again as quickly as possible, rather than risk the king's anger.

"I can turn him aside from many things," he told his son, "but he has set his mind to this and you risk everything by disobeying him."

Sekhemre returned to the Troyu quarry sorrowing, but in the enforced inactivity on board the fishing boat, he thought about the injustice of the king's decision, wondering what could be done. If fate was kind, they would have dug their way through the rubble by now, and freed the trapped men. As soon as he got back to the quarry, he hastened to the mine and found Asen, demanding to know what had happened.

Asen shook his head grimly. "We got through about five paces but the roof collapsed, injuring two men. We tried again, but the rock cries out in protest. I think we must drive through another gallery to go around the zone of weakness."

"The king will not allow it," Sekhemre said bitterly. "He orders the quarry to get back to full production."

"But they will die," Asen protested, "if they are not already dead."

"There might be a way. Assemble the men."

Asen called to the other overseers and had them call the men together in front of the outside wall of the quarry. Sekhemre clambered up onto a great slab of limestone that had fallen from the cliff and shattered into unusable fragments. He looked out over the hundreds of men gathered there.

"You all know that three of our number, Pen, Horem, and Ramose are trapped underground by a rock fall in the 'Glory of Geb' gallery. Many of you have been working to free them, and I know that all of you desire to see them once more in the light of day. I went to Inebu-hedj to ask permission for the quarry to shut down while we rescued our comrades, but I was refused."

The crowd groaned, and a few angry shouts started to stir unrest.

"The king is concerned that production continues unabated, and there is a way we can do that and still rescue our comrades. We have thirty teams of men. I intend to take one team and force a narrow passage through the rock to the 'Geb' workface. In order to keep up production, I ask the other teams to take over the work of the others. If we all work a little harder, for a little longer, we can maintain production as the king requires, and also rescue Pen, Horem and Ramose. I will compel no man to do this, but I ask you in the name of our comradeship. What do you say?"

The crowd murmured, the men fidgeting and looking at one another and then, first a few and then most raised a cheer. Late-comers were jeered at and bullied into joining in, until every man was yelling his agreement.

"Very well," Sekhemre said. "Back to work; we all have a lot to do."

He ordered his overseers to get their gangs back to work, but told Asen to take his team aside, as they would be the ones attempting the rescue. Going back to his office, he pulled out the overall plans of the quarry, noting where each level's galleries ran, and what thickness of rock was to be found between the galleries. After several minutes of searching, calculating, and informed guesswork, he decided upon a course of action.

"'Glory of Geb' is separated from the other galleries not only by depth, but also in direction. The nearest we can get is the 'Rising of Khepri' workface, and that is about eighty *mehi* away, as near as I can estimate. We will have to dig down at an angle and hope to intercept open space, if it is there."

"That is a lot of rock to remove, sir," Asen said. "Even with five men working on the face, it will take hours, possibly days. They could be dead by the time we get to them." He looked embarrassed. "Sorry, sir. I don't mean to sound as if I am complaining."

Sekhemre nodded. "I understand, but we are going to try something a little bit different. We will sink a narrow shaft, not much more than the space two men can work, one breaking the rock, the other gathering it into baskets hauled back on ropes. They work for no more than half an hour before being relieved, so they are always at maximum strength."

Asen nodded. "That could work, sir. There would be no need to take breaks for meals or at the end of the day." He did a few quick calculations. "Five men working in a team, two on the face, two hauling the baskets, and one carting it away. That gives us four teams with an opportunity of resting, maybe even sleeping, between shifts. How long altogether, do you think, sir?"

"Eighty *mehi*, each shift removing one is eighty shifts...forty hours. That might be too long. They have already been down there over a day." Sekhemre thought for a few moments. "We will make it a contest between the teams. The team that shifts the most rock will get a bonus."

Asen grinned. "Sounds good, sir. What is the bonus?"

"I don't know yet, but I promise you it will be worth their while."

They got to work. Sekhemre calculated the best place in the 'Khepri' gallery to start the descending shaft, while Asen organised four teams within his gang, trying to divide strength and agility fairly, so each team would have a fair chance at the bonus. They tossed marked stones for the order of starting and the first team hammered away at the rock with gusto, rapidly carving out a hole in the floor. The next team enlarged the diameter and dug deeper. Work slowed as the space became more confined, but by concentrating their efforts on the bottom of the hole, obvious progress was made with each shift. Men wanted to work longer than their shift, but the other teams clamoured for their turn, wanting to earn the bonus. Shift progress was measured by the number of baskets of rubble hauled up, and after each cycle of shifts, Sekhemre lowered a marked rope into the ever-deepening pit to measure the progress.

As the hours passed, progress slowed as it took longer for each team to change places at the work face. They worked in almost total darkness for a time, but after a few injuries from misplaced hammers and chisels, Sekhemre ordered niches carved every few feet to take a small oil lamp. Thereafter, injuries lessened, but the air grew progressively fouler. The men worked on, but Sekhemre was forced to shorten each shift as the men quickly became exhausted, many getting headaches.

"I will have to bring in more men," Sekhemre said. "Our strength is failing."

"Will you deny us a chance at the bonus?" one of the men asked boldly.

"Will you jeopardise the possibility of rescuing our comrades?" Sekhemre countered. "If they are still alive down there, they have been without water for nearly two days and their air must be getting foul. Bringing in fresh teams is their best chance."

The men grumbled, but allowed the decision was not theirs. "Do not dismiss us entirely, sir. We want to help bring our friends back from the brink of death...as well as earn a bonus."

Sekhemre sent Asen to the surface to bring back another four teams of strong young men. They would join the teams already at work, giving each man longer to recover from his shift. The scheme worked, the new teams doubling the rate at which they extended the tunnel, eager to catch up to their fellow diggers and earn the bonus. Asen's original teams, stung by the enthusiasm of the new teams, redoubled their efforts and, as the hours passed, the line let down into the shaft showed they were nearing the eighty *mehi* mark.

"Are we getting close?" Asen asked.

Sekhemre shook his head. "I think so, but I don't know. There is a bit of guesswork in all this."

"So it could be more than eighty *mehi*?"

"Yes...or less."

"What does that mean?"

"If I have miscalculated the direction, we could have tunnelled right past 'Glory of Geb' without knowing it."

"What can we do, sir?"

Sekhemre shook his head again without answering. An hour later, as one of the teams struggled wearily out of the shaft, he waved back the next one, entering the tunnel himself to have a look. He took Asen with him. The first twenty *mehi* were relatively easy going, the shaft being comfortably wide, but after that it narrowed, leading to cramped conditions at the bottom. Both men were breathing heavily by the time they reached the workface, not so much from exertion as from the foul air. The sputtering oil lamp shed very little light. Sekhemre shifted awkwardly, making room for Asen, touching the rock that enclosed them hardly more than a stretched arm away. He felt panic rising in him at the thought of being entombed in the rock, and he forced it away. It had been some time since he had felt those sensations-- back when he first went underground.

"Where do we go from here?" Sekhemre muttered. "I felt sure we were heading in the right direction, but we should have broken through by now."

"We could miss it by a hand span and never know it," Asen said.

"If we were that near, they would hear us digging and shout out, or tap on the walls or something."

"If they are still alive."

"I cannot just give up on them," Sekhemre said.

"Nobody would blame you if you did, sir," Asen said. "We all supported you wholeheartedly, and you have done everything you could."

"I suppose so. Go on up then, Asen. We will call it off."

Asen turned and grasped the rope attached to a wicker basket, starting to scramble up the steep slope. Sekhemre took hold of the rope, readying himself to follow, and then stopped.

"Are you coming?" Asen called down.

"Be quiet," Sekhemre called. He listened, but the faint noise he thought he had heard was not repeated. "I thought I heard something."

"What did you hear?"

"I don't know. It might have been nothing but a stray noise from above, rock settling...or my imagination."

Rock fragments showered down on Sekhemre as Asen scrambled down again and squeezed in alongside his Overseer. They both listened. All they could hear was their own breathing and an occasional rasp of their kilts on the rough rock as they shifted position.

"I don't..."

"Shh," Sekhemre whispered. "I heard it again...very faint."

On the heels of his whisper, a faint sound reached their ears, a tiny scrape of rock fainter than the sound of a pebble falling down the shaft.

"Did you...?"

"Yes."

"What direction?"

"There...I think." Asen pointed.

Sekhemre nodded. "It could be the men in the 'Glory of Geb' gallery."

"Or rock settling still after the cave-in."

"You may be right, but we cannot ignore it. Send the men down again, Asen. We are changing direction."

The men of the next team came down the shaft, and while it was cramped with Sekhemre there, he stayed to point them in the right direction before dragging himself up the slope. Shifts changed, and the new teams burrowed in the direction from which Sekhemre had thought the sounds came. As time passed, he started to doubt his decision.

"I have made a mistake," he told Asen. "They could be digging away from 'Geb'."

"Or you might be right," Asen said reassuringly. "We should know soon enough."

"How far does sound carry through rock?"

Asen shook his head. "I don't know."

The men worked with renewed vigour, feeling that they neared their goal. Each team jealously hoarded their baskets of rock chips, pouring them onto a great pile accumulating a hundred paces from the angled shaft. Then a shout came from the shaft. Sekhemre lay down and peered into the almost-darkness.

"What is it?" he called.

"A hole...a darkness beyond..." a voice called back, the syllables echoing off the tunnel walls, becoming all but unintelligible by the time they reached the listeners.

"I am coming down."

Sekhemre lowered himself into the shaft, his feet scrabbling for purchase as his arms clasping the rope took his weight. He descended rapidly, pushing his way between the labourers, and then advancing on hands and knees through the new tunnel. A miner, Semet, made way for him as he reached the end, and pointed to a hole the size of his fist in the far wall. Sekhemre stared at it for several moments and then, leaning close to the hole, called out a question.

"Hello. Is there anyone there?"

The hair on his head prickled as a low moan issued from the hole, a disembodied voice drifting from the outer darkness. Semet yelped with fear and tried to push back, but Sekhemre blocked his way.

"It's th...them," he stuttered. "We have found them. Quickly, enlarge that hole."

Encouraged by his Overseer, Semet picked up his chisel and mallet and attacked the edges of the hole, swiftly enlarging it until Sekhemre could push his head and shoulders through. He saw nothing, his body blocking even the faint light issuing from their oil lamp.

"Who is there?" he called.

There was no reply, but he could hear the faint sounds of dust and gravel falling in the darkness. Then a soft moan filled him with hope. Pulling back into the shaft, Sekhemre picked up the oil lamp and wriggled through into the dark cavern beyond, falling awkwardly onto limestone rubble. The lamp flickered, but he held onto it and it did not go out. He looked around at a tunnel filled with rocks and rubble as far as the faint light from his lamp would reach.

"Is anyone there?"

A rock fell with a dust-muffled thump off to his right. Bent double, and coughing from the dust in the air, Sekhemre shuffled toward the sound. As the light fell across a mound, it shifted and Sekhemre almost screamed. A figure...a dust-covered demon with gleaming eyes...rose up and stared at him. The apparition opened its mouth and croaked something formless before falling to its knees. Sekhemre forced himself forward and knelt beside the figure, brushing dust away from its face.

"Horem?" he asked. "Is it you? Where are the others?"

Sekhemre heard a sound behind him and saw Semet crawling through the hole with another lamp and a water skin. Taking the skin, he dribbled water into Horem's mouth. The boy gulped greedily, choking in his haste to drink his fill before it was removed.

"Where are the others?" Sekhemre asked again. "Are they alive?"

"Pen...over there..." the boy gestured weakly. "Ramose...dead."

Sekhemre found Pen lying near the rock fall, and the boy moaned when he turned him over. Water restored a little more life, but there was nothing to be done for Ramose. The man's feet protruded from the fallen rock blocking the gallery. Semet called for others to come down and help and it was less than an hour before both boys and the body of Ramose had been hauled up into the upper gallery.

Emerging into the daylight of the next day, every worker spontaneously downed tools and rushed over to welcome the boys back to life, while heaping praise on Sekhemre. He turned the praise aside, saying that every man there had contributed to the rescue--those who had continued their labour in the quarry to cover for their comrades as worthy of praise as those who had dug the shaft.

"I promised a bonus for the team that dug the most rock, and I stand by that. They will be rewarded, but so will everyone here, even if I have to pay you out of my own purse. Also, I will pay for the funeral of Ramose."

Sekhemre was concerned that there would be repercussions from disobeying the king's express orders, but Imhotep talked the king round, pointing out that the rescue of two small boys could be turned to his own advantage. Imhotep organised people in the street to cheer Sekhemkhet as if it had been his idea all along to rescue the trapped workers. Such was his ability that soon the king himself believed it, and the Tjaty had no difficulty in arranging handsome bonuses for the quarry workers, and a proper funeral for Ramose.

The people believed the king had been responsible, but the quarry workers knew it had been Sekhemre who looked out for them, and his estimation rose in their eyes.

Chapter 21

Nubsekhem was in love.

Despite being stationed at the military garrison of Hut-waret in the north-eastern part of the delta, far away from the larger centres of population, the place was not devoid of women. Men, wherever they are, seek out female companionship, and unmarried males with nothing to spend their pay on, attract women. A town grew up around the garrison, at first supplying only beer and a bit of entertainment, but then all the other professions of modern civilised life followed. Butchers, bakers, seamstresses, launderers, priests, scribes and armourers, pot-makers, weavers, perfumers, paper-makers, and a host of other professions saw a market opening up on the border of Kemet.

Women flocked to Hut-waret also, eager to earn a bit of copper from lustful men, either as musicians, dancers or acrobats, or following an older profession. Many of these women kept to their line of work, but some looked for a more settled life, with children. They married soldiers and started families.

One of the enlisted men, Ament, rose through the ranks to become a senior officer under first Khaba, and then Nubsekhem. He married a musician who was not averse to earning a little extra on her back, and had a daughter, Mennefer, who grew up tall and beautiful, attracting the attention of her father's commanding officer.

Nubsekhem was careful with whom he associated, having one eye fixed on the throne at all times. His emotions warred with his intellect, however, and he fell in love with Mennefer, lusting after her. Desire was completely separate from ambition, after all, and he thought he could satisfy both. He was certain that Ament would have no objection to the marriage of his daughter to his commanding officer, as that could only help to further Ament's own career.

He gave his children only passing consideration. Again, he was marrying Mennefer, not them. Huni was a grown man and Khakhet on the brink of manhood, and both would have households of their own soon enough. No, Nubsekhem was concerned only with his own desires. He had not looked seriously at another woman since the debacle with Ranefert, and he wanted a woman in his life. There had been others, of course, but they had been diversions, a method of stilling the lusts that rose in any healthy male body. Now nearing forty years of age, he desired a beautiful woman to manage his household and, if the gods were kind, be mother to more sons.

"A man cannot have too many sons," he told himself, "particularly if he looks to found a ruling dynasty."

That possibility intruded increasingly on his waking thoughts and even insinuated its way into his dreams. Wary of confiding in others, the only person he ever shared these thoughts with was his eldest son Huni, now twenty years old.

"Sekhemkhet's reign is proving futile. He can father only sickly children whereas I have two strong sons already. I am related to the royal family, and

I have a small but strong army loyal to my person. All I have to do is reach out and grasp the throne to make it mine."

"Yours, father? What of Khaba? He is the head of our family."

"He is old and cautious," Nubsekhem said. "I would like to do this in his name, elevating him to the throne, but I do not think he has the nerve."

"But you do," Huni stated.

"Yes, and you will be my heir. You will need to start your own family so that our line may continue."

"I could always marry Mennefer, daughter of Ament, I suppose. She is only three years younger than me." Huni grinned at his father's discomfiture. "I jest, father. She is a beautiful girl, but I have no interest in her, having my eyes set on another. If you marry her, I shall welcome her as my mother."

Nubsekhem grunted. "Who is this girl you like?"

Huni shrugged. "Actually, there is no particular girl, but if...when...you take the throne, I will have my pick of them, won't I?"

"So you have no objection to me marrying Mennefer?"

"None at all, father, though I am surprised you would not hold out for somebody of higher status. Someone at court, for instance. Forgive my plain speaking, but Ament is nobody, a mere officer under your command."

"I am aware of that, but when I become king I can marry whoever I want. In the meantime, my lust dictates I must seek out what is available."

"You do not love her?"

"Love?" Nubsekhem looked thoughtful. "I think I do, but then I thought I loved the daughter of the Tjaty. Look what love brought me there. No, I like her, I lust after her, and I will have children with her and...who knows? Maybe I will love her in time."

"Well, I wish you joy of her, father," Huni said. "Sincerely."

Huni left the company of his father a little amused by his revelations. He had not thought his father had a young man's juice in him still, or that he would let his member rule his reason. In his place, he would be very careful where he scattered his seed, picking out only the choicest fields. There were more important considerations than a woman's beauty or her willingness to open her legs. If his father ever succeeded in becoming king, then he, as heir, would follow him onto the throne, and Huni was determined to be a strong king, leaving behind a mighty dynasty. If his father did not succeed, then it was quite possible that he, Huni, would anyway.

One thing he was not going to reveal to his father was his choice as a wife. He had his eye on one particular young woman. She a few years older than him, but what did that matter? She would convey a degree of legitimacy to his eventual claim to the throne that not even a successful rebellion could convey. He had managed to keep his intentions from his father and grandfather, and only one other person in the world was aware of his plans.

"She is married," Merekhet said. "You cannot marry her now."

Merekhet was Huni's cousin, his mother Nefert being the sister of Huni's mother Merenebti. He was exactly the same age as his commander, but was of much lower rank, having joined the army later and lacking the connections that Huni enjoyed. For all their differences in background and rank, the two young men had become friends, and Merekhet was the only man Huni trusted enough to share his dreams.

"Where did you hear that?" Huni asked. "It cannot be true."

"I had it from a trader who got in from Inebu-hedj a few days ago. I am sorry to have to tell you she married the king."

Huni scowled. He did not delude himself that he loved the woman--she was a means to an end--but even that might have been snatched away from him.

"It does not matter," he said. "It is who she represents, and I do not need to have an heir with her. Some other woman will do for that."

"It is a pity, though," Merekhet said. "Meresankh was perfect, especially if you could have a son and heir with her. Marriage alone will suffice, I suppose."

Huni nodded. "When my father seizes the throne, he will hold it by the power of his army, and by right. We are descended from the father of a king of Kemet, after all. Then I will marry the only surviving child of another king, and no one can deny my legitimacy."

"And I, sir? What are your plans for your most loyal supporter?"

Huni laughed. "You need have no fear in that regard; I do not forget my friends. What do you want? Gold? Titles? Land?"

"Titles, as long as they are not empty titles, devoid of power. The other things will follow."

"What would you like to be, then? General of the Army?"

"How about your Tjaty?" Merekhet asked.

"You aim high, but yes, why not. Imhotep will be dismissed and I will need a loyal right hand to control the kingdoms."

Huni and Nubsekhem now continued their separate plans for taking the throne, as well as their combined plan. The Northern Army was now almost completely under their control, their scheme to replace officers loyal to the king with men loyal only to them nearing completion. It did not mean that they were ready to strike; only that they could if the opportunity presented itself.

"We could be waiting years for an opportunity," Huni said.

"Then we must create one ourselves."

"How?"

"I am feeding the king reports of unrest among the tribes near the copper and turquoise mines in Ta Mefkat," Nubsekhem said. "Those are of great value to the king. I hope to entice him into leading an expedition into the region. If we can isolate him, surround him with our own men, he might suffer an...uh...unfortunate accident."

"He will have his own guards with him," Huni said.

"How many depends on how secure he feels. He is scarcely going to raise more than a hundred men, while I have five times that number."

"When?" Huni asked.

"Soon. In the meantime, I have other things to attend to."

The marriage to Mennefer went ahead, as most people were in favour of the union. Her father, Ament, was pleased at the thought of being related by marriage to his commanding officer. He could see many advantages flowing from it. Khaba was less pleased when he first heard about it, believing his son was marrying beneath him, but he soon put those thoughts aside.

"It will settle him down," he confided in his estate manager.

What he could not divulge was Nubsekhem's ambitions to become king, and how the marriage might divert him from such a purpose.

Though Ament was pleased with the match, Mennefer had some reservations. She was reluctant to voice them in the face of her father's enthusiasm, and said nothing when the subject was first raised. After listening to him prattling on, envisioning his own rise within the army, she felt she had to say something.

"Is this marriage really necessary, father? You have risen through the ranks because of your own hard work and abilities; will you now take the easy way of advancement?"

Ament looked astonished. "Whatever do you mean? I have risen as far as I can reasonably go without preferment. I need an influential officer to raise me further, and this is the perfect solution. My commanding officer will become my son-in-law, and the way is then open for higher command."

Mennefer looked downcast. "Do I mean so little to you, father?"

"You mean everything to me, daughter. How can you think otherwise? I have secured you a marriage above our station in life, and your sons will be the sons of a General of Kemet. Their opportunities..."

"I know all this, father," Mennefer said, "but is there not another way? Must I offer up my virgin field to such a man?"

"What is wrong with General Nubsekhem?"

"He is old, father. Nearly forty. And I am but sixteen years old. I hoped for a husband who is closer to my own age so that we might rejoice in our youth."

"Youth is overrated," Ament said. "Particularly in men. You should have a man who is experienced as a lover, who can introduce you to the ways of marriage..."

"I am not completely without experience, father."

"Men have sown your field already?"

"No," Mennefer admitted, "Though I have had a lover. A young man, someone who loves me."

"Who is he?"

Mennefer shook her head. "I want to marry him."

"Who is he? Does he have wealth or position? Does he come from a good family?"

Mennefer hesitated before saying, "He is the son of an artisan. His father makes furniture."

"So he will inherit his father's business?"

"No, he is a younger son, but he can set up in business for himself."

"You would have me consign my only daughter to poverty all her life? I can see it now; you would have to hire yourself out as a servant just to bring in wages to sustain your family." Ament shook his head. "Not when I have the opportunity of ensuring she lives in comfort, with servants of her own."

"But I love him, father, and I do not love Nubsekhem."

"Nevertheless, you will marry him."

Mennefer burst into tears, knowing that this last line of defence had worked for her in the past. This time, however, Ament would not be swayed.

"In this you must listen to me, and obey me like a dutiful daughter. I have arranged a good marriage for you and I would be failing in my paternal duty if I gave in to you. General Nubsekhem will be a good husband, and together you will raise many healthy sons."

Nubsekhem married Mennefer, Ament conducting his daughter from his family accommodation in the town to the General's quarters. The marriage feast was lacking in luxuries but was a pleasant enough affair for everyone except the new wife. Townsfolk joined in the celebrations, not because they shared in the food and drink, but because what was good for the commanding officer of the Northern Army was generally good for everyone. The only person in town who wept was a certain young artisan's son.

Nubsekhem showed that despite his advancing years he was still a fit and virile man, vigorously sowing his seed that first night and for many thereafter. The gods evidently smiled upon them as shortly after, Mennefer's *hesmen* was interrupted, and she became pregnant.

Chapter 22

T he feuding between Khawy and Kagemni continued, with both of them now being employed as scribes on the Sekera site. Khawy, despite being the younger, had always believed himself superior to Kagemni at his father Den was Overseer of the King's Works at Sekera, but his self-importance grew with Den's adoption as the son of the Tjaty. He lorded it over the other young man who was, as he loudly told him at every opportunity, only the son of Hor, a minor scribe of Abdju.

"I have never pretended otherwise," Kagemni said mildly. "I am truly grateful to Overseer Den for giving me this opportunity..."

"You mean Overseer Den, son of Tjaty Imhotep and my father," Khawy sneered.

"Yes, that is exactly who I mean. Now, be a good fellow and fetch me the scrolls pertaining to beef production for the workers. They are in a bin in the next room."

"Fetch them yourself. I have other things to do."

"Must I remind you that I am senior scribe in these offices and you are a junior scribe, tasked with doing my bidding?"

Khawy muttered something under his breath, suggesting what Kagemni could do, and stormed out of the room. Nevertheless, he fetched the scrolls and threw them onto Kagemni's worktable, before stamping out again.

Kagemni sighed, noting that at least three of the scrolls had nothing to do with beef production, and he made a bet with himself (soon won) that not all of the ones he had asked for were there. For several minutes, he made notations on a tablet, lifting information from the available scrolls, but soon had to call out for another scribe to bring the missing ones. He finished his calculations, and turned to his next task, which was to work out how much extra pasture was needed to make up the shortfall in meat production. Letters would have to be written to governors of nearby *sepats*, to the priests of various temples owning lands and herds, and maybe even to the treasury who controlled the extensive herds of the king.

He did not enjoy the prospect, as though he had an excellent mind for figures and calculations, he always found difficulty in stringing phrases together. His letters came out stilted and awkward, and he suspected the scribes of the recipients laughed at him as they read out his efforts. What he really needed was a scribe who had a way with words, but he wished that Khawy was not the obvious choice. His cousin could compose beautifully crafted letters, but he knew he had a skill Kagemni lacked, and went out of his way to make life difficult for him. He thought about getting another scribe, but knew that if he was to be successful in getting the extra cattle, he would have to send perfect letters of appeal. That meant using Khawy. The only alternative was to ask Den for access to another skilled scribe, but he knew the answer to that already.

"I have placed Khawy under you so that he might learn, Kagemni. He is skilled in writing, and you are skilled in calculation. Find a way to work together so you can both benefit."

If Kagemni went to him again, he risked appearing incompetent, and that might mean dismissal. He would not risk that.

"Khawy, I want to thank you for bringing me the scrolls earlier. They were just what I needed for the calculations I had to make. However, I have need of you again, but this time for something much more important."

"I see," Khawy said, examining the ink smudges on his fingers. "I am to fetch and carry for you again, am I? It seems to me you need a common labourer, rather than the eldest son of Overseer Den."

"No, no. This is important. I need you to write a letter...several letters, in fact."

"Really? Here I was thinking you were a scribe, capable of writing whatever you wanted."

Kagemni bit back his irritation at Khawy's sarcasm. "We are both capable of writing, but I recognise that you have a superior ability when it comes to constructing persuasive letters. I need that talent of yours today."

Khawy smirked. "So I have something you need, do I? Well, well."

Kagemni tapped a scroll beside him. "I have made some notes about what I want to say, and there is a list of the governors, treasury officials and keepers of the temple funds..."

"I am rather busy at the moment," Khawy interrupted.

Kagemni held onto his growing anger. "Doing what?"

"Oh, this and that. Everybody seems to want me for something today. I might be able to get around to doing something for you tomorrow...or the next day."

"Your father placed you and I together," Kagemni pointed out. "This was so that we could complement each other, and so that you could learn from me."

"There is nothing I need to learn from you," Khawy said. He yawned ostentatiously. "In fact, it looks to be the other way round. Perhaps you need to go back to school to learn how to write properly."

"Must I report this conversation to your father? I do not imagine he will be too happy with your refusal..."

"When have I refused?" Khawy demanded. "All I have said is that I am very busy and it may be a day or two before I can fit you in."

"This is too important to wait. I need you today."

"The other people who need my help will not be happy if I put them off," Khawy said. "What am I to tell them?"

"I do not fornicating well care what you tell them," Kagemni snarled. With an effort, he regained control of his temper. "Perhaps you could explain to them that you work for me..."

"Work with you, you mean?"

Kagemni glared at his young cousin. "However you want to phrase it, your father put us together so that our skills would each help the other," he said patiently. "That is what I require of you now--your help. Do I have it, or must I go to your father?"

"Dear cousin, of course I will help you. You only have to ask."

"I already..." Kagemni clamped his jaws together and took a deep breath, letting it out slowly. "Here are my notes, and the list of recipients. Please construct the letters and have them ready to send by tomorrow."

Khawy smiled and took the scroll, leaving the room. Kagemni leaned back and closed his eyes, wishing that Den had never paired him with his eldest son. Not for the first time, he wished that Khawy could be more like his younger brother Khepankh. Mind you, he thought, Khepankh is not as accomplished a scribe. He started daydreaming about the perfect assistant-- a man with Khawy's skills but Khepankh's demeanour--and from there his mind drifted toward other members of Den's family.

"What do I do about Merit?" he murmured to himself. "She will be beautiful one day, but she is just a child, barely twelve years old."

Her age was the problem, he knew. While girls in Kemet sometimes married when they were that age, it was not something Kagemni wanted. He wanted a companion as well as a mate, someone he could share his life with, someone to come home to at the end of the day and talk to. Merit might grow into such a young woman, but not for years yet.

"I must strike a balance between encouragement and dismissal," he told himself. "I do not want to hurt her, but neither do I want to lead her on."

It was very difficult, and he wondered whether he should have a quiet word with Den. He might be able to gently break it to the girl that her attentions, while flattering, were not appropriate. The trouble with talking to her father was that Kagemni did not want to exclude himself later on. In another three years, Merit would be of marriageable age, and Kagemni was aware that a union with Den's family would stand him in good stead. Being married to a beautiful young girl who adored him would be a bonus.

"What to do? What to do?"

He looked at the position of the patch of sunlight streaming through the window of his office and knew that the noon hour approached. Scratching his head, he wondered whether he should absent himself from work for a time. Merit might call him to a meal at Den's residence, or possibly be bringing him a meal, wrapped up in cloth. If he was there when she came, he would have to talk to her, whereas if he was absent, maybe she would just go away or leave the meal and go.

"I suppose I could go down to the docks on some pretext or other," he muttered, before he slapped the table in frustration. "Why am I being driven away by this girl? Am I afraid of her? Afraid of what I might say to her?"

Kagemni decided he would stay where he was, meet Merit when she arrived, and gently turn aside her obvious adulation for him. He would be polite, and loving, but also firm. Nodding, he smiled to himself.

"What are you smiling about, dear Kagemni?" Merit spoke from the doorway where she stood watching him.

"What? Oh...er...nothing. I did not see you there, Merit. Have you come to call me to the midday meal?"

"Khawy is there today, but father is not, so my brother will be especially annoying," Merit said, easing into the room. "I thought you might like to eat here instead." She held up a wicker basket packed with items wrapped in clean linen.

"That is kind of you, Merit. Thank you. I am a little busy, though, so if you could just leave it, I will eat it later. I do not want to keep you from your own meal."

Merit pouted and put the basket on his worktable. "I brought food and drink for both of us," she said. "We could go outside and sit under a tree. There is a nice breeze."

Kagemni started to grimace, but turned it into a smile. "I really do have to work."

"You could take a few minutes off, couldn't you?" she wheedled. "You have to eat something. Look, I will unpack the basket and prepare something for you, so you do not have to stop your work."

Kagemni sighed as Merit started to lay food and drink out on the table, and he hastily moved a few scraps of paper filled with his calculations. She set out bread, roast goose, chopped vegetables, fruit, and a few small pottery jars filled with delicious looking pastes.

"I got cook to give me some of the plain sesame paste and some of the spicy ones too. And this..."

With a broad smile, she took out a small closely-woven basket covered in wax and broke the covering with her finger. Deep golden honey welled out. Merit put her finger in her mouth and sucked.

"Ish lub-be," she mumbled around her finger. Licking the last of the honey off, she handed the small basket to Kagemni.

He dabbed a small amount of the honey onto a finger and licked it. "Very nice."

"Come then," Merit said, unpacking the last of the meal. "What would you like to drink? I have beer and water...a little wine, too, that I filched from father's store."

"I have to work this afternoon," Kagemni said. "Water will be fine. It should be all you have too," he added as Merit reached for the jug of beer. "You are too young to be drinking beer when you have water."

"Pooh. I am old enough to drink beer. Father lets me..."

"Never while I have been around," Kagemni said. "And without his express permission, you will have water." He took the beer from Merit and put it back in the basket.

Merit scowled for a moment, but then said, "If you say so, dear Kagemni. I would do anything you say."

"Eat your food then."

Merit did as she was told, though she only picked at her food, watching Kagemni. "It is true," she murmured. "I really would do anything you wanted."

"Now that is...ah...silly. Would you jump in the river with your best clothes on if I told you to?"

"Yes."

"There might be crocodiles in the river. They like plump little girls."

"I am not plump," Merit retorted. She thought for a moment, before saying, "You would not tell me to jump in the river if there were any crocodiles around."

"I might not know there were."

"Well, I don't believe you would do such a thing anyway. You lo...like me too much."

"I do like you better than Khawy," Kagemni said with a smile.

"I hope you like me a lot more than that." Merit hesitated and looked away. "I love you."

Now Kagemni hesitated, wondering what words to choose that would enlighten her but not hurt her unduly. "You are too young to be talking about love," he said. "You should be playing with other children, with your toys. You will be a woman soon enough, with womanly cares, without wanting to rush into the responsibilities of adulthood."

Merit went pale, and her eyes opened wide. "I am not a child," she whispered. "How dare you say so?"

Kagemni cursed under his breath, seeking a way to mitigate his bluntness. "Merit, all I meant is that you are on...on the cusp of womanhood and that you should not rush into adult life. Just let things happen naturally and in a few years you will fall in love with a boy your own age..."

"I do not want a boy my own age. They are stupid. I want a man who is worldly and wise, like you. Why can't you see that I am a woman already?"

"Yes, you are a woman...a young woman...but at twelve you are too young to be in love. You do not know what being in love means."

"I know what a man and woman do together when they are in love," Merit said, blushing deeply.

"If a man really loves a woman, he will not want anything for her that will harm her," Kagemni said carefully. "That would include letting her get involved in a relationship before she was ready for it. And if a woman truly loves a man, she will recognise his care for her, and not insist on something that will make him feel uncomfortable."

Merit frowned, trying to make sense of Kagemni's words. There was a word he had used and she brightened as she latched onto it.

"You do not want this because it will harm me?" she asked.

Kagemni looked relieved. "Yes, that is it exactly."

"Then that must mean you love me. By your own words, your actions are those of a man who loves me."

"I...I like you," Kagemni temporised. "A friend also wants what is best for another."

Merit smiled. "You say 'like', but I think you mean 'love'. It is all right, dear Kagemni, now that I know; I will not make you do anything you do not want to. I shall wait patiently until I am what? Fourteen?"

Kagemni grimaced. "Sixteen, at least."

Merit shrugged. "It will be a waste of my youth, but all right, sixteen it is."

"If you find a boy more to your liking in the meantime, I will release you from that promise."

"You are sweet to say so, but it will not be necessary, dear Kagemni. I will not change my mind."

Merit gathered up the remains of the meal and packed up the basket before smiling at Kagemni. "I will leave you to your work then, my betrothed." She turned and almost danced out of the door.

When he was sure she had gone, Kagemni cursed loudly and colourfully. After a while, he calmed down and debated whether there was some action he should take. He considered going to Den and revealing Merit's infatuation with him, but dismissed this on two grounds. The first was that it might embarrass, even mortify, a young girl to have her desires made public, and Kagemni did not want that for her. He could imagine the scorn that would pour from the lips of Khawy, for instance. The other reason was more personal. If Den thought that the proximity of Merit to Kagemni might lead to improprieties, he might dismiss his scribe. After all, he could not very well dismiss his own daughter. That was to be avoided if possible, as he valued his job as his uncle's scribe.

One of the problems, as he saw it, was that of secrecy. He wondered if he could just ignore the young girl's delusions, carrying on as if nothing had happened. Young girls were not good at keeping secrets though, particularly if the secret conveyed some perceived advantage or status. It was likely that Merit would blurt out her secret and then would people believe it was just a young girl's fancy, or would they suspect him of impropriety with his employer's daughter?

He supposed he should talk to someone, get their advice, but he could not think of any sensible adult he could trust. Den was an obvious choice, but he had already rejected him. His father was another, but he knew Hor would have little sympathy and was more likely to seek to turn the knowledge to his advantage. None of the other scribes were entirely trustworthy, he thought, and that put him in mind of Rahotep, the Tjaty's son, who had been in charge at Sekera before Den. He shuddered at the thought of entrusting him with the secret.

Sekhemre then? He was always a decent enough fellow...but I do not know him well enough.

Kagemni cudgelled his mind for an answer, and eventually thought of one person who might be trusted to do the right thing. The problem still remained as to whether the person would keep a secret.

"What choice do I have?" he groaned. "I either do nothing and hope for the best, or reveal my problem and risk everything."

Kagemni went to see Ranefert, the wife of Den, and step-mother to Merit.

"My lady, I turn to you as someone who might understand my problem, and will perhaps have the means to remedy it."

"This is not something my husband can help you with?" Ranefert asked.

Kagemni hesitated. "Possibly, my lady, but I fear he might be too close to the problem to help me."

"You intrigue me, Kagemni. Speak then."

"My lady, Merit, the daughter of Den has become infatuated with me, declaring her love at every opportunity."

Ranefert smiled. "Such infatuation is commonplace among young girls. They feel womanhood pressing in upon them and seek a means of expressing it. Her interest will pass quickly, I am sure."

"I pray that might be so, my lady, but she has displayed her interest for some time, though only today has she spoken of love and of considering herself betrothed."

Ranefert looked at the young scribe sharply. "Have you encouraged her in any way? Speak plainly and honestly."

"My lady, all I have ever done is treat her with respect and politeness, trying not to belittle her in her delusions."

"That was probably enough to encourage her. She will have interpreted your respect as interest."

"How do I make her see that it is inappropriate for us to be together?"

Ranefert considered Kagemni's request. "I will speak to her, but answer me this first."

Kagemni waited, but Ranefert just looked at him intently. He became uncomfortable under her stare. "My lady? You had a question?"

"I want an honest answer, Kagemni."

"Of course, my lady."

"Do you have an interest in Merit as a woman?"

"She is only a young girl," Kagemni protested.

"That is not what I asked. I am aware of her age, but if she was sixteen years old, would you consider her as a match?"

"My lady...she is not...if she was older, I would see her differently, I suppose."

"So your objection to her attentions has more to do with your age difference than a dislike of her as a person?"

"Merit is a lovely young girl, my lady. The man she marries will be very lucky."

"Do you want that man to be you?"

"My lady..." Kagemni flushed and looked down at the floor, not knowing what to say.

"I have embarrassed you," Ranefert said with a smile. "That was not my intention."

"I...I do not want to be thought of as a man who would take advantage of an infatuated young girl, my lady."

"You are seven years older than Merit. That is a lot now, but not so much later. If you asked for her in marriage when she was sixteen, I would argue in your favour, Kagemni. My husband speaks well of you, and I believe you would be a good husband for Merit--should you desire her then, and she desire you, of course."

"I am not sure..."

"Good. I would not like to think you were a man who already desired marriage to a twelve year old girl. Return to your work and think no more of Merit. I will speak to her and make sure she does not pester you. We will leave this until she turns sixteen."

Ranefert talked to Merit, finding out the depth of her feelings for Kagemni, and spoke at length about the proper behaviour for a girl of her age. She also impressed on her the effect her words and actions had on a young man who, whatever his feelings for her, was too decent and upright to take advantage of her. Merit was upset and embarrassed, but saw the sense of her step-mother's words, albeit reluctantly, and agreed to be more circumspect in expressing her affection for the young man.

"Treat him as a brother," was Ranefert's advice.

Chapter 23

Overseer Den was aware of tensions within his family; putting those down to normal disagreements and rivalries between his children. He had suffered under such tensions himself, growing up with an elder brother who went out of his way to elevate his own worth at the expense of his brother.

"It is natural that Khawy should resent the presence of Kagemni," he told himself. "His position as eldest has been snatched from him, but he will learn to work with his cousin."

Disturbances among his younger children did not enter his thoughts at all. If they had, he would likely have dismissed them as passing fancies. In his view, such things were the province of his wife, while his was the oversight and management of the king's works in Sekera. Overall, he was content with the progress of the *mer* and its associated underground tombs.

Initially, he had wondered whether delaying the construction of the great limestone edifice was a mistake. The king demanded progress, and although such progress was being made, it was not immediately visible, which led to visits and complaints to the Tjaty.

"I have every confidence in you," Imhotep told Den after an angry diatribe by the king. "It is just that the king wants to see that his gold is actually achieving something."

"You know these things take time," Den said testily. "Has he inspected the underground galleries? Of course not. If he had he would not complain about a lack of progress."

"Careful, Den. Do not let your frustration lead you into making injudicious comments. I understand and can forgive, but others might report your words to the king, to your detriment."

Den grimaced, but nodded his acknowledgement. "It has only been five years since we started this, and the building is almost exactly where I thought it might be at this time."

"The king looks at his father's *mer* rising above its great enclosure and desires his to look greater immediately," Imhotep said. "He is not a builder and does not understand what is involved."

"You must make him understand."

Imhotep smiled wryly. "One does not 'make' the king do anything. I can apprise him of the progress and tell him that everything is on schedule, but he may not believe me."

"Perhaps you could persuade him to come and view the underground facilities."

"I can do that," Imhotep said, "but I don't think he will be impressed by dimly lit passages and unadorned rooms. Can you do something a little more spectacular? Something above ground, like the *mer* itself. Could you raise up the second level?"

"I am still stabilising the first layer," Den retorted. He grimaced as he considered the problems involved in pushing ahead with a construction that needed careful planning. "I could do something, I suppose," he conceded. "Give me a month, and then bring the king round to view it."

"You can do something that quickly?"

"With the understanding that it will have form but little content," Den said. "He will see a second layer, but it will not be as stable as I would like. Creating this sham will set the whole construction back."

"That is disappointing," Imhotep said. "However, it is a small price to pay if it keeps the king content."

Closer to a month and a half passed before Den sent word that the site was ready for an inspection by the king. In the meantime, he had stripped men from the underground galleries and burial chamber, putting them to work on the more visible *mer*. Although the first layer was not yet complete, Den brought up thousands of casing stones from Troyu that had arrived over the last few years and stored nearby. He ordered the masons to roughly shape them and put them in place on three sides of the edifice, while he kept the fourth side bare so the internal stones of the second layer could be raised up. Here, he had to use a subterfuge, a move designed to deceive the king. It was a risky manoeuvre, but a necessary one if he was to convince the king that progress was further advanced than it was.

Casing stones were raised to the second level and fitted in place on the edges, resting against a thin layer of inner stones. Across the fourth side, Den had a wall built that matched the unadorned first level, giving the impression of a solid construction but was, in reality, little more than a shell. If it could have been seen from above--a gods' eye view--it would have looked like an enclosure wall without a centre. As long as the king did not insist on climbing up to look for himself, the illusion could be maintained.

Hor-Sekhemkhet arrived on his ship and was received with all the pomp Imhotep could muster at Sekera. After ritual greetings and cleansings by the priests of Inpu, Horu, and Re, the dignitaries who had accompanied him from Inebu-hedj formed up around the king and they set out for the building site. The ascending road led past the *mer* and enclosure of King Netjerikhet, and Sekhemkhet scowled as the gleaming edifice came in sight. Imhotep saw the look on the king's face, and sought to lighten the dark thoughts enclosed therein.

"As wonderful as your father's tomb is, my lord, yours will be still more magnificent."

"Yes, but how long is it going to take? I am losing patience."

"Your father's City of the Dead took twenty years to build, but yours will take less than that. It has only been five years since we started, and already it shows the magnificence to come." Imhotep hoped that was true--that Den had achieved enough in the month and a half to placate the king. If not, he did not doubt that they would both feel his displeasure.

The road from the river port debouched only the upper plateau where a vast area had been cleared for the building. Sekhemkhet stopped and looked past the great piles of cut stone, the workers' village, and the lines of labourers passing back and forth on various tasks, to the shell of his City of the Dead. The enclosure wall was only partly completed, rising only six *mehi* at the most, but as Den had planned, its very lack of height accentuated the *mer* that lay beyond it. As intended, the gleaming white casing stones from Troyu soared above the incomplete wall, rising up in two clear levels and holding the promise of greater heights.

Den approached the royal party and abased himself, bowing low and bidding the king welcome. The king could scarcely drag his gaze away from the tomb, so Imhotep stepped in, accepting the welcome in the king's name and bidding the Overseer stand beside them.

"How long before it is finished?" Sekhemkhet asked.

"That is hard to say, my lord," Imhotep temporised. "There are several imponderables that lend uncertainty."

"Such as?"

"I do not want to bore you with the details, my lord, but gold lies at the bottom of every calculation. We must feed and house the labour force, keep them healthy, cut stone in truly prodigious quantities, transport it to Sekera, and build the several parts of your City of the Dead."

"My treasury is being drained already," the king complained. "Now you want more?"

"It all depends on what you want, my lord. If you are content with a tomb that is no greater or even less then your father's, then the savings would be substantial."

"No. I will have a tomb that is greater than that of my father."

"Then you must be prepared to pay for it, my lord. Kemet has never before seen such structures built. We had to build up a dedicated work force from almost nothing in your father's day, but we have been able to use those things to greater effect for you."

The king grunted. "Very well, I understand what you are saying. Show me in detail what my gold is buying me."

Imhotep and Den led the way, a small troupe of overseers and masons following in their footsteps, ready to answer questions if needed. They toured the quarries on the plateau that supplied the core material for the *mer*, and the bulk of the enclosure walls and buildings. It was of obviously poorer quality, but that did not stop the king from complaining once more.

"Why are you not using this rock for the whole *mer* instead of bringing so much in from Troyu and further afield? That would be an enormous saving."

"Indeed it would, my lord," Imhotep said. "It all depends on what you want." He pointed up at the white casing stones. "White limestone comes from Troyu, whereas the limestone of Sekera is brownish. We could build your entire *mer* of local rock, but it would not be nearly as magnificent."

"White is nice," Sekhemkhet conceded, "but gold is gold. I think a *mer* made of local rock would still look good."

"Perhaps my lord king would like to see for himself?" Den asked.

"What do you mean?"

"The two layers of your *mer* are only encased in Troyu limestone on three sides, my lord king. We left the fourth side unadorned, so that we could haul stones up to the higher levels without damaging the casing. If you view the *mer* from that side, you can see what the finished structure would look like."

"Show me."

Den led the king's party round to the western side, where the view was very different. The plain, roughly-hewn stones of local limestone presented a sturdy but unprepossessing appearance, and Sekhemkhet stared up at it for several minutes.

"This is not how I imagined my tomb to look." The king looked troubled. "This is what the *mer* looks like inside? The stones are uncarved and look unfinished."

"There is no need for them to look any different," Imhotep said. "When it is finished, no one will be able to see the core, only the outer casing stones. Even your *ka*, my lord, will only use the passages and rooms created for it below the structure, and will care nothing for the actual structure."

"It disturbs me that perfection is limited to the outside," Sekhemkhet said. "For something as important as my tomb, the inside should be perfect too."

"Imagine the cost, my lord, both in time and gold."

"I am starting to think I must spend more to make my tomb perfect."

"My lord king, might venture a thought?" Den asked. The king looked askance at the Overseer, but Imhotep nodded. "The gods themselves created mankind, of which you are the most perfect example. Yet...and forgive my presumption, my lord...that which lies inside of you, within your intestines, and the organs of your body are...well...not imperfect, though they are messy and...and at times even noisome."

The king was frowning, and Den trembled, regretting his attempt at an analogy.

Imhotep stroked his chin thoughtfully. "I think I see what Overseer Den means, my lord. Your insides, while admirable, do not reflect the perfection of your exterior. The gods have created you with everything you need to function properly. You have lungs with which to breathe, intestines with which to digest your food, bones to hold your body erect, and a member to create new life. The inner parts are not much to look at but they support and sustain the outer body. In the same way, the inner structure of the *mer* may be plain, but it is sturdy and functions to support and sustain the beauty that will be your finished City of the Dead."

Sekhemkhet considered the words of his Tjaty and his Overseer. "I do not like to contemplate the inner workings of my body," he said, "but I see what you mean. We will leave the core of the *mer* as it is."

The king went on to inspect the underground workings, but the air was hot, dusty and full of that which made him short of breath, so he cut short his inspection and went to have a look at the workshop of Bastmose, where the rock carver was creating the king's stone sarcophagus. Bastmose was quite overcome by the presence of so many important people, but with Den keeping close and supporting him, he managed to show the king the beautiful thing he was creating.

"I am intrigued," Sekhemkhet said. "You are hollowing out the block from one end, rather than from the top, as if you mean to stand it on end when it is ready. Do you imagine I will be laid in my tomb standing up?"

"N...n...no, my lord k...king."

Sekhemkhet ran his hands over the stone, remarking on the translucent nature of the stone. "It is almost as if I can see through it."

His royal musings gave Bastmose time to recover his nerve and, with Den's assistance, was able to answer the king's questions without stuttering hopelessly.

"The beauty of the stone is such that I want to keep it as thin as possible, my lord king. This presents me with a problem. A lid of the necessary dimensions would be too thin to be structurally sound, so I am trying something else. The opening will be at one end, with a small sheet of rock that slides into place and can be mortared shut."

"Innovative," the king murmured. He strolled away, the rest of his entourage following him.

Bastmose looked at Den. "So what does that mean? Does he like it?"

"How could he not?"

"I am to continue with it?"

"Of course."

The rest of the inspection went well. Sekhemkhet looked at everything connected with his City of the Dead, and of the construction site. He appeared to like what he saw, and expressed his contentment with all the arrangements.

"Except one," Sekhemkhet murmured when they stood on the dock, just prior to stepping aboard the ship that would take them back to Inebu-hedj. "The sarcophagus disturbs me."

"What aspect of it upsets you, my lord?" Imhotep said.

"It is a beautiful stone, but..." Sekhemkhet frowned, trying to grasp the words that would explain what he meant. "An ala-Bast sarcophagus is suitable for my queen, but not for me. I desire a sarcophagus that reflects my strength and power. I want one made out of granite."

"Then a granite one is what you shall have, my lord," Imhotep said. He turned to the Overseer as the king stepped aboard his ship. "See to it, Den," he said.

Den felt like weeping at the wasted time and effort spent in carving out what was an extraordinary sarcophagus, but knew it was useless to argue against the king's decision.

"What shall I do with the ala-Bast one, sir?"

"Have Bastmose continue with it. It would be criminal to waste such a thing of beauty. It is as the king said; eminently suitable for his queen."

"And the granite one?"

"I thought you had one being produced in Abu," Imhotep said. "Wasn't there one being made originally for the king?"

"That is so, and perhaps the old rock cutter Aha has continued with it. It was never an urgent work though, so I do not know how much progress he will have made."

Imhotep thought for a moment. "I think you should go down and oversee the preparation of the sarcophagus in Abu. You have somebody competent you can leave in charge in Sekera, or should I appoint someone?"

"I can leave Kagemni in charge, sir."

"Do so then."

Den made the arrangements for the building site, knowing he would likely be absent for at least a month, maybe even two. Ranefert would look after the family and Kagemni the actual building site.

"Things should run smoothly," Den told his nephew. "You are young, but competent, and I think you will benefit from the added responsibility. If you come across anything you cannot handle, ask Tjaty Imhotep for assistance."

"Will you also be informing Khawy that I have been left in charge?" Kagemni asked carefully. It was a delicate matter implying that the Overseer's son was the person most likely to cause trouble in his absence.

"I am aware of your disagreements," Den said. "You do not need to worry as I am taking Khawy with me. He can experience a wider knowledge of my work by accompanying me to the quarries in Abu."

Kagemni was pleased that he was going to be left in charge, and even more so that he would not have to put up with a troublesome youth while doing so. "I hope you have a pleasant voyage, Overseer Den," he said.

Khawy, despite his age and inexperience, was disgusted at first that his father had not put him in charge of Sekera.

"It is Kagemni, isn't it? He has maligned me and made you think the worst of me."

Den had to patiently explain to his son that Kagemni was old enough and skilled enough to take over during his absence, and that his cousin had never said anything to make him doubt Khawy's worth.

"You will be coming with me to Abu as my personal assistant," Den said. "I will be too busy to do my own writing, so you will be my scribe."

Khawy was pleased with what he saw as a promotion, and made sure that everyone, particularly Kagemni, was aware that he was now personal assistant to the Overseer of the King's Works.

"I want to go too," Khepankh said. "I am thirteen and my tutor says I am skilled as a scribe."

"My tutor says," Khawy sneered. "You are a child if that is all you can say. My father says I am a scribe, so there."

"He is my father too," Khepankh said. "Tell him, father. I can come too, can't I?"

"I want to go as well," Merit said. "There is no reason a girl can't go."

Den groaned and waited until the tears and recriminations died down. "Merit stays, but Khepankh can go," he said. "This is not a pleasure trip. I only want people with me who can work as scribes..."

"I can write," Merit wept.

"I need you at home," Ranefert said. "I will need help with the babies."

Den felt bad about leaving his wife with the younger children. As well as Merit, there was Khamose, now ten, Khasenet, now six, the twins Neferka and Senefer, now four. Ranefert would, of course, have the household servants to help her, but it was still a long time to leave her and the children behind in Sekera. She said she did not mind, but he was leaving her with five children, not all of them hers.

Den sent word by a swift boat to Nebra and Aha in the southern city, warning of his arrival, and intimating that he hoped to see progress had been made on the original granite sarcophagus. Then he boarded a merchant ship bound for Abu, together with his older sons. At first Khawy was full of his own importance, strutting in front of the ship's crew and telling everyone that his father was Overseer of the King's Works and that he was his personal assistant. The crew had to listen to his boasting, and did so without comment, treating the boy with polite disdain. Their reaction was very different to Khepankh. He was on a great adventure and was determined to make the most of it, asking questions and listening avidly to the answers. They welcomed him, went out of their way to show him things, and the cook brought him little titbits, delicacies that they did not share with his brother.

Den watched how his sons behaved, and was amused at Khawy's pretentions. In his view, the boy was correct to regard himself as superior to the common labourers who made up the crew, but recognised that he needed to learn a lesson in managing those under him. Khepankh, on the other hand, had the common touch, being at one with the crewmembers, but he thought his younger son would have problems if he ever had to order them around.

"By all means be just and honest in your dealings with those beneath you," Den told them, "but always be aware that your status is far above theirs."

"It doesn't seem fair," Khepankh said. "They are nice people."

"I don't dispute that," Den said. "What I do take exception to is treating them as your equals. They know their place in society, but if you give them ideas above their station, they will not thank you for it."

Khepankh frowned at this idea. "Why not? Doesn't everyone want to be happy?"

"Happiness has got nothing to do with it. Look, Khepankh, my father was a scribe and I am a scribe..."

"You are an overseer...in fact, the Overseer of Sekera."

"But I am still a scribe, and now you and your brother are scribes as well. Now, imagine that you get friendly with an oarsman, happy and content with being one, but because of your friendship, he gets the idea that he wants to be a scribe. Can your oarsman friend ever aspire to become a scribe?"

"I suppose he could..."

"How? Does he know how to read and write?"

"He could learn," Khepankh said.

"How would he learn? No one will teach him, and even if he could find someone, it would take years. Look how long it has taken you to train and you have not finished yet. You were able to learn because you were exposed to reading and writing from childhood, with a good tutor to train you, and because you lived in my house. Your oarsman--how is he going to support himself and his family, if he has one, for the years it will take to learn scribing? The answer is, he cannot. Therefore, it is cruel to make him think he can better himself. Society has a place for him--a valued place. We need oarsmen trained to their duty from boyhood, just as society needs trained scribes like you and your brother. Do you understand?"

"I...I think so," Khepankh said.

"Think upon it," Den said, "and you will see I am right."

The voyage continued its slow progress upriver, and Den delighted in showing his sons the wonders of the southern kingdom of Kemet. Green pastures and farmland contrasted strongly with the yellows, browns and reds of the desert, the barren lands pressing close in places or being thrust back by the burgeoning life supported by the wide waters of the river. The river itself teemed with life, from shoals of silvery fish racing to escape the shadow of the ship, to the splash of crocodiles slipping into the water at their approach. Waterbirds thronged the edges, dabbling in the shallows or stalking on long legs to hunt down a frog or small fish. Where the river formed shallow lagoons covered with waterlilies and hemmed about with reed beds, herds of *pehe-mau* wallowed, snorting at the ship's proximity.

The boys thrilled to the approach of game animals where the desert and scrub crept close to the water, with antelope and wild goats drifting through the stunted woodland. Once, as the ship emerged from the lea of an island, they saw two lionesses crouched at the edge of the river, lapping the water. They looked up as the ship came in sight, but they evidently saw no harm in it as they merely watched it out of sight. Khawy had a bow that he sometimes used to hunt ducks, and begged to be allowed on shore to hunt the lionesses, but Den refused.

"Are we royalty to be allowed to hunt lions?" he asked. "Observe and learn. That is your prime function as an aspiring scribe."

Khepankh stared avidly at everything they passed, asking questions of his father or the crewmembers. He identified the gods of Kemet in every creature, greeting him or her by name, much to the amusement of his brother.

"You don't seriously imagine that hawk up there is really the god Horu, do you? Or that crocodile is Sobek? What about the last crocodile we saw, was that Sobek too?"

"Maybe not the god himself, but a representation of him," Khepankh said defensively.

Out of the hearing of Khawy, the ship's captain, Ansep, encouraged Khepankh in his beliefs. "The realm of the gods and the realm of man are separate, but intertwined, young sir, coming together only in the person of the king, who is both of the gods and of men. You are right to respect the hawk, the crocodile, and the lion...even the fish in the river...as manifestations of the gods' presence. They are all around us, sustaining this land of ours, so you believe in them and do not let anyone mock your beliefs."

Khepankh was grateful for Ansep's support, but also confused when he asked the captain how he knew so much about the gods.

"I was a priest once," Ansep said. "Hardly more than an acolyte in a temple of Horu, but I learned something of the nature of the gods."

"But...but if you were a priest, how is it you are...you are only..."

"Only a ship's captain?" Ansep said smiling. "My father was a fisherman, but he had me placed in a temple as thanks for the gods saving his life. I did not enjoy the life, longing for the freedom of the river, so when my father died, I left the priesthood."

"So it is possible to change ones station in life?" Khepankh asked.

"Despite what your father believes, yes." Ansep glanced to where Den was sitting. "I could not help overhearing...it is a small ship. He is right generally, but occasionally a man...or woman...may alter their fate. If the gods allow it, of course."

There was more to see on the banks of the river than the natural world. Towns and villages dotted the shores, each with patches of farmland where peasants toiled, but there were also painted temples, often on a promontory or clifftop. Den would sometimes order the ship to put in, and he would take his sons to see the abodes of the gods. After the stone wonders of

Sekera, the temples were unprepossessing, being simple structures of mud brick, of woven reed panels and timber. They were painted in gaudy colours, however, and banners flew from tall masts, flapping in the breeze.

"They are nothing," Khawy said. "Hovels rather than temples."

"Do you think you could do better?" Den asked.

"I will ask the king to put me in charge of temples, and I will build them in stone instead of mud brick."

"Then you will make a name for yourself, my son."

"I think they are nice as they are," Khepankh ventured. "Homely, rather than grand."

"They are supposed to be grand," Khawy sneered. "These are the homes of the gods, not peasants."

"Even so, when I enter this temple I feel as if I could see the god, talk to him, and if I listened really hard, maybe even hear him. I don't think I could do that in a large, stone building."

"Perhaps there is room for both in Kemet," Den said diplomatically. "Grand places of worship and smaller places where men can feel close to the gods."

At last, they came in sight of the grey, rounded boulders that gave Abu its name, and Ansep guided his ship into the town's dock. Den and his sons immediately disembarked and made their way to the granite quarry. Here he found Nebra at work, supervising the extraction of slabs of the close-grained rock, both large blocks for building purposes and smaller blocks that would be worked into bowls, jars, and statues. He greeted the master mason warmly and introduced his sons.

"How is work progressing on the king's granite sarcophagus?" Den asked.

"So he is going ahead with it then?" Nebra replied. "I heard that he wanted one made of ala-Bast."

Den stared. "Where did you hear that?"

Nebra shrugged. "People talk. Masons all through the kingdoms exchange news and useful information. I heard that Bastmose was making an ala-Bast sarcophagus for the king. Is it true?"

"True enough," Den said. "However, he has changed his mind and wants a granite one after all. That is why I am here."

"Well, are far as I know it is still in production. I do not see Aha very often. He stays in his workshop in the city and I am out here in my quarry. The only time I see him is when I am delivering more raw chunks of granite, and that is not every month."

"All right, I will go and see him," Den said.

Aha's workshop was noisy. He had several apprentices and assistants, and he stalked through the yard, peering at the work on benches or on the ground, making criticisms or offering advice. When Den and his sons walked in, he frowned, and came over slowly.

"Let me guess, you want the granite sarcophagus," he said.

"Indeed I do. Is it ready?"

"Nowhere near ready. Don't tell me the king is dead or sick and needs it now."

"The king is in good health," Den said reassuringly, "but he desires to know how his sarcophagus is shaping up."

"I suppose you had better come and see then." Aha led Den to the back of his courtyard where a section had been cordoned off with wicker screens. Behind the screens, the huge slab of granite lay on the ground with windrows of dust and stone chips heaped about.

"It looks smaller than I remember," Den said.

"You have a good eye and an excellent memory," Aha said with a tinge of surprise. "We had to slice off the top to make the lid. It is over there." He pointed negligently to the back of the screened area. "We will work on that after we complete the main vessel."

Den and the boys looked inside the main block and saw that it had been excavated unevenly to a depth of between one and two *mehi*, the bottom of the basin still littered with tiny fragments and granite dust.

"How is the stone dug out?" Khawy asked. "I thought granite was much harder than copper."

"So it is, young sir," Aha said. "There is no tool hard enough to chip away at it, so we use rounded rocks of a harder rock. Here..." The stone carver picked up a diorite boulder, hefted it in one hand, and gave it to Khawy. "Pounding away at granite with this will reduce the granite to powder. It is a long and laborious process, but it works...ah, young sir, please do not do that."

Khawy had banged the diorite boulder against the outside of the block, and a faint smudge of powdered rock was visible. The boy shrugged and handed the boulder to his brother. Khepankh gave it back to Aha after examining it for a moment.

"There is a lot more to be done," Den observed.

Aha nodded. "There is no pressing need for it, though, is there?"

"I am sure the king will live for many years yet," Den said, "but it is good to have these things nearly completed in case of accident or illness." He made the sign of the Eye of Horu to ward off bad luck.

"I shall keep men working on it then," Aha said. "However, there is the...ah...small matter of payment. The gold you left before is nearly spent and..."

"I understand. I shall leave you a draft payable by the Abu treasury for another sum of gold. That should be all you need, but if not, send word to the Tjaty's office and they will send someone to examine your claim."

Aha frowned at the implied threat and hurried to assure Den that more gold would probably not be needed.

"I cannot foresee everything, though, my lord. If I discover a crack in the lower part of the block, we might have to start again."

Den stared coldly at the stone carver. "Do your very best to not discover anything that might jeopardise the successful completion of the king's sarcophagus. It would be a pity if some other master carver was given the responsibility of creating the king's resting place."

"It will be done as you wish, my lord," Aha hurried to assure Den. "It will be done swiftly and surely, and you will have no cause for complaint."

Khepankh left the carver's workshop with his mind full of thoughts of working with stone, and the varied techniques of wresting useful and beautiful objects from the raw materials of the ground.

Khawy left with excitement at the open display of power his father had wrought over lesser men like Aha. He vowed to himself that one day, he too would hold that power over other men.

Chapter 24

General Nubsekhem sent word to King Hor-Sekhemkhet that tribes in the vicinity of the turquoise mines of Ta Mefkat had rebelled and were endangering production of the precious stone and the equally important copper ore.

"I can take men there myself," Nubsekhem said in his report. "I will smite the enemy most savagely and earn myself much fame and prestige as a warrior. I require only your permission to lead men to certain victory and earn myself a name."

As Nubsekhem anticipated, Sekhemkhet sent word that he would come north and lead the men of the Northern Army himself. The general grinned when the letter was put in his hand, and showed it to his son Huni.

"What did I tell you? He cannot bear for anyone else to earn glory."

Huni read the letter and nodded. "What if he brings his own men?"

"It will not matter. How many trained men can he possibly raise quickly? Two hundred? I have twice that ready to go. We will isolate him and destroy him, making it look like he died in war. Then I will take over."

Huni went off to select the men needed for the expedition, readying everything for the expected arrival of the king within ten days. Hardly had he gathered the men together than news came from the north of an insurrection by men of Kanaan.

"What is all this, and who authorised it?" Nubsekhem demanded. "We already have our proposed excuse to lure the king here. We do not need another one."

"It seems to be genuine, father," Huni said. "The northern tribes really have rebelled, unlike the ones in Ta Mefkat."

Nubsekhem cursed, knowing action would have to be taken against the rebels, but hoping he could put that off until he had killed Sekhemkhet. The king, however, arrived the next day at the head of a hundred men, and immediately called the commanders into a meeting.

"It seems we must fight two enemies at once," the king said. "The rebellion in Kanaan must be put down with all speed if we are to avoid it spreading to other tribes. On the other hand, we cannot countenance a loss of production from the mines of Ta Mefkat."

"May I suggest you ensure the safety of the mines, my lord," Nubsekhem said. "My son, Commander Huni, will accompany you with two hundred of the Hut-waret garrison. At the same time, I will lead two hundred more to Kanaan. In that way, both problems can be dealt with at once."

Sekhemkhet stared at his general. "That is ill thought out," he said. "I have enough men with me to stamp out the tribes threatening the mines. More men will be needed to crush the men of Kanaan, so you will take four hundred men north, General Nubsekhem, while Commander Huni remains in Hut-waret to guard the approaches to Kemet."

Nubsekhem and Huni tried to get the king to change his mind, but Sekhemkhet has fixed on a plan of his own devising and was not to be swayed from it.

"So what are we to do?" Huni asked his father. "Our whole plan revolves around getting the king isolated and overwhelming him with our own men."

"Curse those Kanaanites. If it were not for their rebellion, everything would have worked well. He only brought a hundred men with him."

"Yes, but will a hundred men be enough for him to liberate the mines?"

Nubsekhem stared at his son. "The mines are not under threat. That was a ruse, remember?"

"Ah...er, yes. So what do we do?"

Nubsekhem thought for a few minutes. "The only other choice we have is to fall on his men here in Hut-waret, killing him openly. It is not what I want, but I think we have to do it."

Huni looked confused. "I...I thought that is what you did want, father..."

"Not openly, you fool," Nubsekhem snarled. "I want to kill him in such a way as to look blameless. I want men to look at me and say that I am the logical choice to succeed him, not that I have seized the throne by force." He shook his head. "Now I am forced to do it this way."

"Then let us raise the troops and do it, father. Action is better than words."

They were too late. Sekhemkhet took his hundred loyal men and marched out of Hut-waret that very day, heading southeast toward Ta Mefkat and the supposed threatened mines. There was nothing that Nubsekhem could do but his duty. He marched out of Hut-waret the same day at the head of four hundred men to put down the revolt in Kanaan, which he proceeded to do with great savagery. As far as he was concerned, it was the fault of the tribes that he had not been able to initiate the coup against the king. They would pay for that, he vowed, and dealt death and destruction on the villages along the border.

Not all of the tribes had taken part in the revolt, and they sent envoys to Nubsekhem, pleading their innocence and begging for mercy. Nubsekhem responded by lopping their heads off and sending the decapitated bodies back to their villages. Despite the warning, he had no intention of letting them learn by it, arriving with his soldiers only hours later. Every man, woman and child was put to death, crops were destroyed, and livestock and huts burnt.

People fled from Nubsekhem's fury, leaving behind deserted villages. He raged up and down the frontier, laying waste to the land and leaving it a smoking ruin. As the corpses mounted his rage slowly dissipated, and he realised that taking his anger out on the tribes was ultimately futile. He turned for home.

Huni had stayed behind in Hut-waret with a hundred men to guard the border town. He sat and fumed for a day, angry that he and his father had not reacted more quickly, killing the king before he could leave the city.

"Perhaps it is not too late," he told himself. "I have as many men as he does, and if I surprised them I could overwhelm them. What a wonderful gift that would be for my father."

Shouting for his officers, he had them marshal the troops, selecting only those whose loyalty to his father was assured. He led them out on the road to the Ta Mefkat mines at a fast pace, knowing that he had to overhaul the king's men as quickly as possible. It was a long way to the mines, but a well-constructed road carried ore to the smelters in Kemet, and Huni's men ran at a pace that ate up the distance. Passing around the northern end of the Long Sea, they entered the dry lands on the eastern shore, where tall craggy mountains rose up to block their way. The road hugged the coast, the sun reflecting brilliantly off the water, and Huni wondered how he was going to engineer a surprise attack on Sekhemkhet and his men in such a limiting landscape.

The road left the coast, heading inland through narrow valleys between towering peaks, the way twisting and turning, and Huni knew the king could be very close. Huni sent scouts forward to find out how far ahead the king was, but after the first day, the scouts did not return. He sent more out to find what had happened to them, but scarcely had they run ahead than he rounded a bend in the road and found the king arrayed in battle order facing them.

Flustered, Huni halted his force and drew them up facing the king's men, but he hesitated to take further action. The two armies were evenly matched, but he had lost the element of surprise. While he debated what to do, King Sekhemkhet walked out into the space between the two armies and loudly demanded that Commander Huni advance and attend upon his king. He did so, hesitantly, stopping a few paces from his king. Without thinking about it, he bowed respectfully.

"What in Seth's name are you doing following me, Commander Huni?" the king asked. "I was astounded to learn you sent scouts to spy on me. I captured them and forced the truth out of them."

"N...not spies, my lord."

"They admitted it, so I had them executed. As for you, your orders were to remain in Hut-waret. I want to know why you have disobeyed me."

Huni did not answer at once, weighing up his options. He wondered if he could still take the king. His men were loyal to Nubsekhem, but he was not sure how they would react when his father was absent and facing the king so directly. It was one thing to fall upon a band of soldiers unawares, but quite another to face them in a set battle.

"Well? What have you to say?" Sekhemkhet demanded. "Has General Nubsekhem even gone to Kanaan?"

"He...he has, m...my lord," Huni stuttered.

"Thank the gods someone has remembered their duty. Why are you here instead of at your post in Hut-waret?"

"I...I thought th...that you might need reinforcements, my lord."

Sekhemkhet stared. "I am quite capable of sending for reinforcements if I need them. By your foolish action, you have left Hut-waret and north-eastern Kemet undefended, and that is criminal. You will turn your men around and return to your post at once. I will deal with you when I have restored order in Ta Mefkat."

Huni, intimidated by his king's anger, did as he was told, turning his men around and marching them back the way they had come. He walked well ahead of his men, not wanting them to see the tears of chagrin that stained his face. Now he would have to face his father, not with the gift of the king's death, as he had hoped, but in the knowledge that he had precipitated a crisis, bringing the king's anger down on their family.

"You fool!" Nubsekhem snapped when he returned from his punitive expedition in Kanaan. He listened to his son's excuses impatiently, and then told him to be silent while he considered how he might extricate them from this disaster.

"The only thing that might save us is that the king considers you incompetent rather than dangerous," Nubsekhem said. "If he suspected you of treachery, he would have had you executed on the spot."

"I had the same number of men," Huni muttered. "I could have taken him...I should have."

"Thank the gods you did not. If you had tried, you would be dead. That is why I wanted at least a two to one numerical superiority and the advantage of surprise. Do not underestimate Sekhemkhet or the devotion of his men."

Nubsekhem thought some more. "You have brought the issue to the front, but perhaps we can make something of it. The king suspects you are incompetent, so if the gods are with us, he will return to Hut-waret with the intention of berating me and dismissing you. Instead, we can turn events around and do what must be done." He nodded slowly. "Unexpectedly, you have perhaps brought about the very thing we wanted."

Sekhemkhet spent no time thinking about Huni's actions or the possible reasons behind them. He had rebellious tribes to quell and mines to make safe, so he pushed his men on with all speed toward the small forts guarding the copper ore and turquoise upon which Kemet relied. Their approach had been noted and the commandant of the main fort, Horhotep, came out to greet his king.

"How is it that you cannot manage this region with the men you have?" the king wanted to know. "You have an interchange of guards with Hut-waret."

"My lord king, it has been over a year since we were properly resupplied by Hut-waret. We get some supplies, but for every three men we send back to Kemet, only two return. The few men they do send us are of poor quality, untrained. The only good thing that can be said about them is that they are loyal to their king."

"It seems I have more than one thing to discuss with General Nubsekhem," the king mused. "Very well, Commander Horhotep, I am here with a hundred men. Let us join forces and rid this area of these troublesome tribesmen."

Horhotep gathered together a hundred men, stripping the forts of every able-bodied man and, together with the king, they moved on the main turquoise mine at a place called Hetaw Mefkat, or the Terraces of Turquoise. Here, the extensive excavations gave the appearance of a valley pock-marked with caves, and the tribesmen often descended unseen on the workers, killing several and disrupting the mining process. The local garrisons had done their best to defend the mines, but they were not up to the task. Now, however, Sekhemkhet inspired the soldiers to greater efforts, tracking down the raiders and setting ambushes. Over a period of a month, the king's men killed over fifty tribesmen for the loss of seven soldiers, and captured the main chieftain and a score of his men. This man the king put to death in front of his men; a symbolic death in which the king grasped the hair of the bound and kneeling captive and dashed his brains out with a club.

"So die all the enemies of Kemet," Sekhemkhet declared. He ignored the blood of his enemy that spattered his body and clothing.

Having punished the guilty, Sekhemkhet decided to show mercy to the remnants of the tribe. He nominated a new chief, and then proceeded to take hostages, sending several young sons of the most prominent tribesmen back to Kemet to be educated. Sending for masons, the king had his victory inscribed on smooth rocks at the site, showing him in the red crown and the white crown, so that men would know he was a king of a unified Kemet. When all was ready, he departed the region, having already made offerings at the rock inscriptions left behind by his father Netjerikhet, and Sanakht, both kings having stamped their marks on the land years before.

The king took a different route home, striking through the mountains to the Long Sea and emerged at a fishing village. Here, he rested his men before tackling the long road home along the shore of the sea, and while he was there, a trading ship from far-off Bharat put in to the village. Sekhemkhet took an immediate interest in the crew and entertained the captain of the ship, though the fare he offered was not of high quality.

"I hope you will forgive my lack of hospitality," Sekhemkhet said. "I have been campaigning in the hinterland, and we only have military supplies on hand."

The ship's captain, a dark-skinned man with long, lustrous black hair and a neatly trimmed beard, inclined his head graciously before answering.

"Hospitality is from the heart, King of Kemet. A sparse table is a feast when freely offered. I am honoured by your gift."

"Where are you from and how are you addressed?"

"I am Arjun, styled a lord in my own land of Bharat, far to the south and east of here. I am a merchant, dealing in whatever precious items may be found in these lands. Pearls can be harvested from islands south of here, and I have heard there is a blue-green stone mined here. We call it *perozah*. Perhaps you know of it, lord king?"

"If your stone is what I think it is, then yes, we mine it hereabouts. But what is 'Pearl'?"

Arjun delved into his purse and brought out a rounded object as big as the end joint of his thumb. He held it between thumb and forefinger. "This is a pearl. One of the biggest I have ever found."

Sekhemkhet leaned forward, staring at the nacreous, iridescent lustre of the pearl, greatly desiring such a beautiful object.

Arjun smiled, seeing the greed in the king's eyes. "Perhaps we can trade pearls for *perozah*, lord king?"

Sekhemkhet nodded, his eyes fixed on the pearl.

"Then perhaps you will accept this pearl as a gift, lord king. A token of friendship between us."

"Gladly," the king declared. "You will need to talk to my Tjaty about the details of trade, but I can assure you that if you can offer pearls like this, then the terms will be most profitable to you."

The conversation passed on to other matters, each man describing their own culture and beliefs for the other, exclaiming as they came across similarities and marvelling at differences. Sekhemkhet was interested in Arjun's sea-going ship and the fact that they sailed out of sight of land.

"We sail on our broad river that connects north and south, and sometimes venture along the coast of the Great Sea in the north, though never out of sight of the friendly shores."

"I wondered why you laboriously transported your copper around the sea by donkey rather than taking a direct route across the water," Arjun commented.

"You have visited the far shores? What did you find there?"

"Fishing villages for the most part," Arjun replied. "If my reckoning is right, though, your river valley must lie just beyond the western mountains. I am surprised nobody has made their way across."

"Perhaps because it is easier to sail than to climb the mountains. It makes me wonder, though, whether we could take our copper ore from our mines, across this sea and land it in Kemet directly. If there is a way through the mountains."

"If there was such a direct route, lord king, I could supply ships that would carry all the copper you need."

"How long would it take?"

"That would be hard to answer without knowing land distances, but the sea crossing would take only a day or two."

"And I have the resources to build a proper road over the mountains," Sekhemkhet said, excitement creeping into his voice. He got up and looked outside at Arjun's ship, trying to estimate its capacity. "How many in your crew?"

"Forty," Arjun said. "We have sails as well as oars. I have larger ships too, up to a crew of a hundred."

"Could you take me and my men over the sea?"

"How many men?"

"I have a hundred with me."

Arjun shook his head. "Even packing them in, no more than fifty. My ship is a trading vessel, with room for cargo, but not for people."

"Then take me and twenty of my soldiers. I will pay you well for the passage, and we would be examining the feasibility of making this a regular route."

Arjun frowned. "You are not concerned that you would be at my mercy once we are at sea?"

Sekhemkhet looked at Arjun intently for a minute and then relaxed. "No."

"Then I welcome you aboard my ship as my honoured guest, lord king," Arjun said.

Arjun set sail with Sekhemkhet and twenty well-armed soldiers on board his ship. The other soldiers would be under the command of a junior officer and would take the long, dusty road back to Kemet. It was a novel experience for the king to be aboard a ship on water that was choppy, the motion making him feel queasy. Some of his men suffered more, and Arjun's sailors laughed as several men turned pale, dropped their weapons and ran for the side, heaving out the contents of their stomachs.

"The motion affects some men that way," Arjun said. "You are unaffected, lord king?"

Sekhemkhet swallowed, feeling sweat break out on his brow, but he refused to reveal his feelings to the captain or crew. "The ship moves in strange ways," he admitted, "but I am well."

The king turned and looked back to the Ta Mefkat shore, receding quickly as the wind filled their sails, wishing that he could just order the ship back and have done with this terrible feeling. Instead, he took several deep breaths of air and tried to look nonchalant.

"Is it always this rough?"

Arjun grinned, but quickly hid it. "I regret, lord king, that this is a calm day. Perhaps the gods know that you are aboard and have stilled the waves on your account."

The voyage across the north-western arm of the Long Sea to the main fishing village took almost three days, and Sekhemkhet managed to control his rebellious stomach for that length of time. By doing so, he earned the admiration of his soldiers, and the respect of Arjun and his crew. He even managed to walk down the gangplank without disgracing himself, but as soon as he was in private, vomited. After a wash and a sleep, partaking of a little food, he was ready for the next step of his journey.

Sekhemkhet was gratified to learn that the locals knew of a track over the hills that would bring them to the river somewhere to the north of the Waset trading post. Arjun left him then, promising to return to the fishing village in six months' time. At that time, he would sit down with the king's representative and work out a mutually advantageous trade deal.

The king and his men set out across the western hills with a guide, and ten days later arrived at the lush lands bordering the Great River. Commandeering several small boats, Sekhemkhet reached Inebu-hedj, where he spoke at length with Imhotep, laying out his plans. A road would be built over the hills and the villages at either end of the trail expanded to cope with the new trade. Imhotep was to ready himself to go to the Long Sea when Arjun returned, and work out a trade treaty with the man from Bharat.

"Pearls, if you can, but copper is more important," the king said. "Payment in whatever he wants. He has indicated an interest in turquoise, but all men want gold. He might like other trade goods like hides, wool, grain or statuary. I will leave it up to you."

"Where will you smelt the copper ore?" Imhotep asked. "It does not seem worthwhile taking it all the way north to the existing smelters."

"Build new ones near the village, then only the metal ingots need to be transported."

"In that case, why not build the smelters on the other side, in Ta Mefkat? Then the trader need carry only copper metal. That would be much more efficient."

"Look into it," Sekhemkhet instructed.

With everything that occupied his mind, Sekhemkhet entirely forgot about Huni and when he did at last remember, he dismissed the commander's disobedience and potential treason as excessive devotion to duty, and did not follow up further. He was to regret that oversight.

Chapter 25

Nubsekhem waited for the king to arrive in Hut-waret, readying his men to strike against him. Every man in his little army was personally vetted by his loyal officers, and each man swore again his oath of loyalty to Nubsekhem. Huni sent out scouts to find the king and give warning of his approach, but they were a long time returning, and the report they gave was perplexing.

"Sir, the king's army approaches, but the king is not with them."

Nubsekhem did not know what to make of this, but he did not have long to wait. Eighty men under the command of a junior officer called Absekh arrived at Hut-waret.

"Where is the king?" Nubsekhem demanded.

"He has returned to Kemet by a different path, sir," Absekh said. He went on to describe how a foreign ship had taken the king and twenty of his soldiers out into the Long Sea, leaving Absekh to bring the other men back by the usual path.

"The king was taken against his will?"

"No, sir. He went willingly. It is said that the ship represented a more direct route to Inebu-hedj. If that is correct, he might be there already."

Nubsekhem dismissed the officer and his men, before expressing his concern to his son.

"Are we discovered?" he asked. "Is this the reason he did not return to Hut-waret?"

"You think the king knows of our plans?" Huni asked worriedly.

"Why else would he bypass Hut-waret? He may, even now, be gathering an army to march against us."

"Then we prepare for battle," Huni declared.

"Only if we want to die," Nubsekhem said. "He knows our strength and you can be sure he is raising an army capable of overwhelming us. No, we cannot fight him." The general paced the floor, his brow knitted in concentration. "There is no choice but to flee Kemet. We must gather our wealth and loyal followers and seek refuge in one of the northern cities-- Kebny or Surru perhaps."

Huni looked aghast. "Father, those cities are uncivilised and not worthy of our sojourn there. Surely we have other options?"

"We cannot succeed against Sekhemkhet if he is forewarned. He will raise a large army in the south."

"Let me at least send out scouts to find out his strength," Huni pleaded.

"Very well, send out men swiftly," Nubsekhem said. "In the meantime, we must prepare for flight, but be circumspect. If we reveal our danger before we are ready, many of our men will desert."

So Huni sent scouts south to find out how preparations progressed in Inebu-hedj, and spies to find out what plans were being discussed in the king's councils. The men took fast fishing boats upriver, landing in the capital city and surrounding lands to look for signs of military build-up, but found nothing. One spy even penetrated the palace, speaking to an officer of medium rank, but could find no evidence of anything out of the ordinary. They returned to Hut-waret and made their reports.

"The king has not gathered an army, sir. He is more concerned with building a road connecting the river with a fishing village on the Long Sea for the purpose of trade."

"Can this be true?" Nubsekhem asked his son when he brought him the reports of his spies and scouts. "Sekhemkhet must surely be planning some action against you."

"If he is, then it must be a secret," Huni mused. "I expected a squad of soldiers with orders to arrest me, at the very least. Instead, he seems to have forgotten or dismissed my actions."

"If he has forgotten, then when will he remember?"

Nubsekhem put his plans for flight on hold, but still sent out screens of scouts to warn of any movement of soldiers north against them. In his mind, it was not a matter of if, but of when the king would move against them. He recognised, though, that the situation could not continue.

"If the king will not move against us, then we must move against him," he told Huni.

"You think we should openly rise up against the king?"

"It will be better than just waiting for the blow to fall. We must take the initiative."

"That could be the king's plan," Huni countered. "If we move against him openly, then we become rebels and he can raise up the kingdoms against us. We cannot prevail against everyone."

"Then we must fall back on my previous plan," Nubsekhem said. "I know you do not like it, but we are no longer in a position to be as honourable as we might want."

"Poison? You are right father; I cannot countenance such methods."

"You will limit the weapons at our disposal?"

"It is not honourable."

"That is your final word?"

Huni frowned. "What do you mean by that, father? You know my position on poison. I am not going to change it."

"Then, in the interests of our family, I must curtail your actions. I deeply regret having to do so, but you leave me no choice."

"What?"

"I must have the freedom to act without your open disapproval, and possibly acting against me. You will be confined to your quarters until I have succeeded."

"Or failed utterly, plunging our family into disgrace and death," Huni said bitterly.

"Try to be a little more supportive, my son," Nubsekhem said. "You will benefit from my actions too, becoming king after me."

Nubsekhem called loyal officers to him and had them confine his son to his quarters. They were to afford him every luxury due to his rank, but he was not allowed liberty or to communicate with anyone. Huni remonstrated without effect, but submitted. As soon as he was safely incarcerated, Nubsekhem sent for Sumer, his master of spies, and set in motion his plan to clear the way to the throne.

Sumer was a foreigner, and when he first entered service with Nubsekhem, had long hair in ringlets, and a bushy beard oily with perfumes. Despite his appearance, the man had a cold heart and enjoyed the presence of death. Nubsekhem knew that Sumer's appearance limited his use, so prevailed upon him to change, shaving his hair and dressing as befitted a Kemetu gentleman. Now, he could wander among the populace of any Kemetu city without exciting curiosity. He retained his delight in dealing death, however, and that attribute made him useful.

"I want you to kill several people," Nubsekhem said.

"Thank you, master."

"It will be difficult and dangerous."

"That will add spice then," Sumer commented. "My knife has been dry too long."

"Not your knife; you must use poison."

Sumer grimaced. "Poison is for women, master. A man kills with the blade."

"Not in this case. A few drops in food or drink will kill slowly. The poison mimics a natural illness and it is imperative those who survive think that a sickness has claimed them. Do you understand, Sumer?"

The spy shrugged. "As my master wishes. Who am I to kill?"

"The king and his two sons by his wives. He has other sons by palace women, but they can safely be ignored. Kill the children first, then the king."

"If the opportunity presents itself to kill the king first, should I take it?"

"No. If the king dies, security will tighten around his heirs. Kill them first."

Sumer grinned. "Consider them dead, master."

The master spy made his way down to Inebu-hedj, posing as the agent for a seller of fine linens. Within his baggage were samples of cloth, and a small, tightly stoppered jar. Upon arriving in the city, he hired a room above a moderately classed tavern. He had to pretend a status that would grant him access to the palace, but not so high that he would attract attention. Sumer had acted this role before and was confident he would be able to move around without attracting suspicion.

There was no hurry. Nubsekhem had impressed on him the need for results rather than speed, so Sumer took his time setting up his antecedents in the city before moving on to the palace. By the time he introduced himself to the chamberlains in charge of linen, their queries about him produced only good reports. He spent several pleasant hours in the company of one or other palace officials, plying them with wine bought by his master's gold, and listening to gossip. Information was essential to a successful outcome, so Sumer spent time and gold finding it.

The two legitimate sons of the king, Hor-Re and Hor-Nubkhet, were both to be found in the wing of the palace known as the Women's Quarters, but in suites at opposite ends. It appeared there was some enmity between the mothers of the children. Djeser-Ti was the senior wife, having married Sekhemkhet before he had been king, and Tetimene, a Wawat woman more recently taken as wife. Sumer listened avidly to the gossip; he might be able to exploit the loathing these women felt for each other.

Back in his lodgings in the city, Sumer found a stray dog of similar weight to a small child and, by offering it food, enticed it out of the city, finding a secluded spot near the river. He knew that he would have little opportunity to correct mistakes when he set about assassinating the children, so he needed to know how much poison to administer. Tying it to a tree with a length of rope, he took a cut of meat from a butcher and fed small scraps to the dog until it overcame its innate suspicion and readily ate what he gave it. It even deigned to wag its tail at finding such a generous master. He then measured out a small amount of the poison and rubbed it into cuts in the meat before tossing it onto the ground. The dog fell upon it with gusto, swiftly disposing of it. Then, seeing no more meat being proffered, it curled up in the shade and went to sleep. Sumer sat down nearby and watched the dog, interested to see what effect the poison would have. He did not have to wait long.

The dog woke and moaned, moving restlessly, biting at its stomach. It whined, looking reproachfully at Sumer before suddenly squatting and voiding its bowels. Sumer saw blood in the watery mess. The dog howled, its lean body racked by convulsions, vomiting blood. It staggered the length of the rope in one direction and then the other, whining and moaning, before collapsing. Sumer continued watching, but the end came swiftly now, the dog passing into unconsciousness and after a little while it heaved its flanks once and died.

"Nasty," Sumer murmured, but he smiled with satisfaction. Rather than pick up the dog with its hair matted with vomit and faeces, he cut the rope and dragged the body to the water's edge, leaving it in the shallows for the crocodiles. He returned to the city, satisfied that the poison would work swiftly and decisively.

Now, he faced the problem of introducing it into the food or drink of the young boys. An added problem was the timing. If one boy fell ill and poison was suspected, security on the other would tighten, so there had to be a way of introducing it to both at the same time. Sumer thought about the problem and also considered the possibility of other deaths.

"Rather than try to kill just the boys, should I spread my net wider?" he asked himself. "Poison introduced into a common dish may kill many people, and also obscure the intended target. It might also be easier to deliver the poison."

Poisoning a common dish would call for more poison though; probably more than he had at his disposal, so that would not work. The act would have to be specific or close to it. He needed some food or drink that was certain to be fed to the princes. Drawing up a list of foods that were available, Sumer studied them, hoping for some insight. He found it...or thought he did. Small boys liked sweet things, and honey was much sought after. If he could introduce poison into honeycomb, he could deliver that to the palace and be reasonably sure of it being directed in the princes' direction. Unless servants got greedy, of course. Then they might eat some and get ill before it got near the intended victims.

Sumer grimaced. The poisoning was not going to be as easy as he hoped. It was time for a change of course. He would have to find a way of gaining access to the inner workings of the palace and introduce the poison in a more direct fashion. The first thing he did was make friends with servants in the palace. He had already made himself known to higher officials, chamberlains and other overseers, as an agent for a purveyor of fine linens; now he broadened that to include the lower echelons of servants, male and female, by befriending them in the city taverns. One particular servant became a strong possibility as she served in the dining area in the Women's Quarters, where the children ate. The servant's name was Neferit, and the dark stranger with a generous nature piqued her interest.

Sumer plied her with wine, bought her small gifts of jewellery, and praised her beauty though she was not as beautiful as her name suggested. It was not long before she rewarded his efforts, and after that it was easy to gain access to the inner palace. She took him into the rooms being prepared for royal meals and let him examine the furnishings and the tableware before other servants brought in the food.

"I would love to see the whole meal laid out," Sumer murmured, nibbling on Neferit's earlobe that night as they lay together. "It must be an amazing sight."

"Not really," she replied. "It is only food. The dishes and jars are of a quality not seen in other houses; that is why I brought you to see them."

"I am glad you did, my love, for I have never seen dishes like them. I would think the food would be of a higher quality too."

Conversation ceased as hands and lips explored each other's body, and it was several minutes before they lay back panting, their bodies glistening with sweat.

"I could show you, I suppose," Neferit murmured. "Just a quick look between the food being laid out and the families coming in to eat."

"I will be able to tell my friends in the north that I have actually seen the table set for the king's family," Sumer said. "Tell me, though, what are their favourite dishes?"

Neferit laughed. "That depends on who is here. The wives seldom attend, preferring to eat with the king or by themselves. When they do, Djeser-Ti prefers goose, whereas Tetimene likes her beef. As for the nurses..."

"The princes attend though, don't they?"

"Usually. Sometimes they eat with their mothers alone or with the king, but they are here most days."

"And what do they like to eat most of all?"

"Sweet things," Neferit said. "Milk with an egg beaten in and sweetened with honey most of all. Of course, that is only made up just before they eat, in case they are not going to be here."

Sumer realised that he could not just poison the honey or the milk beforehand, but would need to insert it after it was served. That might be difficult. "Tomorrow?" he asked.

"If I can," she said, reaching for him again.

The next day, as the noon hour approached, Neferit and Sumer entered the Women's Quarters and made their way to the dining area. Servants were just finishing the last touches to the table, and one or two looked up as they entered. They were used to seeing Neferit and Sumer together, so paid no special attention, adjusting the arrangements one last time before withdrawing.

"Look," Neferit said. "They have set out the princes' favourite cups, so that means they must be dining here today."

"When does the food and drink arrive?"

"Just before the women and children. Ah, here comes the first of them."

A line of servants entered the room, each bearing a plate or a bowl, and set them on the table while an overseer ordered their arrangement. Sumer, watching from the edge of the room, saw a servant place a jar of milk on the table, near the cups of the boys.

"Is that the milk for the princes?" he asked.

"Yes. We have to go now."

"One moment." Sumer stayed where he was as the servants withdrew, resisting Neferit pulling on his arm. When the last of them left, he walked quickly to the table. "Watch the door," he told Neferit.

"Why?"

"Just do it."

"They will be here any moment. We should not be here."

"Watch the door."

As soon as Neferit looked toward the door, he removed the tightly-stoppered flask from his clothing, took the plug out and poured a measure of the yellowish liquid into the milk, hesitated, and slopped more in, stirring it with a knife. The metal clinked gently against the pottery. He put the stopper back in the flask and looked up; saw Neferit staring at him.

"What are you doing?"

"I told you to watch the door."

"What is that?"

"This? Nothing."

Sumer tucked the flask away as he came round the table, a fierce expression on his face. Neferit shrank back, her eyes wide.

"Sumer...what..."

He could hear footsteps outside the room, so he quickly grasped Neferit as she drew in a breath to cry out, held her firmly and jerked her head to one side. The sound of her neck breaking was loud in the quiet room. She collapsed in his arms, and as the first women entered the room, Sumer held Neferit, gently cradling her, and moved aside.

"She fainted," he explained as the women stared. "I will take her to her room."

"Who are you?" asked a child.

"Nobody," he replied.

Before any other questions could be asked, he slipped past the women and children, still carrying Neferit's body. Outside, in the corridor, servants looked at the sight of a man carrying a limp woman and Sumer repeated his explanation, asking where she could lie down to recover. He was directed to a small room with a bed, where he laid her, arranging her limbs in a lifelike pose before slipping out. Speed was called for now, if he was to be away before anybody drank the milk, but he knew he would attract attention if he ran, so he managed a purposeful walk toward the kitchens.

He had just reached them when he heard a hubbub break out behind him. Ignoring the increasing clamour, he sauntered into the kitchens, nodding to a few people he knew, and out into the palace courtyard, where he mingled with men and women carrying food, fuel for the ovens, or water from the cisterns. Swiftly, he walked around the palace, out into the street and headed for the city, expecting to hear someone to call out to him to stop. No one did, however, and heart hammering; he made his way back to his rooms. He cursed that Neferit had seen him add the poison and the necessity of silencing her immediately. Now he would not get a chance to poison the king.

"I cannot stay here," he muttered. "They will find Neferit's body and they will quickly associate her with me."

Gathering up his few belongings, he left his rooms and made his way down to the docks. Behind him, on the hill where the palace lay, someone had raised the alarm, and the palace guard swarmed out as if the palace was a kicked ant nest. People from the city started running toward the palace, eager to find out what was happening, and Sumer had to push his way through the crowd. Cries of alarm mingled with grief arose, and rumours spread almost as fast as he could move. He made it to the docks and looked around for a boat for hire, offering copper for someone to take him across the river. One or two fishermen began negotiations with him, but before he could agree on a price, soldiers were pushing through the crowd, bellowing that the port was closed. Before they could reach him, Sumer turned and made his way back into the city, taking shelter in a recessed doorway. From there, he listened to the rumours swirl through the crowds milling on the streets.

"Someone has poisoned the king," a man shouted.

"Not the king, but his children."

"What kind of monster would do that?"

"A foreigner. He and a servant plotted to kill everyone, but she was discovered and the guards killed her."

"Who is dead?"

"The king's son."

"Which one?"

"Both. And their mothers."

"Who did it? Have they caught him?"

"They will find him. Guards are scouring the city."

Sumer scowled as he realised he had put too much poison in the milk. They had not died slowly, as if from an illness, but violently. Still, he was satisfied that part of his assignment had been successfully completed. He wondered whether he should remain in the city and try for the rest of it, but reluctantly decided that the chances of getting close to the king were now non-existent. His personal survival was now most important, but with the docks closed, his only way out was by land.

"North or south?" he mused. "North is toward home, but if they suspect who sent me, they will look for me there. It will have to be south."

They brought the news to Sekhemkhet and great was his anguish. He cried aloud and went straight to where the bodies of his sons had been laid out. The new court physician, Khentu, and Tjaty Imhotep were already on hand, having conducted a cursory examination of the bodies, and they looked up as the king burst into the room. Sekhemkhet stared at his sons with tears streaming down his cheeks, and behind him, wailing and screaming issued from the Women's Quarters, where the mothers of the dead children cried out in grief.

"How did they die?" the king demanded. "Was it sickness? I did not think they were sick; nobody told me."

Khentu looked at Imhotep, pleading silently for him to take the lead.

"It was not sickness, my lord," Imhotep said. "They were poisoned. It is beyond all doubt."

Sekhemkhet stared in horror, but then crossed to the body of Hor-Re and stroked the pale face of his eldest son, shuddering at the agonised expression stamped on it. He looked across at Hor-Nubkhet and saw a similar mask of agony.

"Who has done this?" He stared at Imhotep, but the old man could only shake his head. "How?" was the king's next question.

"It seems the milk was poisoned, my lord. Three children and two adults are dead, two more very sick."

Sekhemkhet looked from the body of one son to the next. "Who are the others?"

"The child was a daughter of yours by a concubine, the adults were their nurses. They drank from a common jar, though the two still living drank less, stopping when the first pains..."

A servant entered the room, looking strained and fearful, crossing to Khentu and whispering in his ear.

Khentu cleared his throat. "One of the others has died."

The king shook his head, fury starting to wipe grief from his face. "Who has dared to lay a hand on my sons?" he demanded. "Find them, Imhotep, and find them alive."

"We are doing what we can, my lord."

"That is not enough. How was the milk poisoned? Put the kitchen staff to the question; drag it out of them."

"I have already ordered interrogations, my lord."

Hours passed before Imhotep secured the information he needed. Nobody died in giving it up, but a few wished for death before it was through. Imhotep took the information to the king.

"I am satisfied that the kitchen staff were innocent of this outrage, my lord. The milk was poisoned later, after it had been brought to the table."

"By one of the women at the meal?"

"No, my lord. One of the servants who brought in the food remarked on the presence of Neferit, one of the ladies who attend upon the Women's Quarters. She was there with a man who was not a palace member."

"You have questioned them?"

"No, my lord. Neferit was discovered dead of a broken neck and the man has disappeared."

"Find him. Somebody must know who he is."

"His name is Sumer and he is an Assuran. That much is known. He had a room in the city but he has fled."

"I want him found, Imhotep; found and taken alive. He will tell me all he knows before he screams out for death."

"We will find him, my lord."

Privately, Imhotep was not sure that the man would be found. By all accounts, the man, though Assuran, looked sufficiently like a Kemetu to pass unremarked among the people thronging the streets of Inebu-hedj. Still, failure would not result from a lack of trying. His position as Tjaty gave him enormous powers, and he intended to use them to the fullest in the pursuit of the king's command.

Imhotep had sent soldiers to the docks and to the city gates, locking this Sumer within the city.

"Unless he has already fled," he muttered. That thought was not to be countenanced as the king's fury at the man's escape was likely to turn against anyone he perceived as failing him.

He gathered any servant who knew Sumer by sight, having spent time with him or the dead girl, whether drinking in the taverns or within the palace, and sent them out with search parties. The population of Inebu-hedj had been ordered inside, no man to step outside on pain of death. Squads of soldiers roamed the streets, looking for men who had disobeyed the command, while others went from house to house, shop to shop, through the warehouses and granaries, demanding the names of every man and insisting on others to vouch for who they were. Failure to provide adequate identification led to instant arrest, and soon scores of men were in custody. Palace servants looked through the prisoners, intent on finding the man who had killed the princes, but after a day of searching, he was still at large.

Sumer made it to the southern gate of the city barely a handful of minutes after the soldiers arrived. He hung back in the shadows to see what they would do. They did not close the gate immediately and were allowing people in and out, though they stopped and questioned any man trying to leave. He thought he would be able to pass for a Kemetu man and stepped out from the shadows, taking several strides toward the gate before he saw a palace servant with the guards. At the same moment, the servant looked up and saw Sumer, yelling and pointing. Sumer turned and ran, the soldiers pounding after him, shouting to people to stop him. Nobody did, hanging back instead, not wanting to get involved.

He ran, ducking into alleys, barging his way through crowds, bursting into a shop front and out through the back, and in an unsighted moment, threw himself down behind sacks of grain. Pounding footsteps came close and passed him by. Sumer leapt to his feet once more and ran off; angling back toward what he hoped might now be an unguarded gate. He was out of luck as two soldiers had stayed behind, and the palace servant was with them. Scowling, Sumer withdrew into a narrow alleyway and sat in the deep shadows, wondering what to do next. He concluded that he should wait for nightfall and try again under cover of darkness.

The number of people in the streets declined, and Sumer heard men talking about the king's command to stay inside while the city was searched. He grimaced, knowing that made his escape harder. When dusk fell, he ventured out of his alley, using shadows and doorways to make his way back to the southern gate, but found it fully manned with soldiers again. He doubled back, dodging patrols, going across the town to try first the western gate and then the northern, but soldiers guarded both. On the way, he saw men in the street accosted by patrols and arrested on the spot, and Sumer knew that even without anyone identifying him, he would be arrested if he was seen. Identification and interrogation would follow, and Sumer knew that he would talk if he was put to rigorous questioning--anyone would. He checked the docks again, but the usually busy wharves were deserted except for guard patrols.

"What in Set's name do I do now?" he muttered. "There is no way out."

Sumer hunkered down in the deep shadow behind a granary and thought hard. He had completed the first part of his assignment and that should be enough to satisfy Nubsekhem. Rewards would be coming his way if only he could break out of the city. That did not seem possible now, so what other action was available to him? The answer, when it came, made him grin.

"I complete my assignment by killing the king."

Is it even possible? he asked himself.

"Probably not, but at least they won't be looking for me at the palace."

Sumer took out the little flask of poison and shook it gently, listening to the sound of the liquid inside. He should get rid of it, he knew. There would be no opportunity to use it on the king; that deed would have to be done with a knife. He shrugged and put the flask back into his clothing--if nothing else, he could use it on himself, though that would be a horrible way to die.

He left his hiding place and made his way through the city toward the palace, noticing that as he got closer, there were fewer patrols. It seemed that he had that right at least--they would not be looking for him to further his crimes against the royal family. There were still guards on the main entrances, so he slipped around the back and, using the darkness and flickering shadows cast from lit torches, made his way into the kitchens and beyond. He made his way through the palace corridors and rooms, drawing closer to the king's suite of rooms, but there were guards on the doors. For a few moments, he considered a quick rush, wondering if surprise would let him get past the first guards and into the king's rooms.

What if he is not there? I would be throwing my life away to no purpose.

Withdrawing, Sumer found a door to the palace gardens and moved round, hoping to find a veranda or window that would give him access, but guards were posted there too. He started to realise that killing the king was a vain hope, and that he should concentrate his efforts on escaping the city.

Enough of this. If you must rush armed men, at least try for those at one of the gates.

Sumer turned away, dropping the flask of poison in the shrubbery, and started back the way he had come. He was almost at the kitchens again when he collided with a hurrying servant.

"Watch where you are going," snapped the man. He half turned away and stopped. "Sumer? Is that...Guards! Help! It is the killer."

Sumer pushed past him and ran for the kitchens, the cries of the man echoing through the hallways, drowned out now by running feet. Something slashed past him, a spear clattering on the tiles, and then he was running past the ovens. A cook saw him and threw a jar; he swerved, knocking over pots, stumbled, and a man crashed into him, knocking him to the ground. Scrambling to his feet, he saw guards pouring into the kitchens, surrounding him with drawn swords and levelled spears.

"Surrender!" called a junior officer. Then, "Take him."

Sumer smiled wryly, drew his knife and ran at the nearest guard. The man, taken by surprise, raised his sword in defence, and Sumer ran onto it. He groaned, noting how painful a sword thrust to the belly was, and then collapsed, the sword pulling free as he fell. Blood gushed out, and Sumer heard the officer yelling at the man who had struck him, while others called for a physician. Sumer felt his life slipping away, and closed his eyes. A hand slapped his face, and he opened his eyes again to see the officer kneeling beside him.

"Who sent you?" demanded the officer. "Speak, you son of a whore. Who told you to kill innocent young children?"

Sumer shook his head wearily as a great lassitude came over him. He heard the man as if from a distance, the light of the kitchen torches dimming around him.

"Who sent you?" the officer said again.

The voice was now very far away as darkness pressed in upon Sumer. He heard noises in his mind, groaning and crying, lamentations and laughter, and he thought of his old gods of Assur, put away these several years. In their eyes, killing was allowed, but not all killing.

Killing children is a crime...the gods will punish me...

Turning his head toward the young officer, staring through eyes that no longer registered light, darkness having overwhelmed him, Sumer whispered, pleading for forgiveness.

"Tell the king what the man said," Imhotep ordered.

The court physician arrived too late to save Sumer's life, so the young officer had to report to the Tjaty the death of the child killer before he could be questioned. He tried to make excuses for the soldier who had inflicted the fatal wound, but Imhotep waved his words away.

"What is done is done. Did he say anything before he died?"

"Yes, my lord." The young officer told him and Imhotep frowned.

"You are sure? Nothing more than that? You couldn't have misheard?"

"It is possible, my lord. He was dying and knew it, but his voice was very faint. His lips moved a lot, but nothing more was audible."

"I want you to tell the king exactly what you heard."

Fear showed on the officer's face. "Must I, my lord? I failed to take him alive and...and the king..."

"I do not hold you at fault and neither will the king, but you must tell him."

Imhotep took the young officer to the king's quarters and told him how the killer had come back to the palace, no doubt wanting to wreak further harm on the king and his family.

"Tell the king what the man said," Imhotep ordered the officer.

"My lord king... he said, 'Sekhem'."

"That is all? Nothing more?"

"No, my lord king."

The king dismissed the officer, who fled, glad to have escaped without punishment. He looked at Imhotep, puzzled. "What does it mean? What was he trying to say?"

"We will never know, my lord," Imhotep said. "He might have been expressing a desire to kill you, but it is my belief he named the man who sent him. That is what the officer was trying to find out when he died."

"Who is Sekhem?"

"Maybe it is only part of his name. He might have been saying...Nubsekhem."

"General Nubsekhem? He is loyal, I am sure of..." Sekhemkhet's voice trailed away as he remembered Commander Huni's recent actions and the investigation he had meant to make. "Do you suspect him of treachery?"

"There is nothing to tie him to the killer save part of a name whispered by a dying man, my lord, but I will investigate his possible involvement."

"Do so, but cautiously," the king instructed. "Much as I want to see the killer of my sons impaled on a stake and screaming his life out, we must be careful. Nubsekhem is the General of the Northern Army and he may lead his men in revolt if he believes his scheme discovered."

"I will be careful, my lord king," Imhotep assured him.

Chapter 26

Investigations take time, but life and death do not wait upon results. A sombre mood cast its pall over the city, the normal turn of events being at variance with the grief that pervaded the palace. Sekhemkhet had anger to sustain him, but his wives Djeser-Ti and Tetimene could only mourn the deaths of their sons. In this time of sorrow, rivalries and recriminations ceased and for the first time, a fragile peace descended over the Women's Quarters. The other deaths were almost forgotten in the face of the king's loss, even that of his daughter Nefsen, only child of his concubine Anset.

Imhotep, in addition to all his other duties, handled the funeral arrangements, and while the preparations were sumptuous for Hor-Re and Hor-Nubkhet, the Tjaty made sure that Nefsen's body was also prepared in a manner befitting a king's daughter. The nurses who died in agony from drinking the poisoned milk were buried in plainer tombs, but the grave furnishings were finer than those their families would otherwise have been able to afford.

"They gave their lives performing their duty toward the king and his sons," Imhotep told the grieving families. "The king desires their afterlife to be above their station in life."

The burials took place in the king's City of the Dead in Sekera. Sekhemkhet spent a fortune on giving his sons the best funeral he could, loading the small rock chambers with every accoutrement the dead boys would need in the afterlife, from toys to fine clothes, all their favourite foods, and weapons for when they grew into men. *Ushabti* stood in ranks, the magical formulae that would bring them to life to do the princes' bidding, painted on their bases. Gold in profusion lined the chamber, enough for both boys to live like the royalty they were; despite the fact it drained the king's treasury.

Once the burial had taken place and the funeral feast completed, Sekhemkhet sent the royal entourage back to Inebu-hedj, staying behind to inspect the progress of his tomb. The king seemed distracted as he toured the site with Imhotep and Den, Tjaty and Overseer uncertain whether the king was actually listening to anything they said. He stared unseeing at the second level of the *mer*, now clad on three sides with gleaming white Troyu limestone, and then abruptly turned away. Imhotep motioned for Den to withdraw, and came close to the king, talking to him in a low voice, asking if there was anything wrong.

"Wrong? What is there about my life that is right?" Sekhemkhet asked bitterly. "My queen killed herself, all my children have died, I have no heir, and now it seems someone is trying to poison my whole family. I do not even mention the lack of a flood this year, which will certainly lead to famine."

Imhotep cogitated for a few moments. He did not want to enter into a discussion on the identity of the poisoner, or the deaths in the royal family, so he chose a marginally safer topic to answer.

"You are young, my lord king, and capable of siring many fine sons. In the meantime, you have another son--Sennenkhet. He is a sturdy and healthy young boy, by all accounts."

"His mother is a slave," Sekhemkhet growled. "I cannot have the son of a slave as my heir."

"Then perhaps you could ensure that his mother gains her freedom? Release her from servitude and make her a concubine. She is comely enough is she not? Sons of concubines can inherit."

"I think the time has come to have a son with my wife Meresankh."

"My lord king, you know the gods have forbidden it," Imhotep said. "Would you risk their wrath?"

"What can they do to me that they have not already done?" the king demanded. "Must I repeat the list of my woes? No, my sister is already my wife. I will lie with her and have a son who shall rule after me."

"Let me talk to the gods first, my lord. There must be a reason for their ban, so let me try and find out how you can propitiate them, at least. In the meantime, I urge you to consider freeing Sennenkhet's mother. You do not have to make him your heir yet, but make the first step, ready in case you do."

Imhotep managed to turn the king aside from an inquiry into his investigation of the killer of his sons, but only at the expense of Meresankh. He knew that she would not consent to having sexual relations with her brother and had only consented to marriage to stave off just such a demand. She would not agree now, despite being the queen.

"I do not care how you do it, Imhotep," she said. "Make up an excuse, lie if you have to, but find a way to keep me out of his couch. I will not lie with him."

"I have already lied for you, as you well know. Misrepresenting the will of the gods is a serious offence, and lying to the king no less so. There might be nothing I can do."

"Find a way, or I will," Meresankh said grimly.

"What do you mean?"

"Just that two people may go to the couch, but only one will get up."

Imhotep looked horror-struck. "You would...you wouldn't...the king?"

"What? No! I would not harm the king, but I will take a knife to my own throat before I let a man part my legs in that way."

Imhotep shook his head. "No, you would not do that."

"Are you so sure? My sister killed herself."

Disturbed to his core, Imhotep muttered that he would do what he could. The problem was a big one, though, without any ready solution. Previously, he had pretended to have a dream from the gods prohibiting the marriage and then, under pressure from the king, had allowed him to marry her and make her queen providing he did not lie with her. He did not think that was going to work again, so he had to find something new that would appeal to the king.

"Rather than focussing on the problem of Meresankh, I should seek to distract the king," Imhotep muttered to himself. "What would distract him from fathering a son on his queen? Another more attractive woman? No, he has any number of beautiful women available right now, so another will not draw him away."

Imhotep paced his room, striding the length before whirling around and striding back. The room was too small to allow him freedom of movement, and he considered leaving the city and walking briskly along the riverbank.

"To what purpose? It is freedom of thought I need. Think, Imhotep. What does the king really need?"

He needs an heir...a son. That much is obvious. That is why he wants to lie with his queen.

"But he already has a son--Sennenkhet."

The son of a slave woman. I have suggested he free her and make their son his heir, but he resists that idea.

"Why?"

Imhotep snorted. *Is it not obvious? The woman is nobody, a rank commoner as well as a slave. Even if he freed her, she has no standing. What sort of an heir would their son make?* He groaned and took his head in his hands, thought and speech silent.

"What if she was not a commoner?" he muttered after a few minutes.

But she is...and a slave.

"What if she is not a commoner?"

Refusing to listen to his inner objections, Imhotep went in search of the woman. Despite being the recipient of the king's sexual generosity, she was still a slave and worked hard in menial positions throughout the palace. Six years of labour had done her no favours, but Imhotep thought she could still be comely enough if she took care of her appearance.

"Do you know who I am?" he demanded of her.

She knelt with head bowed. "Yes, lord."

"You bore the king a child...a son...by the name of Sennenkhet?"

"Yes, lord."

"What is your name and where do you come from?"

She looked up at him, and for a moment a look of pride flitted across her features before she submerged it in subservience again. "I am called Ayah, lord. My people are of the Ribu in the west."

"Perfect," Imhotep murmured. "What is your family's standing within your people?"

"I have none, lord. I am a slave."

"What would it be if you were among your people?"

A shrug. "My father cared for the tribe's horses."

"And the Ribu are a horse people? Your father was looked up to?"

"My father was brother to the chieftain of the local tribe."

"Was he, by the gods?" Imhotep felt his thoughts coming together, coalescing. "The chief was your uncle, so you could almost be regarded as royalty within your people."

Ayah looked up again, and her voice was bitter as she said, "My uncle had five sons, and my father three, whereas I was only a girl. I would have been married off to some sub-chief as a reward for service. I am not royalty, nor is my family royal, for we are just horse herders."

"Let me explain," Imhotep said gently. "The king favoured you and had a son by you, but you will never be more than a slave within his household, and your son can look to be no more than a semi-educated overseer if he is lucky. The reason for this is because the king thinks you are of low birth."

Imhotep bent and helped Ayah to her feet. "I have just found out that you are the niece of one of the petty kings of the Ribu, though, and that changes everything. I think that were I to argue your case with the king, he would see you in a very different way. First, he would free you, because the daughter of a king should not be a slave. Second, you have borne him a son who, because of the recent deaths of his other sons, is now the sole surviving male child. Do you see what this means?"

Ayah shook her head.

"I believe the king will raise your status to that of concubine, and possibly your son will become the king's heir; at least until another son is born to one of his wives."

Ayah stared, her mouth open. "You speak the truth, lord?"

Imhotep nodded. "I will represent you thus to the king. He will question you. Can you identify yourself as the niece of a Ribu king?"

She smiled. "I can do anything if it benefits my son."

Sekhemkhet was astonished when Imhotep brought him the news of the slave woman's identity. "How can this be? Would I not have heard before, when she first came into service here?"

"My lord king, do you concern yourself with the origins of any slave or servant? They are here to cater to your needs and desires."

"That is true," mused the king. "So, this Ayah is Ribu royalty, is she?"

"They have a different concept of what constitutes royalty in the horse tribes of the western plains, my lord. Ayah is the niece of the local ruler, who can be regarded as a petty king. Nothing that approaches your power, of course, but it certainly raises her status."

"Agreed, but to what end?"

"I believe she should be freed from slavery as a first step. After that, my lord, I ask you to consider that she has borne you a male child who is in good health. If you were to marry her, you would give the child legitimacy, and he could be your heir until such time as you beget another."

"I am not sure I want to marry an ex-slave. She would be on an equal footing with my other wives and that would certainly lead to a disturbance of *ma'at* within the Women's Quarters."

"A concubine then, my lord. The child of a concubine can still inherit."

Sekhemkhet frowned, considering his Tjaty's words. "She has been a slave and no doubt other men have sown their seed in her over the years. Do I want to sow my seed in such a field? How could I be sure of the harvest?"

"My lord, there is no need for any further sowing. You already have the good harvest of a son from her."

"As to that, can I be certain the boy is even mine?"

"Of that you may be sure, my lord. Ayah came to your household a virgin at fifteen years and had her first *hesmen* here, as the Chamberlain's records can attest. She then lay with you as her first man and such was your virility that she was immediately with child."

"You are sure I am the father?"

"Yes, my lord."

"Despite your assurances, I still entertain doubts."

"I understand, my lord," Imhotep said. "I hoped that this revelation might ease your mind, but there is always the other alternative--lie with your wives again and have other sons. It will take time, of course, and there will be uncertainty as to whether they will birth sons or daughters..."

"The queen as well?"

"My lord, the gods have not given me any indication that their prohibition has been rescinded."

Sekhemkhet scowled, angry that he was still prohibited from having children with his sister. He might have risked going against the wishes of the gods, but their displeasure was already evident in the failure of the annual flood.

"I suppose the boy might suffice for now," he said. "What is his name?"

"Sennenkhet, my lord."

"He need only be my heir until I have a son by one of my wives."

"That would be a sensible decision, my lord. You need a visible heir and Sennenkhet stands ready to fulfil his duty."

"I will see him before I decide. Send for him."

Imhotep went looking for Sennenkhet. He could just as easily have sent for the boy, but he wanted to impress on the child a few things that were important for his future. There were no lies that needed to be told, the boy was the natural son of the king and Ayah, but he had been reared as just another child spawned by the royal loins, and he lacked some of the social niceties.

"When you enter the presence of the king, keep your eyes downcast, kneel before him and say, 'I am your servant Sennenkhet'. Remain kneeling until he tells you to stand, and do not speak unless you are spoken to. When you do speak, do not chatter, but answer with few words. Understand?" The boy nodded. "The king will likely ask you questions about what you do, what you learn...things like that. I cannot tell you exactly what to say, but remember to be polite, addressing him as 'my lord king'. He is your father, but he has never acknowledged you, so never address him as 'father' unless he gives you express permission."

Imhotep hesitated. "I suppose if there is one response that should be uppermost in your mind; it is that you exist to serve the king in all things. Can you remember that?"

"Yes, my lord," Sennenkhet whispered. "Please, sir, why does the king want to see me?"

"His sons by his wives died, and he needs a son to stand by him, maybe even be his heir. You may be that son, but if the king decides otherwise, you must accept it."

"Yes, sir," Sennenkhet said uncertainly.

"Never mind, you are a brave boy and I am sure you will behave yourself. Come along now, the king is waiting."

The boy did as Imhotep had instructed, entering the chamber with his eyes downcast and only glancing toward the king once or twice as he advanced to the throne, where he knelt.

"I am your servant Sennenkhet," he said in a clear voice.

Sekhemkhet looked surprised and glanced toward Imhotep, but the Tjaty maintained an impassive expression.

"So, your mother is Ayah?"

"Yes, my lord king."

"You speak well for a..." He had been about to say 'slave' but that was not really the case. "You may rise and stand before me."

Sennenkhet rose to his feet and stood with his head downcast.

"Do you know why I have sent for you?"

The boy hesitated, remembering Imhotep's words and thinking of the proper response. "I...I serve the king in all things."

Good boy, Imhotep thought.

Sekhemkhet looked pleased. "Are you being educated properly?" he asked.

Sennenkhet looked puzzled and glanced toward Imhotep.

"Remember he is only a small boy, my lord king," the Tjaty said. To the boy, he said, "Your lessons, Sennenkhet. The king wants to know what you are learning."

The boy looked confused. "I...I don't know, my lord king, except...I learn duties around the palace."

The king frowned. "What duties?"

"I have helped in the kitchens and...and folded linen. Carried water too, my lord."

"All good, I suppose," Sekhemkhet said, "but not duties I would expect of...do you learn how to read and write?"

"A little, my lord king." Sennenkhet's lips started to quiver. "I am not very good at it. The tutor beats me when I make a mistake."

"Well, that will stop...the beatings, I mean. Imhotep, you will arrange a proper tutor for him. It seems he has a lot of catching up to do. No more household duties either. Sennenkhet, do you have weapons training?"

"N...no, my lord king."

"That too, then, Imhotep." Sekhemkhet sighed. "It seems I have neglected one of my sons too long, and now when I need him, he lacks the skills necessary for a prince."

The news that the king had officially recognised his son by the slave woman Ayah raced through the palace and the city, but nowhere did it have a greater effect than in the Women's Quarters. Ayah, newly freed and raised to the status of concubine, fared ill in the Quarters, finding herself almost without allies. Djeser-Ti and Tetimene united in their hatred of her and took every opportunity to make their feelings known. The other concubines joined with the wives and set about making Ayah's life a misery. It had driven others to suicide before, and Ayah might have sought that way out except for two things. The first was her son and the possibility that the king might make him his heir. She dreamed that her son might one day become king, and then her status as King's Mother would enable her to crush petty annoyances like other women. The second thing that kept her alive was the friendship of Queen Meresankh. The king's sister-wife held a strange position in the household--Queen, but not fully wife. She had no son to contend with Sennenkhet nor, she swore, would she have one.

"My fate lies elsewhere," Meresankh said. "I love the king dearly, but as a brother rather than as a husband. I know his heir will not come from my belly, so I offer you my protection, Ayah."

"But I am a slave...I was a slave...my lady. I am grateful for your protection, of course, but I am not worthy of it."

"You are more worthy than any of the other concubines and even the king's other wives," Meresankh said. "Tetimene is the daughter of some subjugated southern tribe, while Djeser-Ti is a commoner. You, however, are the niece of a Ribu king, and worthy of being my friend."

Ayah did not disabuse her of that notion, though she smiled at the thought of uncle as a king. Life as a servant in the palace of the king of Kemet was more luxurious than the life of a Ribu king. She did not miss her early life with the horse tribes, though she did value her newly acquired freedom. Her duties as a concubine were light, and it was unlikely that the king would even demand her physical attentions. Whatever attributes that had drawn the king to her as a girl had vanished with the passage of years of slave labour. With time on her hands for the first time in her life, she wondered what her future would be like, especially with the enmity of those around her. The protection and friendship of the Queen meant everything to her, and she started to think how she could turn that friendship into active assistance for her son.

She was under no illusion that Sennenkhet was ready to become a prince. He lacked education in even the basic things that a ruler would need, but those things could be overcome with a little effort. What he really needed at court were friends, and the knowledge that Queen Meresankh looked upon him with favour would attract many friends.

For Sennenkhet, the recognition of the king opened up a dazzling realm of possibilities, though his young mind could scarcely grasp the complexities of his new life. His lifestyle improved at once. Servants who had once dismissed him as just another product of the king's lust destined for a dull job, now fawned over him. He was moved to new rooms, given fine clothing and jewellery, fed foods of a higher standard than anything he had ever experienced. There were disadvantages too. The lackadaisical attentions of the semi-educated tutor assigned to palace children was replaced by an unsmiling priest determined to make a name for himself by educating this new prince. He worked Sennenkhet hard, often reducing the small boy to tears, but he learned quickly, his young mind soaking up knowledge. As his knowledge grew, Sennenkhet realised that the future held out before him was incredible. One day, he might be king over the kingdoms of Kemet, Ruler of everything, every whim of his instantly granted.

Chapter 27

S cribing work at Sekera settled into an uneasy peace. Khawy and Kagemni realised they had to work together and neither wanted to risk Den's displeasure by causing trouble. Khawy returned from his trip to Abu with his father, and Den put him to work overseeing the arrival of stone from the quarries and the disbursement of blocks to the masons in charge of the various work projects. He was required to keep track of how many arrived, making notes on their size, how many were lost through clumsy handling, and how many finished blocks were carved by each mason. It was exacting work, but in Khawy's eyes it was of far greater importance than Kagemni's work, and therefore pleasing to him. He dreamed of the day when his responsibilities would be expanded to encompass those of his cousin. On that day, he would dismiss Kagemni from service.

Khawy's younger brother Khepankh also returned from Abu and took up permanent duties at Sekera. Den gave him the task supervising the digging out of the underground galleries, keeping track of how many *mehi* of rock was excavated every day and awarding food and drink to each crew on the basis of their work. He was young for a supervisory position, being only fourteen years old, but Den hoped he would grow into the position. As a father, he naturally wanted the best for his children, which was why both of his oldest sons had trained as scribes. The task proved a little much for Khepankh though, and when he submitted his first month's accounts to Den, they were hopelessly jumbled.

Den examined the pages of calculations and the admittedly neat columns of figures, and scratched his head. "How many teams of men are working for you?" he asked.

"Uh...three?"

"You either know or you don't."

"Three then, father."

"In this room, at this moment, I am Overseer Den, not your father. You may address me as 'Overseer' or 'sir'."

Khepankh looked unhappy. "Yes, fa...sir."

"Why, if you have three teams, are there references to only two in some places and..." Den shuffled the papers in his hands, "...three or four in other places. I would swear there are five different teams on this page."

"Er...may I see? Oh, that...yes, there are three teams, fa...sir, but they performed different tasks on different days. I did not want to mix them up, so I separated them."

"I see. So this team..." Den held out the paper with its column of figures, "...is the same as this one?" He held out another column.

Khepankh peered at each column and swallowed hard, a look of desperation taking a grip on his features. "Y...yes, I think so."

"Think so, or know so?"

"No, it is."

Den passed from that to another strange divergence. "This team here, the 'Moles', worked twenty-five days last month and their daily excavation is measured in *mehi* each day, and the total listed below. That is good...I can see exactly how well they have worked. This other team though, the 'Lions', seems to have worked for only eighteen days, but on three of those they excavated far more rock than on others. Why is that?"

Khepankh frowned, examining both columns. He licked his lips and smiled weakly. "They both worked for twenty-five days, sir, but the 'Lions' team leader did not always submit a daily reckoning. Those days..." he pointed to the inflated figures, "...represent two or three days' work."

Den sighed. "It is part of your job to keep accurate records. Have you taken any independent measures of the work done by each team?"

"No, sir."

"Then you really have no idea if that amount of work has really been done, do you? I presume the same overseer who reports on the excavation also collects the daily wages for the team? Do you think it possible that he might inflate those figures so he can draw more wages and keep the difference?"

"I am sure they would not do that, sir," Khepankh said.

"Would you be prepared to gamble your own wages that the figures are accurate? If they have been overpaid, we can always recoup the losses by deducting them from your own wages." Den looked at his son's miserable face and softened his voice. "I do not think we need to do that just now, but really, these records are a mess. How are you going to get them into shape?"

"I...I will try and do better, sir."

"The problem is that you do not really know what you are doing. I am partly at fault, I admit. I thought you were ready for the responsibility, but I see you need a little more tutoring." Den thought for a few minutes. "I will give you into the care of Kagemni. I can find no fault with his record keeping, so he can show you what to do."

Khepankh almost cried with relief. He had anticipated the shame of being dismissed from his position, but his father had spared him the worst of it. His ears burned with the ignominy of letting his father down, but if any man could explain the complexities of the work without shaming him, it was Kagemni. He loved his cousin with almost the intensity that Khawy hated him.

Kagemni liked all the family of Den except for Khawy. He wished he could like him too, but the youth was, quite frankly, obnoxious, and he was very happy to seldom have to cross paths with him. Khepankh was another matter altogether, and when Den approached him, he was happy to help the youth. He imagined it would be something simple, but quickly discovered that Khepankh had little understanding of the complexities of his task. Reading over the records of the previous month, Kagemni grimaced, wondering how he could present the facts logically and simply. He went back to the basics, having Khepankh bring the daily figures back to his office where they could compile them together, setting them out in logical order, and making the necessary calculations based on numbers that could be trusted. Kagemni explained everything, going over each step in detail and showing why each column and entry was important. He also showed Khepankh how his excavation figures meshed with his own that described the whole building site at Sekera, demonstrating how every part contributed to the smooth running of the whole project.

There was a certain amount of grumbling from team overseers, who could see a source of income slipping away, but the honest ones applauded Khepankh's efforts and, after an initial drop-off, the daily work quota increased. Soon, Khepankh was able to show his father improvements in the excavations.

Khawy, working in the stone storage area, also submitted reports to Kagemni for incorporation into the general report Kagemni drew up each month, and he delighted in making life difficult for his cousin. He discovered early on that if he delayed his report, Kagemni was forced to come to him asking for it. A score of excuses resulted in a score of delays, and there was nothing Kagemni could do about it. Endlessly patient, he delayed his own report, working late into the night to correlate Khawy's tardy figures with those from the other departments. Den, unaware of the reason for the delays, started grumbling to his wife and family at night that perhaps Kagemni was not the right person for the job.

"You have to do something," Khepankh told Kagemni. "You are so good at everything else; I cannot understand why you have difficulty turning in the overall report."

Kagemni did not want to tell tales about Khepankh's brother, so said nothing. Khepankh continued to pester his cousin, warning him that Den was even thinking of replacing him.

Perhaps that would be best, Kagemni told himself. *If I cannot manage Khawy then maybe I do not deserve this position of trust.*

Khepankh could not understand this single failing, and kept on trying to worm the answer out of his cousin, and happened to visit him on the last day of the month as Kagemni sat waiting for the last report to come in.

"Why do you wait?" Khepankh asked. "Work on your report now and you will still be able to get it in on time."

"I still need one report to complete my calculations," Kagemni said. "I dare say it will be delivered any time now."

"Is this what happens every month?" Khepankh asked. Kagemni shrugged. "Whose report are you waiting on?"

Kagemni did not answer and Khepankh looked at his cousin keenly. "It is Khawy's, isn't it? Set's hairy balls, does he do this every month?"

"You should not defame the god in such a manner," Kagemni reproved. "Nor should you be swearing at your age. It is not seemly."

Khepankh grinned. "Defame? Are you seriously telling me Set's balls are not hairy? As for swearing, everyone does it."

"All the more reason for you not to. You should set an example for others."

"I will think about it, but getting back to my question, is that Khawy's report and does he do it every month?"

Kagemni shrugged. "Yes, and yes."

"Then you must tell father. He blames you but it is not your fault."

"No."

"Why not?"

"Khawy is young and is still learning. I have no wish to heap further troubles on his head."

"So you would rather stay up all night trying to complete reports that should have been ready days ago? You risk your own job."

"It is no great hardship," Kagemni said. "As for my job, well, perhaps I do not deserve it if I cannot keep my overseers in line."

Khawy continued to hand in late or incomplete reports, leading to Kagemni spending long hours turning them into something that resembled the truth. Den, meanwhile, unaware of the reason for Kagemni's tardiness, grumbled to anyone who would listen, including his family after the evening meal.

"I think I have misjudged my brother's son," he said. "I thought that he was ready for such a responsible job, but I see I was mistaken. His report is late again--that is the seventh time in the last eight months. I have borne his tardiness without complaint, but now I must act. I must remove him and make someone else the overseer."

"I am ready to take over, father," Khawy said.

Den grunted. "Your work has hardly been exemplary."

"At least I get it in in time."

That was too much for Khepankh. "That is not so," he exclaimed. "Kagemni will not tell you so, but the reason he is late submitting his reports is that Khawy delays his own until the last moment, forcing Kagemni to work late."

Khawy flushed and leapt to his feet. "That is a stinking lie!"

"It is not," Khepankh rejoined. "Everyone knows it but fears to speak out."

"Lies!" Khawy yelled. He strode forward and pushed his brother in the chest, sending him staggering backward into the table. Dishes fell to the floor and broke, while the smaller children wailed with fear at the sudden act of violence. Khawy followed up his push with another, taking his brother by the throat.

"Enough!" Den barked. He grabbed Khawy and hauled him off his brother. "What are you thinking?" he demanded. "Apologise to your brother immediately."

Khawy said nothing, just stood and glowered at Khepankh, who rubbed his throat. The crying of the younger children increased and Den told Ranefert to take them into the next room and calm them down; their crying annoyed him.

"Then you control your sons," Ranefert said sharply. "Come children; let us go to the kitchens. I think the cook has some honeycomb." She ushered the children out. Merit resisted, wanting to stay, but Ranefert insisted, closing the door behind them.

"I am waiting," Den said. "You will ask forgiveness of your brother, Khawy."

"Then you will wait a long time, father," Khawy said. He trembled as he spoke his defiance, whether from rage or fear. "I have done nothing to warrant an apology."

Den went pale. "You dare speak to me like that? I will...I will..."

"You will what, father? Beat me as if I was a child? If I am old enough to work, I am no longer a child. Dismiss me, perhaps? Go ahead; I will find other work easily enough."

"I will not lift a hand to you," Den said, "though you richly deserve it. However, you are a fool if you think you can walk away from your position here and hope to get another one as good."

"I am not walking away," Khawy said sulkily. "If I suffer in my life, it will be because you dismiss me."

"All I ask is that you ask your brother's forgiveness for attacking him."

"I merely defended myself."

"How can you say that when you pushed him and tried to strangle him?"

"He started it by lying about me. I defended my good name."

"What good name?" Khepankh scoffed. "Nobody likes working for you, and all the overseers sneer at you."

"There he goes again!" Khawy tried to push past his father, but Den managed to restrain him.

"Khepankh, will you then be the first to offer a hand of friendship to your brother?" Den asked in desperation. "Apologise for your harsh words so that Khawy do likewise for his actions."

"My actions were justified," Khawy said.

"And my words were the truth," Khepankh added. "How can you ask me to reject the truth, father? If you do not believe me, ask Kagemni."

"That son of a whore will agree with Khepankh just to make trouble for me," Khawy said. "He is a liar too if he says I am at fault."

"Kagemni has said nothing," Den said, "but I will ask him."

"And then you will listen to his lies. Father, I am your eldest son, and yet you hold me in lower regard than the son of a man who hated you. We have all heard the stories of how your brother Hor tried to harm you. Well, he failed, but now he tries to sow dissension in your family by using his son to spread lies."

"Enough of all this," Den groaned. "My *ma'at* has been severely disturbed. If you boys will not become friends again..."

"When were we ever friends?" Khepankh muttered.

"...then you must stay apart," Den went on. He hesitated a few moments. "Until I can determine the truth of this, Kagemni is part of this household, and Khepankh is too young, so Khawy, you must move out."

"You turn me out of my own home? Where will I go?"

"Go and live in the workers' village. You are old enough to do so, and it will only be for as long as you decide. Any time you will extend the hand of friendship to your brother and Kagemni, you may return."

Khawy put on a show of bravado, but his face was pale and unsmiling as he walked to the door. "Do not think I will return unless you beg me on your knees, father. I am the one wronged in all this."

Den ordered Khepankh to his room, and though he was old enough to work and should not be considered a child, he obeyed his father. When he was alone, Den sat down and put his head in his hands, groaning and berating himself at having a family determined to rip itself apart.

"I will go to Kagemni and demand to know the truth of it," he told himself. "If Khawy is at fault, he must be punished, but if he speaks the truth, then I must rid myself of my brother's son, no matter how much that might grieve me."

If Kagemni came home that night, it was after Den fell into an exhausted and troubled sleep, so after breaking his fast the next morning, Den decided to confront his nephew in his worksite office. When he entered the office, he found Kagemni asleep at his desk, snoring lightly, papers and inkpots scattered around him. Den stood irresolutely for a few minutes and then, grasping the young man's shoulder, shook him. He came awake slowly, looking around with his eyes bleary and unfocussed.

"Eh... what..." Kagemni saw Den standing beside him and leapt to his feet, stumbling against the table as he did so. He swayed on his feet and stared at his Overseer. "I...you took me by surprise, sir."

"Are you drunk?" Den asked.

"What? No, sir...I am just tired." Kagemni waved a hand at the papers scattered on his desk. "I was working and fell asleep. I am sorry, sir."

"Working on your report?"

"Yes, sir. It is ready; I only have to put it together."

"It should have been submitted two days ago," Den said. "You are late...again."

"Yes, sir. Sorry, sir."

"I do not want your apologies, just that you do your job properly. If you cannot, then perhaps I should find someone who can."

"As my lord wishes," Kagemni said softly.

Den heard the sorrow and resignation in his nephew's voice. He did not want to dismiss Kagemni, but this situation could not continue.

"Khepankh tells me that you are having trouble with Khawy; that he delays his reports so you are late in handing them in."

"Khepankh should not have said anything," Kagemni said wearily.

"Because there is no truth in it?"

Kagemni said nothing for several moments and then shook his head. "I will say nothing against Khawy."

"Is what Khepankh said true?" Den asked. When Kagemni still said nothing, Den added, "What, then, am I to think? Who would you have me believe?"

"I would not presume to speak on the truthfulness of your sons, my lord."

"You will not help me get to the truth of this matter?"

"It is not my place, my lord."

Den sighed, looking troubled. "Then I have to let you go, Kagemni. If you cannot explain your continued tardiness, then I have no option. Please move out of Sekera as soon as you are able to find another position."

Tears threatened to spill from Kagemni's eyes, but he looked down, hiding his emotion. "I will remove my belongings from your house today, my lord, and from Sekera too."

"Very well," Den said. "I think that would be best." He turned to go.

"I am sorry if I have disappointed you, my lord," Kagemni whispered.

Den decided to go to the building site rather than back to the house, not wanting to make things awkward for either of them as Kagemni gathered his belongings. Here, he met his younger son Khepankh, who wanted to know if he had sorted things out with Kagemni.

"Kagemni takes full responsibility for his actions," Den said.

"How can he when it is all Khawy's fault?"

"That is not what he told me. He refused to account for his tardiness. Look, my son, just accept the situation and move on. Whatever the rights and wrongs, it is over now."

"How can it be over if you refuse to believe Kagemni? It will just happen again next month when Khawy does the same thing."

"No, it won't. Kagemni has decided to leave Sekera."

"Leave? No, you cannot let him, father. It is not just. It is all Khawy's fault."

"That is not what he says. He will not accuse Khawy, so I have dispute to arbiter between them. It will be better for everyone if he leaves Sekera."

"Not for me, it won't," Khepankh declared. "He is my friend. And Merit will not like it either. You do know about them, don't you?"

"What...?"

"When is he leaving? End of the month or have you given him time to find another position?"

Den looked uncomfortable. "He is packing up his belongings now...but what is this about Merit?"

Khepankh regarded his father with horror. "You are dismissing him today?" He turned and started running, back home, dust spurting up with every step. As he got closer, he started yelling out for Kagemni, but there was no answer. He burst into the main room of the house and found Merit, tears streaming from her eyes.

"He has gone," she wailed. "He just came, took his belongings and left. All he would say is that it was for the best. What has happened, Hesy-Ra?"

"Father has dismissed him," Khepankh said grimly.

"Why?"

"Khawy got him in trouble."

"Well, tell him to undo it. Father must call him back."

"We might be able to persuade Kagemni to stay. When did he leave?"

"Not long before you got here. Oh, Hesy-Ra, where will he go? I cannot bear to think of him alone out there. We were going to be married when I was older."

"What? Really?" Khepankh shook his head. "Never mind...look, we have to catch up with him. He can only have gone to the docks."

Khepankh and Merit ran from the house, calling to their stepmother Ranefert as they went that they would be back soon. Merit hitched up her dress and kept pace with her brother as they pounded down the road to the docks, dodging and weaving through the workers hauling stone from the Troyu ships, the men and women bringing food and water to the building site, and men returning empty-handed to the ships. They arrived out of breath at the teeming docks but could not see Kagemni anywhere.

"He can't have taken a ship already," Khepankh said, "so where is he?"

Merit ran to one of the ship captain's supervising the unloading of limestone blocks, asking him if any ships had left the port in the last hour. None had, that he knew of, so they were none the wiser.

"Could we have missed him and he has not yet come down from the building site?" she asked her brother. "Perhaps he went to see father one last time to plead for his job."

"It is possible, I suppose," Khepankh said, "but unlikely. From what father said, the dismissal is final."

"We should go and look for him there."

Khepankh shook his head. "Sooner or later, he will have to come to the docks. We should wait for him here; otherwise we might miss him on the site."

They waited, securing a good vantage point where they could see anyone approaching down the long slope from the funeral plateau. Merit could not sit still, forever jumping up and running into the road to see if he was coming. An hour passed, then two, and as the heat of the day approached, Khepankh had an idea that he broached hesitantly to his sister.

"I think we might have missed him altogether. He has taken the road to Inebu-hedj."

Merit leapt to her feet again. "Then we must hurry."

"It will be too late."

"If you are not even going to try, I will go alone."

"I will go with you," Khepankh said.

They hurried to the road that led along the riverbank in the direction of Inebu-hedj, but the road wound its way and there were a number of travellers so it was impossible to see him. Merit started along it, but Khepankh held her back.

"There is no point," he said. "If he came this way he will be in the city long before we got there, and we would not know where to look for him."

"We cannot just give up," Merit said. "I thought you were his friend."

"I am, but there must be a better way of looking for him. Come home, and let us give this some thought."

Khepankh coaxed his sister away from the river road and back to their family home near the building site. Den was there, with Ranefert and the younger children, and when Merit asked if Kagemni was there, he quickly confirmed what Khepankh had said.

"He has gone, daughter," he said gently. "I know you liked him, but he was not right for this position."

"But you hired him, father. You took him into our home and made him one of the family."

"I made a mistake," Den said.

"No, you just refused to believe me," Khepankh said. "I told you who was at fault here but you refused to listen and now a good man has gone."

"That is quite enough out of you," Den said reprovingly. "I am your father and Overseer of the King's Works at Sekera. You must obey me on both those counts, and I order you to say nothing more on this subject."

Fresh protests rose to Khepankh's lips but he bit them back. His father was usually a just man, but in this case had chosen in favour of his eldest son, and his own words would not persuade him otherwise.

"I obey you, father," he said quietly.

"But I do not," Merit said, sobbing. "You have not been fair, father. Kagemni is a good man and you have taken against him for no good cause."

"That is enough out of you too, daughter. My words are the law in this house, so you will obey me..."

"I hate you," Merit screamed, and ran from the room.

"You come back here and apologise," Den called after her. He got up and started to follow his daughter.

"I will speak to her," Ranefert said, putting a hand on her husband's arm. She ushered the younger children out of the room. "Could you not see that her feelings for Kagemni went beyond a sisterly affection? She took it very personally when you dismissed him."

Ranefert spoke to her at length and persuaded her for the sake of family harmony to apologise to her father. She had somewhat regretted her words after her temper cooled, and grudgingly did so. Den accepted it without comment and embraced her. For a time, relationships within the family were strained, but slowly returned to a semblance of normality. Khepankh had special words for his sister, and neither of them mentioned their thoughts to others in the family.

"I will help you look for Kagemni," Khepankh told Merit. "He is a skilled scribe and will soon find another position. We will talk to him and make all things right, you wait and see."

Chapter 28

S
ekhemkhet's sickness returned. A rash developed on his body and he coughed continually, breaking out in a sweat. Diarrhoea racked his body, the stool often bloody, and he took to his bed. Khentu, the new court physician, believed he knew what the sickness was, but was at a loss to explain how the king had it. He took his concerns to Imhotep, desiring to speak with him in private before he started treatment.

"It is a sickness that strikes down farmers and others that wade in stagnant water," Khentu said. "You can see pimples on the arms and legs of peasants where they have been exposed to the water."

"So how did the king fall sick?" Imhotep asked. "He has bathed in the river, but not often, and in company with members of the court. Have others fallen sick too?"

"No, I cannot explain it." Khentu went on at great length about the symptoms of the sickness and possible treatments for it.

Imhotep muttered the occasional word of encouragement to the physician, but his mind was on other things. The king had led an expedition to Wawat two years before, and if memory served him correctly, the sickness had first occurred just after his return. He reminded Khentu of this and the physician nodded.

"I remember. I was still Hesy-Ra's assistant at the time."

"Then you will perhaps remember that the king had occasion to fight the enemy in swampy land. Could the swamp contain the same sickness as stagnant water?"

"What is a swamp but stagnant water?" Khentu asked.

"So that is where the king became sick. The question is whether you can cure him." When Khentu said nothing, Imhotep went on. "This is where you say, 'Of course I can cure him'."

"I wish it was that simple, Tjaty. Of course I can treat the individual symptoms, relieve the itching rash, give him something to bind up his loose bowels, bring down his fever, sooth his throat...but I have no idea what causes the sickness, so how can I treat him?"

"What happens to the peasants who get it?" Imhotep asked.

"Untreated, they die."

"And treated?"

Khentu shrugged. "Nobody lives forever. Look, I know this is not what you want to hear, but it is the truth. The king could live for many years yet, though in pain, or he could sicken further and die next year. I will do my best to keep him alive, but there is no lasting cure."

Khentu did what he could; prescribing poultices that relieved the itch of the rashes on the king's arms and legs. He administered painkillers and febrifuges that moderated the fever racking the king's body, and countered the diarrhoea by feeding the king an astringent extracted from the seed of the aavo palm.

Sekhemkhet complained bitterly about the taste of some of the remedies, but allowed himself to be persuaded by Imhotep to take the medicines. His condition improved, and the king praised Imhotep for curing him, showering him with gifts. In vain did the Tjaty protest that Khentu was the real physician.

"You are too modest," the king said. "You have a great reputation as a physician as well as an architect and builder in stone. Not only are you creating a wonder in stone at Sekera for my afterlife, but you save my life as well. What ingratitude I would show if I did not reward you handsomely."

The best Imhotep could do was make gifts of his own to the court physician. Khentu would never enjoy the fame of having alleviated the king's symptoms, but Imhotep made sure material wealth flowed his way.

Sekhemkhet's health improved, though he started to suffer from swelling in his feet and ankles and shortness of breath. He became thirsty and his water turned darker. Khentu once more approached Imhotep, complaining that as fast as one set of symptoms was done away with, another set appeared.

"I will not even mention the noxious gas he passes in abundance, nor his foul breath and rotten teeth. The first of those is life, and the others are connected, I believe."

"Rotten teeth will often lead to foul breath," Imhotep agreed. "You must have breath fresheners he can use."

"Of course, but short of pulling his teeth, I cannot cure the condition," Khentu said.

"Do what you can to restore our king to health," Imhotep replied. He drew the physician aside and confided in him. "The king's heir is but a child. It would be a catastrophe if he was called upon to assume the throne before he comes of age."

Khentu looked alarmed. "What do you know that you are not telling me?"

"Nothing. Nothing at all. Just make him better."

A persistent thought had been at the back of his mind for some time now, but with the king's continued illness, it insisted on attracting his attention. Hesy-Ra was now in retirement, but Imhotep believed he was the only man he could trust under the circumstances.

Hesy-Ra shook his head wearily when Imhotep raised the subject. "Do not take me amiss, old friend, but you are trying to sell stale fish. You tried to prove this with Netjerikhet and now with Sekhemkhet, but you present no more evidence now than before. The king's sicknesses are natural and common--unless you think this mysterious poisoner is trying to kill thousands of peasants too."

"You mistake my aim, Hesy-Ra. I am not talking about the king's sickness, but at the undoubted poison that killed two of his sons. If it had not been for an overenthusiastic guard, we might have questioned the poisoner and know who was behind it."

"You have not been able to identify him then?"

"His name was Sumer, he was a man of Assur, and he came to Inebu-hedj a month before the deaths of the boy. Several palace servants shared pots of beer with him and the woman he befriended and killed. They gave me what information I have."

"No idea whether he acted on his own or on someone's behalf?"

"How would a man of Assur benefit by the deaths?" Imhotep asked. "The answer, of course, is that he would not. We must look further afield to find someone who would."

"Let me guess," Hesy-Ra said. "That someone lives in the north."

"Where else?"

Hesy-Ra shook his head again. "Do you have any actual evidence? If not, you must ask yourself whether you want it to be Khaba and Nubsekhem so much, your desire blinds you to the real culprit."

"You are right in that I have no real evidence as such, but I do have indications that point to Hut-waret. If the king and his heirs did not exist, the house of Khaba would have a strong claim to the throne. They are military men..."

"Khaba is retired," Hesy-Ra observed.

"He was told to retire by the king. Who knows what resentments he now holds in his heart?"

Hesy-Ra considered the Tjaty's words. "I can see your reasoning, but all these murders have been directed at the king's children. If this really were some attempt to usurp the throne, wouldn't he have tried to kill the king? A king without an heir is still a king, but an heir without a king is his best chance."

"How do we know that he was not going to try and kill the king also?"

"Another unknown," Hesy-Ra commented. "So what will you do next? Where will you look for more evidence?"

"I do not know. If this Sumer came from Khaba, there should be a record of him in Per-Bast or Hut-waret. I suppose I will have to send spies there to find out."

"That might tell Khaba, if he is guilty, that you suspect him. If he feels he has nothing left to lose, you might precipitate a civil war. As you pointed out, they are military men. Can you be sure they are not waiting for just such a pretext to launch their war?"

"Then I must tell the king," Imhotep said. "I will lay out the evidence I have and let him decide what to do."

Imhotep went to the king and asked after his health, listening gravely to the weakness that still afflicted him. He accused Khaba and Nubsekhem of complicity in the murder of the king's sons, presenting the king with all the evidence he had, bolstering it with conjecture and guesswork. Sekhemkhet listened but made no comment when his Tjaty finished.

"My lord king, your northern generals have conspired against you, and have employed men who have struck at your family most viciously. You must strike back in self-defence."

"What would you have me do, Imhotep?"

Imhotep frowned. "These men are on the verge of open rebellion against your rule. You must challenge them immediately. Order them down to Inebu-hedj to defend their actions. Judge them, my lord."

"How do you think they will respond if I order them here to answer those charges? They will either flee into Kanaan and raise an army against me, or march at once with the northern army. Neither prospect appeals to me."

"The former response will give you time to raise an army of your own, my lord..."

"And the latter response will see them claim my throne."

"The northern army is loyal, my lord," Imhotep protested. "They will not march against their rightful king. If Khaba were so foolish as to try it, his officers would rise up and bring him to you in chains."

"You seem very sure of that, yet a year ago I believe there was an abortive attempt on my life by Nubsekhem and his son Huni. If I had not returned home by another route, I think I might have died. Such an attempt could not be made without the support of officers and men."

"If such a thing was planned, my lord, the disloyal faction can only have been very small. A score of men at most."

"Khaba, and Nubsekhem after him, have been in command of the northern army for many years," the king said. "Ample time to suborn loyal men."

"Even so, they cannot have a large army..."

"Size is relative," Sekhemkhet said. "How many would be enough? One hundred men...? Two hundred? They may well have more."

"Then you must meet them with a larger army of men loyal to you. We have soldiers here in Inebu-hedj, we can raise more in the south, in Wawat. Meet your enemy with five hundred trained men and they cannot win."

"I could do as they have done and dispatch a man to the north. He could quickly fix my problem."

"My lord king, you are a better man than that. Your enemies stoop to such behaviour but that is not your way. You rule by law, not by assassination."

Sekhemkhet sighed and gave a wry smile. "You are right again, Imhotep, but if I meet them in battle, I must lead the army myself." He shrugged. "I have a desire to crush my enemies, but my recent illness has weakened my body. No, never mind, I will find the strength to do it. Before you get too smug, it will be your task to raise five hundred men for my army. How long will you need?"

"If we are to look for men from Wawat, six months."

"Too long. Khaba could decide to march against me within a month...two at the most."

"Then I must look for men closer to home," Imhotep said. He thought for a few moments. "Palace guards can be enrolled, and if we stripped the palace of them, that would give us two hundred men with at least some experience of warfare. There is another source of Wawat men close by, but I will need to promise them gold and cattle to volunteer."

"You shall have what you need," Sekhemkhet said. "Where are these men?"

"At Sekera. Several hundred joined the workforce there, but Wawat tribesmen make better warriors than they do common labourers. I think I will be able to persuade them to join your army."

366

"Then do so, Imhotep. Quickly."

Nubsekhem received the report only days later. He had already noted, with great satisfaction, that Sumer had accomplished the death of the children, throwing the succession into doubt once more. The king had even been reduced to making a son of a slave woman his heir. Sumer's death did not concern him as there was no way to tie him to the Hut-waret garrison. Only the king's dilemma interested him.

"That will be unacceptable to most of Kemet's nobility," he told Huni. "Faced with a choice between me and a slave child, it is obvious who they will choose."

The other news that arrived worried him at first. Imhotep had mobilised the palace guards and brought in five hundred Wawat men from the Sekera building site. They were undergoing military training on the fields opposite Inebu-hedj.

"There can only be one reason for this call up of men," Nubsekhem said. "He is going to march against us."

"Would he just launch an attack like that without warning?" Huni asked. "I mean, if he thought you were guilty of something, wouldn't he order you before him or send men to arrest you?"

"Only if he thought there was some doubt as to my guilt. Then he would give me a chance to defend myself. By raising men, he declares my guilt and moves to stop me."

"Guilt about what, father? What does he imagine you have done?"

"The death of his sons."

Huni stared open-mouthed. "That was you? That...that dreadful poison was by your hand?"

"By my order, at least," Nubsekhem confirmed. "I thought Sumer was killed before he could say anything, but they must have discovered who employed him. Well, no matter, it is what it is."

"I cannot believe you did that, father. You said you would not."

"Grow up, Huni. I am doing this because Sekhemkhet is bad for Kemet and I would make a far better king. Do you honestly think he is going to step aside for me? Of course not; he will fight for his life and his throne."

"But innocent children, father? I can barely understand you might kill the king that way, but to kill children?"

"Those innocent children would grow up to be men who would seek revenge. I would be a fool to let them live."

"I do not like it, father. You say it is necessity, but it goes against everything I believe in." Huni shook his head. "I cannot support you in this."

"You would let the king execute me?"

"What are you talking about?"

"Do you imagine the king will bring his army north merely to tell me I have been a naughty boy? He will take me, try me, and execute me, along with my father, my wife and my sons. He will not rest until he has stamped our family into the ground."

"No..."

"Oh, yes. If we do nothing, then this can only end one way."

Huni stared at his father, his mind in a whirl. "If we do nothing? What can we do?"

Nubsekhem grinned. "We oppose him, we defeat him, and I take my place on the throne of Kemet."

"You planned this."

"Well, not exactly, but I thought there was a good chance it might happen this way. At last, all our planning comes to fruition. All the gold we have spent in bribes, all the officers and men we have suborned over the years. Now it comes down to this: the king moves against us openly, and we defend ourselves. The can only be one winner, and I intend that it should be the house of Nubsekhem."

Nubsekhem immediately mobilised the Northern Army, but did not tell the officers the identity of the enemy. Instead, he hinted vaguely that the king was creating a new army to wage war on the same foe.

"I want them ready to fight," Nubsekhem told his son, "but not who they are to fight."

"They will find that out when they face the king's banners," Huni pointed out. "You face the possibility of mass desertions then. Would it not be better to apprise them of the facts now? Then if any are reluctant, you can remove them from the army."

"Your thoughts are noted, my son," Nubsekhem said.

"But you are not going to follow my advice, are you?"

"Do not take it amiss if I do not. I have a plan."

Huni felt uneasy about his father's actions. Nubsekhem had an army of questionable loyalty and he would be pitting it against the king's army. The Northern Army was better trained but was smaller, and Huni did not like to contemplate what might happen if the two armies met in battle. His father might have a plan, but as any good commander knew, a plan did not outlast the beginning of hostilities. There were so many imponderables, so many unknown factors, that it would be impossible to predict the outcome of this impending confrontation.

What do I do? Huni wondered. *Is an attack by the king so inevitable that we must meet it head-on...or can we find another solution? One that will not lead to the immediate extermination of our family?*

Huni wished there was someone he could talk to; someone who knew his father and what he might be capable of, but who would remain loyal to the family. There was Khakhet, of course, but he was only thirteen, barely entering upon that state of a man, and without much experience. He was also related to Imhotep through his mother, who was the Tjaty's daughter, and that was enough for Nubsekhem to doubt his loyalty. Khaba did not seem to doubt it though, so maybe it was safe to talk to him. Khakhet spent most of his days with Khaba on his estates near Per-Bast, but sometimes came to Hut-waret to commune with his father and brother. When he did, he stayed with friends in the town rather than at the military headquarters of the garrison, and by chance, he was in Hut-waret just then.

"You are well, little brother?" Huni asked. "Grandfather gives you everything you want?"

"I am well, thank you, Huni, and as for grandfather, he gives me what I need."

"You do not come to Hut-waret often enough. I know father would like to see more of you, as would I."

"You do not have to pretend," Khakhet said. "I am well aware that father thinks little of me. You are more to his taste." He smiled as Huni started to protest. "I am at peace with the idea, brother, so do not try denying it. You and father are both soldiers and think alike, whereas I am not. My interests lie in priestly realms."

Huni frowned but nodded. "I thought that might have been a passing fancy. You are content to serve the gods thus?"

"I am."

"Studying hard?"

"Of course."

An awkward silence fell between the two brothers until the younger cleared his throat. "Do not think I am not happy to see you, brother," Khakhet said, "but did you really seek me out merely to exchange pleasantries?"

"I wish I could say it was only that," Huni said, "though it touches on the well-being of our family." He fell silent, frowning.

"Say on, brother," Khakhet said. "I must assume it is serious if you do not come out with it straightaway."

"Grandfather is loyal to the king, isn't he?"

"Of course; as am I."

"As are we all," Huni said. He frowned, wondering how to proceed.

"You did not want to speak about just family loyalty, brother, so I suggest you just grasp the thornbush and tell me."

"Father is convinced that the king is gathering an army together and will lead it against our family."

"You cannot be serious. Why would the king do that?"

"I am not privy to the king's thoughts," Huni said, "but whatever the reason; father believes he comes to destroy our family."

"If the king really is coming, then what has happened to provoke him? Has father done something? Is this something to do with the death of Prince Nub-Re? Father swore he had nothing to do with that."

"And I believe him; but what if the king does not? We have enemies at court, Khakhet. I know you are related to him, but Tjaty Imhotep..."

"I am of the family of Khaba, not of Imhotep," Khakhet said firmly.

"That is good to know, as Imhotep is no friend of our family. It might be that he has poisoned the ear of the king against us, but whatever the reason, father believes the king is marching against us."

"What will he do?" Khakhet asked.

"I do not know. March against the king probably. I do not know what to advise him. You are young, but you reside in the house of Khaba and must have learned something of his nature. What would you do...what would Khaba do?"

Khakhet shook his head. "Gods, brother, I am a priest, not a strategist, and if you want to know what grandfather would do, ask him."

"I would if he was in Hut-waret."

"Per-Bast is a day away by boat, brother. If you are concerned, go and speak with him. Father will not even notice you have gone."

Being second-in-command, Huni could not just leave when he wanted, and his duties kept him close to the garrison for several days. He ordered the men into their units, putting the most loyal officers in charge as he and Nubsekhem had previously planned. Anyone in the army that was still of doubtful loyalty was given duties that would not require them to march to meet the king, but in half a month their army was ready.

"Sekhemkhet is still training his men on the fields across the river from Inebu-hedj," Nubsekhem said. "When he is ready, he will likely march his men northeast, following the easternmost arm of the river. When that happens, we will march to meet him."

"You are determined upon this course of action, father?"

"We can do nothing else. If we do not oppose him, we will be executed--all of us. Is that what you want?"

"Of course not...but is there really no other choice? Rebellion is a big thing."

"There is no choice, my son. The king has forced this upon us."

"Very well then, father. When do we leave?"

"Not before he marches. I have spies watching him that will give us good warning."

Huni realised the enforced wait for the spies to bring the news gave him the time he needed. As long as he was circumspect, he could leave the garrison and be down in Per-Bast before anyone knew he was gone. Then an hour or so to talk to Khaba and work out the best thing to do, and a swift boat journey back to Hut-waret. If the gods smiled, his father would not even know he had gone.

Do I still want to go? he asked himself. *I have spent this last half-month doing exactly what my father wants. Does that not mean that I have cast in my lot with him? Going to Khaba is...somehow disloyal.*

"No," he murmured. "I merely seek my grandfather's advice. I will listen to his words and return to my father, at ease with what we must do."

Huni recognised that he would have fully supported his father's bid for the throne if it had not been for the deaths of the princes. That fact alone gave him pause, and the thought of seizing power over the bodies of dead children revolted him.

"It may be that I am too weak to be considered my father's heir, though I believe my response is a noble one. Khaba has great experience and will be able to set my mind at rest, one way or another."

Huni and Khakhet paid gold to the owner of a fishing boat to carry them to Per-Bast, and to escape detection, sailed in the darkness before dawn. They were out of sight of the guards in Hut-waret by the time the sun rose, spreading warmth and light over the turgid flow of the river. Khakhet was young enough just to sit back and enjoy the trip upriver, the boat pushed along by a gentle northerly breeze, but Huni fretted. He was worried that their father would hear they had left and would send soldiers after them, perhaps even believing they were defecting to the king's side. As they got further from Hut-waret, Huni swapped one worry for another. The king might have marched and his army would appear before them, taking them captive.

To get to Per-Bast, they had to sail up the easternmost arm of the river almost as far as Inebu-hedj, before turning into the next arm of the river. This one flowed more to the north and not far down it was the city of Per-Bast. Khaba's estate was a little north of the city, set on a low hillock raised a man's height above the water. They made their way there, and the guard on the gate recognised Khakhet, calling out a greeting to him.

"We must speak with Lord Khaba at once," Khakhet said. "Please send word to him."

Soon thereafter, they were ushered into the presence of Khaba, who expressed surprise at seeing the two of them.

"I was not expecting you back so soon," he told Khakhet, "and I see too little of you, Huni. What brings you here now?"

"Grandfather, I need advice," Huni said.

"Which is why I brought him to see you," Khakhet added.

Khaba sent for beer and bread to refresh his young guests and gestured toward comfortable chairs. "I am always happy to offer advice," he said, "though in my experience, the young seldom take it. However, seeing as you are asking for it, perhaps I can hope for more. What is the problem?"

"It concerns the king, grandfather...and our father."

"I rather thought it might," Khaba said, chewing on a crust of bread. "The king has raised an army of six hundred men who train near Inebu-hedj, though nobody knows what the king intends."

"Father believes the king intends to come north and crush him."

"I was not aware my son was in open conflict with our king. What has happened?"

Huni hesitated, suddenly worried what might happen if he divulged that Nubsekhem had resorted to killing children.

"Father has...has committed a crime against the king."

"Are you sure about this?" Khaba asked. "You are not just reading something into the fact of the king's army?"

"I wish I was, grandfather, but Nubsekhem admitted it to me. It is the reason the king will march against him and try to exterminate our family."

"We have always been loyal to the king," Khaba said. "I cannot imagine why he would turn against us. Your father must be mistaken."

"What was the crime?" Khakhet asked.

"Supposed crime," Khaba said. "Tell me what it is that your father is supposed to have done."

Huni held his head in his hands. "He killed the king's sons."

"What?" Khakhet exclaimed. "How ridiculous."

"He admitted it to me, but..." Huni looked hopefully at his grandfather, "...you know him well, sir. He must be lying for some strange purpose. Surely he would not really do such a thing."

"Did you father tell you the method he employed?"

"Poison, sir." Huni smiled wanly. "It must have been some strange jest."

Khaba shook his head. "This is not the first time he has mentioned such a thing. He admitted making King Netjerikhet sick, and intimated he had made similar attempts on the life of Sekhemkhet and his family." He looked at his eldest grandson keenly. "He now openly admits poisoning the princes?"

"Yes, sir."

"And he believes the king now moves against him?"

"That is what he told me, sir."

"What are your father's intentions? Will he oppose the king?"

"He has mobilised the Northern Army, and readied it for warfare."

"I can verify there are a lot of soldiers in Hut-waret, and that they seem to be preparing for something," Khakhet said.

"He cannot hope to succeed," Khaba protested. "The Northern Army is a good fighting force, but they will lay down their arms at once when they see the king's banners opposing them."

"Maybe once, sir, but we have moulded the army into a force loyal to father rather than to the king."

"He has promised them rewards?"

"Yes, sir. Officers and men."

"A man who fights for gold is never worth a man who fights for honour and his oath to the king," Khaba said in a sneering voice.

"Yes, sir, but once committed to action, such a man will fight if the alternative is execution."

"So why have you come to me with this tale?" Khaba asked. "You are your father are two bricks in the same wall, aren't you?"

"You are right to say that, sir, for I have been a willing participant in my father's plans. I have become an army commander in my own right, and I believe him when he says that our family is every bit as good as the king's. He says our family should rule, sir, and I support that...but not if it means making war on children." Huni gave his grandfather an agonised look. "I want my father to be the king, as I think he would be a good one, but..."

"But?" Khaba asked.

"Killing children is not acceptable, sir."

"No, it is not, but the guilt for that act will settle upon you as much as upon your father unless you dissociate yourself from him."

"How do I do that, sir?"

"You must refuse to take part in his rebellion. Stay here and do not return to your duties with the Northern Army."

"That is desertion, sir. My father would rightly send men to arrest me."

"It is not desertion if you are remaining faithful to your oath of fealty to the king."

Huni looked unhappy. "I want to do what is right, sir, but my father is the authority in the north. The king believes my father guilty and me by association. If I do nothing, it will be the same as if I fought against him."

"Then I will write to the king," Khaba said. "I will explain to him that whatever he believes of your father does not extend to the rest of our family.

It will only take a day or two to get the message to him. In the meantime, stay here with me. I will make some excuse to your father."

"He does not know I am here, sir."

"We slipped away under cover of darkness," Khakhet said with a grin. "It was a grand adventure."

"Then perhaps I will say nothing to your father," Khaba said. "If you have disappeared, it may give him pause, and any delay in the start of a civil war gives us more opportunity to avoid it altogether."

Chapter 29

S ekhemkhet returned from a day drilling his troops on the eastern
plains, tired but content. Even the persistent cough that plagued him
did not discourage him. He drank deeply of cool river water and then
stood while servants sluiced the sweat and dust from his body before
dressing him in clean linens. Calling Imhotep to attend upon him, he tackled
a dish of beef and onions with fresh bread, eating quickly to assuage his
hunger.

"A pleasing day, my lord?" Imhotep asked.

"The troops are coming along nicely," Sekhemkhet said. "I think I shall
have to bring more Wawat men into my army in the future. They take readily
to feats of arms."

"I pray you will have no further need of armies once Nubsekhem has
been taken care of. Except for a few troublesome tribes, there is no need to
wage war on our neighbours."

The king grunted. "War is a noble pastime, and I can always find some
excuse to extend our borders or our influence." He gestured toward the wine
jug. "Have some, Imhotep. It is very palatable and perfectly safe. I have made

sure that none of it comes from Khaba's vines, though I shall drink his wine when it is no longer his."

"I am glad you brought up his name, my lord, for I have had a letter from Khaba."

"Indeed? Trying to stave off the destruction of his family, is he? What flimsy excuses did he use, or does he deny his son's black deeds entirely?"

"Not at all, my lord. He does not seem to deny anything."

"Then why does he write? Is he pleading for mercy? I may do that, you know. If Nubsekhem comes to me on his knees, I might forgive him."

"I do not think that will happen, my lord. As for Khaba, he asks only that you arrest Nubsekhem without resorting to warfare against your own people, giving him a fair and open trial. He professes ignorance of the crimes of which his son is accused, on behalf of himself and his grandsons Huni and Khakhet...the womenfolk too."

"Khakhet is your grandson too, isn't he?" Sekhemkhet asked.

"Yes, my lord."

"I suppose you plead for his life too, do you?"

"I am content to leave his life in your hands, my lord king. You have a reputation for both justice and mercy."

"I will consider his guilt carefully when I put the family on trial."

"Please remember he is only a boy of some thirteen years and can scarcely be caught up in the treasons of his father."

"A thirteen year old boy can be considered a man under the right circumstances, but I take your point. I will consider his case very carefully."

"That is all I ask, my lord."

Sekhemkhet picked up another piece of bread and dipped it into goose grease. Instead of eating it, though, he sat and looked at it, thinking.

"There is one thing you can do in response to Khaba's letter. Tell him that any member of his family who comes to Inebu-hedj and kneels before me will be spared." The king smiled and popped the morsel of bread and grease into his mouth. "Tell him also that if no one does so, then the whole family will be judged as rebels."

"Is there a time frame for this act of mercy, my lord?"

"Yes, I will march against Nubsekhem in ten days' time. If they have not surrendered themselves by then, my mercy is at an end. They will have to take their chances in battle."

It might have only been the worry of the situation that caused Imhotep to eschew a definite date for the ending of the king's mercy in his letter to Khaba. He spent time carefully crafting it, imploring Khaba to listen to the king's words for the sake of his family. The messenger who carried the letter, reached the Per-Bast estates on the third day, and handed it to Khaba, withdrawing to give the retired general some privacy. Khaba read it carefully before calling his grandsons to him.

"The king gives us ten days to surrender and kneel before him. If we do this, he promises our lives will be spared."

"Then we must do so," Khakhet said immediately.

"It would seem the most logical course," Huni said, "but can we trust the king?"

"That is the question," Khaba conceded. He read the letter out loud, commenting on the words of Imhotep within it. "He stresses family, you notice. I think he has you in mind, Khakhet. I think you should leave immediately for Inebu-hedj and go to your grandfather Imhotep. He will protect you when you kneel before the king."

"I am of your family, grandfather, not that of Imhotep. I will go to Inebu-hedj when we all go...or not at all."

"Then we must make a decision as a family," Khaba said. "The three of us are in accord, but we must make an effort to convince your father. If he would join us when we kneel to the king, I believe things would go better for all of us."

Khaba had a letter drawn up revealing the king's offer of mercy, and stressing the date on which the offer would end, ten days hence. He implored Nubsekhem to think of his family and submit to the king, and promised to do his utmost to intercede with the king on his son's behalf.

Huni refused to carry the letter to his father, saying that he risked being forced into his father's rebellion if he went back. The king's messenger, who was waiting for Khaba's reply, agreed to carry Khaba's letter to Hut-waret. He left Per-Bast on the fourth day and arrived at the northern garrison a day later.

Nubsekhem's immediate reaction was to imprison the king's messenger, convinced that he had been sent as a spy. Then he read the letter he carried, and learned that both his sons were in Per-Bast with their grandfather. He cried out in anger that Huni, in particular, should desert him in his time of need, and uttered imprecations against Khaba and Khakhet.

"Surrender to the king and kneel before him? Are they mad? This is merely a ploy to get the family in his power without risking war. Well, I shall teach him what it means to take me lightly."

Nubsekhem read the letter again, noting the ten-day deadline and interpreting it to mean ten days from the writing of the Khaba's letter.

"So the king expects me to bend my knee to him in eight days' time, does he? No doubt he thinks that his army of tribesmen will frighten me into submission. It is time he finds out what manner of man opposes him."

Nubsekhem ordered his army into motion, but because he hurriedly put forward his plans, they marched without adequate supplies. Some of his soldiers, particularly the Wawat archers, had fewer arrows than they needed. When their officers protested to Nubsekhem, pleading to delay for another few days, he angrily refused.

"We must be at the plains across from Inebu-hedj in six days," he told them. "The king is expecting me to tamely surrender eight days from now, but we will fall upon them while they are unprepared, and secure our victory."

Before the army left Hut-waret, Nubsekhem put to death the king's messenger. He was determined to descend upon the king with as little warning as possible, and caused to be killed any man who might be able to carry word south. Every fishing boat they encountered was destroyed, and if the fishermen protested too much, they were killed. As a result, Nubsekhem's army made good time down the shore of the easternmost arm of the river, swiftly reaching Iunu and pushing on toward the plains.

Confident of finding the king's army in a state of unreadiness, Nubsekhem's leading units, advancing casually, ran into forward units of Sekhemkhet's men and reeled back in some confusion. The news was carried to Nubsekhem and he ordered his men into a defensive line even as the king's army surged forward. Two lines of armed men formed up with only a hundred paces between them, and stood uneasily eyeing the other. Both armies were of similar size, though Nubsekhem's men stood confidently, resting upon their spears, while the Wawat tribesmen of the king moved restlessly, chafing against the discipline imposed by their officers.

Now that the enemy had been encountered, neither side seemed sure of the next move. Nubsekhem stared across the intervening space, seeing the king's banners flying, and trying to work out from the placement of those banners where the separate units were gathered. In his mind, the king had once more proved his perfidy, advancing on him before the ten days were up.

"He never intended to give me the opportunity of surrendering, as evidenced by him being here after just eight days. Well, if he thought to take me by surprise, he is confounded."

Nubsekhem turned to give the order to advance when an officer called his attention to movement in the opposing ranks. King Sekhemkhet stepped out and advanced into the open area between the armies, accompanied by a burly man he did not recognise. The king reached the midway point and stopped, looking up and down the ranks of the Northern Army, and Nubsekhem wondered if the king expected him to join him and talk.

"What would be the point?" he muttered. "I am here for a single purpose and I will not be deflected from it by words."

Unexpectedly, the burly man standing by the king started shouting, bellowing out a message to the Northern Army, and Nubsekhem, taken by surprise, was slow to stop it.

"Men of the Northern Army," bellowed the burly man, speaking for his king, "I stand before you as your lawful king. I do not know why your commanders have ordered you to march south, but it can be for no lawful purpose as I did not countenance it. Your actions, and the actions of your officers, are those of rebellion and deserving of death. Yet I will be merciful, knowing that your officers have lied to you.

"Turn, lay down your arms, and march back to your garrison at Hutwaret and I will overlook your actions this day. If you do this, then only your officers, and your commander Nubsekhem, will answer for their actions. If you do not immediately return to your garrison, then I will hold you guilty of rebellion and mete out sentences of death..."

Nubsekhem saw that already some men were talking among themselves, looking around and shuffling their feet. "Attack!" he cried.

The men closest to him, and those under the command of his best warriors, obeyed, drawing their weapons and running forward. Others, scattered through the lines hesitated, many drawing back while their comrades rushed forward. As the Northern Army ran toward the king, the king's army let out a great war-paean and rushed to defend their king. Now, Sekhemkhet stood in the front line of the battle, yelling his defiance and exhorting his men to kill the enemy.

"Let none of them survive," he shouted. "They are rebels and are worthy of death."

Nubsekhem could see his men were faltering already as they examined the loyalty they had promised for gold and found the price too little for their lives. They started streaming away from the battle, and he tried to turn them back, grabbing at men, promising reward or punishment, begging them to remember the oaths they had given. Some he shamed into staying, but others fled, throwing away their weapons as he went.

"Sir, save yourself," one of his senior officers said. "The battle is lost, but we can hold them back awhile to give you a chance."

"The battle is not lost while either Sekhemkhet or I remain alive," Nubsekhem grated. He pushed to the front rank of his steadily decreasing army and looked for the sight of the king surrounded by his men.

"Sekhemkhet, come and meet me man to man. My quarrel is with you, and yours is with me. Allow my men to live if you prevail and I will do the same."

The king shouted for quiet, and answered his enemy, less than twenty paces between them. "I have no need of bargaining with a rebel. Surrender now and I will give you a clean death. Your men will swear fealty to me or die."

"Are you afraid to meet me, Sekhemkhet? Are you such a coward that you, a young man, fears to meet a man twice your age?"

A man who stood beside the king remonstrated with him, arguing that the king held the advantage in the battle and that there was no need to fight the rebel on his own terms.

"What sort of a king would I be if I feared to meet an old man in battle?" Sekhemkhet asked. Louder, he called out, "Stand forth then, Nubsekhem, and prepare for death."

The two armies fell silent as the news spread that the general and the king would fight to the death. They drew back, opening up a small arena of ground littered with dead bodies. Men from both sides ran to drag the bodies away. Nubsekhem stood waiting, armed with a curved sword, a short axe in his belt, and a cowhide shield. He watched as the king divested himself of his jewellery, taking up similar weaponry and testing their weight and balance.

"When you are dead, your men are free to go once they have sworn fealty," the king called out.

Nubsekhem laughed. "And your men are pardoned when you lie dead at my feet."

"That will not happen."

Nubsekhem beat his sword blade on his shield. "Come and meet your death."

Sekhemkhet started forward, angling to one side, circling the other man who moved to keep facing him. The watchers on both sides immediately saw the fighting merits of both men--Nubsekhem was powerfully built and experienced, whereas the king was more slightly built and moved quickly and easily. Aside from the importance the outcome held for all of them, it promised to be a fascinating encounter.

The king leapt forward, feinting with his sword before lifting his shield and slamming it into his opponent, his blade stabbing over the top. Fast as he was, Nubsekhem's blade met his own and then the king was thrown back as the general pushed, his own sword now probing the king's defences.

Now Nubsekhem went on the offensive, slashing his sword at the king, beating down his defences and driving him back. Sekhemkhet moved quickly, but the general's strength started to show as he rained blows on the king's shield. The king stumbled, his foot slipping in blood-soaked mud, almost going down on one knee. Nubsekhem's shield crashed down, forcing the king's shield aside and the general's blade stabbed forward, scoring a line on the king's chest. The wound poured blood, and a great moan of anguish went up from the royal army, but Sekhemkhet staggered back, lifting his shield once more.

"A scratch," he called out. "Is that the best you can do?"

The two men stood close, trading blows blocked on shield or blade, but neither could gain an advantage and after several minutes it was Sekhemkhet who withdrew, stepping back a few paces. Nubsekhem did not follow, and observers could see that the general, despite his greater strength, was feeling the same weariness. They stood and glared at each other, breathing hard, before lifting their weapons and coming together again.

The battle continued, and soon the shields were ripped and torn. Nicks and grooves marred the copper swords too, and during a spell when the fighters drew apart, Nubsekhem put his sword in his belt and drew his short axe. Sekhemkhet hesitated, thinking to do the same, but the general leapt forward, the blade of his axe descending swiftly and burying itself in the rim of the king's shield. The king twisted his shield, hoping to trap the blade, but Nubsekhem wrenched it free and attacked again.

Sekhemkhet retreated again, with Nubsekhem raining blows with his axe, driving the king back as he hacked pieces off the king's shield. This time it was the general who stepped back, resting the edge of his shield on the ground as he caught his breath. The king bent over and vomited copiously, before straightening with a groan, his face pale and sweating.

"Is that from fear or because you are sick?" Nubsekhem demanded.

"You would know if I was sick," the king said. "You poisoned my children and for all I know, you tried to poison me."

Nubsekhem said nothing, though many men on both sides muttered, staring at the general.

"I see you do not deny it," Sekhemkhet said. "How could you when the blood of slain children cries out your guilt?"

"Are you going to talk all day?" Nubsekhem asked. "Fight me, and I will reunite you with your sons soon enough."

The king took out his axe and moved forward. He moved wearily, as if his strength was running out. The wound on his chest had stopped bleeding, though his belly was caked with dried blood that cracked as he moved. Again they met, shields bumping and axes seeking openings to side or top, blocked by the other or failing to find flesh. A blow on the head by the side of the general's axe sent the king reeling back, but Nubsekhem was slow to follow. Breathing hard, he stepped forward, hammering his axe on the king's defences, beating him down. Sekhemkhet retreated again, his shield now dipping lower as if it was too heavy to hold up.

Nubsekhem grinned, anticipating victory, took two strides forward with axe upraised, beating aside the king's shield, but his blade caught in the broken wooden rim and he could not withdraw it for a moment. His right side was momentarily exposed, and Sekhemkhet lunged forward, hacking sideways, and his own axe blade sliced into his opponent's upper arm. The general cried out in agony, his axe tearing loose from the shield as he fell back. His grip on his axe failed and he staggered back as blood cascaded from an arm rendered useless in a moment.

Throwing aside his shield, Nubsekhem snatched up his fallen axe with his left hand and swept it forward, desperately seeking to beat down the king's defences. Sekhemkhet blocked the blows with his own axe and tattered shield, but his legs gave way and he sprawled on the ground. With a shout of triumph, Nubsekhem leapt forward, but his foot slipped on the slime of the king's vomit and he fell to his right. His wounded arm failed to hold him up and he screamed with pain and collapsed. For a few moments, both antagonists lay on the ground only two paces apart.

Sekhemkhet recovered first, dropping his shield and staggering to his feet. He stood over Nubsekhem with his axe held in both hands, staring down at the mask of agony and defeat on his enemy's face.

"For my sons," the king said, as he brought the axe down, splitting Nubsekhem's skull.

There was silence for a moment, and then the royal army erupted in cheers, while the remnants of the Northern Army started edging away, retreating from what they saw as their inevitable death. One of Nubsekhem's senior officers pushed forward though, confronting his bloodied king.

"You promised us our lives, my lord. Will you stand by your word?"

Sekhemkhet stared at the officer, noting that many around him had stopped to hear what he might say.

"My goodwill is conditional," the king said, forcing strength back into his voice. He pointed to one side. "Throw down your arms and kneel in front of me. Utter the oath of loyalty and I will grant you your life."

The officer nodded, tossing aside his shield, his axe, and his whip of office. Then he approached the king and knelt in the mud and the blood and swore loyalty to the king and his heirs. One by one, the other officers did the same, while the men knelt in groups with heads bowed, muttering a semblance of the same oaths. It took a long time, and as each man swore loyalty, he was led off to where the king's officers gave them new assignments. Some were sent back to Hut-waret, others to Inebu-hedj, while others were drafted into the king's own army. At last they were finished, and the king was pale and weak when his officers escorted him back to a hastily erected command tent. Imhotep was there waiting for him, having been sent for as soon as the battle had been won. He helped the king to a chair, pouring him watered wine. Khentu the physician was there too, and quickly set about washing the king's wound, smearing tree resin on the cut edges to hold them together.

"I can do better once we return to the palace, my lord," Khentu said. "Are you in pain otherwise?"

"I am sick," Sekhemkhet said weakly. "My head and my belly hurt and..." he sighed and shook his head. "...I fear I have soiled myself."

Khentu treated the king as best he could, cleaning him up and prescribing medicines to bind his bowels and disperse the pain. "With your permission, my lord, I will go and prepare your rooms for your rest."

Sekhemkhet waited until the physician had left. "I cannot return so quickly, Imhotep, much as I would like to. I have a rebellion to put down."

"I think you have done that already, my lord," Imhotep said. "Nubsekhem was undoubtedly the leader as evidenced by the fact that Khaba was not present."

"That is only because Khaba is an old man. The death of his son will take him hard and he will strike back with whatever forces he has."

"He has almost nothing," Imhotep said. "That old dog is toothless. All he can do is wait on your mercy. Return to Inebu-hedj, my lord, and I will send a man to take his surrender and escort him before you."

Chapter 30

"Your father is dead."

Khaba's words were harsh, though his expression showed the grief he felt at the loss of his only son. All he had left in the world were the two young men who stood before him, looks of horror and grief on their faces. Khakhet choked back a sob, but Huni controlled his emotions, asking only for details of the battle.

"I have few to give you," the old man went on. "The soldier who reported it to me said only that my son fell in single combat with the king. He fled before he knew whether the king would keep his word to extend mercy to the rebel army."

"Why would he?" Huni said. "He has won."

Khaba nodded. "We can expect little mercy from him, so we must decide what to do."

"Avenge him," Khakhet said. "His life was one of violence, but that was only because he was a soldier. He was my father, and I owe him revenge."

"An understandable sentiment," Khaba said, "but one impossible to fulfil. The king has every advantage and we have none. The most we can hope for is to escape the king's wrath."

"How do we do that?" Huni asked. "Where in Kemet will we be safe?"

"Nowhere, which is why we must leave...and soon. We have some small wealth, so we can take a trading ship north to one of the cities of northern Kanaan. The reach of the king will not extend that far."

"I do not want to leave Kemet," Huni said. "It is my home."

"Mine too," Khakhet said.

"And mine," Khaba agreed. "You do realise, it will be death to stay?"

"Better death with honour in our home than a life of shame in a foreign land."

"Nobly said," Khaba agreed, "but your brother deserves a chance to live. He is a boy with a long life ahead of him."

"I am a man, and I can choose my own fate," Khakhet protested, though his voice trembled slightly at the prospect of death.

"So, we stay here and wait for the king's men to arrest us?" Khaba asked.

"I do not relish the thought of sitting here doing nothing, but I am not sure what we can do," Huni said.

Khaba's chamberlain interrupted at this point, reporting that a young officer of the king's army was at the gates, requesting an audience.

"How many men are with him?" Khaba asked.

"None, my lord," the chamberlain said.

"No escort at all?" Huni mused. "What does he hope to achieve alone?"

"Why don't we ask him?"

The officer was shown in, and he looked around the room, noting the presence of the old man, a younger man and a boy. He saluted Khaba as if he was still a general, and cleared his throat.

"Lord Khaba, I am Captain Hornub, and King Hor-Sekhemkhet charges me with delivering a message to you as head of your family. He regrets the necessity of killing your son Nubsekhem and hopes that his death will not prevent sensible discussion between you and him."

"That is my father you so casually dismiss, Captain Hornub," Huni growled.

Hornub looked at Huni. "And you are who, exactly?"

"I am Huni, son of Nubsekhem, and this is Khakhet, my brother. You speak very dismissively of my father, and I take exception to that."

Hornub frowned but bowed slightly to the young man. "Forgive my choice of words, Huni. I did not mean to abuse your father's name but merely to state the facts and the king's wishes in this regard."

"You had better do so then," Khaba said. "I am curious to hear the king's words."

"Yes, Lord Khaba. King Hor-Sekhemkhet bids you and your kin travel to Inebu-hedj, there to bend your knee before the throne and seek forgiveness for the deeds of you family."

"We have done nothing wrong," Khakhet blurted.

"Your father took up arms against the king," Hornub pointed out gently. "He would be in his rights to condemn your whole family out of hand, but he is prepared to be merciful."

"He will guarantee our safe passage to Inebu-hedj and back?" Khaba asked.

"You are not thinking of doing it, are you, grandfather?" Huni asked.

"I trust the king's word. Well, Hornub, is our safety guaranteed?"

Hornub hesitated. "Lord Khaba, I was charged with delivering this message to you and accompanying you and your family to Inebu-hedj. Beyond that, I have no specific instructions."

"I must discuss this with my grandsons," Khaba said.

"What is to discuss?" Hornub asked. "The king has given you a command. Kneel before him in Inebu-hedj or condemn yourselves as rebels."

"Nevertheless, I seek counsel from my kin."

Hornub shrugged. "That is up to you, but I am leaving within the hour. I will, with your permission, refresh myself with food and drink. If you are not ready to leave then, I will have my answer and the king will swiftly respond."

The officer saluted again and strode from the room. Khaba looked at his grandsons and shrugged. "We no longer have the option of sitting and doing nothing. Either we go to Inebu-hedj with Captain Hornub and throw ourselves on the king's mercy, or we flee Kemet at once."

"There is a third option," Huni said. "We go to Inebu-hedj but not with the intention of kneeling before the king. Rather, we oppose him and avenge Nubsekhem."

"Yes, I agree," Khakhet said. "Better that than surrendering."

"March on the king?" Khaba asked. "He has an army--where is yours?"

"There are men still loyal to us," Huni said.

"Not many," Khaba said, "and certainly not an army. No, that is not a feasible response. We must throw ourselves on the king's mercy."

"Never," Huni growled. "I would rather die."

Khakhet listened to his grandfather and brother arguing, but despite agreeing with the idea of opposing the king, could see that his grandfather would win. He was head of the family and it was only a matter of time before he made an irrevocable decision, ordering their surrender. It was inevitable, unless...the germ of an audacious plan occurred to him. He would have to act swiftly and decisively though. Unobtrusively, he slipped out of the room, making his way toward the kitchens where Captain Hornub would be waiting. Trembling with nervousness, Khakhet contemplated his intended deed.

He returned in a little while to find his brother and grandfather still arguing. Khaba was losing patience with Huni's intransigence, his statements become more authoritative, and Khakhet knew he had made the right decision just in time. He cleared his throat.

"I have something to say," he said loudly.

Khaba looked away from Huni, and stared at his young grandson. For a moment, he was not sure what he was looking at, and then Huni voiced his question.

"Is that blood on you, Khakhet? And...a knife. Have you cut yourself?"

"No, but I have rendered this argument pointless. We are opposing the king."

"What have you done?" Khaba rasped.

"I have killed Captain Hornub," Khakhet said. He lifted the knife in his bloodied hand, stared at it for a moment, and threw it aside. "I have never killed anyone before."

"You have killed his envoy, and you have killed all of us, too," Khaba said bitterly. "The king will have our lives for this act, beyond any hope of mercy."

"Well, I say bravely done, brother," Huni said. "Now we can do nothing but fight and conquer."

"More likely die," Khaba said. He shook himself and his eyes gleamed. "We have run out of choices, it appears, so we must act swiftly before news of this murder reaches the king's ears." The old general frowned, thinking. "The king's army is several hundred strong and I doubt we could face it openly with any hope of success. I can raise perhaps a hundred men from the estate and the city," Khaba went on. "Most will be loyal to me as long as we do not stress we fight the king. How many men can you raise in Hut-waret, Huni?"

"That depends on how many fled the battle and are not too demoralised. Two hundred more perhaps."

"Nowhere near enough, but it will have to do. Go to Hut-waret immediately and march south to Iunu as soon as you can. I will meet you there in...what...five days?"

The old man looked more alive than he had in years, and Khakhet rejoiced to see it. He had been disappointed by his grandfather's initial response, but he seemed to have remembered who he was--the head of a proud family related to the royal house.

Huni departed for the northern garrison, and Khakhet busied himself gathering supplies for their little army while Khaba called meetings with local men, exhorting them to stand up to a king who would trample over the basic rights of the noble house of Khaba. He reminded them that as tenants and neighbours of his family, the destruction of one would lead to the demise of the other.

"All I ask is that you accompany me to Inebu-hedj, there to lend me support as I defend my family's good name against the lies that have been leaked into the king's ears."

The estate workers would do as they were told, of course, but other groups in and around Per-Bast, while they looked favourably on Khaba, were more reluctant. They had families to feed, they declared, and could not just lay down their tools, much as they would like to show their support. Khaba gritted his teeth and said he would pay wages to any man who followed him, so that none of their families would go hungry. The estate chamberlain wrung his hands when he heard of his master's promise.

"You know I am loyal to you, my lord, but where will I find enough to feed the men and their families? This will bankrupt the estate."

"Make what promises of payment you have to," Khaba instructed. "If we win the day, then we have the king's treasury to draw upon, and if we lose, broken promises will be the least of our worries."

News came from the north that Huni had enlisted nearly three hundred soldiers, made up of those who had deserted before the battle and others who refused to hold to an oath extracted from them under what they saw as duress.

"We will be ready to come south to Iunu within the next few days. I will look for you in that city, grandfather, but do not delay, I beg you. If the king marches upon me, I cannot hope to defeat him alone."

Khaba sent a swift messenger back saying he would meet him with a peasant army of nearly two hundred. As the units of his motley army came together, Khaba sat down with a sketch map of the area between Per-Bast and Inebu-hedj to work out the best approach. There were really only two options, and both involved crossing the river at some point.

"The logical route would be to march down to the plains opposite the city and ferry the troops across there," Khakhet said. "The only problem with that is gathering enough boats, but we will have to do that."

Khaba tapped the sketch with his forefinger. "Have you forgotten the king's army? As far as I can tell, they withdrew to the plains. If we go there, we will have to fight them."

"Is that not the idea, grandfather? How else can we defeat the king?"

"I have no desire to fight a pitched battle unless I have to. Our men are enthusiastic but unproven, and I think they cannot stand up to even a moderately disciplined force."

"Then where?" Khakhet asked. "Do we sail our army down from Iunu?"

"We do not have enough ships for that, but we will cross the river downstream from the plains, crossing the several arms of the delta until we are on the western bank. Then we march on the city, leaving the king's army on the eastern shore."

"Wonderful," Khakhet exclaimed. "The king will have to surrender then."

"I doubt it will be that straightforward," Khaba said. "If the king stays inside the city walls, it will be difficult to force his surrender."

"Huni could do it. He is a great soldier."

"Possibly. We will see what happens. That is all we can do--prepare and trust in the gods."

Khaba gathered together all the fishing boats he could find, scouring the river north and south, commandeering everything that could float. Then he started ferrying his own men across three branches of the river, leaving Khakhet in charge on the western shore. He took the boats across to Iunu, arriving just in time to intercept Huni and his army, telling him of his revised plans.

"I do not like this sneaking across to the western shore," Huni said. "It looks as if we are afraid. We should meet their army head-on and defeat them honourably."

"The king has a reasonably trained army that far outnumbers ours. By 'sneaking across' as you put it, we avoid conflict while putting pressure on Sekhemkhet. It is my hope that when we appear at the gates of Inebu-hedj he will see sense and surrender."

"And if he does not?"

"Then we storm the city and capture him by force."

A flotilla of small boats and a handful of ships gathered up Huni's small army, taking them upriver and across into the westernmost arm, dropping them off with Khaba's estate workers and Per-Bast volunteers. Together, they made up a multitude, but Khaba knew that if they ever faced a professional force of soldiers, they would shred like a scroll of papyrus in water. It was his intention not to let that happen. Leading with Huni's soldiers, Khaba led his little army south. They saw the king's army on the far shore, and a scattering of small boats trying to transport the men across the river.

"We must prevent that." Khaba sent instructions back to his flotilla of boats that they were to sail south and intercept the enemy boats, beating them back. "We cannot spare soldiers to man the boats," he told Huni, "so the best we can hope to do is disrupt and delay them."

Scattered units of the royal army landed on the western shore before Khaba's boats could arrive, but Huni's soldiers hunted them down and only a few made it to the safety of the city. Khaba expressed satisfaction as his small army arrived outside the city to find the gates barred. Ordering his men to set up camp, he conferred with his grandsons before having a letter written to send in to the king.

Sekhemkhet had arrived back from his victory over Nubsekhem to rapturous celebrations, and despite feeling unwell, insisted on walking through the streets to enjoy the praise of the populace. He displayed his chest wound openly, and let soldiers around him tell the tale of his single combat and how he had overcome the rebel general. The procession took all his strength, though, and by the time he arrived back at the palace, he was close to collapse.

"Hide my condition from people," he instructed Imhotep, "and send for Hesy-Ra."

"Khentu is the court physician now, my lord," Imhotep reminded him.

"Eh? Oh, very well...as long as you are there too. I value your medical knowledge."

Khentu arrived quickly and had the king undress and lie down while he examined him carefully. "The wound is superficial. I will apply an unguent and bandage it, but my lord, your illness has returned."

"I am just very tired," the king protested. "I should have cut short my procession through the city, but it was required of me. Did you see how the people cheered me, Imhotep? With one swift action I have restored the country's *ma'at*."

"Yes, my lord," Khentu said as the king dismissed him.

"By all accounts, it was a magnificent victory, my lord," Imhotep said. "I hear you have summoned Khaba to appear before you?"

"Yes. I expect him within five days."

"You really think he will come, my lord?"

"Why not? He has no choice."

"That is what I mean," Imhotep said. "A man who has no choice may do the unexpected."

Sekhemkhet laughed, but his laughter turned into a coughing fit that left him red-faced and gasping for breath. "What can he do?" he wheezed.

"He was a general in the army," Imhotep pointed out.

"A general...without...an army," the king panted. "He can do...nothing. Now send for Khentu again. He can make me up a sleeping draught."

The king took his medicine and slept, waking hours later with a fever and aching muscles. Khentu attended upon him once more, prescribing febrifuges and heated herbal compresses, but the king threw these off and insisted on getting up and bathing. It was a mistake, the king experiencing an attack of diarrhoea, followed by a seizure in the stream of cold water, and had to be carried back to his bed where he lapsed into unconsciousness.

"Do something for him, Khentu," Imhotep said.

Khentu grimaced. "I can try to bring down the fever, but he needs to be conscious to drink the liquid. I can give him painkillers, apply poultices, bind prayers to his limbs and seal up his bowels, but I cannot cure him. Look at his belly; the sickness causes it to distend and it will attack his inner organs soon."

"He is dying?"

"That is with the gods..." Khentu saw the look on Imhotep's face and shrugged. "Unless they intervene, then yes."

Over the next three days, the king regained consciousness but could not stir from his bed. Khentu and his assistants ministered to him continually, while Imhotep managed the affairs of the kingdom. He received reports that Huni was up in Hut-waret, raising troops, while Khaba enlisted the help of locals in the Per-Bast region.

"I knew it," he muttered. "You gave him no choice, so he risks all."

Imhotep hurried to the king's chamber and found him in a lucid moment. He explained the situation, and suggested they send the army north to put down Huni's men before they had a chance to properly organise.

"No," Sekhemkhet said. "They swore loyalty to me before I let them go. Whoever Huni has found can only be a handful of men. They are no danger."

"What of Khaba's men?"

"Farmers and artisans. He will find them all but useless. Ignore them and they will go away."

"My lord, we should not dismiss the danger so casually..."

"Who is the military man here?" the king asked. "Do nothing, Imhotep; that is an order."

Sekhemkhet dismissed his Tjaty then and slept, awaking hours later to retch violently and vomit blood. Khentu fussed around, doing what he could, but it was little more than making his patient comfortable. He sent for Imhotep and together they stood over the once more unconscious form of the king. Khentu lifted one of the king's eyelids, showing him how the white of his eye had turned yellow.

"The disease has reached his liver," he said. "His skin has taken on a yellowish tinge too, though that is hard to see in this light." Khentu drew back the sheet over the king's body and gently pressed his fingers into Sekhemkhet's distended belly. "Feel for yourself; it is hard and swollen."

Imhotep did so, adding in a few basic procedures of his own. He felt the little ripple beneath his fingertips in the king's neck--faint and rapid; the effect of the king's breath on a feather--weak and slow; and smelled the king's breath--his nose wrinkled in distaste.

"Have you smelt his breath?"

Khentu bent over the king and sniffed; his expression grim as he straightened up. "How would you describe it?" he murmured. "Fishy?"

Imhotep shrugged. "Like urine, I would have said. Either way, it is a bad sign."

Khentu looked sombre. "You know what it means?"

"His life is to be measured in days, at most. Can you do anything for him?"

Khentu shook his head. "You know the answer to that as well as I do. I can make him comfortable for now, but he will not last long. This is when you should bring in his heir and prepare him."

"His heir is a young boy without learning or experience," Imhotep said.

"His mother then, to act as regent?"

"Even less learning and experience."

"Then it must be you, Imhotep. You are the Tjaty, second only to the king. You have ample learning and experience. Take up the symbols of kingly power and rule the kingdoms until his heir is old enough."

Imhotep shook his head. "It is not something I relish, but I will consider it."

He left the king in Khentu's care and using his own authority, called together the principal members of the royal family--the king's mother Khemtet, Queen Meresankh and her mother Hetephernebti, and the king's wives Djeser-Ti and Tetimene. Also present was Ayah the concubine and her son Sennenkhet, who was now the king's heir.

"Ladies," Imhotep said, then bowed briefly in the direction of Sennenkhet, "...and young sir, I regret to be the bearer of bad news but the king's sickness is mortal. He will not rise from his sickbed, or if he does it will be but briefly."

He waited while the king's women openly cried aloud with grief at the confirmation of all they had known and feared. Sennenkhet looked frightened and clung to his mother. Imhotep went on.

"We face a crisis of succession..."

"My son is the king's heir," Ayah said, looking defiantly at the other women.

"Only until another son is born to his wife," Djeser-Ti countered. "I am pregnant, and when my son is born..."

"If a son is born," Tetimene interrupted.

"...then he will be heir," Djeser-Ti finished.

They all started arguing, dividing into factions supporting one or other of the filial candidates, until Imhotep called for silence.

"Ladies, cease this unseemly bickering, I implore you. Let me stress the situation as it stands. The king rules while life remains in his body, but I, as Tjaty, am empowered to act for the king in his absence or incapacity. I can say quite categorically that the king is, at present, incapacitated, and I am therefore the temporary ruler of Kemet."

"What is this?" Khemtet demanded. "You will dispossess my son to grasp power for yourself? What is next? You will crown yourself king?"

"I do not need to grasp power," Imhotep said, stung by the king's mother's remarks. "They are mine already by order of the king."

"Then what are you saying?" Hetephernebti asked.

"What I am saying is that the king's commands must stand, and I have the power to enforce it if I must."

"The king's commands being what, exactly?"

"In the absence of a son of the king's body by one of his wives or his queen, then Sennenkhet, son of the concubine Ayah, is the presumptive king following the imminent death of Hor-Sekhemkhet."

A look of triumph flitted across Ayah's face and she held her son close, while Djeser-Ti and Tetimene cast looks of hatred in her direction.

Meresankh shrugged. "It is all one to me. I am my brother's queen, but I have no son in contention. Let it be done as the king commands."

"I agree," Hetephernebti said, echoed by Khemtet.

"Then it is decided," Imhotep said. "Sennenkhet will rule after Hor-Sekhemkhet, and I will act for him until such time as the new king can rule by himself."

"That was not agreed," Ayah said. "I am Sennenkhet's mother, and I speak for my son until he is of age."

"I am sorry, Ayah, but that is unacceptable," Imhotep said. "It is inconceivable that a concubine rule Kemet, even in the king's name. You have no learning, no experience. You are completely unsuited to the task of governance. I will continue those duties."

"I support Imhotep's contention," Djeser-Ti said, "but only until my own son is born. Then he must become king, and I will be his regent...though I am willing to share those duties with our loyal Tjaty."

"And if you have a daughter instead?" Tetimene asked. She looked sour, but then decided to cast her support where it would do her the most good. "Sennenkhet is the obvious choice as the next king, with Imhotep as regent."

There was further argument from Djeser-Ti, but it rapidly descended into grumbling. Sekhemkhet only had one living son--Sennenkhet--and in the absence of another male contender, he must become the next king. Ayah disputed the choice of regent, but she could not hope to prevail against the united support of the other royal women.

Sekhemkhet's health continued to fail. Khentu camped within the king's chamber so he could be on hand to minister to him, and Imhotep looked in on him several times a day. Imhotep continued to govern the kingdoms, and now had the added task of educating Sennenkhet, so that when the time came, the boy would have some idea of his duties and responsibilities. It was a lot for an older man to do, and though at fifty-five Imhotep was still in good health, he found himself wishing he had not taken on the added burden of the regency. He said as much to Khentu, on one of his visits to the king.

"You had no choice," the physician said. "There is no one better qualified for the task. I can prescribe you a tonic, if you like; something to make you feel younger and more energetic, if only for a day."

"No thank you, my friend," Imhotep replied with a tired smile. "I have tasted your concoctions, and I prefer to be tired."

Khentu sniffed. "You have medical expertise, so prescribe something for yourself."

There was a knock at the door and a messenger hurried across to Imhotep and murmured in a low voice before hurrying out again.

Khentu saw the grim expression on Imhotep's face. "More bad news?" he asked.

"An army approaches Inebu-hedj. It is led by Khaba, and I would guess he has taken up his son Nubsekhem's rebellion."

"We still have the king's army though?" Khentu asked.

"It is on the other side of the river. Khaba has turned our flank." Imhotep rubbed his face with both hands, stretching the flesh on his stubbled cheeks. "I will leave you, Khentu. I must go and lead the city's defence against the rebels."

"No," came a whisper from the bed, "that is my duty."

Khentu and Imhotep stared in consternation at the king, who stirred and struggled to sit up. He looked like an animated corpse, but his voice, though rasping, was firm.

"It is my duty as king to lead the defence of the city. Help me up, for although my determination is strong, my body is weak."

Chapter 31

ord of the king's recovery sped through the palace and as Sekhemkhet tottered out of his suite on the arms of his physician and Tjaty, the palace servants cheered. He insisted on walking through the city to the walls unaided, refusing to be carried on a chair.

"I am their king," he said. "How would it look if I was carried into battle? Would any man have confidence in my ability to lead them to victory?"

The thin and wasted man stumbling through the streets of the city toward the North Gate did little to inspire the people, however. Cheers turned to a shocked silence and then a groundswell of muttering induced Imhotep to send for extra palace guards. They formed a cordon around the king, while Imhotep physically supported the man.

"You should not be here, my lord," he whispered as the king shuffled along. "You are just out of your sickbed and need rest and strengthening tonics. Go back to the palace and let me deal with this upstart ex-general."

"No...I am the king...I will do it."

They reached the gate and Sekhemkhet laboriously climbed the steps to the lookout on the top of the wall, from where he could see Khaba's small army. Imhotep pointed out the banner that denoted the presence of the general, and the king nodded, holding onto the wall for support.

"I should send out my army to destroy him," the king muttered.

"We do not have an army, my lord. It is on the other shore."

"Then signal him that I will talk," Sekhemkhet said.

"Bring him closer and our bowmen can swiftly end the threat."

"Where is the honour in that? I will guarantee him safe passage."

Imhotep raised the banner that proclaimed a desire to talk, and after a short delay, two men strode out from the rebel ranks and walked close to the gate where they looked up at the king and his Tjaty.

"My lord king, I regret it has come to this," Khaba called out.

"We can end this quickly," the king replied. "Surrender and swear allegiance to me, you and your family."

"I cannot do that, my lord. You have taken the life of my son, Nubsekhem."

"He was a traitor, taking up arms against his king."

"He has paid the price for his folly, my lord, against which I counselled him. However, we all know the penalty commonly exacted on the families of traitors. I cannot risk that."

"I have told you that you only need bend your knee to me, Khaba."

"In the hearing of everyone here, my army and the people of Inebu-hedj, you swear that me and my family will live, and that you will exact no vengeance against us?"

"Nubsekhem killed my sons."

"Against all my counsel."

"You knew of it?"

"After the fact," Khaba admitted. "To return to my question, my lord, do you swear to grant me and my family our lives?"

Sekhemkhet closed his eyes, holding onto the wall. "Do you doubt my word?"

"It pains me to say it, my lord, but trust seems to be in short supply at the moment. Yet I will trust your word if you publicly swear it in the presence of army, people, and gods."

"You doubt my word as your king if you would have me swear such an oath."

"Do you swear, my lord?"

"No. I give you only my word, which should be enough."

"Then it seems I have my answer," Khaba said, turning back to his army.

Sekhemkhet's body sagged as he turned away, and he clutched at Imhotep for support. His face was the colour of ashes and his eyes stared past his Tjaty unseeing.

"Take me home, Imhotep," he whispered. "I want to rest."

Imhotep knew the king could not manage to walk back to the palace so called for a chair on which to carry him, unmindful of appearances as the bearers ran back through the streets. People stood in silence, watching their king as he was carried past, his head lolling, his hands gripping the arms of the chair. Khentu had the king carried to his rooms where he examined him.

"He should never have been allowed to go," the physician fumed.

"You were there when he insisted," Imhotep pointed out. "I did not hear you refuse permission then."

"He is the king," Khentu muttered.

"Exactly. Who will gainsay any decision he makes."

Khentu took Imhotep by the arm and drew him aside. "He has made his last decision," he said in a low voice.

Imhotep looked across at Sekhemkhet lying on the bed, his face pale and sunken, breathing torturously as he struggled to remain alive.

"He is dying?"

"His excursion took the last of his strength."

As he spoke, a sputtering noise issued from the king and the stink of faeces filled the room. Sekhemkhet had lost control of his bowels.

"Call servants to clean him up," Imhotep said. "He should face death with dignity. When all is in readiness, call for his women so they can bid him farewell."

Imhotep and Khentu watched as the king was stripped of his soiled garments, washed clean and new clothes fitted. The dirty sheets were carried away and perfumes liberally sprinkled around the room to mask the stink before the women were admitted.

The king lapsed into unconsciousness as the women wept over him, held his hands or stroked his wasted body. Their cries of grief anticipated his death, but the king summoned strength from somewhere and clung to life. As the hours dragged by, Imhotep ushered the women from the death chamber, telling them that he would continue to keep watch, notifying them of any change in the king's condition.

"How is he?" the Tjaty asked, when he and the physician were alone once more.

"I do not know how he is still alive," Khentu said. "His body has ceased to function, yet he still breathes."

Imhotep stared at the body on the bed, seeing the slow rise and fall of the king's chest falter, stop and restart. Sekhemkhet's skin colour had a waxen look, as if the blood had been drained from his body, the flesh of the face fallen away as if anticipating the embalmer's work.

"I do not tell you your business," Khentu said, "but it might be the time to prepare the heir for what must surely come today."

"There is more than that to consider," Imhotep said. "General Khaba sits outside our city with an army. He desires the throne for himself. Sennenkhet is incapable of ruling, so it falls to me to do something."

"You will march out and defeat Khaba?"

Imhotep bared his teeth in a mirthless grin. "The palace guards I have at my disposal are almost useless. It would hand Khaba a swift victory and the right to dictate terms."

"What then?"

"I must negotiate."

Imhotep sat down in a corner of the king's chamber to consider the problem of negotiating the succession of Sennenkhet while Khaba stood poised to rip the kingdom apart in civil war. He tried to think about what would be the best for Kemet, and what could reasonably be expected in the circumstances.

"The best outcome is that Sennenkhet is crowned king and I manage his affairs until he comes of age," he murmured. "Of, course, Khaba would have to swear fealty, disband his army, and return home, and I cannot see that happening."

The Tjaty sent for food and drink and continued his deliberations while the king lay dying and Khentu kept watch, ministering to his few needs. Toward evening, Khentu alerted him that the king was nearing death, and Imhotep came to the bed to see Sekhemkhet's struggle for life fail. A feather at his nostrils showed no breath within the body, and the king's eyes, when his eyelids were drawn back, were blank, filming over.

"The king is dead," Imhotep said. "You concur, Khentu?"

"Yes, my lord."

"Please send for the embalmers. I will notify the family and issue instructions to maintain order within the palace and city."

Khentu hurried off on the Tjaty's bidding. Imhotep stood for a time, looking down on the king's body, knowing that a time of trial lay ahead. As the first of the embalmers entered the room to take charge of the body and prepare it for eternity, Imhotep went to call on the ladies of the Women's Quarters.

He informed them of the death of the king and waited as lamentations filled the entire wing of the palace. The grief was largely formal, as the women had been prepared for many days for this event, but it was real enough for Khemtet, the king's mother, his sister Meresankh, and Djeser-Ti who had been his wife since before his accession. Imhotep did not tell them of his intended talks with Khaba, though he knew they would soon find out.

The next day, Imhotep sent a messenger to Khaba, asking him for a discussion of the future, suggesting they meet in a tent erected outside the city walls. His suggestions were accepted, and he supervised the erection of the tent, and the disposition of guards from the palace and from Khaba's army. Then, with refreshments provided, he sat and waited for Khaba. The general turned up in the company of his grandson Huni, looking around suspiciously.

"Where is Sekhemkhet?" Khaba asked. "I should be dealing with him rather than his servant."

"The king is dead," Imhotep said. "I represent his heir, so you may talk to me."

"What heir?" Huni demanded. "He has no living sons."

Imhotep looked at Huni curiously. "So you know about that?" he asked. "I wondered if Nubsekhem's crime extended to his family."

"If you are referring to my son's involvement in the killing of children, then I knew about it after the fact," Khaba said stiffly. "The same applies to my grandson Huni. Neither of us approved of the action, and we both deplored it. That is why we took no part in his insurrection."

"Yet here you both are."

"We all know the penalty for insurrection," Khaba countered. "Death to the rebel's family. Did you expect us to stand idly by, waiting for the executioner's axe?"

"The king offered peace in return for fealty," Imhotep said. "You spurned his offer."

Khaba shrugged. "Blood had been spilled on both sides; I could not be sure of the king's mercy. Anyway, what is past is past; we must decide what happens now. You mentioned an heir--who is this?"

"Sennenkhet, son of the king by his concubine Ayah."

"I have never heard of him," Khaba said. "Is he a newborn?"

"Seven years old. Being the son of a concubine he was never in the line of succession until Nubsekhem cleared the way for him."

"Someone will be thankful for his actions, then."

Imhotep glared at Khaba, disdaining his flippant remark. "Such is the situation," he said. "Sennenkhet will be crowned as king, and I will act as his regent until he comes of age. What we must decide now is what assurances I can give on the new king's behalf that will make you feel safe."

"I am not sure there is any assurance you can make," Khaba said. "Sennenkhet is the son of Sekhemkhet and as such will always feel antagonism toward me and my family."

"I will be regent and I can give you my personal assurances," Imhotep said.

Khaba weighed the Tjaty's words. "I trust you, Imhotep, as you are a man of honour, but Sennenkhet is a child. How can I trust his word, even when made through you?"

"Then it seems we are at an impasse," Imhotep said.

In the silence that followed, Imhotep offered wine, but was turned down by Khaba and Huni until Imhotep poured a cup for himself and drank it. Then they accepted it.

"Too much has happened to sow distrust," Imhotep said. "I accept your word that you knew nothing of your son's actions until after the fact, but once the idea of poison has been voiced, suspicion is everywhere."

"Poison is for cowards," Huni muttered.

"I agree," Imhotep said. "But now it is in all our minds, as evidenced by your suspicions when I offered the wine."

Khaba nodded. He drained his cup and refilled it, matching cup for cup with Imhotep. "So how do we get out of this impasse?" he asked.

"There is a way," Huni said. "Sennenkhet is not the only royal male."

Imhotep smiled. "Yes, I am the brother of Netjerikhet and uncle to Sekhemkhet, but I have no desire to sit upon the throne. That is no solution."

"I did not mean you, Tjaty Imhotep."

"Who then?"

"Khaba. His father was brother to Khasekhemwy's father. Khasekhemwy was..."

"He was my father," Imhotep said, "and father to Netjerikhet. Yes, I see what you are saying--Khaba belongs to the same family." He smiled wryly. "All relatives together." Looking directly at Khaba, he added, "You claim the throne for yourself?"

"I have never considered it before, but I would make a better king than an unproven boy of whom nobody has heard...and I have an army to back up my claim."

"Sennenkhet has an army too, under my command."

"Which is stuck on the other side of the river," Huni pointed out. "Ours is here, outside the gates of Inebu-hdj."

"Nobody wants an army breaking into the city to conquer it," Khaba said. "Even under strict orders, anything could happen."

"You would threaten the people of Inebu-hedj?"

"Of course not, but anything can happen in war. Why take the chance. Let us negotiate a peaceful solution to the issue of succession."

"Involving you being king, I suppose?"

"It would be the most logical way forward," Khaba said.

"Where does Sennenkhet fit into this scheme?" Imhotep asked. "Or will he quietly disappear?"

"I do not make war on children. Sennenkhet is only a boy and has yet to prove himself capable of ruling. I propose that I become regent, ruling Kemet through him for...let us say, ten years. If he proves worthy, I will step aside and he can rule alone." Khaba gave a wry smile. "I am sixty-seven years old; I will be seventy-seven in ten years if I am still alive, and will welcome the opportunity to put the cares of a regency aside."

"What of Huni? You want nothing for him? You do not want him to follow you onto the throne?"

"I have in mind something else. You have great experience in governance, Imhotep. I want you to remain as Tjaty and to train up Huni as your replacement. I know that neither of your sons want to follow you into government, but this way you still have the opportunity to mould the future."

Imhotep sat and thought hard, his mind in turmoil. Khaba had laid out a plan that might bring peace to Kemet instead of civil war--if he could be trusted.

"What about the royal women?"

"What about them? I have no interest in another wife, even for form's sake, but I am willing to marry one, if only to give some assurance that I mean Sennenkhet no harm. I will leave the girls that have sprung from Sekhemkhet's seed for the boy king when he reaches maturity."

"Let me think about this," Imhotep said. "I cannot decide the future of Kemet on an instant."

"Do so then," Khaba said, rising to his feet, "but do not take too long. At the first sign that the army across the river tries to cross, I will assume you have refused my offer. Then I will take the city by force."

"You will have my answer tomorrow."

Imhotep returned to the city and took counsel with the royal women, but their reaction was more warlike than his own. They would readily consign the city to the horrors of war rather than countenance surrender. The sole exception was Ayah, who saw Khaba as the means to secure her son's hold on the throne.

"I will take Khaba as my husband," she told Imhotep. "In that way, he takes my son Sennenkhet as his own and will protect him. For the rest, I leave that in your hands."

Meresankh's concern was for her continued abstinence and asked Imhotep to continue to protect her. He could offer no guarantee, but said that he would do his best.

"Be hopeful in that Khaba does not seem to want a wife. If he accepts Ayah, then he will not want you."

Imhotep also took counsel with Minhotep, the captain of the small city garrison, telling him of Khaba's offer and asking his advice.

"They do not pay me to make such decisions, my lord," Minhotep said.

"I will be making the decisions," Imhotep replied, "but I need ideas from someone with a military background. In your view, can we withstand the rebel army?"

"Only if we can get our army across the river, my lord."

"And what are the chances of that?"

"You have seen the fleet of small boats that blocks their passage?" Minhotep asked. "Unless you can get rid of them..." he shrugged.

415

"Can we defend the city without it?"

"No, my lord."

Imhotep frowned, but he nodded. "Thank you, Captain, your comments have been most useful. I have reached my decision."

"May I ask what that is, my lord?"

"I will surrender the city to Khaba."

"I believe that under the circumstances you can do nothing else, my lord."

The next day, Imhotep met with Khaba again and told him of his decisions. "I will surrender the city to you, Lord Khaba, in the interests of preserving the peace. You must, however, swear to uphold Sennenkhet as the king, with you acting as regent until he reaches the age of sixteen, at which stage you will step aside and let him rule alone. I will continue to act as Tjaty."

"That is acceptable," Khaba said.

"You will marry Ayah, the concubine of Sekhemkhet and mother of Sennenkhet, protecting the boy as if you were his father."

"I have no desire to marry, but I will do so."

"As regards the sister of Sekhemkhet, Queen Meresankh, you will not take her as wife, nor allow anyone within your court to do so without her express permission."

"That is a highly unusual requirement."

"The gods themselves have prohibited her from having relations with any man, including Sekhemkhet, though he made her his queen."

"If the gods command it, who am I to say otherwise?" Khaba replied. "What else?"

"You will not exact vengeance against any man or woman for any act they might have taken prior to you becoming regent."

"That seems reasonable. I want to restore order and justice to Kemet. I believe that the lack of a flood and expected famine is a result of upsetting the *ma'at* of the kingdoms."

"There is one last provision," Imhotep said. "You must swear that you will uphold these things before the gods, taking the oaths in their holy presences within their temples in Inebu-hedj. This must be done before the gates are opened to you."

"You want me to enter the city alone, leaving my army outside?"

"I give you my word as Tjaty of Kemet and speaker for the new king that no harm will befall you. I will escort you to each temple and back again. When you have sworn the oaths, the city will be open to you and your men."

Khaba considered Imhotep's conditions for several minutes. "You are an honourable man, Imhotep, and I will accept your word." He called Huni to him and explained what was to happen.

"You cannot do this, grandfather," Huni exclaimed. "You are putting yourself in the hands of your enemies."

"Imhotep is not my enemy," Khaba said.

"Even if he is not, he is one man. What if someone takes it into their head to do you harm? How can he prevent that?"

"I am doing this, Huni."

Huni looked hard at Imhotep. "Be aware that in my grandfather's absence, I command his army. If anything befalls him, I will raze this city to the ground and kill every man within it."

"That will not be necessary," Imhotep said calmly.

Imhotep made the arrangements and the next day escorted Khaba through the streets of Inebu-hedj with Captain Minhotep and a squad of soldiers as an honorary guard. Khaba also brought a few men solely as an escort, and after a few small tensions, both parties relaxed. Men and women of the city followed the little party through the city, chattering and gossiping in the street while Imhotep and Khaba went inside each temple. There, in the presence of the Hem-netjer of each of the principal gods of the city, Khaba swore the necessary oaths.

When all the oaths had been sworn, Khaba returned to his camp while Imhotep organised the official opening of the gates and welcome. The army would stay outside the walls, though he brought soldiers into the city in numbers to match the city garrison and palace guards. Everything went smoothly, and the royal women bowed to the inevitable, receiving lord Khaba graciously.

Sennenkhet was proclaimed as titular king, his official coronation to take place at a later date. Khaba was invested with the powers of the regency, and his marriage to Ayah, mother of the king, announced. The new regent then made a speech to the gathered nobles and important citizens that he was there to restore peace and prosperity to the kingdoms, claiming the right to do so because of his family relationship to the new king.

"I hold the regency," Khaba said, "until such time as the king is capable of ruling on his own."

Chapter 32

Huni sat with his grandfather on that first evening after Khaba assumed the regency, enjoying a cup of wine, while Khakhet drank beer as befitted a boy of his age. They talked of small matters while the servants were around, but as they withdrew, the subject of their discussion changed, becoming more serious. Khakhet sat to one side, playing with a kitten.

"I do not understand why you accepted the regency, grandfather, instead of the throne," Huni said. "You had an army and could easily have imposed your will, seizing the kingdoms."

"There would have been bloodshed."

"So what? The first step in preparing the dinner is killing the goose. I can think of a few people I would not mind getting rid of. It would make life easier."

"This way is better," Khaba said. "If I had taken the city by force, seizing and killing the principals, others of the nobility, court officials and those looking for their own power would have masked their thoughts. Any treachery nascent in their breasts..."

"What is 'nascent', grandfather?" Khakhet asked, looking up from his play.

"It means something just coming into being," Khaba said. "Like your bedtime if you interrupt me again." He paused, collecting his thoughts. "As I was saying, budding traitors would have hidden, and it would be harder to see from where the next threat was coming. This way, people will assume I am a harmless old man who selflessly takes on the task of raising the young king."

"And you are not?" Huni asked.

Khaba leaned forward, lowering his voice despite there being nobody close by. "I mean to have the throne for my own, and you will be my heir; king after me."

"What about Sennenkhet?"

"He is not fit to be king. Do you know his mother Ayah was a slave when he was born? I will not allow him to ascend the throne."

"What about Imhotep? He will obstruct you."

"There are certain men...and women too...who must be removed if my plan is to work. Imhotep is one of them."

"You will kill him?"

"I would rather not; he is too valuable. I must neutralise him, however."

"Who else?" Huni asked.

"Sennenkhet, of course. His mother. The old queens maybe...I have not decided. Sekhemkhet's mother Khemtet may prove troublesome; she has a stake in her grandson's continuance. There are a handful of court officials I must consider too."

"What of Meresankh?"

Khaba looked at his grandson with a smile. "Lust after her, do you?"

Huni flushed. "All I meant is that if the gods forbid her to procreate, then of what use is she? Do you intend getting rid of her too?"

"While she lives, she must inevitably become a focal point for anyone seeking to supplant us. Marriage to her would strengthen a man's claim to the throne."

"Then why not marry her yourself?"

"I thought about marrying her to you."

For a few moments, Huni's eyes came alive. "She is beautiful enough, I suppose, but I would prefer a wife I can plough, have sons with."

"The gods might be prevailed upon to change their minds," Khaba said. "After all, it was only through a dream of Imhotep that their will was made known in the first place. Another dream might change all that."

Huni grinned. "I will be happy to do the will of the gods...and King Khaba."

The story of the Pyramid Builders continues in Book 3: Khaba

Glossary of Egyptian words used in the story

Abu

Elephantine, city on the border of Egypt and Nubia

Abdju

Abydos, an ancient sacred city of Egypt

Ala-Bast

Alabaster, sacred to the goddess Bast

ba

the personality of an individual

deben

a unit of weight, about 13.6 grams in the Old Kingdom

Djesa

the Giza plateau

Hatnub

an alabaster quarry in the eastern desert near Amarna

Heb-sed

also known as Sed, a festival that celebrated the continued rule of a king

Heka

shepherd's crook that symbolised kingship

Hem-netjer

High Priest

Hery-heb

a lector priest, one who read out the magical incantations

Hesmen

menses, the time of menstruation

Hut-waret

later Avaris, modern Tell el-Daba

Inebu-hedj

Memphis, an ancient capital city of Egypt

Iter

unit of length, about 10.5km

Iunu
Heliopolis, city of the sun, a major religious centre

ka
the vital essence of an individual

Khet
unit of area, about 27.56 square metres

Ma'at
concepts of truth, balance, order, harmony, law, morality, and justice

Mehi
unit of length, about 52.5cm

Mer
pyramid

Mer-netjer
beloved of the gods

Nekhakha
flail that symbolised the fertility of the land

pehe-mau
hippopotamus

Per-djet
mastaba or bench-like tomb

Per-netjer

House of the God

Sed

also known as Heb-sed, a festival that celebrated the continued rule of a king

Sepat

a regional division of the country

Serdab

a chamber in which the ka statue stood

Serekh

heraldic crest containing a royal name

Setat

unit of area, 100 khet, about 2,756 square metres

Shabti

a figurine intended to act as a servant in the afterlife

Tjaty

Vizier, the highest official to serve the king

Tjenu

Thinis, an ancient capital city of Egypt

Waset

Thebes, modern Luxor

Wawat

northern Nubia

If you enjoyed this author's book, then please place a review up at the site of purchase, and any social media sites you frequent!

You can find ALL our books up on our website at:

https://www.writers-exchange.com

All our Historical Novels:

https://www.writers-exchange.com/category/genres/historical/

All Max's Books:

https://www.writers-exchange.com/max-overton/

About the Author

Max Overton has travelled extensively and lived in many places around the world--including Malaysia, India, Germany, England, Jamaica, New Zealand, USA and Australia. Trained in the biological sciences in New Zealand and Australia, he has worked within the scientific field for many years, but now concentrates on writing. While predominantly a writer of historical fiction (Scarab: Books 1 - 6 of the Amarnan Kings; the Scythian Trilogy; the Demon Series; Ascension), he also writes in other genres (A Cry of Shadows, the Glass Trilogy, Haunted Trail, Sequestered) and draws on true life (Adventures of a Small Game Hunter in Jamaica, We Came From Königsberg). Max also maintains an interest in butterflies, photography, the paranormal and other aspects of Fortean Studies.

Most of his other published books are available at Writers Exchange E-Publishing, https://www.writers-exchange.com/Max-Overton/ and all his books may be viewed on his website: http://www.maxovertonauthor.com/

Max's book covers are all designed and created by Julie Napier, and other examples of her art and photography may be viewed at www.julienapier.com

If you want to read more about books by this author, they are listed on the following pages...

A Cry of Shadows
{Paranormal Murder Mystery}

Death is only the beginning...

When a young woman is savagely murdered in a dark alley in Illinois, Lieutenant John Barnes is drawn into a case that quickly becomes personal. With the victim mistaken for someone else, the investigation reveals a twisted tangle of jealousy, obsession, and calculated identity theft.

Half a world away, at an Australian university, Professor Ian Delaney pushes the boundaries of ethical science. His work restoring lost memories with taipan venom has brought him acclaim--but it's his secret research into the final moments of life that truly consumes him. Delaney believes he can measure the soul... and perhaps even retrieve it.

As Barnes closes in on a killer, and Delaney inches toward his unthinkable goal, two paths converge--one of justice, the other of madness. In a world where murder, memory, and metaphysics collide, the shadows hold more than secrets. They whisper of something waiting beyond.

Publisher: https://www.writers-exchange.com/a-cry-of-shadows/

Adventures of a Small Game Hunter in Jamaica
{Biography}

In 1959, fresh from boarding school and driven by a love for nature, Max Overton embarked on a journey that would shape the rest of his life. Journeying to Jamaica with his parents, he found himself captivated by the island's lush beauty, rich culture, and fluttering population of butterflies.

From the hills of Jack's Hill to the mystique of Hellshire, from humorous school mishaps to dangerous encounters with disease and superstition, Max recounts his time as a "small game hunter" with honesty, charm, and a hint of mischief.

Each chapter is a vignette of discovery--of insects, people, and himself. As he wrestles with lizards, braves banana truck rides, or reflects on the poetry of rot and renewal, his love for the island and its creatures shines through.

This is not a guidebook. It's not just a travelogue. It's the lived experience of a young boy chasing wings and stories in the heart of Jamaica.

Publisher: https://www.writers-exchange.com/adventures-of-a-small-game-hunter/

Ascension Series, A Novel of Nazi Germany
{Historical: Holocaust}

The Ascension Series chronicles the rise and fall of Nazi Germany through the eyes of Konrad Wengler, a man caught in a harrowing contradiction: born of a Jewish mother, raised with German pride, and enlisted in the SS. As the Third Reich expands and the atrocities mount, Konrad's internal war threatens to destroy him even before the bullets do. This unflinching trilogy explores moral complexity, survival under tyranny, and the desperate pursuit of redemption in a world where humanity is rapidly being consumed by ideology.

Book 1: Ascension

Konrad Wengler believed in his country.

He wore his father's army tunic with pride and joined the war effort like every young man in Germany--until he saw the truth behind the flags and speeches. With a Jewish mother and a legacy of violence rising all around him, Konrad finds himself buried in guilt and shame. From the muddy trenches of WWI to the civilian police of WWII, he tries to reconcile his past with the horror unfolding before his eyes.

But conscience is dangerous in Hitler's Germany.

As he rises through the SS ranks, Konrad walks a tightrope of survival, deception, and inner torment. His heritage is a death sentence. His silence is complicity. And when the moment comes to act, he must choose between protecting the life he's built--or confronting the evil he has helped uphold.

Publisher: https://www.writers-exchange.com/ascension/

Book 2: Maelstrom

Konrad Wengler cannot sleep. Not because of the war, or the cold, or the sound of Allied bombs falling over German cities--but because of the people he's killed.

A Jewish mother. Her daughter. Entire families. All buried in shallow graves while he looked on--or pulled the trigger himself. Once a loyal German, now a haunted man, Konrad is desperate to find a path to redemption. His only hope lies in confronting the powerful Nazi official responsible for the corruption and cruelty that set him on this path: Heinz Falk.

But with every step toward the truth, Konrad walks deeper into danger. Every revelation tightens the noose around his neck. And as the tide of war turns against Germany, time is running out--for Konrad, for his family, and for the truth to ever be heard.

Publisher: https://www.writers-exchange.com/maelstrom/

Book 3: Dämmerung

The end of the war is near.

For SS officer Konrad Wengler, it cannot come soon enough. Haunted by nightmares, paralyzed by guilt, he clings to the only thing that has kept him alive--his wife Ilse, their daughter Wilhelmina, and their baby son, Gregor. But even family cannot shield him from the past.

Germany is collapsing, yet justice remains just out of reach. The man Konrad has tried for years to expose--Heinz Falk--continues to prosper. His only witness is dead. His authority dwindles. His soul is fraying.

When Konrad returns to the front, he knows it may be his last campaign. But even amid retreat and ruin, he refuses to stop searching for truth. For justice. For redemption.

Publisher: https://www.writers-exchange.com/dammerung/

Fall of the House of Ramesses Series,
A Novel of Ancient Egypt

{Historical: Ancient Egypt}

The towering legacy of Ramesses the Great casts a long shadow over Kemet as the Twentieth Dynasty begins to fracture. In this gripping historical trilogy, Max Overton brings to life the final collapse of Egypt's most illustrious house, where every title bears a burden, every heir bears a curse, and every act of loyalty may yet become betrayal.

From the aged Merenptah's struggle to hold a disintegrating kingdom together, to Prince Seti's short-lived reign and untimely death, and finally to Queen Tausret's desperate bid to secure the throne for her infant son against political rivals and regency plots--this series charts a slow descent into dynastic ruin with unflinching historical depth and dramatic intensity.

A richly imagined tale of blood, ambition and the fall of a royal house, grounded in the dusty scrolls of history.

Book 1: Merenptah

Kemet is a kingdom rich in tradition--and cracks. As age and illness take their toll on King Merenptah, son of Ramesses the Great, the line of succession begins to fray. His sons, Seti and Messuwy, are princes of the same house but men of very different character. In the corridors of Men-nefer, political maneuvering becomes more dangerous than battle, and alliances shift with the river winds.

Seti, the favoured son, walks a path of honour but cannot escape the storm that brews in his brother's heart. Messuwy, perhaps illegitimate, perhaps merely passed over, seeks more than his due. As Merenptah's reign wanes, the seeds of Egypt's greatest family's collapse are sown in ambition, bitterness, and silence.

Publisher: https://www.writers-exchange.com/merenptah/

Book 2: Seti

When King Merenptah dies suddenly, suspicion runs like poison through the palace walls. His son Seti, returning from the Great Field, finds a throne barely waiting and a kingdom already plotting. Beside him stands his queen Tausret, sharp-tongued and fiercely loyal--but behind them loom enemies old and new: the ambitious Chancellor Bay, the enigmatic Sethi, and Messuwy, a brother whose loyalty cannot be trusted.

As Seti begins his reign, he must face the truth that thrones are not inherited--they are defended. Every choice holds the weight of empire, and every delay could mean his end. The gods may have made him king, but men still hold the knife.

Publisher: https://www.writers-exchange.com/seti/

Book 3: Tausret

The House of Ramesses has fallen into disarray. King Seti is dead, his infant son too young to rule. Queen Tausret--once a soldier, now a widow--becomes regent in a court divided. To avoid war, a compromise is struck: young Siptah, son of the late king's rival, is crowned under Tausret's guidance, with the promise that her son Seti-Merenptah will one day rule beside him.

But peace built on political compromise is fragile. Old enemies like Messuwy whisper from prison cells, new ones move behind silken curtains, and Siptah himself--crippled in body but not in ambition--may not be content to share the throne. In this gripping final volume, Tausret must outwit traitors, command armies, and protect her son from forces that would erase his legacy before it begins.

Publisher: https://www.writers-exchange.com/tausret/

Glass Trilogy
{Paranormal Thriller}

What if the mind held the key to humanity's forgotten past--and its uncertain future?

From a carved stone in the Australian wilderness to a machine that alters thought beneath a Californian mountain, and finally to a shattered time thread that leads thirty thousand years into prehistory, The Glass Trilogy follows the journey of three unlikely allies: a sceptical entomologist, a determined journalist, and a photographer haunted by visions.

Bound together by psychic links, ancient artefacts, and forces beyond understanding, James Hay, Samantha Louis, and Marc Lachlan uncover a truth deeper than science--a legacy etched into the glass of memory itself.

As past and future collide, the fate of the world may depend on what they discover... and what they choose to believe.

Spanning continents, consciousness, and time, this trilogy blends archaeological mystery, metaphysical exploration, and emotionally grounded science fiction in a gripping and original narrative.

Book 1: GLASS HOUSE

When research student Rick Jennings discovers a carved black stone in the remote Australian wilderness, he doesn't expect it to tear apart his mind. The moment he touches the strange object, something awakens--something powerful, ancient, and dangerous.

Entomologist and researcher of strange phenomena, Dr. James Hay, is called to investigate. Thousands of miles away in Illinois, journalist Samantha

Louis finds herself inexplicably drawn to James by a psychic link neither can explain. Together, they are pulled into a world of fractured memory, ancient mysteries, and unspoken truths.

Alongside photographer Marc Lachlan, they follow the stone's trail to evidence of a lost civilisation--and something even darker waiting in the shadows. As hidden forces close in, the trio must unlock the secrets of the past to protect the future.

From the rainforests of Australia to the depths of the human mind, *Glass House* is a story of discovery, danger, and the shattering of everything you thought you knew.

Publisher: https://www.writers-exchange.com/glass-house/

Book 2: A GLASS DARKLY

Dr. Andromeda Jones thought she was accepting a standard research position. But the underground lab in California is far from ordinary--and so is the technology it hides.

As work intensifies on the Vox Dei machine, a device capable of influencing the human brain, Andi begins to experience strange phenomena--shadowy figures, distorted thoughts, and visions that blur the boundary between reality and delusion. Recruited as a spy by a clandestine organisation, she must walk a razor-thin line between truth and deception.

Is the machine merely an experimental breakthrough? Or a tool for a darker purpose? And as its creators push forward, is there anyone left they can trust--including themselves?

As the mind bends, so does the world around it.

Publisher: https://www.writers-exchange.com/a-glass-darkly/

Book 3: LOOKING GLASS

It should have been a breakthrough. But when an experimental portal malfunctions, James and Samantha Hay lose their infant daughter, Gaia-- vanished into the unknown.

What follows defies science. Gaia is alive... but trapped thirty millennia in the past. From the scorching lands of prehistoric Australia to the icy intelligence of Neanderthal scientists, the journey to find her will test the limits of belief, memory, and humanity itself.

Time is fractured. Civilisations collide. And a child holds the key to repairing a broken reality.

To save Gaia--and the world--James and his companions must walk into the heart of the past and face truths that were never meant to be known.

Publisher: https://www.writers-exchange.com/looking-glass/

Haunted Trail A Tale of Wickedness & Moral Turpitude
{Western: Paranormal}

1877. Dakota Territories. A condemned man scratches his life story in rough pencil from a prison cell in Hammond's Bluff.

Ned Abernathy never set out to be a killer. But a hard life on the frontier, a reckless temper, and forbidden feelings for a rancher's daughter set him on a path soaked in dust and stained in blood. From the raw boredom of ranch life to the lure of whisky, poker, and women with no illusions, Ned's story is anything but romantic.

He tells it like it is--with poor spelling, harsh humour, and no excuses. He writes of betrayal, misguided loyalty, and the brutal shootout that sealed his fate.

In his own words: "The West ain't romantick... I wish I cood goes back an do it all agin... seein as ow it wuz me ot temper an jellusy wots gonna get me anged."

Haunted Trail is the unflinching voice of a man condemned by both law and conscience... and a frontier that offered no second chances.

Publisher: https://www.writers-exchange.com/haunted-trail/

Hyksos Series, A Novel of Ancient Egypt

Egypt's golden legacy fractures beneath foreign rule, civil war, and the rise of kings not born to the throne.

In a time of drought, division, and dynastic collapse, Kemet stands vulnerable. As the 13th Dynasty crumbles, noblemen betray their kings, foreign warlords seize cities, and alliances shift with the Nile's tide. From the fall of Avaris to the battles for Waset, the rise of the Hyksos--rulers of foreign lands--redefines Egypt's future.

Across seven epic volumes, Max Overton weaves a sweeping historical saga of ambition, brotherhood, betrayal, and faith. Generals become kings. Sons rise against fathers. Queens manipulate nations. And a new generation must choose: preserve the past or forge something entirely new.

Based on the real events of Egypt's Second Intermediate Period, the Hyksos Series *brings a lost age of war, strategy, and honour to unforgettable life.*

Book 1: Avaris

Avaris was meant to be a stronghold. Instead, it became a crucible.

As the once-proud dynasty of Kemet begins to fracture, King Sheshi faces an unexpected betrayal from within his own ranks. Urubek, once trusted, turns against him--and the city's future spirals into uncertainty.

In the aftermath, alliances shift like desert sands. General Khakherewre, noble-born but politically outcast, must navigate a city on the brink. Abductions, double-crosses, and the creeping presence of foreign powers threaten to unravel what little order remains.

Before Egypt was conquered, she was betrayed. Avaris is where it begins

Publisher: https://www.writers-exchange.com/avaris/

Book 2: Conquest

The Amurru have taken Avaris. Now they want everything.

With the city of Avaris under foreign control, the balance of power in Egypt has shifted--and native dynasties begin to fall. From Ankh-Tawy to Tjenu, noble houses must choose: serve the new masters, or face annihilation.

Samuqenu's sons, each a potential heir, carry the flame of conquest southward, but the road to domination is treacherous. Kemet is not a land easily governed. While one son builds through diplomacy, another turns to espionage--and others to violence.

Conquest traces the rising tide of Hyksos ambition and the resistance of Egypt's divided rulers. Allegiances are tested. Crowns are claimed. And Egypt will never be the same.

Publisher: https://www.writers-exchange.com/conquest/

Book 3: Two Cities

Two cities. One land in turmoil.

In the north, the Hyksos consolidate their conquests. In the south, ancient traditions cling to life--but rebellion simmers under the surface.

When Wepwawemsaf returns home to Tjenu after the sudden death of his father, he expects a funeral. Instead, he finds a power vacuum, a dead brother, and an uneasy city council desperate for leadership.

Reluctantly, Wepwawemsaf steps into a role he never wanted. But in a land shadowed by invaders and spies, power brings danger--and every move could be fatal.

Two Cities continues the sweeping saga of Egypt's Second Intermediate Period, where faith, ambition, and bloodline collide.

Publisher: https://www.writers-exchange.com/two-cities/

Book 4: Possessor of All

The king is dead. But the real battle is only beginning.

In the ancient city of Waset, civil strife flares as the throne of Kemet falls vacant. Monthhotepi, son of Queen Monthhotep and presumed heir, declares himself king. His half-brother Nebiryraw stands beside him--loyal, calculating, and dangerous.

As Kemet's south reels from famine and rebellion, and the Hyksos strengthen their hold on the north, alliances must be made across rivers, kingdoms, and bloodlines. Monthhotepi seeks legitimacy. Nebiryraw sees a deeper truth: only one man can reunite Egypt--and it may not be the one with the crown.

Possessor of All is a gripping exploration of fractured royalty, shifting power, and the birth of a dynasty that will either save or sunder Egypt.

Publisher: https://www.writers-exchange.com/possessor-of-all/

Book 5: War in the South

In a kingdom still reeling from invasion, a new king dares to challenge fate.

With the death of Sewadjenre, his son Nebiryraw rises to power, promising peace--but peace is a fragile lie. His brother Semenenre plots treachery in the name of justice, and far to the north, Hyksos King Khayan eyes the Nile with conquest in his heart.

As intrigue festers in Waset and enemies gather at Egypt's borders, the fight for Kemet becomes a crucible of loyalty, ambition, and survival. From battlefields to inner chambers, *War in the South* reveals the cost of leadership in a land no longer at peace.

Publisher: https://www.writers-exchange.com/war-in-the-south/

Book 6: Between the Wars

The battle is won, but the war is unfinished.

After a hard-fought victory against Hyksos forces, King Rahotep returns to the south hailed as Egypt's hope. Yet within the walls of Waset and across the kingdom, peace proves elusive. Ambassadors arrive with hidden agendas. Cities change hands. The young heir to Amurru rises.

Even as Egypt rebuilds, cracks emerge between generals, brothers, and kings. And beneath it all, the ancient gods seem silent.

In *Between the Wars*, Max Overton continues the sweeping saga of Kemet's Second Intermediate Period, capturing the quiet tensions, political manoeuvres, and fragile triumphs that shape an empire on the brink of rebirth--or destruction.

Publisher: https://www.writers-exchange.com/between-the-wars/

Book 7: Sons of Tao

In the desert winds of southern Kemet, a father fights to reclaim a nation--and his sons prepare to inherit both glory and burden.

Senakhtenre Ahmose wages war against the Hyksos, but it is his sons, Nebmaatre and Tao, who will shape the land's fate. While Nebmaatre upholds the old ways and the weight of lineage, Tao challenges ancient tradition with fresh strategy and relentless will.

As rebellions ignite and alliances are forged across Nile and sand, *Sons of Tao* tells a story of brotherhood, ambition, and the final spark of revolution.

The war for Egypt is ending--but the battle for her soul is just beginning.

Publisher: https://www.writers-exchange.com/sons-of-tao/

Kadesh, A Novel of Ancient Egypt

The city of Kadesh smoulders with ambition, rebellion, and the clash of empires. In the fourth year of his reign, Pharaoh Ramesses II sets his sights on reclaiming a legacy lost to the Hittites. But war is never so simple.

As alliances shift and old borders fracture, warriors from across the ancient world are drawn into the conflict. Mutbaal, a Sherden pirate spared from execution, must trade his freedom for honour in service to Egypt. Amentep, a young charioteer with more recklessness than rank, dreams of glory beyond his station. Psaru, a fiercely disciplined Kushite archer, becomes the iron spine of the Pharaoh's campaign. And far to the north, an Anatolian stableboy named Amaradu is swept into the machinery of Hatti's military might.

When diplomacy fails and swords are drawn, these lives will converge at Kadesh--a city whose fate will tip the scales of history.

An epic tale of war, loyalty, ambition, and the men who carved their names into legend.

Publisher: https://www.writers-exchange.com/kadesh/

Scythian Trilogy
{Historical}

Exiled from empire. Embraced by enemies. Marked by destiny.

When Nikometros, a wounded cavalryman in Alexander the Great's army, is left for dead on the eastern frontier, fate delivers him into the hands of the Scythians--a nomadic people who value strength, loyalty, and the favour of their gods above all.

In the savage rites of the Massegetae, he should have died. Instead, he survives, earning a place not just in their tribe, but in their hearts. As war leader and lover of a priestess, he becomes the Lion of Scythia. But honour is a dangerous gift in a world of jealous kings, ruthless warlords, and crumbling empires.

Across the windswept steppes and into the courts of Persia, Nikometros must fight to protect what he has built, to rescue those he loves, and to clear his name before the empire brands him a traitor.

From ritual combat and betrayal to forbidden love and empire-spanning trials, the Scythian Trilogy *weaves a gripping saga of courage, faith, and identity in a world where justice wears many faces.*

Book 1: LION OF SCYTHIA

Wounded in the campaigns of Alexander the Great, Nikometros is left in a distant outpost with little hope of advancement. But fate has other ideas. When his patrol is ambushed by Scythian warriors, Nikometros faces a deadly ritual challenge--one that will determine whether he lives or dies in a land that views outsiders with suspicion.

Against all odds, he survives.

Taken in by Chief Spargises and adopted as a brother, Nikometros becomes the tribe's war leader. His strategies turn battles. His presence commands respect. But when he falls in love with Tomyra, the tribe's priestess, they violate the sacred laws of the Mother Goddess. What follows is a storm of betrayal, vengeance, and exile that will pit him against the very people who once called him brother.

In the land of the horse and the spear, honour may be won... but never without blood.

Publisher: https://www.writers-exchange.com/lion-of-scythia/

Book 2: THE GOLDEN KING

Areipithes, son of Spargises, wears the golden crown--but at what cost? With his father and sister gone, the throne of the Massegetae is his... yet loyalty cannot be commanded, and justice will not sleep.

Tomyra, priestess of the Mother Goddess, is missing--captured by the cruel Dimurthes, a rival chief whose ambition matches his appetite for violence. But Tomyra is no helpless victim. Her faith runs deep, and the *Owls*, her warrior guard, are not far behind.

Meanwhile, Nikometros risks everything to find her, trailing danger through snow-covered forests and across crumbling alliances. The world is shifting. Enemies wear familiar faces. And sometimes, a former brother becomes the most dangerous foe of all.

Winner of the 2005 EPIC Ebook Awards.

Publisher: https://www.writers-exchange.com/the-golden-king/

Book 3: FUNERAL IN BABYLON

The road to Ekbatana is long--and every step brings Nikometros closer to judgment. Branded a traitor by a false witness, the warrior once hailed as the Lion of Scythia must stand trial before the highest powers in the empire.

Beside him rides Tomyra, the woman he loves, and within her, a child not his own. Caught between Macedonian law and Scythian honour, they navigate suspicion, sorrow, and simmering danger.

But darker forces stir. Scorpion, hired killer and master manipulator, weaves a web of deceit that stretches from the steppes to the Persian court. If Nikometros fails to uncover the truth in time, not only his life--but the fragile peace between nations--will be lost.

Winner of the 2006 EPIC Ebook Awards.

Publisher: https://www.writers-exchange.com/funeral-in-babylon/

Sequestered
By Max Overton and Jim Darley
{Action/Thriller}

In the quiet forests of Oregon, something is stirring beneath the ground.

Dr Maxwell Hay is pulled from his quiet research lab and thrown into a world of secrets, surveillance, and shadowy power. At the behest of a global energy mogul, Max joins a scientific team investigating unexplained gas activity linked to an ancient volcanic lake.

But the more he uncovers, the more disturbing the truth becomes. A haunting tragedy, a buried facility, and a deadly silence threaten to repeat themselves--and this time, the consequences could be far worse. Max finds himself in a race not just for discovery, but for survival.

Inspired by real science and rich in suspense, *Sequestered* is a taut, intelligent thriller set against the striking backdrop of Oregon's volcanic terrain.

Recipient of the Life Award (Literature for the Environment):  "There are only two kinds of people: conservationists and suicides. To qualify for this Award, your book needs to value the wonderful world of nature, to recognize that we are merely one species out of millions, and that we have a responsibility to cherish and maintain our small planet."

Awarded from http://bobswriting.com/life/

Publisher: https://www.writers-exchange.com/sequestered/

Strong is the Ma'at of Re, A Novel of Ancient Egypt

{Historical: Ancient Egypt}

In Ancient Egypt around 1200 BCE, ambition festers behind palace walls while gods turn their faces away from the land. Ramesses III, son of a usurper and heir to a turbulent kingdom, strives to rebuild the glory of the past. Taking on the throne name of Usermaatre--"Strong is the Ma'at of Re"--he wages war, builds monuments, and raises sons to secure his dynasty.

But within the royal court, conflict brews. Tiye, the first wife of Ramesses, watches her hopes of queenship and legacy fade with each son she loses. The rise of a new heir, born to the king's sister-wife, fuels bitterness, intrigue, and desperate ambition. As famine, unrest, and divine silence grip the Two Lands, treachery seeps into the palace itself.

This gripping trilogy reimagines the life and death of Ramesses III and the chilling conspiracy that brought Egypt's last warrior pharaoh to his knees. From the heights of power to the depths of betrayal, Strong is the Ma'at of Re *explores the cost of empire, the weight of legacy, and the perilous divide between faith and fate.*

Book 1: The King

Ramesses III ascends the throne on the promise of revival. With the memory of his legendary namesake looming large, he takes the name Usermaatre and dedicates his reign to emulating the greatness of Ramesses the Great. He fights, builds, and raises sons in the same mould. He believes, fiercely, in the destiny of kings.

Yet beneath the polished stone of monuments and the gleam of gold, decay spreads.

Wives war in whispers. The priests grow richer than the crown. And the love that once grounded his reign is slowly eclipsed by loss, age, and the demands of succession. Ramesses battles to hold together a kingdom unraveling at the seams--and to silence the doubt growing louder in his own heart.

Will his name stand the test of time, or be buried under the weight of a legend he can never equal?

Publisher: https://www.writers-exchange.com/the-king/

Book 2: The Heirs

Egypt's throne is never safe--not even from within.

Queen Tiye once basked in the glow of power, her sons destined to rule. But time has been cruel. Sons have died, others grown disinterested in kingship. And now, the line of succession bypasses her completely in favour of the king's sister-wife and her son, Crown Prince Ramesses.

Even marriage ties her daughter to this hated rival.

While Ramesses III is consumed with distant campaigns and fragile trade missions, Tiye moves through the corridors of the palace, whispering, watching, weaving her plans. Her youngest son must be elevated--but to do that, she may have to sacrifice everything.

Even peace. Even Egypt.

Publisher: https://www.writers-exchange.com/the-heirs/

Book 3: Taweret

The throne of Egypt shudders. Not from foreign attack--but from within.

Ramesses III, the last true warrior pharaoh, is dying. As the gods veil their faces and the people cry out in hunger, the palace echoes with silence and suspicion. In his name, the Crown Prince rules--but the shadows behind the throne grow longer.

Queen Tiye has watched her dreams shrivel. She was never crowned. Her sons were never chosen. But she still has one son left--and one last plan to seize the future she believes was stolen.

What begins as a whisper of discontent will become the most infamous conspiracy in ancient Egyptian history. In its wake lie broken oaths, spilled blood, and the question every kingdom must ask:

Can a throne built on divine order survive when faith itself is betrayed?

Publisher: https://www.writers-exchange.com/the-one-of-taweret/

The Amarnan Kings Series, A Novel of Ancient Egypt

{Historical: Ancient Egypt}

Set against the splendour and upheaval of 18th Dynasty Egypt, The Amarnan Kings *series reimagines one of the most mysterious chapters in ancient history--through the eyes of a forgotten princess. Beketaten, known as Scarab, is daughter, sister, and mother to kings, yet history has all but erased her. Until now.*

When a team of modern archaeologists uncovers a hidden tomb in Syria, they find not just a burial site, but a written chronicle preserved in thousands of hieroglyphs. Within these walls, Scarab recounts her life: her loyalty to Akhenaten, love for the soldier Paramessu, rivalry with Tutankhamen, and betrayal by Ay and Horemheb. Through war, faith, exile, and loss, Scarab endures--and shapes a legacy that will echo through the reigns of Ramesses and beyond.

As ancient voices call across centuries, truth and myth collide in a story of power, survival, and the unyielding will of one remarkable woman.

Book 1: SCARAB - AKHENATEN

Buried beneath a Syrian mountainside lies a secret the world was never meant to find: a lost tomb from the age of ancient Egypt, its walls filled not with treasure, but with truth.

Inside, a modern archaeological team discovers the preserved words of a princess long forgotten--Beketaten, the youngest daughter of Amenhotep III and sister to the infamous Akhenaten. Known in her time as Scarab, she lived through the religious revolution that changed Egypt forever. As gods fell and temples emptied, Scarab's life was shaped by palace intrigue, political ambition, and a forbidden love that could cost her everything.

In this vivid first volume of *The Amarnan Kings*, Scarab tells her story as she saw it--from the rise of the Aten to the fall of the House of Amenhotep. Her voice, silenced for centuries, speaks at last.

Publisher: https://www.writers-exchange.com/scarab/

Book 2: SCARAB- SMENKHKARE

Egypt is broken. The House of Aten is in ruins, its worship condemned. But in a remote land, a lost king stirs.

Smenkhkare, brother to the heretic Akhenaten, cheated death once. Now, years later, he returns to Egypt to claim what is his. With him is his sister Beketaten--Scarab--who must act as diplomat, advisor, and protector as enemies rise to meet them.

The road to the throne is paved with betrayal, and the blood of gods and men. Scarab must find strength in her past and courage for the future, even as the world she knew crumbles around her.

In this second volume of *The Amarnan Kings*, ancient truths, lost loyalties, and divine legacies unfold through Scarab's eyes--revealing a chapter of Egyptian history that was never meant to be remembered.

Publisher: https://www.writers-exchange.com/scarab2/

Book 3: SCARAB - TUTANKHAMEN

In the silence of a hidden tomb, a story unfolds--one of two brothers at war, and the sister who held their fates in her hands.

Tutankhamen is no longer the boy in the shadow of his elders. Backed by powerful generals and priests, he challenges Smenkhkare for Egypt's crown. The city of Waset becomes a battleground of intrigue, ambition, and secrets older than dynasties.

As Scarab watches history unfold, she must face the cost of loyalty, the agony of loss, and the responsibility of truth. For the battle is not just for power--but for the soul of Egypt itself.

Finalist in 2013's Eppie Awards.

Publisher: https://www.writers-exchange.com/scarab3/

Book 4: SCARAB - AY

The gods are silent. The people mourn. The king is dead.

But behind the veil of ceremony, Egypt seethes. Tutankhamen lies in his tomb, but his legacy is far from safe. Into the power vacuum steps Ay--manipulator, schemer, and now, pharaoh.

He demands Scarab as his queen, seeking to legitimise a throne built on treachery. Trapped between survival and resistance, Scarab must navigate palace politics, divine warnings, and the memories of those she's lost.

And all the while, beneath the cliffs of Syria, her testimony waits in silence... ready to reveal the truth.

Publisher: https://www.writers-exchange.com/scarab4/

Book 5: SCARAB - HOREMHEB

He was the last pharaoh of the 18th dynasty. She was its forgotten heart.

As Horemheb claims the double crown of Egypt, he brings a brutal end to the House of Aten. Statues fall. Names are struck from records. Scarab, last living daughter of Amenhotep III, is erased from history.

But history underestimates her.

From exile and silence, Scarab writes. She tells of gods and kings, of broken temples and enduring truth. She names names, exposes lies, and claims the legacy denied her.

This is the reckoning of Scarab.

Publisher: https://www.writers-exchange.com/scarab5/

Book 6: SCARAB - DESCENDANT

History buried her. The gods remembered.

In the deserts of Syria, Dr Danielle Hanser uncovers what no one was meant to find--an empty tomb hidden for millennia, sealed with royal seals, inscribed with a woman's voice.

That voice is Scarab's. Her chronicle ends, but her influence echoes.

As the truth threatens to shatter long-held beliefs and the line between past and present grows thin, one final legacy is revealed.

She was daughter, sister, lover, mother, queen. Now, she is the voice beneath the stone.

Publisher: https://www.writers-exchange.com/scarab6/

The Pyramid Builders, A Novel of Ancient Egypt
{Historical: Ancient Egypt}

At the dawn of Egypt's pyramid age, innovation met ambition--and history was carved into stone.

The Pyramid Builders series explores the lives of the pharaohs who oversaw the earliest monumental tombs, beginning with Djoser and the revolutionary Step Pyramid at Saqqara. Set during a period of rapid advancement in architecture and statecraft, these books trace the evolution of pyramid construction and the political, religious, and personal forces behind it.

But this is no dry chronicle of engineering. With a focus on the rulers, architects, and advisors who risked everything to shape a legacy of permanence, the series brings to life the human drama at the heart of Ancient Egypt's golden age. From court intrigue and dynastic struggles to the breakthroughs that allowed stone to defy gravity, each book is grounded in what historians know of the time--presented with compelling, character-driven storytelling.

The Pyramid Builders is historical fiction rooted in reality--an immersive journey into the minds and motivations of the people who raised the world's first pyramids.

Book 1: Djoser

He was not born to rule--but the crown came to him all the same.

Djoser, second son of Pharaoh Khasekhemwy, never expected to inherit the throne. But with his elder brother dead and his father gone, the burden of kingship falls to him. What follows is a reign marked by bold decisions, fierce loyalty, and dangerous enemies.

Faced with rebellion, drought, and a nation still healing from division, Djoser must unify his people and prove his legitimacy. Alongside his gifted architect Imhotep, he undertakes a tomb-building project unlike anything attempted before--one that will reshape Egypt's future.

Told with meticulous attention to historical detail, *Djoser* is a vivid exploration of a man, a kingdom, and the beginnings of an enduring legacy.
Publisher: https://www.writers-exchange.com/djoser/

Book 2: Sekhemkhet

To follow in Djoser's footsteps is to walk a perilous road.

Sekhemkhet ascends to the throne after one of Egypt's most influential rulers, stepping into power during a period of optimism, but also fragile balance. Seen by many as a stopgap ruler, his legitimacy is questioned even before he can issue his first decree.

As internal divisions rise and his own pyramid project struggles to match the splendour of Saqqara, Sekhemkhet must fight to prove he is more than a forgotten name in history. But enemies surround him--some cloaked in ceremony, others masked as allies.

In *Sekhemkhet*, Max explores a ruler often lost in the margins, painting a compelling portrait of a pharaoh whose story deserves to be told.
Publisher: https://www.writers-exchange.com/sekhemkhet/

Book 3: Khaba

He was born into the legacy of pyramids--but must prove himself to build one of his own.

Khaba, royal grandson of Pharaoh Djoser, has always lived in the shadow of greatness. As a child of the royal court, he has seen the brilliance and burden of kingship--but never expected it to reach for him so soon.

With Djoser gone and power shifting in Memphis, Khaba is swept into the dangerous currents of succession. Allies and enemies surround him, each with their own vision for Egypt's future. And at the heart of it all lies the unfinished dream of stone rising from the sand--a monument not just to the dead, but to a dynasty.

In *Khaba*, Max continues his masterful recreation of early dynastic Egypt, revealing the uncertainty, ambition, and courage of a prince poised on the edge of history.

Publisher: https://www.writers-exchange.com/khaba/

Book 4: Huni

A king's duty is to preserve peace--but peace never comes without a price.

Pharaoh Huni, son of Khaba, rules a unified Egypt. Yet his reign is anything but settled. As threats rise from without and ambitions stir within, Huni must rely on his experience, his alliances, and his understanding of both war and statecraft.

His greatest concern, however, is the one every pharaoh must face: the matter of succession. For while the monuments may stand for generations, only a strong heir can secure a king's legacy. And among those who circle the throne is a prince whose name will reshape Egypt forever.

Huni is a thoughtful, character-driven entry in *The Pyramid Builders*, capturing the twilight of the Third Dynasty--and the dawn of an empire that will rise even higher.

Publisher: https://www.writers-exchange.com/huni/

Book 5: Sneferu

He was not content to follow tradition--he would redefine it.

Pharaoh Sneferu enters history as the builder of not one, but multiple pyramids. Yet his legacy reaches far beyond architecture. At a time when Egypt is poised between dynasties, he offers strength, stability, and the will to shape a new vision of kingship.

But true leadership demands more than vision. It requires sacrifice, diplomacy, and unwavering resolve. As Sneferu navigates shifting alliances, expanding territories, and the challenge of shaping a future worthy of his ambitions, one question remains:

Will Egypt remember him for what he built--or who he was?

Sneferu continues *The Pyramid Builders* with the rise of a king whose name would mark the beginning of Egypt's greatest age.

Publisher: https://www.writers-exchange.com/sneferu/

Book 6: Khufu

Greatness runs in his blood--but now the burden is his alone.

When Khufu ascends the throne, Egypt stands united, prosperous, and inspired by the vision of his father, Sneferu. But the weight of legacy is heavy, and the young pharaoh is determined to surpass it.

Driven by ambition and the desire for eternal remembrance, Khufu sets in motion the construction of a pyramid more immense than any before. But the stones of Giza will not be raised by force alone. To see his vision realised, Khufu must navigate the shifting loyalties of the royal court, manage the labour of thousands, and survive the political and personal tests that come with absolute power.

Khufu brings to life the early years of the Fourth Dynasty in vivid, historically grounded detail--revealing the man behind the monument.

Publisher: https://www.writers-exchange.com/khufu/

Book 7: Djedefre

A crown, a kingdom, and a family divided.

Djedefre, son of Khufu, ascends to the throne in the wake of his father's death--surprising many by claiming the crown ahead of his half-brother,

Kauab. What follows is a reign caught between spiritual devotion and political resistance.

As Djedefre shifts royal traditions and provokes powerful enemies, he finds himself isolated within his own court. His queen, his advisors, even his priests carry their own ambitions. And when buried secrets threaten to undo his fragile rule, Djedefre must confront the cost of leadership in a world where betrayal is as enduring as stone.

In *Djedefre*, Max continues *The Pyramid Builders* with a haunting portrayal of a ruler whose struggles were carved not just in monuments--but in blood.
Publisher: https://www.writers-exchange.com/djedefre/

Book 8: Khafre

Khafre was never meant to rule.

With the death of his father Khufu, all eyes turn to Djedefre--the rightful heir. But ambition doesn't always follow the bloodline. When opportunity knocks, Khafre seizes it, setting in motion a ruthless pursuit of power.

In a land where gods walk among men and stone speaks louder than words, Khafre is determined to carve his name into eternity. As he lays the foundation for the second great pyramid at Giza, whispers of deceit and betrayal ripple through the court. Friends become enemies, and the cost of glory may be higher than the weight of stone.

From palace intrigue to desert labour camps, from divine rituals to brutal confrontations, *Khafre* explores the human heart behind the stone façade of a legend. History remembers the monuments--but what of the man?
Publisher: https://www.writers-exchange.com/khafre/

Book 9: Menkaure

A king in decline. A kingdom in waiting.

Menkaure, Pharaoh of Egypt, has secured his throne--but not his future. Wracked by illness and shadowed by unrest, the king sees his strength fail even as his pyramid reaches skyward. With death a looming certainty, his son Shepseskaf must shoulder the burdens of rule and prepare for what lies ahead.

But Egypt is not idle. General Userkaf rises in power, aligning himself with the powerful priesthood of Ra. Amid this political turbulence, the gifted Peseshet dares to dream beyond her station--to heal, to lead, to rise.

Menkaure explores the personal and political in a world shaped by stone, legacy, and survival. As old powers fade and new ones stir, the future of Egypt hangs in the balance.

Publisher: https://www.writers-exchange.com/menkaure/

Book 10: Shepseskaf

Shepseskaf, last son of Menkaure, never wanted the throne--but fate left him no choice.

Born into the splendour of the Fourth Dynasty, Shepseskaf's world is one of ritual, architecture, and ancestral glory. As he ascends to power after his father's death, he must navigate a realm where expectations are carved as firmly as the stone monuments around him. Yet Shepseskaf is not his father--and his vision for Egypt sets him on a different path.

The pyramid may be a symbol of divine rule, but Shepseskaf seeks to leave his own mark, not merely echo the past. While his advisors urge tradition and the priesthood demands favour, Shepseskaf's inner turmoil mirrors the shifting sands of his realm. Can he preserve the sacred lineage, or will Egypt fracture under the weight of change?

A richly drawn tale of loyalty, ambition, and a leader torn between legacy and innovation, *Shepseskaf* is the compelling next chapter in Max Overton's gripping *The Pyramid Builders* series.

TULPA
{Paranormal Thriller}

From the rainforests of tropical Australia to the cane fields of the North Queensland coast, an ancient horror awakens.

It began as a teenage experiment--something to break the boredom of small-town life. Inspired by stories of Tibetan mystics, four high schoolers and a university student attempt to create a tulpa: a being made from pure thought. But their experiment spirals out of control. Something terrible takes shape--something real.

As the creature begins to kill, panic spreads. The police are baffled, helpless against a force they cannot see. With terror escalating and more lives at risk, the teens must face what they've created. Joined by a student of the paranormal, two seasoned hunters, and a handful of brave children, they search for a way to stop the unstoppable.

But how do you kill what the mind has given life?

Publisher: https://www.writers-exchange.com/TULPA/

We Came From Konigsberg

{Historical: Holocaust}

Königsberg, 1945. The world is crumbling around her, but Elisabet Daeker refuses to surrender.

With the thunder of war closing in, Elisabet clutches her children close and begins a harrowing journey from East Prussia to the distant hope of freedom in West Germany. As starvation, separation, and danger stalk every step, she must draw on a strength she never knew she possessed.

We Came From Königsberg is more than a wartime story--it is a mother's story. Based on the true memories of her children, this powerful narrative captures the heart of a woman who defied history to keep her family alive.

Her name may have changed. Her voice may have been lost to time. But her story lives on.

Winner of the 2014 EPIC Ebook Awards.

Publisher: https://www.writers-exchange.com/we-came-from-konigsberg/

You can find ALL our books up our website at:

https://www.writers-exchange.com

All our Historical Novels:

https://www.writers-exchange.com/category/genres/historical/

All Max's Books:

https://www.writers-exchange.com/max-overton/

www.ingramcontent.com/pod-product-compliance
Lightning Source LLC
Chambersburg PA
CBHW051939020726
47501CB00001B/194